THE BURNS CODEX
THE FIRE SALAMANDER CHRONICLES BOOK FOUR

N. M. THORN

N.M. THORN

THE BURNS CODEX

THE FIRE SALAMANDER CHRONICLES • BOOK FOUR

The Burns Codex

By N.M. Thorn

Copyright © 2020 by N.M. Thorn. All rights reserved.
nmthornauthor@gmail.com
This is a work of fiction. Any resemblance to actual persons living or dead, businesses, events, or locales is purely coincidental. Reproduction in whole or part of this publication without express written consent is strictly prohibited.
Cover art design by
www.originalbookcoverdesigns.com

PROLOGUE

* * *

**Sixteenth Century
Moscow, Russia.**

A MAN SAT IN THE WINDOW FRAME, STARING ABSENTLY INTO THE obscurity of the night. It was clear he didn't care about the midnight view as his thoughts were far removed from it. His right hand was stroking his long beard mechanically and his wide-open eyes remained slightly unfocused as if he were traveling through the labyrinths of his memory.

The downpour became heavier, the water falling behind the window like an impenetrable wall. The noise of the rain morphed into a continuous loud rustle, occasionally interrupted by a mighty boom of thunder. The man flinched, torn abruptly from his thoughts by the racket of the storm, and looked around wildly. The lightning flashed again, splitting the darkness of the sky and the thunder rolled over the Kremlin, making its walls tremble.

The man crossed himself, whispering a quick prayer, and stepped on the floor with his bare feet. Shaking his head, he made his way to the bed and grabbed his long, fur-adorned robe from a chair. While shrugging it over his wide shoulders, he shuffled his feet in search of his shoes. Finally, he put them on and headed toward the door, muttering under his breath.

"I hate thunderstorms. They are nothing but a display of God's displeasure with mankind. And these nightmares... Seems like during the storm they are more realistic and more terrifying than ever. If any of it is real—"

He shuddered and halted, placing his hand on the door handle. A long vertical crease cutting through his forehead got deeper as his thick eyebrows met above his narrowed eyes. Then he rubbed his temples, noticing the wetness of perspiration under his fingers, and pushed the door open.

Two guards, who were standing outside his chambers, immediately bowed to him, ready to follow him wherever he was going like two loyal dogs. He observed the two men, registering the vibe of fear in their eyes, and waved his hand dismissively, stopping them in their tracks.

"Stay here," he ordered with the kind of harsh authority that no one in their right mind would attempt to challenge. "I don't need shadows when I wish to be alone."

"*Velikij Knyaz* — Your Majesty—," started one of the guards, but the man glared at him and the guard fell silent, shrinking under his heavy gaze.

Leaving his chambers behind, the man followed the long corridors of the Kremlin, moving briskly and soundlessly toward the basement. He knew this path well enough, walking it almost every day, so he didn't need extra light to follow it. Soon, he reached the end of the corridor and halted in front of a beautiful tapestry. He lifted it, uncovering a narrow door positioned in a deep niche in the wall.

Nevertheless, he didn't rush to open it, but instead observed the corridor over his shoulder just to make sure one more time that no one had followed him here. Even though he didn't meet a soul on his way in, the nagging sensation of being watched didn't leave him for a moment, making the hairs on his neck stand on end.

He grunted, irritation prominent in his every move, and carefully pushed the door open. With his height of almost six feet, he had to bend down to make it through the tiny opening, and his wide shoulders didn't do him any favors as he had to turn his body sideways a little.

As soon as he closed the door, he found himself in the kind of darkness where he wasn't sure if his eyes were opened or closed. He stilled, swallowing hard—he had never liked the darkness—and probed the wall on his right with his hand. The roughness of the white bricks' surface felt familiar and somehow comforting to his stretched nerves. A few seconds later, his fingers found what he was looking for—a wooden shelf with a stack of candles on it. He grabbed one of them, feeling another one slipping under his fingers and rolling off the shelf. A second later, he heard a distant thud as it landed on the floor of the room.

"*Ignius*," he muttered, pointing at the candle he was holding, and a small flame ignited at the end of its wick, partially illuminating a large empty space with low, arched ceilings.

He stood on a small platform with a narrow wooden staircase leading down, the last few steps of which disappeared into darkness. Counting the steps, he slowly walked down the stairs, careful not to slip. As he planted his feet on the steady floor, he sighed with relief and headed to the right.

He stopped in front of a heavy oak door, locked with a giant iron padlock, made by old masters. Even though he had a bunch of keys on a large iron ring attached to his belt, he didn't bother looking for the right one. Instead, he touched the massive lock with his fingers and whispered, *"Recludius."*

The padlock screeched mournfully and fell open, hanging on the staple. The man pulled the lock out, throwing it on the floor next to the door and pushed it open. Just like the first door, this one was too small for his frame and it took him a moment to pass through it. Warm stuffy air surrounded him, and he grimaced as a musty, unclean smell reached his nostrils.

He walked fast through the dark corridor, his right hand gliding over the rough stonework. He counted out three openings on his right and turned into the fourth. He kept walking, once in a while taking side passages until he finally reached a solid wall made of roughly cut white stones.

Muttering something under his breath, the man waved his arm in a wide arc and the air in front of him glowed with the soft white light of wards. He touched the invisible shield, and it disappeared. As soon as the shield was gone, the white wall shimmered like a mirage and slowly dissipated.

With the illusion gone, the passage continued leading into the darkness as if the wall had never interrupted it. The man kept walking until he reached another dead-end. This time it was real. He whispered a spell, and a door materialized in the wall. He pushed it open and walked inside.

"My Golden Library," exhaled the man, observing the room with love and adoration in his eyes, as if he were gazing upon his lover.

The room was filled with books and scrolls, and a hardly noticeable scent of dust lingered in the air. A few large shelves embedded into the walls were stuffed with books in heavy leather bindings. A few of the scrolls were unraveled on top of a massive oak table positioned in the center of the room, and a large book with thick yellow pages covered in hand-written Latin letters lay open, partially concealed by the scrolls.

This library had been started by his grandfather and it contained books, manuscripts and scrolls from all over the world, including the works of Greek and Roman writers, Chinese texts, and manuscripts from the famous Library of Constantinople as well as from the Library of Alexandria.

He had continued collecting the rare volumes, enriching the library with the works of Arabic authors after he had conquered Kazan and Astrakhan. Most of the books were of religious, scientific or philosophical content, but among them there were also books of magic and witchcraft.

The man pulled a massive chair out and sat down, his fingers fumbling nervously with a piece of paper, slowly rolling and unrolling it. He loved reading, and this library was his sanctuary, a place where he could forget about the heavy burden he carried on his shoulders since he had been just a boy. Even if it was for a short time only.

He sighed and leaned back in the chair, closing his eyes. Tormented by nightmares, it had been a long time since he'd had a good night's rest. The library was protected by wards and spells, and he felt safe here. He wasn't sure if he fell asleep or if his exhausted mind drifted off, but a wisp of cold wind to his face woke him up with a start.

He jolted up and then froze, his heart thundering in his throat. A young woman, no more than twenty-eight, was standing in front of him. She wasn't quite standing, but rather levitating a few inches above the floor. She was beautiful with that unearthly beauty of a bodiless spirit, sad and slightly translucent. She was gazing at him, a longing smile lingering on her lips.

"Anastasia..." he breathed out, pressing his hand to his chest.

"Ivan, my love," she whispered, her voice just as bodiless as her appearance.

"Is it you, my dove?" he asked, stretching his trembling hand toward her. "But how?"

"My heart, I am here just to deliver a message to you," she whispered, her large blue eyes sparkling with tears.

"What? A message?" Ivan asked, barely comprehending her words, his steady gaze fixed on his late wife. "I do not care about that. I just want to be with you, hear your voice… just one more time."

"We do not have time for that, husband," she said with notes of impatience in her voice, drifting closer to him. "We have but a few minutes together."

A wave of cold air enveloped him at her approach, and a chill rushed through him as the reality of what was going on finally settled in his mind.

"Anastasia, how did you get here?" he asked, taking a step back, his every muscle tense. "You are no longer of this world and this room is warded against anything magical."

She ignored his question, gliding closer to him. Her translucent hand caressed the air over his cheek without touching him.

"Your beard, my love," she said softly, tears running down her face, sparkling like small diamonds, "it used to be as bright as a sunshine on a summer morning, but now it shines with strands as pure as snow…"

Driven by pain and longing, he forgot about caution and lifted his hand to take hers. His fingers slid through and he dropped his arm powerlessly. Torment shadowed her beautiful features, sending his heart into an abyss of agony.

"What happened, my dove?" he asked softly. "Are you not at peace?"

"No, I am not at peace. I can never be," she replied, shaking her head, her thick braid swiping from her back to her chest.

"But you can change it, Ivan. You are the only person who can help me."

Her words set his naturally sharp and suspicious mind to high alert. He narrowed his eyes at her, slightly cocking his head to the side, as if he was trying to gaze into the depth of her very soul. As much as he wanted to believe that the spirit in front of him was indeed his first wife whom he loved with all his heart, his intuition told him it wasn't the case.

"What do you need me to do?" he asked, cold tones of reservation in his gruff voice.

She smiled—a hardly visible twitch of her full lips. "My spirit is tormented in the Dark Nav, my love," she explained, her whisper so soft that he could barely make out her words. "And the Lord of the Dark Nav wants something you have here, in your possession. Give him what he wants, and I shall be free to move on to the Light Nav."

"Dark Nav?" he echoed her words, crossing himself as his suspicions grew stronger. "It is not possible. You are—um—were a God-fearing Christian woman. Surely a pure soul like yours should be with our ancestors in heaven, not Nav, Dark or Light. Who are you? Whoever you are, you are not my wife."

Anastasia froze in midair for a moment, staring at him with widened eyes. "Ivan, I am begging you..." she pleaded, her voice trailing into a heavy silence.

"You are not my wife!" he growled, his face an iron mask. "Who are you and what do you want from me?"

Anastasia stretched her arm to him again but then waved her hand dismissively and hooted laughing as her appearance started to morph into something entirely different. It was still her features—the tender oval of her face, her soft full lips—but the terrifying face of undiluted evil was staring at him through her eyes. An ugly snarl distorted her mouth, wiping away the last resemblance with his beloved wife. Her eyes lit up with a sickening yellow glow and the stench of sulphur permeated the air, making his stomach twist.

"Hello, Ivan," said the monster, his voice deep and raspy. While he partially kept Anastasia's appearance, now he stood taller, almost as tall as Ivan, and his broad shoulders looked strange clothed in the long dress of a woman. "You finally figured it out, did you not? No, I am not your sweet and boring Anastasia. Nevertheless, you want to listen to me carefully and do as I say."

"And why is that?" asked Ivan through gritted teeth, folding his arms over his chest. His strength and self-assurance sprung to life fueled by rising anger.

It wasn't the first time in his life he had to face evil—human or supernatural. The fact that whatever evil creature he was facing now had the audacity to assume his beloved wife's appearance had him shaken, but now he was back to his normal self and the very same fact was making him boil with rage.

The monster cackled, shaking his head. "Aw, Ivan, what a sweet question you asked. I thought with your experience, you would know that I cannot take the shape of your wife without touching her. Well… her soul, in this case."

Ivan shivered as if the temperature in the room had just dropped by a few degrees. "Who are you?" he hissed, his voice trembling with anger as he realized the truth of that statement.

"Wrong question, Ivan," replied the monster mockingly. "Should you not be asking what you can do to save your wife?"

"What do you want!" yelled Ivan, his hands clenching into fists by his sides as he struggled to contain his rage. "Leave Anastasia alone! She deserves to be at peace."

"And I deserve—," started the monster furiously but cut himself off and cackled, his lips stretching even wider. "Never mind that. All I want is one book from your famous collection, Tsar Ivan Vasilyevich. You give me that book, and I swear, Anastasia will rest in peace, in any Death domain of your choosing."

"And what book might that be?" asked Ivan, but he knew the answer before the monster had a chance to explain.

"The Dark Codex," said the monster, a vibe of gluttony palpable around him.

Ivan's initial reaction was to say no, but he forced his turmoil of emotions under control and met the nauseating gaze of the monster with a deadpan expression.

"I need time to think," he said in a no-nonsense tone, a crooked smirk gracing his hard face. "You did not think I would just hand it to you, did you?"

The monster gaped at Ivan, unconcealed shock reflected in his eyes.

"Aw, you did. How sweet," jeered Ivan, firmly taking control of the situation. "No, I am not going to hand it to you. I need time to think. The Dark Codex is my favorite book in this entire library"—he waved his hand around nonchalantly—"and I love it above all, my dead wives included. I hope it is not a problem?"

Since Ivan had been just a young man, dealing with boyars who were tormenting and disrespecting him, weaving sticky webs of conspiracies around him, he learned how to take control of any situation, no matter how scared he was. Boyars thought they could use him, make him a faceless pawn in their dirty power struggle. How wrong they had been! Fear would never rule him.

A low growl rumbled in the monster's chest. "You have twenty-four hours, Tsar," he grumbled. "I'll find you then and you better be ready to hand the Codex over or your Anastasia will—let's put it this way, Christian Hell has got nothing on me and what I can do to her."

The monster cackled and his body shimmered as he vanished from the room. For a split-second, his glowing yellow eyes remained in the air and then slowly dissipated, too. Ivan exhaled, wondering how long he had been holding his breath and dropped into the chair as his last strength abandoned him.

*　*　*

Ivan left the library, quickly restoring all the wards and spells as he headed back to his chambers, walking as fast as he could muster without switching to running. After all, he was the first Tsar of all Russia and it wasn't fit for the Tsar to dash across the Kremlin like some commoner.

The same two guards were still standing by his door. He grabbed one of the men by his shirt and pulled him inside his chambers, slamming the door shut behind them. Once inside, he headed to his desk and sat down, shrugging his long robe off. It fell on the floor in a heap of silk and furs, but he didn't care.

For a moment, he just sat with his hands pressed together, his lips moving in silent prayer. He prayed every day, confessing his sins in genuine repentance, regretting his past deeds, and begging God for forgiveness. But right now, he wasn't praying for himself. He pleaded with God for Anastasia and her innocent, beautiful soul. If God could take care of her, he would deal with the monster on his own terms.

A few minutes later, he made a decision and reached across the desk for a blank page. As he pulled it closer, he picked up a writing quill and deepened it into the ink, wiping the excess on the edge of the bottle. He wrote a single word and waited until the ink dried out. Then he folded the page two times, without sealing it, and motioned the guard to approach him.

"What is your name?" asked Ivan, taking in the guard's appearance. He was young, his blue eyes bright under his dark eyebrows. Nervous and scared, he shuffled from foot to foot, his hands squeezing his hat.

The man bowed reverently, almost touching the floor with his hand. "Aleksey, Your Majesty," he said, his voice trembling with fear.

"I need you to do something for me, Aleksey," said the Tsar rising.

He leaned down to the guard's ear and whispered a few words. The guard's jaw dropped, and he gaped at him in awe.

"Do you understand everything you need to do?" asked the Tsar, pursing his thin lips.

"Yes, Your Majesty." The young man nodded vigorously. "I shall find the priest and bring him over to your chambers at once."

Ivan handed the note to the guard and tapped him on his shoulder. "You may leave now," he ordered with a dismissive wave of his hand. The man bowed low again and backed away to the door. "And remember, if you want to see another day, do not tell a word to anyone." He frowned, narrowing his eyes at the guard to impress the severity of his last words upon him.

The open threat in his voice made the guard blanch and bow even lower. "No, Your Majesty. My lips are sealed."

The Tsar waved his hand, and the guard looked more than happy to rush out the door.

* * *

BEFORE THE FIRST RAYS OF SUNRISE TOUCHED THE WALLS OF THE Kremlin, Tsar Ivan Vasilyevich was walking through the dark corridors of the labyrinths under the Kremlin again, this time followed by three men. The men were dressed in long black robes of Russian Orthodox Priests, but the way they moved and held themselves left no doubt—these men were trained warriors. And Ivan suspected that somewhere under the folds of their robes, they were hiding swords.

He removed the wards from the library and let the priests inside. They observed his collection in awe, and as their eyes wandered over the priceless tomes and manuscripts, their faces got transformed by the undying hunger for knowledge Ivan could relate to.

"Your collection is admirable, Your Majesty," said the oldest of the three, slightly inclining his head at the Tsar.

"Yes, it is," agreed Ivan, his fingers stroking the page of the open book gently. "In the hands of wise people, a collection of knowledge like this is a powerful tool which can be used to benefit our motherland and our people. But in the hands of evil, these books can be a terrible weapon capable of destroying the world as we know it."

In so many words, he told the priests everything that happened a few hours ago, without leaving out even the most personal details of his conversation with the yellow-eyed monster. As the men listened to his words, their expressions hardened.

"How is that possible?" asked the eldest one. "I saw your wards. They are quite potent, especially for a person who was not trained in magic formally."

"Not potent enough," objected Ivan, his expression hardened. "I fear the Dark Codex is no longer safe with me and I have no time to transfer it into the Wardens' Library. It was hubris of me to think I could keep it safe on my own..." For a moment, he fell silent, averting his eyes. "Whatever this monster is, we cannot allow him to put his hands on this book. This is why for the first time since I had met the Master of the Wardens Order, I had to request his assistance. I want to lock my library forever, so no one—neither human nor monster—can ever put their hands on these books."

The eldest Warden bowed his head. "What a shame," he whispered. "But you are speaking the truth, Great Russian Tsar. There is no safe way to transfer the Codex, and I fear if we try to take it outside the Kremlin's labyrinth, the monster will detect its magical energy signature swiftly as the three of us are not powerful enough to suppress it. Just keep in mind, Great Tsar, even if we conceal your library, you are not going to be safe in your palace. This monster, whatever it is, will find you sooner or later."

Ivan chuckled bitterly. "I am never safe," he said quietly. "Men or monster, what's the difference? But I shall never give in to fear. If he wants to seek my death, he is welcome to try."

For the last time, Ivan observed his precious collection, a heavy weight settling inside his soul, and walked out the door, followed closely by the Wardens. He locked the library and silently observed the men as they wielded their magic. They raised their arms and the air between them and the door into the library lit up with a brilliant white light. As they kept chanting, the light grew brighter and brighter until he could no longer see anything, black and red spots dancing in his vision in a wild merry-go-round.

When his vision returned to him, Ivan could no longer see the door. It was gone, the stonework of the wall looked as even and untouched as if it was never there.

"Your Majesty, our work here is done," said the older Warden, inclining his head respectfully. "Between our magic and the wards you had placed on this whole wing of the labyrinth, no one ever will find your library."

"Not enough," exhaled Ivan. "I do not deal in half-measures. If I do anything, I do it all the way as it is the only way appropriate for a Tsar."

Ivan closed his eyes, and he saw a page from the Dark Codex in his mind so clearly, he could read every single word of the Dragon Tongue inscribed on it. Slowly he started to chant the words that seemingly made no sense, but as he kept repeating them over and over, he felt a surge of magic traveling through his body and exiting through his hands.

As he kept chanting, a strange exhaustion overwhelmed him, soreness settling in his very bones. He swayed but strengthened up and kept repeating the words of enchantment over and over. The Wardens moved closer, providing him with the steady support of their strong arms, and he caught a reflection of concern in their eyes.

He wasn't sure how he knew it, but when he stopped chanting, he was positive that his work was done. Slowly, he looked down, staring at his trembling hands. His skin was wrinkled and covered in brown spots he hadn't had before. He grabbed a strand of his long hair, pulling it forward so he could see it and smirked—it was ghostly white. He ran his fingers over his face, sensing the deep creases crossing his forehead.

"What did you do? Did you use a spell from the Dark Codex?" asked the older Warden, horrified. "Every spell in this book is built to feed on the life energy of those who dares to use it."

"Did you not think, I knew that?" The Tsar chuckled darkly, staring at his shaking hands. "I do not care about my life. There are things I fear more than death…"

Ivan lifted his head, carefully observing the three Wardens. He got used to people averting their eyes, the fear of him visible in their slumped shoulders and lowered heads. The Wardens, however, met his furious gaze calmly, gazing at him with respect.

"Anyone who dares to seek the Dark Codex or any book from my library will be cursed forever," Ivan said icily, cutting the air with his hand. His voice crackled like the voice of an elderly man and he cleared his throat, straightening his back. "Blind and disoriented, they shall wander the labyrinth driven by fear. A man or a monster, they shall be imprisoned here forever with no way to escape."

CHAPTER 1

~ ZANE BURNS, A.K.A. GUNZ ~

Modern day
Miami Beach, South Florida

The narrow suburban street was dark and empty. Every single streetlight was out, and nothing was moving in the dead of night. The approaching tropical storm was making its presence known by driving the winds and veiling the starless sky with heavy clouds. The palm trees bent their crowns and the soft hissing of ruffled leaves accompanied every gust.

Even though it wasn't raining yet, Gunz could feel the gathering moisture in the air and his Salamander senses were screaming bloody murder, warning him about the presence of the opposing element.

"Is this the place Akira told you to check out?" Gunz asked, throwing a quick glance at Yaroslav.

The vampire nodded, slowly unsheathing his katana. He was dressed all in black, but his long golden mane was telegraphing his presence from far away.

"I don't sense anything," said Aidan, approaching them.

Another one with blond hair, Gunz thought and chuckled. "You guys should wear something to cover your hair. I can see you from a mile away, even in complete darkness."

"So what?" Yaroslav shrugged nonchalantly with a wide grin that showed the points of his long fangs. "Let them see me—I welcome any monster who is fast enough to catch my hair."

"Shh," whispered Aidan, his eyes slightly glowing with the white light of his magic. He extended his arm, muttering something under his breath and a long sword materialized in his hand. As Aidan raised his sword assuming a combat stance, the weapon glistened like an icicle, looking deadly in his hands. "Something is coming."

Gunz expanded his Salamander senses, probing the area and nodded to Aidan, confirming his statement. He reached into his pocket and pulled out his Swiss army knife, turning it into a sword. There was something in the area that hadn't been there just a few minutes ago and its menacing presence was getting stronger with every passing moment.

"Well, that's a new one," murmured Aidan, jerking his chin toward the road as six large SUVs with tinted windows came to a screeching halt in front of them.

"No shit," muttered Gunz, raising his blade to his shoulder. He squeezed the grip of his sword tighter, wondering why it felt heavier than usual.

At least eight men walked out of each vehicle and spread around surrounding them in a wide circle to block all possible ways out. The dark energy of their ominous magic overwhelmed Gunz's senses, and he grunted, directing some of his fire toward his sword. As the flames went up in his eyes, he felt Aidan stepping next to him ready to fight.

"Aw, so much fun!" Yaroslav laughed, flashing his vampiric grin as he took his position, back-to-back with them.

A split-second later, the air was thick with the strikes of dark magical energy and the stench of demonic essence as all the men charged them at the same time. Their fighting style differed from anything Gunz had ever seen before. It wasn't his first confrontation with demons. Usually demons were disorganized and chaotic, each demon caring for no one but themselves. This team was fighting like a well-oiled machine. With each step properly calculated and coordinated, they moved as one, breathed as one, and struck as one. Advancing at them like a menacing wall, they presented a true danger.

"Protect Yaroslav," Aidan hissed into Gunz's ear as he channeled his power.

"Praecidio Amnia," muttered Gunz, manifesting a thick power-shield around the vampire. Once done, he turned to Aidan and yelled, "Now!"

A blast of white light expanded around Aidan, assailing the advancing enemies. Gunz expected them to fall back as demons, vampires, or any other types of supernatural beings couldn't withstand a full assault of Aidan's godly powers. To his shock, the men staggered back just a little, moved by the sheer force of the blast, but none of them suffered even a mild injury.

"What the hell?" Aidan hissed, gathering more of his power. But the second blast produced just as little effect as the first.

"My turn," growled Gunz, watching Aidan wrap his protection shield around Yaroslav. *"Ignius Amplio!"*

His sword went up in flames and a smoldering jet of fire hit the advancing men straight in their chests. The fire flowed around them doing no damage whatsoever. Gunz increased the heat and potency of his fire strike to no avail. The fire magic seemed to be useless against them and using his elemental power wasn't an option as he was in the middle of a suburban neighborhood.

"Aidan, take this shield off of me," yelled Yaroslav, his eyes lighting up with a hungry scarlet glow. "Let's do it the old style."

As soon as Aidan brought down his shield, Yaroslav disappeared. He didn't teleport, but he moved so fast it was impossible to see him without using magical sight. Immediately, his katana wreaked havoc among the opposing party as they recovered from Gunz's and Aidan's assaults and resumed their steady forward motion.

The screams of pain and furious growls accompanied Yaroslav's progress and the stench of blood, mixed with the reek of demonic energy filled the cool night air. Gunz and Aidan exchanged a quick look and joined Yaroslav, putting their swords to business.

Gunz channeled more of his fire through his sword, making it burn brighter. He swung it down, slicing the man in front of him in two, and realized that he was just a demon—not even a demon in its pure form, but a human body possessed by demonic essence.

How is it possible that neither my fire magic nor Aidan's godly powers worked against run-of-the-mill demons? A thought flashed through his mind and quickly disappeared as he had no time to dwell on it. Three men attacked him at the same time, and he spun around, avoiding their direct strikes. His Salamander senses told him that two of his attackers were demons, but the third one was a dark wizard who was wielding not only magic but also a dangerous looking sword, which meant he wouldn't be easy to kill.

As fast as Gunz moved, he could never be as fast as Yaroslav and today he felt slower and heavier than usual. One of the demons caught his thigh with his blade and Gunz dropped to his knee, a pain-infused grunt escaping his lips. The dark wizard didn't wait for him to recover and blasted him with a powerful magical strike. Gunz cried out and fell on his back. He hit the ground hard, losing his breath, and his fingers unlocked. His sword dropped to the warm asphalt with a loud clang.

The wizard cackled and struck him with his magic again, overwhelming his senses and sending his mind into a wild frenzy. The wizard raised his sword ready to push it through Gunz's chest, and with horror, Gunz realized that he was completely immobilized by dark magic. Helpless and desperate, he watched the blade slowly lowering down, only one thought clear in his mind—if he died now, hundreds of humans would die with him.

"No…" he exhaled, struggling against the hold of dark magic.

A second before the sharp end of the blade pierced his chest, the mighty strike of a katana deflected it. One more strike and the head of the dark wizard rolled off his shoulders, hitting the road with a sickening thud. Bright red blood pumped from the headless neck and a second later the dead body dropped to its knees and then collapsed forward. Before the lifeless corpse fell on top of Gunz, Yaroslav's hand jerked him up to his feet.

"What's wrong with you, Salamander," hissed the vampire, thrusting Gunz's sword back into his hand. "You're slower and weaker than usual. If that's even possible."

Gunz rolled his eyes at him and sidestepped the next attacker, allowing Yaroslav to swing his katana one more time, slicing the demon in half.

"Yaroslav is right."

Gunz heard Aidan's voice somewhere on his left but had to ignore him, engaging the demon who attempted to punch him in his face. Easily avoiding his attack, he seized the demon's arm, flipping him over his hip. The demon fell to his side and Gunz twisted his arm at a painful angle, while running his blade through his neck. The dark shadow of the demonic essence separated from the body and shimmered into the night.

The shrilling sound of police sirens sounded somewhere in the distance and flares of multicolored lights illuminated the air at the far end of the neighborhood. To Gunz's surprise, the remaining men took off. They hopped into their SUVs and a heartbeat later all vehicles were gone.

Gunz lowered his sword, taking in his surroundings. At least fifteen dead bodies were sprawled motionless on the asphalt, their black eyes staring into the dark sky. Severed heads and body parts were floating in puddles of blood. Aidan and Yaroslav stood with their blades down, their blond hair now more red than gold, their clothes torn and covered in scarlet stains of blood—theirs and their opponents.

The first drops of rain fell from the sky and Gunz flinched from the touch of water to his skin. The police sirens now sounded closer and he didn't think it was a good idea for local authorities to find the three of them standing with their swords over a pile of corpses. FBI agent or not, Jim would have a hard time explaining all of this to both the police and his superiors.

"Aidan, Yaroslav, you need to leave," he said, turning to his friends. "I'll take care of the dead bodies. Police can't see this battlefield."

"How are you going to do it, Pyro?" Aidan asked, a light smirk playing on his face covered in blood splatters. "You can't use your elemental power here and fire magic won't do the trick fast enough."

"I can't," agreed Gunz, returning his smirk, "but I know someone who can. Now leave, both of you."

Aidan's lips parted, forming the shape of a letter "O" and he nodded to Yaroslav. "I'll see you both tomorrow for training in my school." He snapped his fingers and vanished from the street.

"Zane," said Yaroslav wiping his katana on the ripped sleeve of his shirt, "are you sure you're going to be okay?"

"Yes," replied Gunz impatiently, "but I need you to leave, Slavik. Something tells me you are not going to appreciate the fire show."

A wide grin split the vampire's face, and he was gone in a heartbeat. Gunz raised his hand up and tapped his finger on the surface of his wristwatch.

"Mishka, I need your help," he said quietly.

With a light pop, Mishka the wyvern materialized in front of him.

"I'm here, boss, what can I—"

The wyvern fell silent, twirling in the air, circling above the improvised graveyard. As he returned to Gunz, a sarcastic glimmer shone in his igneous eyes.

"Wait. Don't tell me," said the wyvern hovering in the air in front of him. "Clean up on aisle three, Mr. Burns?"

Gunz nodded, guilt swirling through him. But as the bright lights of the approaching police vehicles lit up the street, he forgot about feeling guilty.

"Mishka, please," he hissed, throwing his hands in the air. "I can't leave this Deadsville for the police to find! And I can't use my elemental power around humans. So cut the crap and help me clean this mess up, would yah?"

Mishka huffed, rising back up in the air. "Fine, fine, but you'll owe me one."

"I owe you more than one, my friend." Gunz chuckled, turning his sword back into the Swiss army knife and shoved it into his pocket. He waved his hand, unfolding the fire curtain of his portal and turned around.

"Now go!" yelled Mishka, the cloud of fire energy surrounding him. "When Mishka the Cleaner is at work, little fire lizards should run." He tittered, spitting tiny fireballs.

"Are you sure—," Gunz started to say, but Mishka waved his wings vigorously interrupting him.

"The police are going to be here in a minute," he hissed, showering him with fire and smoke. "Fire Salamander—go!"

Gunz nodded and walked through his fire portal.

CHAPTER 2

~ ZANE BURNS, A.K.A. GUNZ ~

Gunz walked out of the portal in the middle of his backyard in Coral Springs and sighed with relief. It was dark but blissfully empty. He probed it with his Salamander senses but didn't detect anything out of the ordinary. Slowly, he took the first step toward his house when his leg gave in, and he fell to one knee.

With shock, he stared at the large dark stain slowly growing in size on his thigh. He touched it, feeling the rough fabric of his jeans thick with his blood. The memory of the demon's sword slicing through his leg flashed in his mind and all of a sudden, the pain sprung to life with full force. Gunz grunted, holding down a scream, and leaned forward, bracing himself against the ground. For a moment, everything went dark and he took a deep breath fighting the fatigue.

Flesh wound... blood loss... The thoughts were scrambled in his mind and he had a hard time focusing. *I need to get inside and revert...*

He pushed himself off the ground and straightened up, slightly swaying on his feet. Limping heavily, he made it all the way to the house when abruptly his vision went dark and he collapsed on the steps, hitting his forehead against the door. He regained consciousness a few minutes later and found himself lying next to his house.

With a moan, he sat up, resting his back against the door and stared down at the puddle of dark blood under his leg. *Both Yaroslav and Aidan were right,* he thought miserably, guilt tormenting him. *What the hell am I thinking? I'm slow and weak, and I can't go on like this... I'm endangering my friends. I need to do something about these—whatever they are—dreams? Nightmares? Visions? I need to be able to get some sleep...*

He raised his arm up and found the door handle above his head. As soon as his fingers touched it, his Salamander senses came to high alert. Something was off. Ignoring the pain and weakness, he got up to his feet and put his hands flat against the door, probing his house with his other sight. All his wards and protection spells were gone. All of them. The house stood completely unprotected.

Gunz silently backed away from the door, chills running down his spine—he never left the house without arming all his wards and protection spells first. Something was terribly wrong. He spun around and sharpened his senses, surveying the area around his backyard and in front of the house. His breath came out almost like a gasp as muddy waters of dark energy enveloped him.

He pulled his knife out of his pocket, manifesting his sword and froze in place, all his senses at the highest alert. Stormy clouds veiled the sky, obscuring the moon, and the weak glimmer produced by two porch lights couldn't illuminate every corner of his property. Dark shadows shifted and swayed as the wind picked up.

He felt the ominous presence somewhere close by, yet still he could see nothing out of the ordinary. His heart pounded in his chest as a dreadful feeling of upcoming trouble spread through him. *"Stop trying to see with your eyes. Look through your elemental power."* Kal's voice sounded in his mind and he shut his eyes, channeling as much elemental fire as he could without reverting.

As he slowly opened his eyes, his magical sight presented an entirely different view. He reinforced his sight by directing more of his elemental fire toward his eyes and it worked better than he expected, revealing the true picture that made his blood run cold.

Ten shadowy figures stood in his backyard just a few feet away from him. Keeping under control so much elemental power within his body for a prolonged period of time was draining him physically and magically, and since he was already hurt and exhausted after the earlier fight, he knew he couldn't keep this state much longer. He closed his other sight, letting go of his elemental power and extended his sword toward the intruders.

"I know you're here. Show yourselves!" he shouted, the tension making his voice ring.

Loud whispers were the answer to his words. A silvery laughter sounded somewhere on his right and he felt a soft touch to his shoulder. He snapped to the right, but there was no one there. *Vampires? Who else could move this fast? But why can't I see them...*

He didn't want to use his elemental fire to enhance his sight again, but these cat-and-mouse games were playing on his nerves. He didn't see the invaders moving—he felt the movement with his skin and when a blade softly hissed through the air, he met it with his sword. A few sparks flew in the air as the two blades collided, and for a split-second Gunz could see the face of his opponent. This quick flash of light was enough for him to notice the glowing red eyes and long fangs.

Vampires or Upirs. Not Akira's...

A sharp pain originated on his cheek and he pressed his hand to his face, feeling the sticky wetness of blood under his fingers. More soft whispers, giggles and shifting around followed his movement.

"Ostendium," he muttered a spell and a thin layer of his magic surrounded him, revealing everything that wasn't visible to a human eye.

He saw nine men and a tall, slender woman standing in front of him in a half-circle. They were observing him with carnivorous smirks on their faces, their fangs and glowing eyes revealing their vampiric nature.

No silver, no wood. What would Henry VIII do? Beheading it is, decided Gunz, raising his sword to his shoulder, an icy smirk splitting his face.

"He wants to fight." A tall vampire in front of him cackled with an amused expression on his face, slowly clapping his hands. "Let's give the little lizard a fight he'll never forget."

At his last words, the vampire crouched and pounced at him, his hands with curved claws extended. As fast as the vampire moved, Gunz saw him coming through the thin mirror-like layer his spell created. He took a step aside and swung his sword, decapitating the monster in midair. As the severed head bounced on the soft grass of his backyard and immediately disintegrated into ashes, Gunz stepped forward raising his sword again.

"Anyone else stupid enough?" he growled, pointing his blade at the remaining monsters. But as strong as he made himself sound, he knew it was nothing but a pointless bravado. Between sustaining his spell, blood loss and pain in his injured leg, he had no chance of winning the fight against nine vamps. And most likely, his adversaries knew it too.

He needed help, and he needed it as soon as possible. He couldn't use more of his energy to summon Aidan, or Mrak Delar, or Kal, as even minimal use of his magic or elemental power was depleting his strength. *Yaroslav... he can hear me...* A short while ago, he was forced to create a psychic bond with

Yaroslav, and all the time since then, he couldn't wait for it to wear off. But now, for the first time, he was actually happy he still had it.

"*Yaroslav,*" he called desperately in his mind, using their psychic connection. "*Slavik, I need help! Now!*"

There was no answer. Gunz grunted, worry gnawing at him. Yaroslav had always answered his calls before, arriving in a heartbeat, no matter why he called him. With everything going on, his silence was unsettling.

"Hold him," hissed the woman, and the remaining eight vampires pounced at him from every direction. As weak as Gunz was, it didn't take them long to restrain him and pin him against the wall, leaving his sword lying on the ground at his feet.

The woman approached him without any rush, swaying her hips flirtatiously and halted just a step away. Her lips stretched into a derisive smirk and she took one more step, invading his personal space. The heavy presence of her vampiric energy engulfed him and Gunz turned his face away from her, closing his eyes.

She cackled, and he felt her raiser-sharp claw slicing through the skin of his cheek. He grunted, clenching his teeth and opened his eyes, meeting her scarlet stare. She showed him her finger coated with his blood and slowly brought it up to her lips. Her tongue flicked in and out as she licked the blood off, an expression of pure bliss on her face.

"Mmmm..." she exhaled, a drunk smile stretching her blood-stained lips. "I've heard about the qualities of the Fire Salamander's blood, but I never thought it was that good."

She grabbed a handful of his hair and yanked his head to the side, exposing his neck. Gunz jerked against the iron hands holding him pinned to the door, but quickly realized that in his condition he couldn't fight the hold of a few vampires and decided to stop wasting his energy.

"Aw, sweetie, don't be scared," she purred into his ear, "it's not going to hurt much. Just a pinch…" She licked his neck, her long tongue running all the way from his clavicle to his ear, and he cringed involuntarily as his skin crawled with disgust. "But you already knew that… I heard you have a bond with Yaroslav Potemkin." She pulled away for a moment, staring at him, gluttonous light in her scarlet eyes. "I think I can please you in a way Potemkin never could, little Salamander. I know you're not into boys. What do you say?"

"Sure," growled Gunz through gritted teeth, "you can please me in a way Potemkin never could—by simply dying. Seeing you disintegrating into a pile of hot ash would send me straight into an earth-shattering climax."

She squealed, anger distorting her cold features, and sunk her blade-like fangs into his neck. Gunz cried out, but his scream morphed into a soft moan as the sticky pleasure of the vampire bite spread through him, suppressing his desire to resist. He felt her hand slowly progressing south, moving down his chest and stomach, and settling over his groin, but he had no will to object, even as she squeezed her fingers a little.

A second later, she lifted her face, smiling over the bleeding wound on his neck and licked it, purring like a giant malicious feline. "So, little Salamander, tell me… it feels good, right? No more pain… just pure pleasure… say yesssss…"

Gunz moaned, unable to speak, and she stared down at him, gloating over his vulnerable state. Then she snickered softly and nodded to the other vampires. "I think he's ready," she said to them and her shrilling voice was an unwelcome sound in Gunz's fogged mind. "We can bind and take him now."

She took a backpack off her shoulders and dropped it to her feet. Reaching inside, she pulled out a few rolled ropes and threw them to one of the vampires.

"It's fireproof," she pointed out, more to Gunz than to the

vampire, "he can't escape this one. Bind him well and don't be gentle."

She stepped away and the vampires who were still holding him against the door finally let him go. Gunz collapsed, lying sprawled on the ground, helpless and powerless. His magic was depleted, his physical strength gone and his power of will suppressed by the effects of the vampire's bite.

A beefy vamp kneeled next to him and wrapped the fire-resistant rope around his neck. Gunz stared at him, following his every move, asking himself why he wasn't fighting this giant undead jackass. But the only thing he wanted was to be left alone. He moaned and closed his eyes. Like in a nightmare he felt someone's hands running down his thigh and suddenly a jolt of sharp pain pierced his body as the vampire attempted to bind his legs, placing the rope over his open wound.

Gunz cried out and his eyes flew wide-open while his mind got instantly cleared. Without looking, he reached down to clasp his wound. Instead, his fingers fell upon the cold slick surface of his sword. He grabbed the blade, ignoring its sharp edges and swung it, placing all the physical strength he still had, in one mighty blow. The vamp fell back, his jaw crushed by the pommel of the sword.

Gunz felt fire igniting in him, fueled by pain and anger, and he flicked his wrist, unfolding the fire curtain of his portal right next to him. Before the vampires realized what just happened, he rolled through the portal followed by angry shouting and multilingual curses.

CHAPTER 3

~ YAROSLAV ~

It didn't take Yaroslav long to get from Miami Beach to Ft. Lauderdale. Even though he owned a vehicle, he moved a lot faster without it. In the dead of night, when the air was cool and fresh, he preferred to enjoy a free run as opposed to driving in the confinements of a metal box humans called a car.

He had been walking this world for many centuries, gradually learning and getting used to the advancement of technology and modern-day lifestyle. Yet when he was alone, some things he preferred to do the old way, ignoring the technological inventions of the twenty-first century. Cars were one of those modern inventions he didn't care about.

Yaroslav halted in front of the high-rise with the large logo of *EverSafe Security* on it—his mother's building. He could have gone straight home, but the events of this fight bothered him and since Akira was the one who sent them there, he wanted to speak with her about everything that had happened. He could sense Akira's presence from anywhere, and he knew she was still in her office.

He smirked, thinking about the lecture his mother would give him about not using the car, and ran his hands through his windblown hair trying to organize it the best he could. His hair was stiff with blood and thick with dirt, and soon he gave up his futile attempts to make himself look presentable.

Quickly, he ran up the steps and headed toward the large glass door. As he put his hand on the door handle, he sensed a hardly noticeable presence behind him and stilled. He was no longer alone. Yaroslav reached under his trench coat and wrapped his fingers around the grip of his sword, staring at the reflection of the street in the mirror-like surface of the door.

Two dark SUVs were parked across the street from the *Ever-Safe* building. He didn't notice any people inside the vehicles, but it didn't mean they weren't around. Yaroslav cursed under his breath. How could he miss something like that? For a quick moment, he considered going inside the building, but then changed his mind. He pulled his sword out and spun around in one lightning-fast motion.

Before he finished his movement, he saw eight men advancing at him with the speed that rivaled his own. *Vampires*, thought Yaroslav, raising his katana. Two swords came together in a mighty clash, the loud clutter of metal on metal ringing through the empty street. Yaroslav growled, pushing his opponent back, but the man was just as strong and as fast as he was. And he wasn't alone.

The men surrounded Yaroslav, maneuvering him away from the building and forcing him down the steps. The attackers were giving him a hard time, and he had no doubt that these vampires were just as old if not older than he was. His vampire speed and strength were no longer his advantage as he was fighting his equals.

Nevertheless, he was still a better swordsman than they were, and it didn't take him long to outmaneuver them. One at the time, he beheaded four of them, leaving steaming piles of ash on the marble steps. He spun around, and his katana—a silvery blur in the blueish light of the streetlights—carried death with every strike. A few minutes later, he had two more of his opponents reduced to ashes and the remaining two were slowly retreating toward the road, struggling to deflect his fierce attacks.

Silent and fast like death itself, he quickly moved forward. His katana swished through the air, decapitating one of the remaining two vampires. As the headless body hit the asphalt, quickly dissolving into ashes, Yaroslav turned toward the last man. With a swift flick of his blade, he captured his opponent's sword near its hilt and moved it around in a circle, disarming him. His attacker's sword flew up in a large silvery arch and landed on the road with a loud clang.

The vampire staggered backward and lost his balance, falling flat on his back. At full speed, Yaroslav covered the distance between them, pressed the man's chest down with his foot, and placed the blade of his katana under his chin.

"Who sent you after me and why?" Yaroslav hissed, his long fangs expanding.

The vampire stared at him but there was no fear in his glowing eyes. His lips slowly stretched into a snarl, displaying a set of fangs just as dangerous as Yaroslav's. For a moment, his eyes lingered on something behind Yaroslav's back and his smile grew wider and more sinister.

Before Yaroslav realized that something was going on, a thick silver chain wrapped around his neck, forcing him to his knees. He grunted as silver came in contact with his skin. His hands trembled, and he dropped his katana. A second chain wrapped around his chest, pinning his arms to his body.

Yaroslav pushed against his restraints, ignoring the burning pain around his neck and the weakness inflicted by silver, but the man who held him just squeezed the chain tighter. Another vampire seized Yaroslav's hair, wringing it around his arm and yanked his head backward.

"Prince Yaroslav Potemkin," he hissed into his ear, "stop

struggling, boy. I have an order to bring you in either alive or as a pile of ashes in a small box. You are going with me, one way or the other. How you are going to go is entirely up to you."

"It's been centuries since someone dared call me a boy, dumbass," growled Yaroslav, his muscles straining under the chains.

The first vampire got up and approached him. Slowly he put a pair of thick leather gloves on and then ripped Yaroslav's shirt, pressing the silver chains to the bare skin of his chest and stomach. Yaroslav grunted as searing pain took hold of him, weakness slowly turning his muscles into mush.

"That's a good boy…"

He heard the voice of the man who held him restrained, pulling his head back, but it sounded hollow and distant. Somewhere on the outskirts of his mind he heard another voice. Gunz… His friend was calling him, using their psychic connection. He was asking for help, and for the first time since they had met, Yaroslav couldn't be there for him. His hands tightened into fists and he howled, pushing against the chains with whatever strength the silver had left in his body.

The vampire standing in front of him pulled his leg back and kicked him in his face. His head jerked to the side and blood filled his mouth, spilling between his lips to his chin, trickling down to his chest. He coughed, spitting the blood, and received another kick, this time to his stomach.

For the next few minutes, the vampire kept punching and kicking him, not holding anything back. Affected by the silver, his wounds weren't healing and when the vamp finally stopped, Yaroslav had no energy left in him. The other man finally let go of his hair and his head dropped to his chest, thick drops of blood dripping from his mouth.

Yaroslav felt a touch of something sharp to the bare skin of his chest and he cracked his eyelids open. A sharp wooden stake was positioned right over his heart. He stared at the stake for a moment and started to laugh. A quiet chuckle in the beginning, it became louder and finally he was laughing hysterically, unable to stop.

"What's so funny, your royal assholeness?" hissed the man, pressing the stake deeper into his chest.

Yaroslav watched a few drops of blood escaping from under the wood and just shook his head no, unable to put two words together.

"Well, *I* think it's funny."

He heard a familiar girlish voice and raised his head with effort. A young woman was standing a few feet away from him. She had a round face, covered in a multitude of freckles and her azure eyes were sparkling with anger. She frowned, taking a step closer to them and waved at someone behind Yaroslav's back.

"Hey, dipshits," she yelled, planting her hands on her hips, clothed into tight blue jeans. "Is that any way to treat ancient royalty?"

"Peyton," whispered Yaroslav, "run…"

Peyton's large eyes halted on his face and a lopsided smirk curved her full lips. "Why should I?" she asked, winking at him, her expression cold and slightly arrogant, and added in a deliberately loud whisper, "I think your undead friends overstayed their welcome and it's time for them to leave… Hastily."

The vampires barked laughing, and Yaroslav clenched his teeth as he felt the wooden stake slithering deeper into his chest. Peyton probably noticed that too because she extended her arms forward and yelled, *"Ignius!"*

A blazing jet of fire escaped her hands, almost as powerful as Gunz's and Yaroslav winced, expecting the fire to hit him square in his chest, but her targeting was beyond reproach. The fire rushed past Yaroslav, engulfing him in smoldering heat, but didn't touch him even slightly. Unfortunately, Peyton's fire strike didn't produce the result he was hoping for.

Just like earlier, the fire wrapped around the men, doing them no harm.

She didn't seem to be discouraged but rather switched her tactics. *"Ventius!"* she yelled, and a powerful blast of wind rushed toward the vampires. This time Yaroslav knew her spell was going to impact him, but he had no way of avoiding it.

The powerful blast of air slammed him in the chest, and he fell back, propelled a few feet away. Together with him, the man who was holding the stake against his heart also fell, but not before he drove the stake all the way into his chest. Yaroslav screamed as pain, the likes of which he had never felt before, contorted his body. His fingers wrapped around the stake involuntarily and his body arched. Peyton was by his side in two long strides, but she hardly glanced at him.

"Ventius Amplio!" she yelled again, and the second blast of wind, more powerful than the first one, propelled the rest of his enemies across the street.

A moment later, Yaroslav heard the sound of a vehicle taking off at high speed. He groaned as agonizing pain twisted his body, making his every muscle spasm. The young woman stepped over him, her legs positioned on either side of him and made a circular motion with her hand.

"Oprimenta Amnia," she whispered, and the soft yellow glow of a cloaking spell erupted around them. She stepped aside and kneeled next to him, carefully exploring the piece of wood protruding from his chest. Then she scratched the back of her head and arched her copper eyebrows at him. "Just curious. Why aren't you dust?"

"He missed my heart." Yaroslav grunted, squeezing the stake tighter, but he had no strength to pull it out. "Peyton, you need to pull it out. Just do it slowly and carefully. And no matter what you do, don't—"

Peyton wrapped her fingers around the stake and yanked it out. Yaroslav howled as his body arched in response to the sharp pain and cringed inwardly at the crunching sound accompanying her move.

"Oops..." She stared at the stake in her hand with a sheepish grin on her face, probing the broken tip with her finger.

"That's exactly what I was trying to avoid," growled Yaroslav. "You left a piece of wood in my chest. Now, you have to fish for it."

"Not a chance," she objected, throwing the blood-smeared stake away, disgust curving her lips.

"Peyton, you left a piece of wood in my chest," Yaroslav repeated with a groan, pressing his hand to the gaping hole right above his heart. "Unless you pull it out, I can't regain my strength."

"Are you crazy?" yelled Peyton, jerking her hands up. "I will not to put my hand inside you! Vampire cooties. Ew!"

"Ugh, Peyton!" Yaroslav yelled and cringed as the next wave of pain spiraled through him. "We don't have time for that. The people who attacked me can come back at any time. And I can't fight! Goddamnit! I can't even walk! Put your hand inside this hole and find that piece of wood you left there. This is the only way I can regain my strength and heal."

"Fine," muttered Peyton, "here is what I'm going to do. I'll take you wherever you want to go, but I ain't putting my hands anywhere next to your holes—"

A painful laughter escaped Yaroslav's lips and dark, thick liquid trickled from the corner of his mouth. "Sweetie, I don't want you touching any of my holes either. Just find that goddamn piece of wood in my chest. That's all I want. Trust me, I've been a vampire for centuries. I already forgot what disease means. You're not going to get the bird flu by touching my blood."

"How about syphilis?" she asked snidely.

"Peyton!" shouted Yaroslav raising his head, his eyes lighting up with a furious scarlet glow. This effort took his last strength, and he fell back with a soft moan. "Please…"

"Fine, where do you want me to take you? Your mother? We are right next to her *EverSafe Security* building."

Yaroslav thought for a moment and shook his head no. "Not my mother. I don't want her involved in whatever this is. Take me to Aidan McGrath. His penthouse is warded so heavily, it's like a magical fortress—no one can get in or out without his permission."

"And how exactly can I get in then, oh bright one?" asked Peyton, a cold sarcastic smirk splitting her face.

"Have you ever heard of knocking on the door?" Yaroslav chuckled and regretted it immediately, clasping his hand to his wound. "Did you know you can try these good old-fashioned human ways? Not everything needs to be solved by magic."

"I had no idea," muttered Peyton, rolling her eyes. "This concept is absolutely foreign to me."

She pushed her arms under his armpits and attempted to pull him up. Yaroslav clenched his jaw and a low growl rumbled in his chest.

"What are you doing? Are you set on torturing me?" he managed to say as she pulled him up into a kneeling position.

"Taking you to Aidan's fortress," she muttered while circling around him.

"And how are you planning to do that?" he asked snidely. "If you just listened to me and removed this piece of wood from my chest, I wouldn't need your assistance."

She ignored his statement. "Help me get you up to your feet." She groaned, as she strained to pull him up to no avail.

Yaroslav sighed but picked up his katana and sheathed it beneath his trench coat. Then he gathered whatever strength he could find and slowly got up to his feet, leaning heavily on her shoulder. The world around him spun, and he swayed, grasping at Peyton's shoulder to stop himself from falling.

"Are you going to open a portal?" he asked through clenched teeth, pressing his hand to the bleeding hole in his chest.

"Do I look like a frigging Master of Power to you?" she retorted furiously. "I can't open a portal and I can't teleport either."

"Then how are you planning to take me there!" yelled Yaroslav, throwing his free hand in the air. "I'm at least a foot taller than you and probably a hundred pounds heavier. Please enlighten me!"

"I'll use the new kind of magic," she replied dryly, carefully directing him toward the road. "It's called a 2016 Nissan Altima." She waved her hand at a small sedan parked at the side of the road.

Peyton was a lot stronger than she appeared, but it still took them a few minutes to make it all the way to the car. Once there, Yaroslav leaned heavily on the side of the vehicle, resting his head atop his folded arms as he waited for her to unlock the doors.

"Your Highness," she said with a mocking bow, opening the passenger door for him, "your royal carriage has arrived."

Yaroslav rolled his eyes and pushed himself off the vehicle. There was only one step from the place he was standing to the front door, but he couldn't make it. Everything was dancing around him, and his body was a giant aching knot. She probably noticed his struggle, because she wrapped her arm around his waist to steady him and helped him to sit down.

He heard the soft click of a seatbelt and smiled faintly. "I'm a vampire, remember..." he whispered without opening his eyes. "I don't need a seatbelt... can't die in a car crash."

"I can see that," muttered Peyton, starting the engine and then added, "Royal pain, that's what you are."

CHAPTER 4

~ AIDAN ~

Aidan teleported to the dark beach behind the high-rise where he lived. He was exhausted, drenched in blood and some other sticky substance, but he wanted to think a few things over before going home. For him, a stroll on a dark beach was always the best way to focus and think clearly. He took his shoes off and headed toward the stormy ocean, stepping on the cold sand barefoot. The wind picked up and a soft drizzle hung in the air, but he ignored the weather conditions and slowly walked by the edge of the water.

Who were these men? It seemed like they were expecting Gunz, Yaroslav and him to be there at that exact time. How had they known? They were demons and vampires, but he doubted they belonged to any of South Florida supernatural organizations.

Both demonic queens Akira and Aisling kept their subjects under strict control, and they wouldn't tolerate any disobedience. Well aware that Aidan and his team were at peace with *EverSafe*, they wouldn't dare cross them. And come on… Akira would never send someone after her own son.

Assuming a vampire could experience such a strong

emotion as motherly love, what Akira felt toward Yaroslav could have been described as such. Yaroslav was her only weakness. *Not really,* Aidan corrected himself with a smirk. *I think she also adopted Zane. I don't know how he did it, but the infamous Scarlet Queen cares for him more than she wishes to admit.*

His phone vibrated and buzzed in his pocket, breaking his train of thought. He dropped his shoes before pulling the device out and answered the call. His security company was notifying him that the intrusion alarm was triggered inside his school. Aidan frowned, wondering if this incident was somehow related to the mysterious group of demons they had been fighting earlier.

He checked the video feed of the security cameras inside the school but didn't notice anything or anyone in the dark dojang. Aidan frowned, staring at his phone—nothing was moving. What could have triggered the alarm? A feeling of unease spread through him, chilling his soul. He grunted as he shoved the phone in his pocket and snapped his fingers, vanishing from the beach.

AIDAN MANIFESTED IN THE MIDDLE OF THE SMALL PARKING LOT AT the back of his school. It was empty, dark and silent, just the way it was supposed to be at this time of night. The weather seemed to be a lot worse in Parkland. The temperature had dropped, and the rain was throwing streams of cold water at him, soaking his clothes through. He shivered, just now noticing that he was barefoot.

Carefully, he channeled his magic and surveyed the building with his other sight. While he didn't sense the presence of any magical energy, something still bothered him. He pulled the keys out and slowly approached the backdoor. Trying to produce as little noise as possible, he unlocked it and stepped inside.

As soon as he crossed the threshold, dark magical energy, which he hadn't noticed before, slammed into him, overwhelming his senses. Gasping for air, Aidan staggered back to find the door shut and locked. He fumbled with his keys, searching for the right one, when dark energy spiked up around him to a new high.

He had no time to think. He had no time to transition into his full godly form. He hardly had any time to react. *"Praecidio Amnia,"* muttered Aidan, dropping to his knees, and wrapped his arms over his head as he bent all the way to the floor.

Triggered by magic, an explosion sounded right next to him. The ceiling and the walls collapsed, burying him under a pile of concrete, rocks and debris. Even though the protective dome of his spell held, shielding him from serious injuries, the sound was so loud that for a while he couldn't hear anything except a blaring buzzing in his ears. Everything went dark in front of his eyes and his thoughts scrambled into uncontrollable turmoil.

It took him a little while to calm down and start thinking straight. Whoever had done this didn't know he was a god. Otherwise, why would they use a bomb, or any mundane weapon for that matter? Yes, an explosion could have damaged or even destroyed his physical body, forcing him to return to the Otherworld, but once he had healed, he would be back with a vengeance...

Once I heal? Wait. Maybe they do know that I'm a god... Aidan tried to organize his thoughts, but they were escaping him, slithering away like slippery serpents. *Someone wants me out of this realm... at least for a few days. Why?*

A dense curtain of dust still hung in the air obscuring his vision. Carefully, he opened his magical sight, checking the area outside his protection spell, and now all his doubts were gone—he wasn't alone. As his mind finally cleared, fury slowly boiled up in him. He channeled his power and assumed his godly form. The blinding white light expanded around him, and he roared, rising to his feet, as if there wasn't a pile of bricks, concrete and debris lying on top of him.

A blast wave of undiluted power rushed in every direction, disintegrating concrete into nothing more than dust. Aidan stood in the middle of a disaster area that used to be his school, his chest rising and falling with heavy breaths, his eyes blazing with the brilliant light of his magic.

A ringing sound of slow clapping bounced in his ears. He flinched and snapped around. As the dust slowly settled down, he saw that he was surrounded by at least twenty men, if not more. All of them were dressed in tactical uniforms and in their hands, they held assault rifles, pointed at him. The malignant energy of their magic and the stench of their demonic essence polluted the air, leaving no doubts in his mind—he was dealing with a group of demons, powerful ones.

Aidan spread his arms wide, a slow smile stretching his lips. "What are you waiting for?" he asked frostily. "Here I am. Fire!"

They did.

The dry bark of automatic weapons tore the silence, and the air boiled with flying bullets. Aidan lifted his hand and the bullets froze in midair. Then he snapped his fingers and every single bullet fell on the floor. The heavy odor of gunpowder mixed with dust and smoke lingered in the air. He inhaled and slowly turned around, his eyes sliding from one masked face to the next.

"My turn," he whispered and the blast wave of his power spread around him.

The same power blast had just evaporated concrete, but the group of men surrounding him just staggered back a few steps, otherwise completely unaffected.

What the hell?

As the demons backed away from their original position,

Aidan noticed a glowing yellow line on the floor, curving around him. He spun in place, realizing that he was locked in a circle created by some type of a dark spell. Chills went down his spine and he felt cold sweat trickling down his back—if it was God's snare, he was trapped. He took a deep breath, quickly probing the circle. It was glowing yellow instead of white, so it wasn't God's snare. Besides, he could freely channel his power within the circle and the God's snare would drain his magic, severing his connection with the outside world.

What kind of magic is this?

He took a couple of steps forward and ran into an invisible wall. Ignoring the pain on his forehead and the snickering of demons, he placed his hand on the barrier and attempted to break through. Even a full blast of his godly power had no effect on this strange spell. It buzzed angrily and lit up with a bright yellow glow but didn't budge. Soft chuckles and then outright laughter surrounded him as he attempted to bring down the barrier again.

After a few futile attempts, Aidan gave up. He lowered his arms and glared at his captors, struggling to keep overwhelming fury from boiling over.

"What do you want?" he growled, and the floor trembled as his turmoiled emotions made him lose control of his power for a moment.

A tall demon stepped forward, almost touching the circle of magic. "Aodh mac Lir, we want you to return to the Otherworld and never come back. Do that, and we're not going to hurt you."

"Hurt me," repeated Aidan, having a hard time believing what he was hearing. "As it seems, you are well aware that I am a god. How are you planning to hurt me?"

"Like this," replied the demon, baring his teeth in a wolfish grin.

He squatted down in front of the glowing yellow line on the floor. As he touched the circle of magic with his fingers, muttering something under his breath, multiple lightning bolts erupted from the invisible magical barrier, striking Aidan from every direction.

Every muscle in Aidan's body contracted, and he collapsed, his fingers spasmodically grasping at the floor. He screamed, his jaws locked together by the electric shock. The demon let go for a moment, just to strike him again. Aidan howled, shocked to hear that his vocal cords could produce such a gut-wrenching sound, feeling as if his body was taken apart cell by cell. As an unbearable torment crippled him, he blacked out for a moment.

When he regained consciousness, he found himself lying on the floor, still surrounded by the demonic team and trapped by the circle of unknown magic. He turned his head to the side, not sure he could speak.

"Aodh mac Lir," the same demon addressed him, his voice laced with arrogance and superiority, "now you know we're quite capable of hurting you. Let me also assure you—we can keep you locked in the circle of this spell for as long as we deem necessary. Having said that, we're willing to let you leave in one piece, as long as you go back to the Otherworld and never return."

Aidan slowly raised his hand in a peaceful gesture, gasping air with his mouth open. He struggled to sit up but couldn't, electricity still surging through his body, making his muscles contract involuntarily. After a moment, he raised his hand again, but instead of replying to the demon, he quickly drew a rune in the air above him. In one swift motion, he infused it with his power and slammed his palm against it. As the next electric assault arched his body, he growled Uri's name through his clenched teeth, summoning him.

A bright golden glow flooded the area and for a moment everything quieted down—the electric shocks ceased, and the demons fell silent. Aidan exhaled, his breath coming out in a soft moan. A tall man was slowly descending, supported by large golden wings. Even though his body was enveloped in golden flames, there was neither heat nor smoke.

He stepped down next to Aidan, folding his wings behind his back and gave him a curt nod. Then he approached the yellow circle of the spell, carefully probing it with his fingers. An icy smile touched his lips as he turned back to Aidan and offered him his hand.

"Uri, thank you," Aidan managed to say, taking his hand and got up with a soft groan, every muscle in his body aching.

"Aidan, it's not going to be easy, but I'll get you out of this trap," said Uri quietly. "When I tell you to run, teleport out of here, do you understand me?"

"I can't leave you here alone," mumbled Aidan, "these demons—"

"If I'm not mistaken, these demons are powered by the energy of Chaos, and you need to figure out what's going on. Live today to fight tomorrow. I'll be fine," Uri cut him off and turned around while unsheathing his sword.

Aidan stood behind his friend, unease twisting his gut. How could he leave Uri alone to face at least twenty demonic entities, fueled by the energy of Chaos? As if hearing Aidan's thought, Uri glanced back at him and his brows drew together.

"Do what I say when I say it," he ordered, opening his golden wings to full extent.

The sword in his hands got engulfed in golden flames and Uri swung it, crashing it at the invisible shield of the dark spell with his full might. A wave of fire spread around him, yet it wasn't burning. It wrapped around Aidan, embracing him, gentle and soft, but didn't penetrate the shield.

Uri closed his eyes and slowly moved his head from left to right, rolling his shoulders. Then he opened his eyes and laughed, a cold and dangerous sound. The demons backed away from him, a shadow of fear reflected in their eyes visible through the slits of their mask. But they recovered quickly and started to chant.

The yellow circle of their malignant magic shone brighter, and the shield buzzed like an angry beehive. Uri held his sword with both hands and brought it up to the full extent of his arms. A glowing beam of light projected up from his flaming blade, disappearing into the dark, stormy sky.

With no rush, he brought his sword down, cutting through the shield like it was nothing but a piece of paper. For a brief moment, the shield became visible and Aidan could see a thin, dark fracture in its poisonous-yellow glow where Uri cut through it with his sword. The demons saw it too because they roared and shifted closer to them, holding their automatic weapons at the ready.

"Aidan, now!" shouted Uri, slicing the shield with his sword again.

The shield crashed with a thunderous bang and the demons opened fire. Uri held his hand up, freezing the bullets in midair and smirked. Slowly, he stepped across the yellow slimy line and brought his sword to his shoulder.

"Next," Uri said softly, and the demons shuddered at the sound of freezing hatred in his voice.

Aidan swallowed hard, feeling like a traitor but snapped his fingers and vanished from his demolished school.

CHAPTER 5

~ AIDAN ~

Aidan manifested on the dark deserted shore, ravaged by the approaching tropical storm, and dropped to his knees, breathing hard. The rain intensified and cool streams of water ran down his face and shoulders, his half-torn shirt clinging to his body. A powerful gust of wind rushed through the beach, ruffling his wet hair, but he didn't feel the cold.

"I shouldn't have left him alone," he whispered, his voice hoarse. "What did I do?" Tormented by remorse, he bent forward, pressing his palms to his eyes and stilled, considering teleporting back to make sure Uri survived the encounter with the demonic team. *Live today to fight tomorrow.* Uri was right... He had to figure out what was going on first. Raising his head, he allowed the cold streams of rain to wash over his face, wiping away his doubts.

He got up and slowly started on his way to the swimming pool area of his condominium building. He passed through the gate and stopped, observing the area. The deck and bar were empty which wasn't a surprise. Besides the fact that it was late, all the residents were in their tightly shut apartments, riding out the storm. The dim light of the outdoor deck lights barely illuminated the area, but it was enough for Aidan to see and what he saw made his blood run cold.

Peyton sat on the floor, leaning her back against the wall of the bar. Gunz lay next to her, his head resting on her lap. Even though her hand, covered in brown stains of dried out blood, brushed absentmindedly through his wet hair, he didn't react to her touch. He didn't react to the rain drenching him with cold water either. With his eyes closed and his lips slightly parted, he appeared to be sleeping, but the tears silently sliding down Peyton's face told Aidan that it wasn't the case.

Yaroslav sat on her other side, his hand pressed to his chest, and thin red streams of blood mixed with rainwater ran between his fingers, down his arm. His head was bowed down low and his wet hair matted with blood and dirt fell in limp strands over his face.

"Peyton," mumbled Aidan, paralyzed by fear, his legs filled with lead.

As quietly as he spoke, she heard him and looked up. "Aidan, thank God," she said quietly, her eyes lighting up with hope. "You're a god, right? You can heal him, right? Zane... I think he's—"

"No," Aidan growled, covering the space between them in a few long-legged strides. He dropped to his knees next to Gunz and quickly scanned him with his magical sight. Gunz's heart was barely beating in his chest and the fire energy had risen to a dangerous level within him. Except for a deep laceration on his leg, he didn't notice any other injuries, but the cut was still bleeding, and a dark puddle of blood spread under him.

"You can heal him, Aidan. Right?" Peyton repeated, gazing pleadingly at him.

"No... I'm not that kind of god. I have no healing power," he whispered, shuddering. "We can't let him die, Peyton. If Zane dies a human death... Oh, God..." He let his gaze wander over the buildings surrounding them, frowning. "All these high-rises are full of humans... they will all be dead."

"I can heal him," said Yaroslav faintly, lifting his face. "I told her, but she doesn't listen to me and I'm too weak to move because of the friggin' piece of wood she left in my chest." He tried to get up but fell back with a strained moan, his ashen face contorted with pain. "Aidan, take my blood and give it to Zane."

Aidan carefully lifted Gunz and got up to his feet with a grunt, holding him in his arms. With horror he watched his friend's arms limply hang down, his head thrown back lifelessly. He took one step toward Yaroslav and halted, holding his breath. The same dark energy signature he had sensed when he had been attacked at his school earlier was present in the area. Coming from far away, it wasn't strong, but he recognized it immediately.

"No time..." he exhaled.

Before he knew it, the malevolent energy signature increased, becoming powerful enough for Peyton to sense it.

"What is it?" she asked, pressing her hand over her mouth and nose.

"Help Yaroslav get up," ordered Aidan, ignoring her question. "We need to leave, and we need to do it fast."

Reacting to the urgency in his voice, she didn't ask anything else but wrapped her arms around the vampire and tried to pull him up. He was too heavy for her and she let go, dropping him without much care if he would get hurt.

"Dammit!" hissed Aidan.

He lowered down to his knees and carefully placed Gunz over his shoulder. Then he seized Yaroslav's arm and turned to Peyton.

"Can we go to your apartment?" She nodded, and he continued, "Hold on to me—"

His words were swallowed by a loud explosion. The air shuddered with a blast wave and a thunderous echo rolled through the midnight neighborhood. The fire alarm howled, and the terror-infused screams filled the area as people started to run out of the building.

Aidan slowly raised his head up and stared at his penthouse. The windows were shattered, and hungry flames were quickly devouring everything inside. Someone just blew up his home and whoever they were, they weren't kidding. They wanted him out of their way bad enough, so they were willing to do pretty much anything to achieve their goal.

"Dammit," he cursed again, his every muscle tense with fury. He made sure that Peyton was holding tight to him and snapped his fingers, teleporting all of them to the staircase in front of her apartment.

* * *

IT WASN'T THE FIRST TIME AIDAN VISITED PEYTON'S APARTMENT building. Since she had started working with Agent Jim Andrews, there were a few occasions when he had to pick her up from her home, waiting by her door, but she had never invited him to come in. Nevertheless, he knew the area around it well and teleporting wasn't a problem.

"Why didn't you teleport straight inside the apartment," asked Peyton, shoving her hand into her pocket angrily, searching for the key.

"Because I have never been inside before—that's one reason. And the second reason is Yaroslav," replied Aidan tiredly, gently lowering Gunz to the floor. "Come on, Peyton, don't you know anything about the vampires and upirs? Their blood has healing properties and they can't walk into your home uninvited."

"I know more than enough," barked Peyton, forcing the key

into the door lock. "Dirty, disgusting, bloodsucking leaches—that's what they are. I don't want to have anything to do with them."

"Not all of them, Peyton," Aidan objected quietly, throwing a quick glance at Yaroslav. The vampire lowered his eyes and his exhausted face grew a shade paler, if it was even possible. "Invite him in."

"Fine." Peyton pursed her lips, not even trying to hide her aggravation. "Hey, royal pain," she said dryly, gesturing at Yaroslav, "you can come in. I will uninvite you later."

Yaroslav didn't move. He didn't even lift his eyes, staring at his hands, covered in red and brown stains. Aidan gave her a frosty look, his mouth set in a hard line. He had never seen Peyton so mean and rude. Normally, she was the sweetest, slightly awkward girl and everyone loved being around her. She had seen Yaroslav before but had never had to work with him, and now that he thought back, he couldn't remember her ever approach and talk to the vampire.

Aidan shook his head slightly, wondering what that was all about, but right now he had no time to think about it. He lifted Gunz and carried him inside the apartment where he put him on the floor. With horror, he noticed that the bleeding had almost stopped, and Gunz's fire energy rose so high, Aidan could see it without using his other sight. Gunz was a step away from the human death and the Fire Salamander in him was quickly taking over.

"Dammit," he cursed and rushed out the door.

Yaroslav still sat in the same position, a puddle of rainwater spreading around him. As a vampire he could sit without moving for hours, but there was something desperate and eerie in his stillness now. Aidan had no doubt that it wasn't only his injury that made him so unresponsive—Peyton's words hurt him worse than the wooden stake through his chest.

"Slavik," said Aidan, squatting next to him and Yaroslav slowly lifted his face, a haunted expression in his bloodshot eyes. "I know you don't want to go inside, but Zane is dying, and you are the only one who can heal him. Besides, I need to get that piece of wood out of your chest, so you can heal yourself. Please, help me."

"You want me to help you?" Yaroslav chuckled mirthlessly and grunted, pressing his hand to his chest. "I need *your* help to get up," he added quietly and looked away, the vibe of discomfort getting heavier around him.

Aidan helped Yaroslav to his feet, wrapping his arm around his waist to steady him, but as soon as they made it across the threshold, Yaroslav froze, every muscle in his body tense. His eyes widened in shock and his fangs expanded, as a low hiss escaped his lips.

Aidan looked around, realizing with a shock that everything inside Peyton's apartment was vampire-proofed. The walls were covered in runes, wooden crosses and some other artifacts Aidan couldn't recognize, but no doubt that they had something to do with vampires. He even noticed a few bunches of garlic hanging by the window. Things like crosses and garlic were just urban legends, and they didn't really affect vampires. But most of the runes and artifacts on her walls were the real deal.

"Aidan, get me out of here, please," Yaroslav panted, leaning heavily on Aidan's shoulder. "A bloodsucking leach… like me… shouldn't be here…"

"As soon as we heal Zane," Aidan murmured, helping Yaroslav to sit down in the center of the room, away from the walls.

"Get a cup," said Yaroslav, his voice almost a whisper. He bent his legs with a low grunt and rested his arms atop his knees, leaning forward.

Aidan quickly walked into the kitchen and found Peyton

standing there, leaning against the counter. She glanced at Aidan, her face void of emotions, and waved at the cabinet next to her. "Glasses are up there."

He shook his head reproachfully, grabbed one glass and walked out of the kitchen. Everything inside him was screaming in indignation and most of all, he wanted to give Peyton a piece of his mind, but he couldn't waste his time on this conversation right now.

As soon as Aidan walked back into the living room and approached him, Yaroslav bit his left wrist, allowing thick red liquid to spill into the glass. Aidan lifted Gunz's head and pressed the glass to his opened lips, letting a few drops of the vampire's blood trickle into his mouth. Then he put the glass on the floor and pressed on his jaw, closing his mouth. Gunz remained motionless, and his Adam's apple didn't move.

"I was too late," Aidan muttered under his breath, cold sweat trickling down his back, blending with the rainwater. With his heart pounding against his ribcage, he wondered if his power shield could contain the elemental energy of the Fire Salamander in his natural state. His second thought was conjuring a God's snare, but he doubted he had enough energy in him to place and sustain such a complicated spell.

"No, you weren't," objected Yaroslav. "I can hear his heart beating."

Struggling to his knees, he crawled closer to Gunz and sat down next to him. With an effort, he lifted Gunz's head and pressed his bleeding wrist to his lips.

"Now, Gunz, just like old times, my friend," the vampire whispered into his ear, gently tugging at his jaw. Gunz didn't react. "God knows I didn't want to do it to you."

Gently, Yaroslav lowered Gunz's head on the floor and leaned forward. He found the deep laceration on Gunz's thigh and squeezed it with his hand, his sharp vampire's claws digging into his wound. Gunz jerked away from him and cried out.

"That's it, you're back, alive... now drink," Yaroslav muttered. In one swift motion, he pressed his bleeding wrist to Gunz's lips again and grabbed his arm, sinking his fangs into it above the elbow.

"What are you doing, leach?" yelled Peyton, her features distorted by searing rage. She bolted toward the vampire with a wooden stake in her hand, but Aidan seized her wrist and yanked her back.

"If I didn't know you any better, I would—," he growled, cutting himself off before he said something he would regret later.

He kept squeezing her wrists in his iron grip until she unlocked her fingers and the wooden stake dropped to the floor with a loud clatter.

"Please allow me to explain." He jerked Peyton closer and leaned down, now staring directly into her eyes. "Yaroslav just saved Zane's life and the lives of hundreds of humans in this apartment complex. Zane was unconscious and since we don't have ammonium salts handy here, hurting him was the only way Yaroslav could wake him up. Then he bit him because the vampire's bite has pain-suppressing quality."

As a proof of his words, Gunz moaned and seized Yaroslav's wrist, pressing it tighter to his mouth. A few seconds later, Yaroslav pulled away and lay down on the floor, closing his eyes. "He should be okay now," he said faintly.

Gunz opened his eyes and sat up, looking disoriented and mildly surprised by his surroundings. "Where am I?" he mumbled, his fingers massaging his thigh absentmindedly.

His foggy gaze stopped on Aidan and then moved to Yaroslav, who was sprawled on the floor next to him. His eyes widened as he noticed the dark hole in the vampire's chest and he leaned over him, gently shaking his shoulder.

"Yaroslav!" he called. "Slavik!"

The vampire opened his eyes and the corners of his lips

lifted ever so slightly. "Gunz," he whispered, "I'm sorry, but I had to reinstate our psychic bond. I know you hated it—sorry about that…"

"What are you talking about, man?" Gunz smiled, squeezing the vampire's shoulder slightly. "You saved me and all the people around here. Thank you."

"Sorry, I couldn't be there when you called me earlier," Yaroslav said barely audible, and his eyes rolled back.

Gunz turned to Aidan, a shadow of fear crossing his face. "Aidan, what is wrong with him? Why is he not healing?"

"A long story." Aidan stared at Yaroslav sprawled on the floor and frowned. "But here is the short version. A piece of wood is stuck in his chest. I need to remove it."

He lowered down next to Yaroslav, just now noticing how sore and exhausted he truly was. Even though he hadn't been injured during the earlier explosions, he felt like there wasn't a place in his body that didn't hurt. He placed his hands over Yaroslav's chest and grunted—gray with dust and dirt, his arms were shaking uncontrollably. He pulled his hands back, locking and unlocking his fingers.

"Aidan, are you sure you can do it?" asked Gunz, staring at his friend with concern. "What happened to you? You look like a building collapsed on top of you. And Yaroslav? Who did that to him?"

"Well, a building did collapse on top of me—my school to be precise. I'll tell you everything later," he promised, gently shaking Yaroslav awake. "Yaroslav, I'll use my magic to remove that splinter from your chest. You'll feel some discomfort, but it's going to be fast. Just try not to move while I'm doing it. Okay?"

"Go for it," replied Yaroslav. "I think I can handle some discomfort."

Aidan placed his hand over Yaroslav's chest, channeled his

magic, and whispered just one word, "*Transvectum*." The vampire didn't move, but his eyes flew wide open and he screamed like someone was tearing his heart out of his chest.

"It's over," said Aidan soothingly, showing him a piece of wood in the palm of his hand. "Sorry, Slavik, that was the only way."

"Some discomfort? Motherf—" Yaroslav panted, pressing his hand to his chest, and then added a few more choice words in Russian that made Gunz do a doubletake. Carefully, he lifted his hand and peered down at his chest. The wound was no longer bleeding and the edges were slowly closing. "Thank you, Aidan."

"I thought you forgot most of your Russian," said Gunz, observing the vampire with a lopsided grin.

"The important words I still remember," growled Yaroslav, but the corners of his mouth lifted in a weak smile.

A few minutes later, he got up, straightened his ripped shirt and pants and made sure that his sword was still safely sheathed beneath his trench coat. His eyes fell on Peyton and for a moment, he visibly stiffened, a look of torment crossing his handsome features, but quickly recovered and bowed to her displaying the best manners of a medieval courtier.

"My lady," he said calmly meeting Peyton's gaze but not addressing her by her name, "thank you for your assistance and for allowing me to enter your home. You can perform a spell to uninvite me, but I swear on my honor, I'll never cross your threshold again."

Yaroslav turned around and headed toward the door, but as soon as he put his hand on the door handle, he hissed and jerked his hand away. He turned around, a guilty look on his face and sighed.

"Aidan, can you please open the door for me?" he asked through gritted teeth. "The door handle is silver."

Maybe it was all the stress of this endless night or the fact that he just lost his home and his school. Or maybe it was the fact that he almost lost two of his best friends and he still didn't know what had happened to Uri, but something snapped inside Aidan. He spun around to face Peyton and a dangerous white light lit up in his eyes.

"What the hell is wrong with you, Peyton!" he yelled and the walls of the apartment building trembled like it was a house of cards. "Yes, Yaroslav is an ancient vampire. Yes, he lives on a liquid diet. But it's been years since he fed and killed a human. His vampiric nature doesn't make him a soulless bloodsucking leach, the way you put it. Yaroslav is our friend! Every day he stands by our side, fighting for the people of our city! He saved both Zane and me countless times—"

"And what did he do before he had met you? What did he do hundreds of years ago when his mother—the deadliest vampire in human history after Dracula himself—turned him?" Peyton yelled, her hands in tight fists as she took a step closer to Aidan, rising on her tiptoes to be closer to his face. "How many people did he drain and discard like empty milk cartons? Did you count that?" She took another step toward Aidan, her chest rising and falling with angry breaths. "He saved you and Zane? Big friggin' deal! Let me remind you—you are a god of the Celtic Otherworld, hence immortal, and Zane is an immortal Fire Salamander. How much saving do the two of you need?"

She stopped talking, her eyes blazing with fury, her tiny frame trembling. Aidan didn't reply, just silently shook his head. It was Gunz who reacted to her heated speech. He walked to the door and put his hand on the silver door handle.

"We're leaving, Peyton," he said calmly. "You're right about everything you said, except one thing. I have no idea how Yaroslav was centuries ago when Akira turned him. He probably was the monster you described, but he's no longer that. I'm not going to go into a long explanation—it's probably a waste of my breath. There is only one thing you need to know—human or vampire, Yaroslav is my friend and I'll die before I let anything happen to him."

He pushed down on the door handle and opened the door. A heavy wave of dark magical energy barged in, invading every corner of the room and an earsplitting rocketing of automatic weapons split the silence.

CHAPTER 6

~ ZANE BURNS, A.K.A. GUNZ ~

Yaroslav's reaction was immediate. At his full vampiric speed, he threw himself in front of Gunz, blocking the doorway with his body. A few bullets hit him, penetrating his chest and legs, ripping chunks of his flesh on exit. A terrible howl of pain escaped his lips, but he braced himself with his arms against the doorframe, his body trembling with strain.

Aidan gathered his power and raised his hand up, stopping the bullets in midair and for a moment everything silenced. Nevertheless, Gunz could sense the presence of dark magical energy all around them, and he knew the reprieve was temporary. Yaroslav was still standing in the doorway, his head bowed down, blood streaming from the gunshot wounds on his back and chest, and once again Gunz had to wonder why the vampire wasn't healing right away.

Carefully, he approached the door and noticed that Yaroslav's hands were burnt to the bone. The doorframe was covered in strange runes, strips of silver embedded into the wood. Carefully, he peeked outside and saw some men in black tactical suits with assault rifles in their hands. Fire was blazing from the barrels and the bullets were lingering in midair. Just to make sure, he probed the area with his Salamander senses. He detected an overwhelming amount of dark energy but besides the few men who stood in front of the door, he couldn't see anyone else.

"Zane," called Aidan, his face strained, "I can't hold the time bubble forever. We need to get out and find a place where we can be safe at least long enough to come up with a plan."

"I think I can give us a few minutes," said Gunz. "No more than that."

He approached Yaroslav and carefully unlocked his damaged fingers. The vampire groaned and slowly started to fall. Gunz caught him and pulled him away from the doorway. Then he channeled his magic, intertwining it with some of his elemental power, and made a circular motion with his hand.

"*Ignius Praecidio Amnia*," he whispered, and a dense wall of fire energy mixed in with a basic protection spell rose around the perimeter of Peyton's apartment.

She gasped and her eyes darted to a smoke detector for a moment. Gunz noticed it and smirked mirthlessly.

"This is just an elemental energy, not actual fire. It's cold and there is no smoke. In combination with a basic protection spell, it's harmless to humans," he explained and turned to Aidan. "Aidan, you can let go of the time bubble. This spell should give us about five minutes of peace."

Aidan snapped his fingers, and the small pieces of metal that were lingering in the air dropped with a loud jingle. He exhaled heavily and swayed a little before lowering himself to the floor next to Yaroslav. The vampire sat with his hands up as the burns left by the silver and anti-vampire runes were slowly healing.

"What is this spell?" Aidan asked, observing the wall of cold fire in awe. "I've never seen anything like this."

"And you'll never see it again." Gunz smirked darkly as he sat down in front of his friends. "I invented it about a year ago when I was spending all my time in different libraries. It's a basic protection spell infused with the elemental fire. Kal said I shouldn't use this spell for more than a few minutes because it feeds on my own energy, so here is what we are going to do," he said, wiping cold sweat from his forehead with the back of his hand. "When I came back from California, Jim built a safe house for me. It's fireproofed and warded by Mrak Delar and it has a safe room where I can revert if I have to. No one knows about this place except Jim, Mrak and yours truly."

"How are we going to get to your safe house?" asked Aidan. "I've never been there, so teleporting is not an option. And I hate to state the obvious, but we're still surrounded and can't just walk outside and take a bus."

"There is only one way," said Gunz, throwing a quick glance at Yaroslav, "my portal."

"A Fire Salamander portal?" asked Yaroslav, shuddering. "Me —the unholy bloodsucking leach—and your purifying fire don't really work well together. Last time you took me through your portal, it nearly killed me."

Gunz sighed, giving Peyton a dirty look. "Slavik, do you trust me?" he asked quietly. "My portal will affect you, but I swear, I'm not going to let anything happen to you."

Yaroslav met his eyes, and a smile touched his pale lips. "With my life and beyond."

Gunz got up and waved his hand, unfolding the burning curtain of the Fire Salamander portal.

"Aidan, you're first," he said, motioning toward the portal. "Yaroslav and I will be right behind you."

Aidan nodded and walked through the fire, disappearing on the other side. Gunz turned to Yaroslav.

"You know what I have to do, right?" he said, ready to conjure a protection shield around the vampire, but Yaroslav raised his hand stopping him.

"Gunz, you can't leave her here," he said jerking his thumb in Peyton's direction. "She can't walk through your portal without your help and it's not safe for her to stay here. Take her first. I'll wait."

Gunz grunted but turned to Peyton. She shrunk under his heavy gaze and lowered her eyes.

"I'm going to carry you through the portal. As long as you're with me, the fire is not going to hurt you," he explained, irritation breaking through in his every word.

He approached her, and she just stood with her arms down, shifting uncomfortably from foot to foot. He didn't say anything else but lifted her and threw her over his shoulder without much care about how she felt about it. Then he nodded to Yaroslav and walked through the fire.

A moment later, Gunz emerged on the other side of the fire curtain and unceremoniously dumped Peyton on the floor. Catching Aidan's shocked gaze, he just shrugged his shoulders.

"Yaroslav refused to go until I brought her here," he said bitterly. "Being a soulless bloodsucker as he is, he couldn't leave her in danger. I was—"

Gunz didn't finish his statement, just waved his hand dismissively and rushed back through the portal. He appeared on the other side and found Yaroslav sitting on the floor in the same place he left him. The cold fire of his protection spell was slowly dwindling down and it was a matter of seconds before it would dissipate, opening the entry to the dark forces that no doubt were waiting patiently behind the barrier he had erected.

"Slavik, we need to rush," he said urgently, kneeling next to the vampire. "You know you are a lot bigger than I am, so do me a favor and be helpful for once."

Yaroslav bit his lip to stop himself from laughing but allowed Gunz to lift him and place him across his shoulder. Gunz got up with a strained grunt and whispered, *"Praecidio Amnia"*—he made a circular motion around himself and Yaroslav—*"Praecidio Amnia Circula Archni."*

Gunz closed his eyes and swallowed hard. Supporting the

Fire Salamander portal, the protective barrier around the apartment and the double protection shield over Yaroslav was quickly depleting his magic and his strength. He stepped heavily through the portal and walked to the other side, falling to his knees with the last step. He waved his hand over his shoulder, closing his portal. Then he gently lowered Yaroslav to the floor and touched his arm, whispering, *"Incanto Comlium".*

As he removed the protection spell, he gently shook the vampire. Yaroslav opened his eyes and a wide grin split his youthful face. "Did you call me fat back there?" he asked, his blue eyes twinkling with humor.

For a moment, Gunz just stared at him silently and then burst out laughing. Slowly, he got up to his feet and offered Yaroslav his hand, still chuckling. The vampire took it and got up.

* * *

THE SAFE HOUSE JIM CREATED FOR GUNZ WAS JUST A SMALL HUT in the heart of the South Florida everglades. There were no populated areas for miles around this place and even if for some reason, wards and protection spells failed, Gunz could still safely assume his natural state without fear of harming anyone.

The hut was hardly furnished, but it wasn't built for luxury. It was designed for efficiency and survival. There was everything here to live for at least a couple of weeks without the need to ever leave it and since it was located in the middle of the everglades, it wasn't easy to access. Besides that, the perimeter of the property was protected by a state-of-the-art alarm system as well as magical anti-intrusion spells to warn Gunz if anyone was approaching uninvited.

The walls of the house were infused with wards and protective magic, designed to keep intruders—magical and mundane—out as well as to keep his fire energy inside. When Mrak Delar placed the wards, he made sure that Aidan and his team, as well as Yaroslav, could cross the threshold without any problems. He also made sure that anyone who was under the protection of Gunz's Fire magic could cross into the safe house without triggering the wards.

A large metal closet stood by the wall. Its doors were slightly open, presenting a view of all sorts of modern weapons, standard ammunition and clips with silver bullets, an assortment of swords, throwing knives and daggers. At the opposite wall there was another metal door, but it was locked with regular door locks and a few runes were drawn at each corner.

Besides that, the hut had modern plumbing and power systems, so things like a washroom with a full-size shower and a small kitchen were available to him if he ever needed to stay here longer than a few hours.

Aidan shifted closer to the wall and stretched his long legs, his face gray with exhaustion, but possibly it was the layer of dust and dirt covering him from head to toe that made him look like this. Yaroslav sat down next to him. He didn't look much better than Aidan with his matted hair and clothes soaked in blood and God knows what else.

Gunz took in his friends' appearance and sighed. He felt just as bad as they looked, and he doubted he looked any better than them. Nevertheless, their safety was his main concern at the moment. Quickly, he scanned them with his other sight and with relief registered that as tired as Aidan was, he was still shadowing his godly powers.

The vampiric energy around Yaroslav was bright and clear, but there was nothing the vampire could do to cover it up. He could also sense Peyton's magical energy, but since he didn't know her well enough, he wasn't sure if the young witch knew how to shadow it.

"Peyton," Gunz called turning to her.

She was sitting on the only bed, her head bowed down. As

soon as he called her, she raised her face but quickly averted her eyes under his gaze.

"Do you know how to shadow your magical energy?" Gunz asked, silently cursing at how harsh and cold his voice sounded. "We don't know who these people are and why they are after us and shadowing our energy signatures will make it harder for them to find us."

She shook her head no, a blush rising in her cheeks. "No, sorry," she mumbled. "I mean I learned how to do it, but I'm not very good at it."

"I can shadow her," Aidan offered, and Gunz felt the presence of Aidan's power softly surrounding the young witch. "Hopefully, we can take a breather for a few hours before someone will shoot at us again." He sighed, rubbing his eyes with his fingers like he had a hard time keeping them open. "I still can't believe what just happened. I only wish I knew if Uri survived."

In a few words, he told Gunz and Yaroslav what had happened at his school and the situation he had left Uri in. They quickly exchanged information, each telling how they were ambushed and what the attackers wanted from them.

"Each one of us was attacked separately," mused Gunz, unease spreading through him as his mind processed everything he just heard, "but I have a feeling, it was the same person who orchestrated all these attacks. Whoever they are, they want to capture me alive and get the two of you either dead or out of the way. Interesting."

"And what did they want from you, Peyton?" Aidan asked, raising his eyebrows at her.

"Nothing," replied Peyton, lifting her shoulders in a tiny shrug. "I don't think they know I exist. I was just at the wrong place at the wrong time."

"What do you mean?" asked Gunz.

"Well, I was driving by the *EverSafe* and I noticed a man

being attacked by at least ten assholes, fighting alone against all of them." She looked down, fumbling with a small ring on her right hand. "I couldn't leave him alone. Besides, all the hostiles were vamps and that fact alone was enough for me to intervene." She raised her eyes for a moment holding Gunz's flat stare. "When I got involved, I didn't realize it was your pet-blood—vampire under attack. Anyway, like I said—wrong place, wrong time."

"So, if you had known it was Yaroslav, you wouldn't have helped him?" asked Gunz flatly, staring somewhere over her head. He was afraid that if he met her indifferent eyes, he wouldn't be able to control his aggravation.

"Of course not! An internal vampire altercation? As far as I am concerned—let them all kill each other," Peyton huffed throwing her hands in the air. "Listen, Zane, I don't know you well, but from what I've heard from Missi and Agent Andrews, you're a good man, so I'm not going to lie to you. The truth is simple—I despise vampires and I have a reason for it, which is none of your business."

"But it is our business," Aidan objected, slightly leaning forward. "Whether or not you like it, you're stuck with us now. When you got involved to help Yaroslav—accidently of course—whoever was targeting us, drew a nice shiny bullseye on your back too. So, guess what?"

He took a short pause, but even his silence was overflowing with sarcasm. Peyton held his mocking gaze, her fingers fiddling with her ring nervously, pulling it off and placing it back on.

"Seems to me, if you want to survive, your safest place is with us. You know? A god and a Fire Salamander"—Aidan arched his brow at Gunz with a cold chuckle—"who can protect you better than us? So, do yourself a favor and accept the fact that Yaroslav is our brother-in-arms, and neither I nor Zane will ever give up on him. So, your choice is rather simple—you come clean and learn to work with him side by side, or I teleport you to any place you want to go, and you are on your own."

"Really? Then screw you all! I don't need your protection!" Peyton jolted up, her nostrils flaring. "Zane, take me back to my place. I'll deal with those masked assholes on my own, let them co—"

"Hey, all of you, stop!"

Yaroslav jumped to his feet, interrupting their heated conversation, his voice coming out as a feral growl. With his long hair in disarray and his eyes glowing with unconcealed irritation, he looked more dangerous than ever. Both Aidan and Peyton fell silent and turned to him, staring at the vampire flabbergasted.

Yaroslav raised his hands up and closed his eyes for a moment. When he opened his eyes and spoke again, his voice was calm and even, and his face was void of emotions. "No one goes anywhere. Not until we figure out who is after us and why." He turned to Peyton and pointed at the bed. "Peyton, why don't you lie down and take a rest. We are all tired and hurt. In this condition, we shouldn't be making any serious decisions. I think we can afford a couple of hours of sleep. I promise, Peyton, I'll keep my disgusting bloodsucking self as far away from you as I can."

Peyton flushed hot red, the color of her cheeks matching the scarlet glow of Yaroslav's eyes. She didn't say anything but climbed on the bed and turned to her side, facing the wall.

Gunz also got up and stretched his shoulders, feeling his body aching all over. The vampire's blood healed his wounds but wielding all that magic and carrying Peyton and Yaroslav through the portal took a lot of his strength and magical energy. The stress of this night finally caught up with him and he felt drained and sore.

He turned to Yaroslav and Aidan, giving them a hardly visible smile. "There is enough floor-space here for the two of you to get some sleep. I need to go into the safe room and revert," he said apologetically. "I probably should stay there until I regain my strength. Just in case."

"Go," said Yaroslav with a dismissive wave of his hand. "I'll stay awake and let Aidan get some rest. Someone needs to keep an eye on things."

"Thank you," said Aidan. He stretched on the floor by the door, placing his arms under his head and was asleep right away.

Gunz nodded to Yaroslav and headed to the door locked by the runes and enchantments. He touched it with his hand, infusing the runes with his fire energy and the locks clicked open.

He threw one more glance at his friends—half-dead and gray with exhaustion—and sighed. They didn't recover from the encounter with the dark soul of Rasputin and already they had to face some unknown evil.

And this time, whatever the new evil which tore into their lives was, it was prepared and immune to their magic and powers.

CHAPTER 7

~ ZANE BURNS, A.K.A. GUNZ ~

"Well, hello Zane..."

Gunz heard a familiar voice and jolted to his feet, staring around the small dark room he locked himself in earlier. After he had reverted, he felt better, but exhaustion took over and he fell asleep right there on the dusty hard-wood floor.

The way the runes were placed on this heavy metal door, only his fire energy could open it, so no one could enter it without his consent. Besides, Yaroslav wasn't sleeping, so a stranger couldn't pass him by unnoticed. Yet there was no mistake—there was someone in this room with him.

He knew this voice. He loved it and was terrified of it at the same time.

"Angie," he moaned, his hand grasping at his throat as if her mere presence was suffocating him. "Why? Why are you doing this to me?"

"Doing it to you? Hardly." Angelique sat down on the floor next to his feet and tugged at his pants, inviting him to join her. "I miss you, silly."

Barely able to breathe, rigid with trepidation and twisted by internal torment, he lowered himself to the floor by her side. She wrapped her arm around his neck, pulling him closer, and placed her head on his chest. He inhaled her familiar scent, and his head spun as longing and desire sprung to life, bypassing the desperate signals of his brain.

"I can hear your heartbeat," she whispered, bunching up his shirt, her voice high and dreamy. Her breath touched his bare skin as her lips slowly made their way up his chest, sending shivers down his spine. "Tu-thump, tu-thump... I love that sound."

"Angie..." he moaned, pain of loss and guilt tearing through his soul, making him bleed inside. "I love you and I miss you every moment of my life, but this... this isn't you... please leave..."

"But it is me, my love," she whispered pulling away just a little. "You told me your heart belonged to me, remember? Are you taking your words back now?"

He finally looked down, meeting her gaze and shuddered. Her eyes were glowing with a malignant yellow light, her pupils the vertical slits of a snake. While his mind clearly realized that it wasn't his Angie, his body refused to comply, and this knowledge didn't make it any easier on him.

"Angie, please," he pleaded, painfully aware of what was coming next, but unable to do anything about it.

Angelique's eyes shone brighter and her right arm went up as a long dagger materialized in her palm in a puff of dark smoke. At the same time, she walked the fingers of her left hand up his stomach and drew a large circle over his heart. He screamed as she plummeted the blade down, slicing his chest open.

Blood gushed from the open wound, infusing the air with its heavy copper odor. As an unbearable agony tormented his soul and crippled his body, Gunz started to fall back. His fall seemed to be nightmarishly slow and when his back finally hit the floor, he didn't feel it, as an all-consuming pain in his chest turned his world inside out. Like from above, he saw himself lying powerless, sprawled on the floor, thick scarlet streams gushing from the terrible wound on his chest, while the woman he loved more than life itself was staring down at him with malice.

"I can see your traitorous heart now, my little Salamander," she purred. Her fingers dug deeper into the laceration, wrapping around his desperately beating heart. "Was it you or your heart that betrayed me, leaving me to die under a pile of dead sand? You killed me twice, my love."

She pulled her hand out, ripping his heart out of his chest and he screamed for what seemed like forever, not fully comprehending if his pain was physical or if it was his soul crying, torn to shreds by the only woman he ever loved.

Angelique laughed, demonstrating his heart in the palm of her hand coated in his blood, large red drops falling to the floor from the tips of her fingers. It was still contracting and expanding, pumping spurts of bright scarlet liquid with every beat. She lowered her lips to it, glowering at him over it. Her forked tongue slid in and out of her mouth, tasting his blood and a monstrous smile stretched her bloodied lips, showing horrifying serpent-like fangs.

He gulped air, unable to fill his lungs with oxygen, his mind blank, his soul consumed by despair and fear. "You're not her... and this is not real," he croaked, "leave me alone, Zmey."

A loud knock pulled Gunz out of the bloodcurdling nightmare, and a terrible howl tore from his lips, cold perspiration covering his forehead, trickling down his back. Forcing himself to sit up, he clasped his hand to his chest, ragged breaths shuddering his body. As blood slowly seeped between his fingers, he lifted his shirt with a trembling hand and saw a hideous gash crossing his chest. The edges of the wound were slowly closing as if he were a vampire and possessed self-healing powers.

"Zane, open the door! Gunz!"

The sound of Yaroslav's voice cleared Gunz's feverish mind, and he slowly scrambled to his feet. He took two unsteady steps and leaned slightly, resting his forehead against the cold slick metal. Placing his palms on the door, he channeled his fire to unlock it. He staggered forward, almost falling, when Yaroslav swung the door open.

"Gunz, what the hell?" the vampire asked, his voice laced with fear, observing the bloodstain on his shirt. "What happened here?"

"Nothing," Gunz snapped, not meeting Yaroslav's eyes, his arm rising to his chest of its own accord.

Before he could say anything, Yaroslav's arm shot forward. He threw Gunz's hand off and tore the shirt apart. The laceration was gone, but his skin was crisscrossed by thin white lines in the place where Angelique ripped his heart out of his chest every time he fell asleep.

"What the hell are these white lines?" the vampire whispered, horrorstricken.

"Those are scars left by magic. From what I've heard, they never disappear."

Both Yaroslav and Gunz spun around to see Aidan standing in the doorway. The god of the Otherworld was leaning against the doorframe, his arms folded across his chest, his eyes blazing furiously with the light of his magic.

"Care to explain?" Aidan asked, the crease between his eyebrows getting deeper.

"No, I don't," Gunz cut him off, backing away from his friends until his back hit the opposite wall.

"Then allow me to explain," said Yaroslav firmly, quickly closing the distance between them.

As he detected slight notes of irritation in the vampire's voice, Gunz glanced at him and felt all blood drain from his face. "Slavik, I don't want to talk about it," he said and cleared his throat, noticing how weak and shaky he sounded. "It's personal—"

"It's not personal," objected Yaroslav, a shadow of sadness crossing his features. "Not if what happens to you affects all of us."

Gunz bit his lip and dropped his head. Aidan closed the door all the way, making sure that the lock clicked. Then he approached Yaroslav and Gunz and sat down on the floor, gesturing at them to join him. Gunz slid down, his back pressed against the wall, and wrapped his arms around his bent knees, pulling them closer to his chest. Just the mere thought of discussing his nightmares with anyone made his blood run cold.

"Zane," started Yaroslav with a sigh. His eyes lost their scarlet glow and now he looked just as tired as he sounded. "You know we have a psychic bond, and a few hours ago, when I healed you, I made it stronger. I didn't do it to spy on you. Anyway, there is something you should know. Every night when you have your nightmares, I can hear you screaming. I can feel your pain and fear. You have no idea how many times I ended up in your backyard in the middle of the night, not sure if I should walk in and wake you up just to make sure you were all right."

"Slavik, I'm sorry," mumbled Gunz, mortified, cold sweat trickling down his back.

"Yaroslav is right, Zane," Aidan chimed in quietly. "I'm a god of the Otherworld and I can hear human souls. Every night I hear yours, screaming. Unlike your psychic bond with Yaroslav, my power doesn't show me exactly what's going on. I just know you are in pain. At first, I thought you were still grieving and the pain in your soul was related to that. But when you started to show the symptoms of sleep deprivation, I began to suspect that there was more to it than just grief."

"You must tell us what's going on," said Yaroslav, gently

tapping Gunz on his shoulder. "We're your friends and we'll do whatever it takes to help you."

Gunz stared at his hands vacantly, rubbing his knuckles with his thumb. Thousands of thoughts were crowding his mind, but only one was loud and clear—he didn't want to endanger his friends by getting them involved in his situation. Skiper-Zmey had already taken his love and he couldn't allow this monster to hurt his friends. He didn't think he could survive the loss of another person he loved.

"No," Gunz objected firmly. His eyes halted on Aidan's face and then darted to Yaroslav's. "No, my dreams are my personal business and while I appreciate your concern, I don't want either of you involved. I'll get it under control and my nightmares are not going to affect what we're doing in any shape or form."

Aidan and Yaroslav exchanged a quick look and identical uneven smirks appeared on their faces.

"Yeah... no," said Aidan, "I don't think so." He nodded at Yaroslav, and before Gunz could do anything, he was yanked up to his feet and pinned to the wall by a pair of strong hands.

"Don't you dare burn me," Yaroslav hissed into Gunz's ear and pulled away slightly, showing him his long fangs, "or I swear, I'll bite you."

"Guys, come on—," Gunz started to say, but Aidan shook his head, his lips pressed into a straight line.

"I know it's not going to be pleasant, Zane, but I have to do it," he said sounding almost apologetically. "You don't want to tell us the truth because you're trying to protect us. So, this is the only way we can protect you from your own stubbornness and stupidity."

"I don't think you have that kind of power, god of the Otherworld. Stupidity is an incurable disease, and in his case, it's fatal." Gunz heard a high-pitched voice and raised his head. Mishka the wyvern was hovering in the air above Aidan.

"Mishka!" Gunz yelped, hope rising in him. "Can you get these two jackasses off me?"

"Sure, I can," replied Mishka, a wide dragon-like grin on his face, "but I'm not going to. I don't fight people when they're trying to do the right thing, especially because it happens so rarely. Besides, your nightmares don't let me rest either, and I need my beauty sleep. I'll see you when it's over, boss." He pivoted in the air, facing Aidan and motioned with his golden wing. "Go on. Don't let me stop you."

Mishka winked at Gunz and vanished with a light pop, leaving a few bright sparks behind.

"Traitor," mumbled Gunz, "I'll deal with you later."

"Brace yourself," Aidan growled, channeling his power, "you know that it's not going to be easy for you."

"Just some discomfort?" Yaroslav smirked, giving Aidan an arched stare.

"Yeah, something like that," murmured Aidan, locking his eyes with Gunz's.

"Aidan…" Gunz whimpered, unable to break their eye contact.

Aidan pressed his right hand to Gunz's chest and Gunz pushed against Yaroslav's hold. As Aidan started to read his soul, he felt like the god of the Otherworld was turning him inside out, scanning his insides with his glowing white eyes. A low growl rumbled in his chest and the fire started to rise within him, responding to his struggle.

It wasn't the first time Gunz was on the receiving end of Aidan's godly powers. When he met him for the very first time, Aidan had given his soul a quick read. But it wasn't anything like what he felt now. He cried out again, fighting Yaroslav's grip while trying to suppress the fire within him at the same time, but it wasn't possible.

"Aidan…" he panted, his chest shuddering with short, strained breaths. "Stop… I can't… control… fire…"

"Almost done," muttered Aidan, hardly paying any attention to him.

His eyes lit brighter, and suddenly he placed his left hand on Yaroslav's chest over his heart. The vampire stiffened but didn't move. A moment later, the bright glow in Aidan's eyes subsided. He dropped his arms and slowly lowered himself to the floor.

Yaroslav finally released Gunz and gently helped him to sit down. With cold sweat running down his face, Gunz sucked in a deep breath trying to equalize his erratic heartbeat. The vampire sat down next to him, his shaking hands sporting nasty-looking blisters of burns.

"When were you planning to tell us?" Aidan asked, his unnerving silvery-white eyes staring at Gunz with reproach.

"Tell you what? That every time I close my eyes my dead girlfriend visits me to cut my heart out?" Gunz lifted his shirt pointing at a grid of thin white lines on his chest. "Or maybe I should have told you that even though I know it's not her, I still love her so much that I can't fight her? What the hell did you want me to tell you, Aidan!" he shouted at the top of his lungs, then leaned forward, hiding his face in his hands.

"No, Zane," replied Aidan, his voice almost a growl. "I wanted you to tell me, or Yaroslav, or anyone you trust, that the Skiper-Zmey has you on speed dial. Do you know what it means?" He slammed his fist into the floor, making a sizable dent in the wood. "It means the goddamn curse Veles placed on Mount Karasova is failing!"

Aidan fell silent, a muscle twitching in his jaw, and for a few moments all of them didn't say a word. Finally, Yaroslav broke the prolonged silence.

"Aidan, what did you do?" he asked.

Aidan smirked. "You know that nifty psychic bond you have with Zane?" he asked and continued without waiting for his response. "Well, now all three of us are psychically connected.

Anything else happens to this firetwat"—he jerked his thumb in Gunz's direction—"we both will know."

"Oh, nice one, Aidan," Gunz huffed, shaking his head. "As if having a vampire in my head wasn't enough. I needed a god there too."

"Well, at least now you have something in your head," retorted Aidan snidely. "Seems like before, you had the Torricellian vacuum there."

"Aidan!" Yaroslav scowled at him. "Take it down a notch on the sarcasm."

"You're right," replied Aidan, and his shoulders sagged a little. "I'm sorry, Zane. But do me a favor and don't try to protect us anymore. Both Yaroslav and I are big boys and we can take care of ourselves. Right now, what we need is to be completely honest with each other.

"We have an unknown and powerful adversary who seems to know everything about us and is immune to our power and magic, while we know nothing about them. This is why I created this psychic bond between the three of us—not to spy on you, Zane, but to have a way to communicate. We stand together, or they will take us out one by one."

"They've tried it already," added Yaroslav.

Aidan nodded at Yaroslav and continued, "Zane, you were right when you said earlier that these people are not after me or Yaroslav but after you. They know I'm a god and they can't kill me, so they want me out of this realm. They know who Yaroslav is, and perhaps they don't want to get Akira involved, so they are willing to spare his life as long as he doesn't interfere. But they wouldn't hesitate to kill him if push comes to shove. The only person they wanted alive was you. It means from now on, you are not going to be alone even when you sleep."

"Especially when you sleep," chimed in Yaroslav.

Gunz bit his lip. Everything Aidan said was true, yet he couldn't help feeling violated by what he had done and a little rebellious. He lowered his eyes, so his friends wouldn't see how he felt, staring stubbornly at his hands.

"You realize that now we can sense your emotions. Don't even try to hide your teenage rebellion," said Aidan, chuckling. He got up, smirking down at him. "I'm sorry. What I did was invasive, but I had to create this bond between us. I promise, as soon as we figure out what's going on, I'll remove it. At least my side of it."

Gunz finally met Aidan's eyes and swallowed hard, shoving his injured pride into his pocket. "You were right," he admitted. "I wish I knew who is behind all this."

"This is why I am going to leave you with Yaroslav right now. I have to try to get in touch with Gwyn. If there was ever a time to ask the oldies-club for help, it's now."

"Aidan, to open a window to the Otherworld, you'll have to use your full power," muttered Gunz, rubbing his face tiredly. "You'll expose our location. I'm sure whoever is searching for us is scanning this world day and night for our energy signatures."

"I know," agreed Aidan. "As soon as you hear the intrusion alarm activated, be ready to run."

Gunz leaned back against the wall, running his hands over his face and exhaled. "I wish I had something stronger than water in this hole—"

He didn't finish his statement when Mishka materialized in the room with a light pop. In his left paw he was holding a small bottle of vodka, a tiny white napkin thrown over his right paw. He landed next to Gunz, placed the bottle on the floor next to him and quickly wiped the bottle with the napkin.

"Mishka the waiter is at your service, boss," the wyvern sung, spraying everyone with a fountain of sparks. "Neat and straight up, just the way you like it."

"Now, that's not a codependent relationship at all," muttered Aidan, suppressing his laughter. "Mishka, why are you enabling this alcoholic?"

"My Salamander is not an alcoholic," the wyvern snapped at Aidan defensively, his eyes two burning pits. "In his case, this is not alcohol. It's a highly recommended stress-relief medication, calls *fuckitall*. You probably heard of it—take as needed."

Gunz, Aidan and Yaroslav exchanged a look and burst out laughing. Mishka landed on Gunz's head, spreading his golden wings over him. Gunz lifted his arm, allowing the wyvern to migrate down from his head and stroked his scaly back. The sleep deprivation was taking a toll on him. He was weak and disoriented, and all his moves felt jittery like he was running a fever.

"Mishka, you spend way too much time on Facebook and Instagram," Gunz said once he stopped laughing.

The wyvern huffed, puffing out his chest. "I have thousands of followers. How many do you have? Oh wait, you don't have social media presence at all, do you? Firetwat."

"And on this note, I'm going to go and check on Peyton," said Aidan, his eyes twinkling with laughter. But then he took in Gunz's demolished appearance and sighed. "Listen, I'll give us one more hour of rest before I contact Gwyn. Maybe Mishka is right..." He rubbed his chin covered in golden stubble. "Drink, hopefully it'll help you get some sleep. Just don't get drunk. You need to have a clear mind in case we have to fight our way out of here."

"It takes a lot more than this for me to get drunk," replied Gunz, raising the small bottle. "The fire in me burns it out, I guess. I used to get drunk a lot faster before."

Aidan gave him a curt nod and snapped his fingers, vanishing from the room. Mishka fazed into Gunz's tattoo muttering something about crazy Salamanders who don't know what they're doing. Gunz twisted the cap off and offered the bottle to Yaroslav. The vampire accepted it, took a swig, and gave it back to him.

Gunz held his breath and swallowed a large gulp. He closed

his eyes as the harsh liquid slowly rushed down his throat, spreading warmth through his body. He felt heavy and drowsy, but he was sure it wasn't the alcohol. He took another swig and dropped his hand with a half-empty bottle to the floor.

"Sometimes I wish I could get drunk, get completely wasted," he muttered, his heart wrenched with sadness. "You know? Like the good old days, when I could sit down with my friends at a kitchen table and just relax. When I didn't have to worry about obliterating everyone if I let go for a moment." He chuckled humorlessly. "I had no idea how easy it was being human…" His voice trailed off and he took another swig of vodka.

"You *are* human, Zane. More human than some mundanes out there," replied Yaroslav, shaking his head. "Is being human what you miss though? From where I sit, it sounds like you miss your friends, your land, your former lifestyle."

Gunz chuckled uncomfortably. "Are you suggesting I'm homesick?"

"You tell me." Yaroslav smirked, finally meeting his eyes. "Perhaps it's your sleep deprivation talking. It makes you more delusional than you normally are. Why don't you get some sleep now? I'll keep an eye on things and wake you up in case—you know."

"Yeah, I know." Gunz nodded and lay down, folding his arm under his head, but then turned his face toward the vampire and asked, "Slavik, do you believe Peyton didn't recognize you when she stepped in to help you."

"Not in the slightest," the vampire replied, a crooked smirk curving his lips. "How many men do you know of my size with my hairstyle? She knew who I was when she stepped in."

Gunz frowned. "Then why did she lie? And the way she treats you—"

"She probably has her reasons for hating vampires." Yaroslav stretched his long legs, resting his back against the wall. "Still, we should be careful. I'm sure Aidan realizes that too. Now sleep. Who knows how much time we have before we need to run again."

Gunz nodded and finally closed his eyes. He heard Yaroslav humming softly under his breath and little by little, his tired mind gave in to peaceful oblivion.

CHAPTER 8

~ AIDAN ~

Aidan materialized in the main room next to Peyton. The young woman was fast asleep, still in the same position facing the wall. For a moment, he stood next to the bed, silently observing her. In their current situation, he couldn't trust anyone outside his immediate circle of friends and a few things Peyton said made him doubt her honesty.

He couldn't believe she didn't recognize Yaroslav. The vampire had a unique appearance and no one in their right mind could forget a face like his. She claimed to hate vampires, yet she risked her life to help him.

A long time ago he learned that every move on the Board of Destiny was predefined and nothing was ever coincidental. So, what was the young witch doing by the *EverSafe* building and why did she step in to save a vampire she claimed to despise?

Right place, right time? I don't think so, thought Aidan, rubbing his forehead. All these thoughts were giving him a headache and all he wanted to do was lie down and sleep, but he didn't have the luxury of falling apart now. Not when they were being chased all over the realm and Gunz was dealing with these weird dreams or visions which were making him bleed inside and out.

Aidan sighed and headed to the exit door, trying to produce as little noise as he could. Carefully, he probed the wards and protection spells and with satisfaction found out that they were built to let him go in and out uninterrupted. He unlocked the door and quietly walked outside.

It was still dark and the fresh air of the everglades, infused with the scent of damp earth and greenery, enveloped him. Aidan inhaled it, enjoying the absence of the habitual stench of a big city—a mix of car exhaust and dust. He sat down on the small porch, resting his back against the wall and closed his eyes. He promised Yaroslav and Gunz one hour of rest and he needed it just as much as his friends.

HIS INTERNAL CLOCK WOKE HIM UP EXACTLY ONE HOUR LATER. Aidan stretched, rubbing his hands over his cheeks and got up. Far on the horizon, the first rays of the rising sun colored the dark silhouette of a tropical forest with a soft pink glow. Despite the early hour, it was getting warmer and together with the temperature, humidity made its presence known.

He channeled his power and drew a glowing white rune on the side of the house, thinking that right now his energy signature was screaming at anyone who cared to listen. He had to move fast. Who knew how quick the demonic forces could mobilize and get here?

"Gwyn ap Nudd, I summon thee," he whispered, placing his hand over the rune.

A large oval window materialized in place of the rune and with relief, Aidan saw that this time, Gwyn didn't make him wait. His mentor stood in front of the window, searching Aidan's face with a deep frown on his face.

"Father, hi," said Aidan, his voice shook, breaking at the end. He took a step closer to the window and braced himself against the wall, placing his arms on either side of it.

"Father?" repeated Gwyn ap Nudd and his silvery eyes lit up with the light of his magic. "What happened, Aidan? You look like hell and you call me Father only when something is wrong. Spit it out."

Aidan smirked—Gwyn knew him too well. "I don't know what happened, Father," he said quietly, "but someone is chasing us all over the realm. Right now, by talking to you, I am projecting our location. It's only a matter of minutes before they show up here. My powers and the Fire Salamander's magic are useless against them. We need to disappear at least for a short while so we can figure out what to do next."

"Who is *us*?" Gwyn ap Nudd asked coldly, anger ringing in his voice.

Aidan gave him an extremely abridged version of what happened, including whatever he knew about Gunz's strange nightmares and the information Uri had given him when they had fought the demonic team at his school. Gwyn listened, nibbling at his lip, and with every word Aidan said, his sharply angled cat-eyes lit up brighter and brighter. When he finally finished talking, Gwyn took a deep breath and ran his fingers over his thin black mustache.

"Okay," said Gwyn urgently, "all of you need to come here, to the Otherworld. Teleport to the labyrinth—you know the place —and I'll open the door for you. We'll discuss everything when you get here. Don't waste your time. You look too exhausted to fight."

"The others look worse than me. I'll see you soon."

Aidan nodded at his mentor and closed the communication window. Since the moment he channeled his power, projecting his energy signature into the world, the countdown started. And now, their clock was ticking, counting the seconds to the next demonic attack. He rushed inside the house, locking the door and quickly shook Peyton awake.

"Peyton, we'll be leaving in a minute. It's no longer safe here."

She blinked at him sleepily and rubbed her eyes but got up, straightening up her shirt and jeans. Aidan snapped his fingers and teleported inside Gunz's safe room. He found Yaroslav sitting on the floor, wide awake. Even when Aidan popped up right in front of him, the vampire didn't move, but his bright blue eyes got wider. Gunz lay on the floor, sleeping.

"Is everything okay?" asked Aidan, motioning at Gunz.

"Yes," replied Yaroslav in a soft whisper.

"Wake him up. I talked to Gwyn and we must leave immediately, before—"

He didn't finish his statement as a loud screeching filled the room. Gunz jolted to his feet, in one swift move manifesting his sword. His fire energy spiked up around him, small flames appearing on his arms and shoulders. Yaroslav hopped aside, raising his arms to protect his face from the unbearable heat the Fire Salamander was emitting.

"Zane, what the hell is that?" yelled Aidan, pressing his hands to his ears.

Gunz waved his hand muttering something under his breath and the screeching ceased just to get replaced by a loud ringing.

"Dammit!" Gunz cursed and rushed toward the door. He put his hands on its surface, channeling his fire energy, just to remember that he didn't restore the runes earlier. He turned the door handle and the door swung open.

Peyton was standing in front of him, pressing her hands to her ears. "What is this, Zane? What's going on?" she yelled over the noise, her eyes filled with fear.

"The screeching was the magical intrusion alarm," Gunz explained as he ran to the small panel on the opposite wall. "The ringing is the mundane alarm. Someone is here and close enough to trigger first my spells and now the motion detectors of the alarm system." He pushed a few buttons, and the ringing stopped.

In a split-second, dark energy rose around the house to a level he had never experienced before. The putrid stench of demonic essence polluted the air. Peyton pressed her hand over her mouth and nose, her eyes watering. Both Yaroslav and Gunz tensed, swords in their hands.

"I talked to Gwyn," said Aidan through gritted teeth. "We're going to the Otherworld. No one can get there without Gwyn opening the door. Let's go."

He put his hands on Yaroslav's and Gunz's shoulders and Peyton wrapped her arms around his waist. Aidan snapped his fingers.

Nothing happened.

He channeled more of his power and tried again to no avail.

"Something is blocking my power," he hissed, worry clawing through him. As the level of dark energy spiked up, it became hard to breathe. "Zane, try to open your portal."

"I can try, but even if I can open the portal, I don't know the final destination," he muttered and waved his hand, channeling more fire.

Nothing happened.

Using his other sight, Aidan scanned the area around the safe house. As he realized what was going on, anger swirled through him and he swore colorfully, punching the air with his fist.

"We are trapped," he explained in a low growl. "The same spell kept me trapped within its circle earlier this night. I couldn't break free, but Uri's purifying fire had been able to create a small fracture in their magic, so I could teleport out."

Gunz laughed and his laughter, short and sharp, seemed to be inappropriate for this tense moment. "Aidan, thank you," he said. "I know what I have to do now. But before I do anything, I need you to shield Yaroslav and Peyton." He stilled, thinking, his narrowed eyes fixed on Aidan. "Come to think of it, shield yourself too. Kal Junior is coming to town."

"What are you going to do? Revert?" asked Aidan, conjuring the shield around himself, Yaroslav and Peyton.

"No, I don't think your shield is powerful enough to contain the pure state of the Great Fire Salamander at such close proximity," he replied with a guilty lopsided grin and turned his sword back into a knife, putting it into his pocket. "But I'll be damn close to it, so brace yourself."

Gunz channeled his power, and fire energy surrounded him like a cloud. It was so dense that Aidan could see it without using his other sight. Fire broke through his skin, playful flames dancing on his arms and shoulders, wrapping around him like silky ribbons.

"*Exitius,*" he roared as he stretched his arm up. A stream of a blinding white light erupted from his hand and hit the ceiling, creating a large opening, and a chain of dark fractures webbed away from the hole.

Gunz lowered his arm and observed the opening. "Get ready to teleport," he said quietly, but his voice, infused with fire energy, seemed to come from every direction at once. "Let the show begin."

He channeled more of the fire energy and started to transform, slowly growing in height until he stood as tall as Kal. He brought his flaming arms up, clasping his hands together and redirected the undiluted stream of elemental energy up, through the hole in the ceiling. As he channeled more and more fire, his body gradually dissolved into flames, a wave of smoldering heat spreading around him.

"Oh my God," whispered Peyton, staring at Gunz in awe. "He's magnificent... I've never seen anything like that."

"Close your eyes, Peyton," whispered Aidan, watching Gunz's every move, "it's about to get extremely bright and hot."

Just as he said it, Gunz spun and a fiery twister took his place, interweaving the stream of elemental energy with physical fire. Yaroslav grunted, wrapping his arms around his head and bent down as purifying Fire energy leaked through Aidan's shield. Aidan channeled more power, reinforcing his shield, and pulled Peyton into his chest, to give her some extra protection.

Soon, a blazing inferno took over the hut, and the dark spell that held them captive responded to Gunz's assault with a loud angry buzzing. Its ear-splitting noise resonated within Aidan's chest and he grunted, struggling to hold his shield. With awe, he had to admit to himself that Gunz's power was equal to Kal's in its potency and just as dangerous.

A moment later, the dome of malignant energy that encapsulated the safe house cracked. Gunz returned to his human form and grabbed Aidan's shoulder. "Teleport!" he growled, breathing laboriously.

Still holding Peyton, Aidan put his hand on Yaroslav's arm and snapped his fingers, vanishing from the safe house.

THEY MATERIALIZED IN THE DARK CAVE OF THE HIDDEN underground labyrinth under the Glastonbury Tor. Aidan unlocked his arms, allowing Peyton to step away, and conjured a few small light orbs, sending them in the air. Yaroslav sat down, resting his arms atop his bent legs. For a moment, Gunz stared at Aidan with widened eyes, his chest rising and falling with short breaths, then he smiled wearily and lowered himself to the cold sand.

Aidan glanced down at the shoulder where Gunz held him just a moment ago and cringed. His shirt was burnt through and his skin was covered in blisters.

"You burned me," Aidan mumbled, covering his shoulder with his hand.

Gunz chuckled. "Aw, I'm sorry," he said, an evil lopsided grin playing on his exhausted face. "It was an accident; otherwise the burns would be a lot worse."

"Firetwat." Aidan rolled his eyes at him and focused on summoning his mentor. As soon as he finished the spell, a bright rectangle of white light materialized in front of them.

"This is our door," said Aidan pointing at the blazing light. He offered Gunz his hand and pulled him up to his feet, just now noticing how truly exhausted his friend was.

"This last bit of magic was harder than I anticipated," said Gunz apologetically, leaning heavily on Aidan's shoulder. "I think it drained me a little."

"A little?" asked Yaroslav, offering him support of his shoulder from the other side.

"We'll be safe in Gwyn's house. You'll get your chance to rest and recharge," promised Aidan and turned to Peyton, letting her go through the door first.

CHAPTER 9

~ ZANE BURNS, A.K.A. GUNZ ~

Gunz crossed into Gwyn ap Nudd's house and halted swaying slightly, supported by Yaroslav and Aidan. He was drained to the point where holding his head up was an effort. He wasn't surprised—what he had to do to break through the malignant spell encapsulating the safe house, had called for all his magic and a lot of purifying Fire energy. Besides, he had already been at the end of his rope between all the events of the night.

All four of them stood in the middle of the sparkling-white living room of Gwyn's glass house, dripping dirt and shedding dust to the white marble floor. Gunz stared at his reflection in the mirror-like polished tiles, thinking that they all resembled dogs who just rolled in the mud after the rain and now stood in front of their stern owners with an extremely guilty look in their sad round eyes. *I wonder if we stink like wet dogs too. Hmm, probably worse...* He had to bite his lip to stop himself from laughing.

Gwyn ap Nudd and Mrak Delar met them with freezing silence. Even though the King of the Otherworld with his height of seven feet dwarfed the Master of Power with his puny six-foot-four, both managed to look equally intimidating. They stood with their arms folded, identical frowns on their hard faces. Gwyn's unnerving white eyes scanned all of them and he exchanged a quick look with the Ancient Master.

Gunz didn't expect to meet Mrak Delar here, and he wasn't sure how he felt about it. On one hand, he was glad to see his friend. On the other, he knew he'd have a lot to explain and Mrak's natural sarcasm wasn't going to make it easy on him. He glanced up at the Master of Power and sighed. While the Ancient Master looked appropriately stern and concerned, a humorous twinkle was already playing in his obsidian eyes.

"Father—," Aidan started.

"Uh-huh," Gwyn ap Nudd hummed, interrupting him and Aidan fell silent. The King of the Otherworld turned to Mrak Delar and jerked his thumb toward Gunz. "Mrak, can you deal with that one and I'll take care of the other three."

"No one needs to deal with me," grumbled Gunz, annoyance flaring through him, "I am not a child. I just need a place to clean up and get some rest."

"Planning to get some sleep while you're at it?" asked Mrak Delar snidely, arching his eyebrow at him.

Gunz dropped his head, avoiding the Master's sarcastic gaze. *"Aidan,"* he called through their psychic link, *"what did you tell Gwyn?"*

"Everything," replied Aidan dryly. *"We need their help to deal with the situation. It means they must know everything, including the small issue of your insomnia."*

"Gunz, this is one of those cases, where you have to come clean and tell Mrak Delar the truth," added Yaroslav. *"Perhaps the Ancient Master can stop your nightmares."*

"Aw, how cute," purred Gwyn ap Nudd, a tiny smirk hiding under his black mustache as he rested his large hand on Aidan's shoulder, heavily. "Mrak, these three imbeciles created a psychic bond with each other, and they think I can't hear them."

Mrak Delar chuckled darkly, but there was no humor in his laughter. "Actually, all things considered, it was probably the right thing to do," he said, half-turning to Gwyn.

The Master of Power approached Gunz and gave him a quick once-over. "Can you walk?" he asked with a sigh. "With my sight I can see that you're drained, so don't try to lie."

"I never lied to you, Mrak," Gunz snapped irritably, the words slipping off his tongue before he could stop himself. "Can you say the same about yourself?"

"Okay," growled Mrak Delar, the elemental power around him spiking with new strength. He took Gunz's arm off Yaroslav and easily lifted him, draping him over his shoulder. "I'll let it slide, assuming it's your sleep depravation talking. We'll get back to this conversation when you're back in your right mind."

"Well, you may end up waiting forever then." Gwyn ap Nudd chuckled, shaking his head. "You can use any room upstairs, Mrak," he told pointing up, at the second floor. "I'll make sure no one will interrupt you."

"Yeah, do that," muttered Mrak Delar, heading toward the stairs. "When Kal comes in, tell him to wait until I'm done."

"Hmm," hummed Gwyn ap Nudd, narrowing his cat-eyes. "Kal is not big on complying with orders when it comes to his children, but I'll do my best."

Mrak Delar ran upstairs skipping steps, as if carrying an adult man on his shoulder was nothing for him. Gunz seethed inwardly at the way the Master was treating him but wisely decided to keep his annoyance to himself, at least for now.

The Ancient Master kicked the door open and walked inside a room, slamming it shut with his foot. He halted by the bed and dumped Gunz on top of it, ignoring his constrained grunt. After that, he walked back to the door and locked it. Once he was sure the door was locked and no one could bother them, Mrak Delar turned around and stared at Gunz heavily, folding his arms over his chest.

Gunz pushed himself up, lowering his feet to the floor, and sat down on the edge. "Mrak, all I wanted was—"

"I know what you wanted, Gunz, and I don't give a damn." Mrak Delar made his way to the armchair and sat down, crossing his long legs at the knee. "Now we are going to do what I want."

Gunz dropped his head into his hands, leaning forward. "Mrak, please—"

"Why didn't you tell me about your nightmares?" the Ancient Master growled, his eyes flooding with darkness as he struggled to control his emotions.

Gunz threw a quick look at Mrak Delar and shuddered—even though his voice was overflowing with aggravation, a haunted expression was imprinted on his face.

"I could understand if you didn't trust me anymore after what happened in California," continued the Master of Power, "but why didn't you tell Kal? I thought you already learned how to ask for help when you needed it."

"Mrak…" Gunz whispered, covering his face with his hands as an overwhelming anguish expanded in his chest, taking his breath away. He knew that he had to say something, but his constricted vocal cords refused to function. "Mrak, I—I can't—"

Mrak Delar got up and approached him, halting just a few inches away. "Lie down," he ordered quietly. "Don't argue with me. I'm going to put you into an enchanted sleep."

Gunz stared up at him, and his heart pounded desperately against his ribcage as fear twisted his gut. "Mrak, don't. I can't sleep. If I have to survive it one more time…" His voice trailed off, and he pressed his hands to his throat.

"Survive what exactly?" asked Mrak Delar, frowning. "Aidan told Gwyn some crazy nonsense and I need to understand what's going on if I stand a chance of helping you. Lie down, Gunz."

Gunz sighed but lay down, intertwining his fingers over his stomach. His body buzzed with exhaustion and his eyes started to close involuntarily. Arguing with the Ancient Master was useless, and he knew it, but the idea of seeing the woman he loved possessed by the ultimate evil was far worse than any torture he'd ever been through.

Mrak Delar sat down on the edge of the bed and then in one fluid motion pulled the half-torn shirt off Gunz's chest. Gunz tensed but didn't move, knowing perfectly well what the Master saw.

"Scars left by magic," whispered Mrak Delar, his voice shaking a little, but swallowed and continued louder, "Let's start by restoring some of your Fire and your strength."

He placed his hands on Gunz's forehead and his scarred chest and channeled some energy of Fire through him. Gunz exhaled with a moan and relaxed, enjoying the feeling of his element flowing through him, taking away the pain and giving him some of his strength back.

Like through a wall, he heard Mrak's voice. "That's good, Gunz, let it go. Now, I am going to put you to sleep and you are not going to fight me. You understand?"

"Mrak, I don't think I can survive one more time of seeing her like that," he whispered, a single tear slipping between his tightly shut eyelids. "My fault... I didn't protect her..."

He felt Mrak Delar remove his hands but didn't open his eyes. His muscles were no longer sore, and it made the dull ache in his soul so much stronger.

"Do you trust me, Gunz?" asked Mrak Delar, and Gunz cracked his eyelids open. The Ancient Master of Power was standing now, his black eyebrows connected above his blazing eyes. "I swear, I'll be with you every step of the way. I must see what's going on in this stubborn head of yours. You're my friend and there is nothing I wouldn't do for you, but something tells me there is more than your life at stake here. So, do you trust me, Fire Salamander?"

"Yes, I always trusted you," replied Gunz, "even when no one else did."

Mrak Delar's expression hardened as he wielded his magic and touched Gunz's forehead with two fingers, whispering something. Gunz felt his eyes closing and a velvety, soft darkness surrounded him.

* * *

A SOFT TOUCH TO HIS SHOULDER SENT AN ICY SHIVER THROUGH him. He opened his eyes unwillingly and immediately turned away, a deep crease cutting through his forehead. Even though he expected it when Mrak put him into the magical coma, he still wasn't ready. The truth was, he could never be ready seeing her like this.

He felt her fingers gently brushing over his cheek, tracing the shape of his jaw but remained still, everything inside him tense like a tightly wound spring. Angelique seized his chin, her fingernails cutting into his skin, and forced him to look at her. He met her eyes, flooded with the nauseating yellow glow of Chaos, and crumbled inside. Fighting back the tears, he sat up on the bed, putting his feet on the cold marble floor.

She smiled, lowering down to her knees in front of him. Gently, she placed her arm on his lap, resting her head on top of it. He glanced down at her, and before he realized what he was doing, his fingers found their way into the dark mane of her hair, threading through it softly. She lifted her face, locking her serpent-like eyes with his and her hand moved up to the waistband of his pants.

Her fingers fumbled with the button for a quick moment and then pulled the zipper down. The sound of the zipper made him cringe, and he put his hand on hers trying to stop her. She didn't insist. Rising on her knees, she tore the remains of his shirt off, throwing it on the floor.

"You're still my beautiful strong boy," she whispered, her hands moving down from his chest to his stomach. "Do you love me, Zane?"

He nodded.

"Say it," she demanded, her sharp nail tracing the squares of his tensed abdominal muscles.

He moaned as his weakness and desire turned his muscles into jelly. He knew that what he felt was induced by dark magic, but this knowledge didn't give him the strength he needed to fight it, to resist what she was doing to him.

"I love you..." The words rolled off his tongue before he could stop them and he couldn't recognize his voice, so much pain and longing were in it.

Angelique got up and leaned forward, her warm breath caressing his cheek, the familiar scent of her skin invading his senses, and his lips parted involuntarily, expecting her kiss. It didn't come. Gunz opened his eyes and saw her standing in front of him, a dagger gleaming ominously in her hand.

She brought the blade up, carefully running its sharp tip over the side of his face. "You have no idea," she said mockingly, planting a soft kiss on his forehead. "Desire itself can't look as desirable as you do right now." She seized his chin, lifted his face up, and crushed his lips with hers.

It wasn't the kiss he remembered. Real Angie would never kiss him like that, biting his lips to blood. He grunted as the metallic taste filled his mouth and turned his face to the side, breaking whatever it was—he couldn't call it a kiss. Her fingers seized the back of his neck, pushing him down to the floor.

He didn't have to guess what was coming next. He knew it, but he couldn't fight it, anyway. Everything inside him was destroyed, and the remains of his soul were bleeding profusely, flooding his entire being with undiluted torment. The only thing he wanted was for all this to be over. All of it...

Gunz kneeled before her and drew a circle over his heart with his finger. "Do it," he said, hardly moving his bleeding lips. There was no defiance in his voice, just acceptance. He dropped his arms by his sides and squeezed his eyes shut in expectation of pain.

There was no pain.

There was nothing.

He heard a loud clang as the dagger hit the floor and cracked his eyelids open. Mrak Delar was standing behind Angelique, both his hands placed on either side of her face.

"Mrak," Gunz mumbled, gazing up at his friend in awe. He had never seen the Ancient Master wielding so much of his power. His eyes were swirling with all the colors of the magical spectrum and his jet-black hair fanned around his face. The muscles on his arms and chest bulged, straining, and a thick blue vein pulsed on his neck as if he were lifting a heavy weight.

Mrak Delar ignored him, channeling more of his power through Angelique. Slowly, the yellow gleam faded away, and her eyes returned to their normal color. She glanced down at Gunz who still was kneeling before her and tears ran down her pale cheeks.

"Zane," she whispered his name, and it sounded like a prayer in the way she said it.

"Talk to him, Angelique," growled Mrak Delar, his voice shaking with strain. "I can't hold Zmey for long. Zane needs to hear it from you, my lady."

"Angie..." Gunz stretched his trembling hand to her.

She took his hand, gently squeezing it with her fingers. "Zane, my love," she said, "you need to stop blaming yourself for what happened to me. You didn't kill me. I chose to sacrifice myself to save you and the realm. And if I had a choice, I would do it again."

He brought her hand to his bleeding lips and kissed it, leaving a few scarlet drops on her marble skin. "I'm so sorry," he moaned.

"Zane, listen to me. It's important," she interrupted him. "Something awful is coming, and it's coming for you, my love. I can't even imagine how painful it must be for you to see me like this." She pressed her fingers to her mouth, and her face scrunched up as she fought back the gathering tears. "His supporters are not going to stop until the Skiper-Zmey rules this realm again. You already made a terrible mistake and because of it, Zmey can communicate with the outside world now."

"Mistake?" Gunz asked, chilling fear settling somewhere in the pit of his stomach, making his heart thunder in his chest. "What did I do?"

Angelique took a rugged breath. She raised her arms, covering Mrak's hands with hers, pressing them tighter to her temples. "Veles' curse is failing. Find Tessa… Perun… must save this world again," she managed to say. "I love you. You're my perfect world…"

She trailed off and her eyes slowly lit up with the yellow light again. Her pupils turned into dark-red vertical slits and a malignant smile stretched her lips, morphing her tender face into a terrifying mask. With a cry of pain, Mrak Delar jerked his hands back and vanished. Moving deliberately slow, Zmey picked up the dagger and pointed it at Gunz. With a loud cackle, he gradually dissolved into the darkness until only his glowing eyes were left lingering in midair.

A moment later, the yellow light got extinguished and Gunz fell powerlessly on the cold marble tiles, feeling nothing but the emptiness in his chest where his heart used to beat. And this place was quickly filling up with a twisting, debilitating pain far beyond a level he could handle. He squeezed his head with his hands and screamed, placing all the twisted, raw anguish he felt into one blood-curdling howl.

* * *

Gunz woke up screaming, cold sweat covering his face and chest. Mrak Delar was kneeling by the bed, holding his arms up like a doctor ready for surgery, blood trickling down from the damaged palms of his hands. Gunz sat up, his strenuous breaths coming out in short gasps.

"Kal is here. Unless you're ready to face your father's wrath, I suggest you get your emotions under control," said Mrak Delar, his voice raspy. He sat back on his heels and dropped his head to his chest.

Gunz sensed the spike in the energy field around the Master of Power as he started the healing process. His hands stopped bleeding and the wounds on his palms closed. Mrak Delar exhaled and raised his face. He raked Gunz with his heavy gaze and shook his head.

"What did you do, Gunz?" he asked quietly. "What mistake was she talking about?"

Gunz just lifted his shoulders in a light shrug. "I have no idea," he replied, fear chilling his soul at the thought of Zmey breaking free. "I didn't do anything."

Mrak Delar nodded and got up. He pulled the armchair closer to the bed and sat down, stretching his legs in front of him. For a few long moments, he remained silent and Gunz didn't want to bother him. In his mind, he replayed his short conversation with Angelique, but he still couldn't think of anything he had done that could have allowed Zmey to communicate with the outside world.

"I think I know what to do to stop Zmey from entering your mind while you're asleep," said Mrak Delar slowly, as if he was still processing something in his mind. "Let's just hope Gwyn has everything I need here."

"Thank you." Gunz dropped his shoulders, feeling more exhausted than ever. "It's been a few weeks since I had restful sleep. I need a break."

"I'm afraid you need a lot more than I can give you right now, my friend, and rest is not something you're going to get any time soon," said Mrak Delar rising heavily. "You heard Angelique—big bad is rising, and it's specifically after you. To be honest, I've been sensing the fluctuation in the magical energy of this world for the last few days, but I couldn't figure out what it was. I still can't." He rubbed his face with his hands, like a person who hadn't slept for days. "Ready or not, we need to go and speak with the rest. Including Kal."

The Master of Power headed toward the exit, but as soon as he placed his hand on the door, he turned around and his usual sarcastic grin split his face.

"Your Father is here and he's about to give you a serious time-out, boy. He is not happy. Ready?"

"No," exhaled Gunz, cringing. He got up, discarded the leftovers of his shirt, and walked to the door, while Mrak Delar opened it.

Kal stood in the hallway. His massive arms were folded over his chest and his entire frame was breathing with the fire energy as anger ignited smoldering flames in his deep-set eyes.

"Father," said Gunz, his mouth dry, and took one knee before the Fire Elemental.

Kal raked him with a furious gaze and switched his attention to Mrak Delar, leaving Gunz on his knees. "Master, were you able to figure out what this idiot got himself into this time?"

"Partially," replied Mrak Delar. "Let's go downstairs. I don't want to be repeating everything twice. Things are a lot worse than I thought."

The Great Salamander bent down, seized Gunz's shoulder and yanked him to his feet. Luckily, Gunz had no shirt on, otherwise, Kal would have torn it apart by the way he was handling him.

"Let's go," Kal growled, hardly awarding him a look. "I'll have a tête-à-tête with you after we decide what to do next."

"Sounds promising," muttered Gunz, but unfortunately, he wasn't quiet enough. Both Mrak Delar and Kal turned around to face him.

"Shut up," they said at the same time as Kal pushed him out the door into the hallway.

As he slowly walked downstairs, following Kal, Mrak Delar fell into step with him and whispered into his ear, so only he could hear, "By the way, you do realize that when you are having alone time in your nightmares, you are not with Angelique there. You're with Zmey and he is a man."

Gunz looked up at the Master of Power and found his obsidian eyes twinkling with humor. Heat creeped up his face, coloring his ears and cheeks into a bright shade of magenta.

"Ugh, shut up, jackass," Gunz murmured, pushing him in the shoulder.

Mrak Delar laughed out loud and hopped over the railing, landing softly on his feet like a large cat. He winked at him from the first floor and headed toward the living room. Gunz smirked, leaning over the railing following his progress, but Kal's firm hand yanked him back.

"No, you don't," growled the Great Salamander. "You and Mrak are always joking around, no matter what the situation is. Thirty years old or three hundred years old—doesn't seem to make a difference. When the Ancient Master is around you, he is too relaxed and the two of you behave like teenagers. You're going to stay by my side and behave in the way a Child of Fire should."

"Maybe when everything around us crashes and burns is the best time to joke around, Father," Gunz objected quietly. The

Great Salamander halted, glowering down at him. "Maybe because we don't take these evil bastards seriously, both Mrak and I have been able to survive everything they put us through and have ended up on top?"

The grip of Kal's hand on his shoulder lightened up and the Great Salamander frowned, small flames surfacing on his arms.

"Maybe," Kal replied softly, a shadow of sadness crossing his features. "Possibly you're right… but not today, my boy. Get yourself in a serious mood. I'm afraid none of us is going to like what's coming."

CHAPTER 10

~ ZANE BURNS, A.K.A. GUNZ ~

Gunz walked into the living room fully intending to behave like a Child of Fire should, but the thought of his state of undress didn't help him achieve the proper mindset. He threw a guilty gaze at Kal and sat down on the couch next to Aidan. Peyton glanced at him and averted her eyes, a touch of pink coloring her cheeks. She picked a place the farthest from Yaroslav, which didn't surprise Gunz in the slightest but still made him smirk.

While Gunz had been in his enchanted sleep, Aidan, Yaroslav and Peyton had enough time to take a shower and change into fresh clothes. Thanks to Gwyn's magical closets, each of them had found something fitting their size and taste. *One day I have to ask Gwyn how his closets work. Possibly this magic works only in the Otherworld.* He caught himself on this thought, wondering why he cared about a thing like that when his entire world had just crashed around him.

Kal walked up to Gwyn ap Nudd and Mrak Delar and for a few seconds they conversed about something in hushed tones. Then Gwyn waved his hand, opening a door blazing with a blinding white light, and Mrak Delar left through it.

Neither Gwyn nor Kal looked approachable at the moment, and as much as Gunz wanted to find out what this was all about and where the Master of Power went, he decided it would be safer to keep his mouth shut. He leaned back, folding his hands on his lap and closed his eyes, one more time going over everything Angelique told him.

"Mrak is summoning me, Kalidus. Are you ready?" Gwyn's voice brought Gunz back from his thoughts and he opened his eyes.

"As ready as I can be," Kal grumbled, lowering himself into a large armchair.

"I know you're not very happy about being confined by the shield, my friend, but we're welcoming a human here." Gwyn sounded apologetically. "It has been a while since a living human walked the Otherworld."

Kal didn't reply but gestured at Gwyn to proceed. A magical energy field spiked around the King of the Otherworld, and a dense shield of white light surrounded Kal's massive figure. The Great Salamander sighed and pursed his thin lips.

"Human?" Aidan asked, giving his mentor an arched stare.

"Yes, human," replied Gwyn ap Nudd frostily. "Lord Jim Andrews. I believe your friend"—he jerked his chin at Gunz —"calls him *'boss'*."

This day can't get any stranger, thought Gunz, but again decided to exercise the fifth amendment and wisely remained silent.

Gwyn opened his door, but it wasn't Jim who walked through it. The Scarlet Queen emerged through the blazing wall of light and halted, her gaze slipping from one face to the next. She was dressed in her usual business attire, and her tiny frame exuded a vibe of self-assurance and unyielding authority that could rival that of the Great Salamander himself. Yaroslav got up, and his eyebrows rose as he met his mother's heavy gaze.

Before he could say anything, Gwyn folded his massive

frame into an unexpectedly elegant bow. "Your Majesty, the Scarlet Queen," he purred, "welcome to my modest home."

Akira Ida's lips formed a tiny duty smile as she greeted him, slightly inclining her head. "Gwyn ap Nudd. The White Son of Night. The King of the Otherworld. The Lord of the Wild Hunt," she counted his titles, her voice soft and insinuating, and it wasn't clear if she was trying to greet him or seduce him. "Thank you for your hospitality and for providing the safety of your realm to my son."

"It was my pleasure, Your Majesty," replied Gwyn ap Nudd, offering her an armchair.

Gunz threw a puzzled look at Yaroslav, but the vampire just rolled his eyes and sat back down. Once Akira made herself comfortable in the armchair, Agent Jim Andrews walked inside the room, accompanied by Mrak Delar. Even though Gwyn was shielding Kal's elemental energy with his magic, the Master of Power wrapped an additional shield of his power around Jim. While Gwyn's shield was dense and restrictive, confiding Kal to one spot, Mrak Delar's shield was a lot lighter, and it allowed Agent Andrews complete freedom of movement.

The King of the Otherworld observed the FBI agent, his eyes swirling with white light and a crooked smirk curved his lips. "My lord, Agent Andrews, it's been a while since the last human walked my realm and lived to tell the tale."

A black mask flashed over Gwyn's face for a brief moment and disappeared. He folded his massive arms over his chest and cocked his head as his smile grew wider.

"Master Mrak Delar said you needed me." Calm and unfazed, Jim shoved his hands into his pockets, meeting Gwyn's blazing gaze without a moment of hesitation. "I see Mr. Burns is here, and that tells me we're already in the middle of some new magical mayhem. So, what can a puny human as myself do for this mighty assembly of magic and power?"

For a few seconds, Gwyn stared at Jim without blinking. Then his eyes darted to Kal, and they both laughed.

"You were right, Kalidus," Gwyn murmured when he stopped laughing. "I like him already." He turned back to Jim and gestured at an empty chair. "Agent Andrews, welcome. Please make yourself comfortable. We need to talk."

Once everyone had settled, Mrak Delar got up. Gunz raised his eyes at the Master of Power and shivered like from a chilly breeze. The Ancient Master was cold and serious—not a touch of sarcasm or humor in his jet-black eyes.

"Just to bring everyone on the same page," started Mrak Delar. "Agent Andrews is right—we're in the middle of magical mayhem. And worst of all, we have no idea what's going on. Gunz, Aidan and Yaroslav were attacked by unknown demonic forces. The only thing we know is that they wanted Aidan back in the Otherworld, Yaroslav captured or dead—they didn't seem to care either way, and they wanted to take the Fire Salamander alive."

"So, the two explosions last night were of a magical origin?" asked Jim, throwing a furious gaze at Gunz. "A phone call with a quick report would have been helpful."

"Yes," replied Aidan, "the demons were targeting me. Sorry, Jim, we had no time to notify you."

"Let me disagree with you, Master. This is not the worst," objected Gwyn ap Nudd. "The worst part was that whoever attacked them knew all of us well. They knew how we thought, how we functioned and what kind of magic we possessed. Aidan's godly powers as well as the fire magic of the Fire Salamander were useless against them. They also knew that in the realm of humans, the young Salamander wasn't going to use his elemental power."

"It means Gwyn ap Nudd and Kalidus are also vulnerable," murmured Akira, her face as calm and emotionless as ever. Slowly, she crossed her legs at her knee and leaned back in her armchair, the unwavering gaze of her narrow eyes lingering on Gwyn.

"Why?" asked Jim, the tones of annoyance clear in his voice. "I'm sorry, but all this magical mumbo-jumbo is not my strongest suit and there are things I don't understand."

Akira threw a cold glance at the Agent and pursed her full lips into a tiny bow. "Aodh mac Lir, or Aidan as you know him, is a mere shadow of Gwyn ap Nudd. The King of the Otherworld shared his powers with his child. So, if our adversary was not affected by Aidan's power, they're most likely immune to Gwyn's as well. And Kalidus is nothing but another Fire Salamander—ancient and giant, mind you—but not much different from his mini-me." She pointed at Gunz with her well-manicured hand. "If they know how to subdue the little Salamander, most likely they know how deal with the bigger one."

"How about your son, Ms. Ida?" asked Jim. "He is a vampire. He doesn't have any special magic or powers, outside of what he is. Why was he attacked?"

"I don't believe he was. He is my child and I would sense if he was in distress," objected Akira lifting her narrow shoulders in a tiny shrug, her angled eyes halting on Yaroslav. The vampire raised his hand to say something, but Peyton interrupted him.

"Oh, he was attacked, alright," she retorted with a dismissive wave of her hand, her lips curved in distaste. "Right in front of the *EverSafe* building as a matter of fact. And they had him on his knees, bundled up in silver like a helpless babe. I was there."

"It's impossible," hissed Akira leaning forward, the mask of indifference gone from her face. "You're lying, witch. Yaroslav is an unmatched fighter—Mrak Delar can attest to it. He has powers beyond that of an ordinary vampire. Besides, I was in my office and if my only son was in distress, I would have known that!"

"I am not lying!" Peyton hopped to her feet, anger making

her tremble from head to toe. "Your son is nothing but a disgusting common vamp," she shouted, her hands clenched into tight fists. "These other vampires had him in no time and if I didn't get involved"—she took a step closer to Akira—"you would have one vamp less in your company. If I had known it was him, I would have let the demons finish what they started."

"Disgusting vamp?" hissed Akira Ida, a dangerous scarlet glow in her eyes.

Yaroslav and Gunz jumped to their feet, but both were too slow. One second the Scarlet Queen was sitting in the armchair, the next moment Peyton was dangling in the air, Akira's fingers squeezing her throat, holding her a few inches above the floor.

"Mother! Let her go!" yelled Yaroslav. He grabbed Akira's wrist, but she wouldn't let go and he wasn't strong enough to counteract a few thousand-years old vampire.

"Akira," said Gunz, trying to sound as peaceful as he could muster, "Peyton wasn't lying. She chose the wrong words to express herself, but she told you the truth—Yaroslav was attacked and almost killed."

"Mother, I owe her my life or at least my freedom," Yaroslav added quietly, letting go of Akira's arm and bowed his head.

Akira's angled eyes darted to Yaroslav and back to Peyton and she slammed her to the floor. Peyton hit the marble tiles hard and whimpered, tears shining between her fluttering eyelashes. The Scarlet Queen leaned forward ever so slightly and smiled, and her smile was far more terrifying than her outburst of anger.

"Witch, you will show proper respect to my son," she hissed, her fangs slowly expanding.

No one in the room moved. Gwyn and Mrak Delar exchanged a quick look, and both folded their arms. Kal just smirked and Gunz was positive that even if Gwyn's shield wasn't keeping the Great Salamander in place, he wouldn't interfere. Aidan remained motionless and silent. Jim was too shocked or too smart to try to fight an ancient vampire. Only Gunz and Yaroslav were standing ready to act in case things got out of hand.

Peyton's eyes, wide with fear, were glued to Akira, but at least she finally got the point that insulting an ancient Demonic Queen wasn't such a bright idea.

"If you're stupid enough to ignore Yaroslav's dangerous nature," continued Akira quietly, "you will respect his status. He is my only son, and that makes him the Prince. Twice. If you call him a vamp one more time..." She trailed off, straightening and stepped away, an expression of disgust on her elegant face as she threw her long ponytail back. "Beg him for forgiveness, witch. Do it now and if Yaroslav can forgive you, I'll let you live."

"Mother, begging won't be necessary," objected Yaroslav, offering Peyton his hand. "There is nothing to forgive. I owe her, Mother. Instead of doing what you're doing, let's try to figure out why you didn't feel my presence when I was fighting just a few feet away from you."

For a moment, Peyton stared at Yaroslav's hand but then took it and got up. Akira gave her a murderous stare, following her with her glowing eyes.

"Isn't it obvious?" asked Kal, his deep voice unexpectedly loud in the quietness of the room. He threw his flaming hair off his face and looked around, but since no one said anything, he continued, "Someone is blocking your connection with your son. Just like someone found a way to deflect the Fire Salamander's magic and Aidan's godly power. Whoever it is, they got these three exactly where they wanted them—running for their lives, powerless and vulnerable."

"Gunz, I'm sorry, but I have to ask. In your nightmares, has Skiper-Zmey ever asked you any questions?" asked Mrak Delar. "Do you know what he wants from you?"

Everyone turned to Mrak Delar, staring at him flabbergasted, and just now Gunz realized that the Ancient Master hadn't disclosed the nature of his nightmares to anyone. At least not yet.

"No," replied Gunz, clearing his dry throat. "You saw everything, Master. Every time it's the same—he comes, tortures me by pretending to be... her." He bit his lip, taking a brief moment to deal with the rising wave of grief. "Then he cuts my heart out. He has never asked me any questions or made any demands of me. He has never asked me for anything, period." Involuntarily, his hand when up to his chest where a grid of white lines marred his skin, and he looked away, hiding his internal turmoil.

"The Lord of Chaos is talking to you in your dreams?" growled Kal, fire igniting at the bottom of his eyes. "And you never bothered telling me about it? Anyone? How could you allow it to happen in the first place, Salamander?"

"How could I stop him?" yelled Gunz, throwing his hands in the air. "Do you think I enjoy him cutting my heart out of my chest every time I close my eyes? I can't sleep, Father! I haven't had one restful night since I returned from California! My hands are shaking, and I can barely move." He met Kal's burning gaze, his chest rising and falling with heavy breaths.

"Is there anything else you failed to tell me, my child?" asked Kal through gritted teeth, his fingers squeezing the arms of Gwyn's armchair, leaving holes in its white leather upholstery. Gunz glanced at his mentor and shivered like from a touch of cold rain, grateful for Gwyn's shield holding the Great Salamander in place.

"Yes, Father. There is one more thing," he said quietly, slipping a quick glance in Mrak Delar's direction. The Ancient Master frowned but gave him a small nod. "Master Mrak Delar was able to free Angelique's spirit for just a short while. There were a few things she said that you all should know." Gunz fell silent for a moment, bracing himself for Kal's explosive reaction to what he was about to say. "She said that we must find Tessa and Perun. Only Perun can fight the Lord of Chaos and finally put an end to all this."

"Find Tessa?" asked Aidan, a pained expression crossing his face. "What do you think I've been doing since I came back from California? I can't find her! I can't sense her anywhere. Uri, Svyatobor and Angel have tried and failed. No one can find her! And now Angel just disappeared without a word, Svyatobor is nowhere to be found, and Uri..." He trailed off, dropping his hands on his lap powerlessly.

"I'm sorry, Aidan," said Gunz, "I'm just delivering the message—"

"Go on," muttered Kal, interrupting him. "I'm sure there is more. Otherwise you wouldn't be avoiding my eyes, looking like a little mouse under a broom."

Gunz raked his fingers through his matted hair uncomfortably and continued, "Yes, there is more. She said I made a terrible mistake, Father, and my mistake allowed Zmey to communicate with his supporters despite Veles' curse. But I swear, I have no idea what I've done. I've done nothing!"

The silence in the room became absolute. No one spoke. No one moved. Gunz bit his lip, wishing to be anywhere but here. It was Mrak Delar who broke the silence.

"Does it really matter what the mistake was?" he asked, placing his hand on Gunz's shoulder. "Whatever mistake he made, it wasn't intentional. Knowing what that was won't help us. Now we have to deal with the situation."

"Gunz," growled Kal, "after Agent Andrews leaves, I need to have a word with you."

Before Gunz could respond, Mrak Delar let go of his shoulder and rose a few inches off the floor. His eyes flooded with darkness as the energy of his elemental power surrounded him. He levitated for a few seconds before softly lowering down, then leaned forward, placing his hands on his knees for support, breathing strenuously.

"Gwyn," the Ancient Master said as he straightened up, wiping perspiration off his forehead with a white handkerchief, "I need you to open the door for me. I must go back to Kendral. Immediately. The Master of Kendral is summoning me and it's urgent."

"Do you know—," Gwyn ap Nudd started to ask, but then changed his mind and just waved his hand, opening the brilliant white rectangle of his door.

"I don't know. He didn't give me any details. I'll try to come back here as soon as I can," he promised and disappeared behind the blazing light.

As soon as Gwyn closed the door behind Mrak Delar, a pain, abrupt and unyielding, flattened Gunz like a car crusher. He gasped, unable to take a breath and squeezed his head with his hands. The room spun around him into a nightmarish shaky blur and he collapsed, falling flat on his back. He hit the marble tiles hard, but he didn't feel the impact as the agony inside him consumed everything else.

Images of blood and horrors were flashing in his mind non-stop, turning his reality into a twisted and gruesome ordeal filled with pain and suffering beyond any measure. He couldn't focus or recognize any of them. Sticky fear poisoned his soul, and he screamed, flaming tears running down his face. As the next wave of pain rattled him, turning him inside out, his body arched. His arms dropped at his sides, his fingers clawing at the floor.

"Gwyn, do something!" roared Kal and his loud voice bounced in Gunz's head adding to his torment.

He felt Gwyn ap Nudd's hands on his shoulders. Through the veil of horrors presented by the whirl of images, he saw Gwyn's lips moving, his features shadowed by concern, but he couldn't hear a word he was saying. Aidan dropped to his knees next to him, his eyes blazing with his magic, fear imprinted on his face.

He didn't know how long he was in this state—maybe hours, maybe just a few minutes. He couldn't scream anymore, and only silent tears were escaping his wide-open eyes. Aidan sat by his side. Gunz could no longer see him, but strangely he could sense his and Yaroslav's presence.

He didn't notice when the continuous flashing of hideous images in his head slowed down, becoming blurry and distant. Mrak Delar's face emerged on the foreground, pushing further back the living nightmare his existence had become.

"Gunz, look at me. Focus on my voice." The voice of the Ancient Master sounded like thunder.

"Mrak... help..." Gunz whispered to the image of his friend, not sure if he was real or just another illusion in his tormented mind.

"I'm here, Salamander. Just hang in there... almost done."

Gradually, the flashing stopped completely, and the pain subsided. Finally able to see, Gunz glanced around and found himself still lying on the floor, his head on Mrak Delar's lap. The Ancient Master's hands were placed on either side of Gunz's forehead as he was muttering something under his breath.

"Is it over? What was it? What happened?" asked Gunz as Mrak Delar removed his hands, gently helping him to sit up. Then the Master held his hands up, revealing red spots and blisters of burns.

An unfamiliar deep laughter bounced through the room and the crystal chandelier jingled, responding to it. Everyone stilled, looking around. Both Gwyn and Aidan assumed their true forms, and the room got flooded with the brilliant light of their magic, but their powers had no effect. The man kept laughing, mocking all their fruitless attempts to stop him or discover what he was.

"That was just a small demonstration of my power. Your magic is useless against me," stated the voice frostily. "Stop wasting your energy. All I want is a Fire Salamander. Either of them will do. A Fire Salamander must come to the City of Gold alone. If you comply with my request, I'll leave the rest of you and your realms be. You have ten days."

"I had something like this happen to me before," said Gunz, grabbing Mrak Delar's arm. "I mean this bodiless voice. I've experienced something like this before. Years ago. When I just moved from Kendral to Florida. Remember—"

"Disobey me and your worlds will be destroyed." The voice laughed again, and everything went silent.

CHAPTER 11

~ ZANE BURNS, A.K.A. GUNZ ~

Gunz got up, supported by Aidan, and made his way to the couch. The pain was gone, but the weakness was overwhelming. He leaned back and took a deep breath, fighting the nausea. Like through a fog he saw Mrak Delar approaching him, his image blurry and shaky like a mirage. He felt a light touch to his forehead and a wave of fire energy surged through him, partially restoring his strength.

"Mrak—," started Gwyn, but the Master of Power shook his head no, pressing his finger to his lips in a silencing gesture.

A moment later, he let go and arched his eyebrows at Gunz, giving him a thumbs up. Gunz nodded, answering Mrak's silent question. While the pain was gone and the energy boost did what it was supposed to do, something still felt off.

"*Oprimenta Amnia*," whispered Mrak Delar and the yellowish light of the cloaking spell filled the room. "*Praecidio Amnia*." He held his hand up, asking everyone to remain silent and added in a whisper, "Gwyn, now yours."

Gwyn ap Nudd nodded and transformed into his true form. Terrifying as he was with the black mask over his face and his eyes blazing with blinding light through the slits of his mask, when he started singing, no one could take their eyes off him. The words of an unknown tongue built a complicated spell, and as Gwyn continued singing in his deep, musical voice, the yellow shine of the protection spell Mrak Delar placed got intertwined with the brilliant glow of Gwyn's magic. When he finally fell silent, Gunz exhaled, just then realizing he had been holding his breath all this time.

"We can talk now," said Mrak Delar, sitting down, his every move filled with fatigue.

"I didn't see that coming," said Gwyn ap Nudd quietly, shaking his head. Then he punched the air with his fist, anger making his eyes shine brighter. "This is the first time someone dared to attack me in my own house. In my own realm! Dammit!" He slammed his hand on the wall and the glass sung under his touch. "Fire and ice! This is *my* domain! No one can enter the Otherworld physically or psychically without my consent! It's warded and protected by ancient magic the likes of which no one knows anymore. No one but me! The wall of magic surrounding the Otherworld is impenetrable. Even the Masters of Power can't teleport in and out of here without me opening the door! What the hell is going on?"

"Here is what's going on," said Mrak Delar, his face void of emotions. "The Master of Kendral summoned me to let me know that Kendral was attacked from the outside. He is sealing all the doors in and out of the World of Magic as we speak."

"No," snapped Kal, "he can't do it! It'll weaken the flow of magic and elemental energy in this realm! It is weak as it is here."

"Yes, he can, Kal. He is the Master of Power and the Master of Kendral. And frankly, I agree with his decision," objected Mrak Delar. He leaned forward, propping his elbows on his lap, and bowed his head as if he had no strength left in him to keep the upright position.

"Fire almighty," growled Kal, throwing his arms in the air.

"Why, Mrak? You're his mentor. Did he ask for your advice and you told him it was the right thing to do?"

"Yes," confirmed the Ancient Master with a cold determination he never displayed while talking to the Great Salamander. He lifted his face, regarding the Fire Elemental calmly. "Do not interrupt me again, Kal, let me finish."

Kal fell back in his chair, staring at the Master of Power with shock. The fire in his eyes slowly subsided as he shook his head, resigned.

"Lady Gatekeeper of the Land of Dreams is also in Kendral," continued Mrak Delar.

"What?" Kal and Gwyn shouted at the same time.

"Lady Gatekeeper never leaves her place," Akira said, furrowing her brow. "Even when she visits our realm, she always stays close to the door into the Land of Dreams. She would never abandon her duty to travel to Kendral."

"Exactly, she wouldn't," agreed Mrak Delar, inclining his head in Akira's direction, "yet, she did. The Land of Dreams was attacked and taken over by unknown demonic forces. The flow of magical energy and elemental power in the nexus was polluted by demonic essence and the energy of Chaos. To stop this malignant infection from spreading outside the boundaries of the nexus, Lady Gatekeeper sealed the Land of Dreams. This is why all of us feel weaker, magically speaking. This is why the wards and protective spells of the Otherworld are no longer as impenetrable as they used to be."

"So, the Land of Dreams is sealed. The World of Magic is sealed, and the Isle of Legends had been sealed by the Destiny Council centuries ago. The three out of four magical realms are blocked, leaving the human world severely deprived of magical energy," Kal pointed out, shifting uncomfortably in his chair.

"Precisely," said Mrak Delar wearily. He pressed his hands to his eyes for a brief moment and then slowly ran them up, throwing his long hair off his face. There was something so dismal and fatigue in the Ancient Master's gesture that Gunz cringed inwardly.

"It leaves the world of humans vulnerable to a demonic attack," continued Mrak Delar. "The Master of Kendral gave me the choice to remain in Kendral by his side or to come back here and help you defend the realm of humans."

"That's nice. We're supposed to protect the world of humans from some unknown powerful dark force with hardly any magic available," muttered Aidan, scratching the back of his head.

"Yeah, we can try that," said Gunz. With surprise, he noticed that while his voice was strained and hoarse, it sounded firm. "We can take a defensive position and wait for them to attack again, fighting on their terms, by their rules—powerless without our magic, and blind with no knowledge of whom we're facing or their goals." Gunz got up, swaying slightly on his feet. "Or we show these demonic scumbags that they're playing with fire and beat them at their own game."

"What are you saying?" asked Aidan, confusion written all over his face.

"I'm done running from them, Aidan," replied Gunz, shaking his head, his eyes searching the faces of his friends for support. "They want a Fire Salamander? Fine! I'll give them what they want. I'm going to the Land of Dreams. It's time we learn who they are and take the war to their territory." He shrugged, a cold lopsided smirk playing on his lips. "To stop the demonic infection and restore the flow of magic, we must fight them, but we can't fight them here, surrounded by humans. The only way to destroy this hornets' nest is by blowing it up from the inside."

A heavy pause lingered in the room as everyone stared at him.

"He is out of his mind, Mrak," muttered Kal, "demons probably fried whatever tiny amount of brains he had."

The Master of Power glanced at the Fire Elemental, and a

light smile lit up his face. "Maybe he is, but maybe he's not," he objected. "I think your boy has a point."

"Gwyn, do you think this demonic infection is contagious?" asked Kal turning to Gwyn ap Nudd, angry flames rising in his eyes. "They both are out of their goddamn minds! We can't give demons what they demand. We don't know who they are and why they want a Fire Salamander! And to boot, they're immune to the Fire Salamander's magic and power! Gunz will be powerless against them!"

"Wait, Kalidus," said Gwyn peacefully, "let's hear them out—"

"No!" shouted Kal. "It's a suicide mission!"

"Kal, please keep your fiery personality under control for a few minutes! It's no longer about our individual lives or safety. It's about saving magic itself! In all the realms!" Mrak Delar growled furiously, but then drew in a long breath to calm down and continued, "Just a few weeks ago, we were dealing with the followers of Chaos led by Grigori Rasputin. Who's to say that these demons are not organized by another dark soul?"

Kal didn't interrupt him, but his shoulders sagged and the fire in his eyes dimmed down.

"These demons were overflowing with the energy of Chaos, so whoever runs this freak show has to be one of the dark souls Morena released last year," Mrak Delar continued, calm and composed once again. "Sending Gunz to explore the situation in the nexus and check out the City of Gold"—he swallowed hard, almost choking on the name of the city—"is the only chance we have to find out who stands behind these attacks and eliminate them. We must restore the flow of magical energy between the worlds as soon as possible."

"You want to send my child to the City of Gold after everything *you* went—" Kal didn't finish his statement and smirked humorlessly, his deep eyes sad and cold. "I will not allow that. Period. He is too young, Ancient Master. Young and inexperienced. How can I send him out there alone and unarmed, without his magic?" He ran out of steam and a low growl rumbled in his chest as he struggled within the restraints of Gwyn's shield. "If we need to send someone to the City of Gold, I'll go."

With a heavy weight settling in his heart, Gunz approached the Great Salamander and kneeled before him.

"Father, no," he objected. For a moment he fell silent, searching for the right words. "I'm sorry to disobey you, but it has to be me."

"Gunz, we both are Fire Salamanders," said Kal, gazing down at him. "Demons don't care if it is you or me. I'm old... too old. You're just a boy. I can't risk your safety and possibly your life, my child."

"You're right, Father. We both are Fire Salamanders, but I'm the only one among us all who's equipped to recognize the dark soul and send a message to Chernobog," Gunz said, placing his hand to his side as he got up. "If you remember, Voron gifted me with a rune, which allows me to do it. This is the only way we can find out who is running this show and I'm the only person who can do it. I have no choice. I must go."

Kal dropped his head and long strands of his flaming hair fell over his face, concealing it.

"You can't go alone, Zane. I am going with you," said Aidan, rising heavily. He threw a quick glance at Gwyn ap Nudd as if asking his mentor for support. The King of the Otherworld didn't look happy, but he gave Aidan a curt nod.

"So am I," Yaroslav stated matter-of-factly. He got up and halted next to Gunz and Aidan, a wide grin on his face. "You didn't think I would let the two of you have all the fun, did you?"

At his words, Akira tensed. If before, she had been sitting still with only her narrow eyes alive on her face, now she looked like a statue with a mask of fear. Nevertheless, she said nothing to her son.

"Friggin' three musketeers," Peyton muttered, rolling her eyes. She said it softly and if she had been in the company of humans, no one would hear her. But unfortunately for her, she was surrounded by beings of magic and elemental power whose senses were a lot sharper than those of a regular human.

As soon as her careless words escaped her lips, everyone in the room turned to her.

"Three musketeers?" hissed Akira, only too eager to spill someone's blood right about now.

"Oops," Peyton whispered, shrinking into her chair.

For a moment, no one said anything, and it was Jim who broke the uncomfortable silence.

"As far as I can see," the FBI agent said dryly, scrutinizing Peyton with his wintry eyes, "it's four musketeers, Ms. D'artagnan. For an unknown reason, demons marked Gunz, Aidan and Yaroslav, but I believe as soon as you got involved, they marked you too. So, your choices are limited, Peyton—you either go with them, assuming they don't mind you tagging along, or you go back to the city and deal with the demonic forces on your own." He cocked his head, staring at the young witch with distaste. "Oh, and by the way, you're fired."

Gwyn ap Nudd exchanged a look with Kal and chuckled, his cat-eyes crinkling at the corners. "I do like him," he said to Kal and arched his brow at Jim. "After you cross the veil, Lord Agent, which deathly realm are you planning to go to?"

"Um..." Jim murmured, visibly cringing. "I'm trying to avoid making this decision. For quite some time, hopefully."

Gwyn nodded and turned to Peyton, humor gone from his white eyes. "So, what do you want to do, witch?"

"I don't think it's a good idea for her to go with us," interjected Aidan, folding his arms across his chest resentfully. "With her animosity and attitude toward Yaroslav, she'll be nothing but a liability. Zane?"

Gunz shrugged, biting his lip. He wasn't sure how he felt

about it. He liked the Peyton he knew before, and he found her current behavior strange and unsettling. Nevertheless, Aidan had a point—Peyton's attitude toward Yaroslav could endanger their mission. On the other hand, he realized that Peyton couldn't stay in the Otherworld, and returning to the city was her death warrant. She was relatively strong as a witch, but she wasn't experienced, and with the lack of magic in the human realm, she was a sitting duck.

"Perhaps we should think about it, Aidan," he suggested peacefully.

"She is coming with us." Yaroslav cut the discussion in a no-nonsense tone. "I'm indebted to her. She got marked because of me. Leaving her alone in the city is equivalent to killing her. I'm not saying that our trip through the demon-infested Land of Dreams is going to be all butterflies and rainbows, but at least she won't be alone."

"As you wish, Slavik," agreed Gunz, "that's fine with me."

Aidan frowned but nodded.

"Nobody cares what I want to do?" Peyton squeaked, throwing her hands in the air.

"No," replied Gunz dryly, with surprise hearing Yaroslav and Aidan echoing his words.

"So, it's decided then," said Gwyn ap Nudd. "Aidan, Yaroslav, Gunz and Peyton will travel to the City of Gold and try to discover who stands behind the followers of Chaos this time."

"How?" asked Akira and for the first time Gunz caught signs of nervousness in her movements. Her angled eyes lingered on Gwyn's massive figure before she leaned back in her chair with a light wave of her hand in Mrak's direction. "The Ancient Master made it clear—the magical nexus was sealed. It means the door is locked and no one can teleport there. How are they going to cross over?"

"There is only one way," replied Kal, "through the Fire Salamander's portal. Fire doesn't know borders and restrictions. It exists everywhere. We, the Fire Salamanders, don't travel like the Masters of Power who teleport or Wizards who use their magic to open portals. Our portals burn through the fabric of reality itself. Nothing can hold us. As long as we know where we are going, we can open our portals anywhere in this world or the others."

"The purifying Fire of your portal will kill my son," said Akira with a frosty tone in her voice. She got up and approached the Fire Elemental. Even with him sitting and her standing, he was still taller than her by at least a couple of inches. "I won't allow it." She slashed the air with her hand, as if it was her infamous katana.

"It's not going to kill me," objected Yaroslav. "I already did it three times and I'm still here. I trust Gunz to protect me."

The Scarlet Queen pursed her lips into a tiny pink bow and turned to Gunz, "Young Salamander, the life of my son is more precious to me than my own. I believe you will not betray my trust?"

The Scarlet Queen behaved like any mother who was worried about her only child. Yet, at the same time, her words sounded like the most terrifying threat Gunz had ever heard.

"I can't promise that any of us will be safe, travelling through the nexus taken over by the forces of Chaos," said Gunz, feeling unease spreading through him. "But I can promise you one thing—Yaroslav is going to be absolutely safe passing through the Fire Salamander portal."

The Scarlet Queen just nodded, lowering down into the armchair. Even though her face looked as emotionless and calm as ever, Gunz knew it was just a façade she loved to keep up on display. Inside, Akira was a bleeding mess of doubt and worry. Despite the fact that she was a dangerous ancient vampire, when it came to Yaroslav, the term *motherly love* wasn't good enough to describe her feelings toward her son. It was so much more, and it also made everything a lot more dangerous as she would do anything to keep him safe.

"We need to protect the human realm from the followers of Chaos," said Mrak Delar. "Besides that, we can't leave the Otherworld unprotected. The Isle of Legends is also a magical nexus and the only way in, is through your domain, Gwyn. We must be ready to defend it." He caught Gwyn ap Nudd's reproachful gaze and sighed. "Gwyn, we all are deprived of magical energy and weaker than we were before. And the longer Kendral and the Land of Dreams remain sealed, the weaker we all are going to become. You need someone to stay behind with you. Just in case."

"I'll stay behind with Gwyn," volunteered Kal. "I can't use my elemental power in the world of humans and if the Master of Kendral needed me, he would have summoned me by now. Besides, Gwyn and I go way back. We fought together before any of you youngsters existed." He chuckled, winking at Gwyn ap Nudd.

"Fine," said Mrak Delar, turning to Jim. "Agent Andrews, you need to get your human team ready to control possible riots and other effects of demonic activities and energy of Chaos. Do what you need to do, Agent. We don't know what to expect and how far the demonic infection will spread."

"I'll start preparations as soon as you take me back home, Master," replied Jim, as calm and determined as ever.

"*EverSafe* will stand by your side, Agent," promised Akira, rising.

"Mrak, how about you?" asked Gunz, turning toward the Ancient Master.

"I have to stay behind with Agent Andrews," replied Mrak Delar, throwing a quick nod to Jim. "With both Aidan and you gone, he will need magical reinforcement." He sighed, lowering his eyes. "I wish I could go with the four of you, but it is not a good idea for many reasons. Now, I have to take Akira and

Agent Andrews back home, but I'll be back before you leave in the morning."

He tapped Gunz on his shoulder and nodded at Gwyn ap Nudd. The King of the Otherworld opened the door and Mrak Delar walked through it, followed by Akira and Jim.

CHAPTER 12

~ ZANE BURNS, A.K.A. GUNZ ~

Gunz lay on top of the bedcover, his body buzzing with exhaustion like an angry beehive. As soon as the meeting was over, he went upstairs and hopped into the shower, not quite sure he had enough strength to do anything but sleep. Nevertheless, the amount of dirt and blood on him didn't seem to agree with the whiteness of everything in Gwyn's house, so the shower wasn't optional.

Now, he was lying on the bed dressed only in pajama pants he found in Gwyn's closet and stared without blinking at the immaculately white ceiling, terrified by the idea of closing his eyes. The soft knock on his door made him flinch, and he jolted up into a sitting position. As he probed the area with his other sight, he recognized Kal's energy signature and slowly lowered his feet on the cold marble floor.

His gaze halted on his pants and he chuckled—the black pajama pants were covered in pictures of small golden fire salamanders. Some of the lizards were on fire, but some were hiding behind rocks, their cartoonish eyes round and terrified. Even Gwyn's closet had some sense of humor.

Kal is going to have a field day with this, he thought with a sigh and then yelled, "Father, come in!"

The door opened, letting in the giant figure of the Great Salamander. Kal crossed the distance between the entrance and the bed in one step and sat down on the edge next to Gunz, making the springs moan and sink under his weight. He took in Gunz's appearance, his eyes lingering a moment on his pajama pants and a wide grin stretched his thin lips.

"How appropriate," he murmured, tracing the shape of a terrified lizard on Gunz's knee. "Afraid to sleep?"

"Yes," Gunz replied through gritted teeth. There was no sense in denying it now that Kal knew everything.

Kal nodded, all mirth gone from his eyes. "Why didn't you tell me?" he asked, his voice hoarse. "Why are you insisting on fighting through everything on your own?"

"Because—" Gunz bit his lips and fell silent, looking away.

"Because you are afraid that by involving people you love, you'll get them hurt or dead?" supplied the Fire Elemental.

Gunz raised his eyes at his mentor but didn't find the usual mockery in his gaze. The Great Salamander was serious and a little sad. Gunz nodded, his fingers fiddling absently with the edge of the bedsheet.

"Look what I did to Angelique," he said, realizing that he wasn't capable of sounding louder than a whisper. "It's my fault, Kal. Everything is. The vision Rasputin showed me back in California... You have no idea... oh, God..." He moaned, hiding his face in his hands. "The only thing she did wrong was falling in love with me. If she hadn't followed me to Mount Karasova, she would still be alive. My fault..."

"This is exactly why I'm here right now," said Kal frowning. "You must stop blaming yourself. Do you understand me, my son?"

"I don't think that's possible."

"You have to," objected Kal. "You have no choice, or you will become an easy prey to the first demon you meet in the nexus."

While Kal's voice was still soft and kind, Gunz caught some iron notes in it. "I'm not sure I can just—"

"Then you're not going anywhere. I'm taking your place," Kal cut him off, slamming his fist on the bed, making it wobble.

"Why?" Gunz croaked, shrinking under Kal's furious gaze. "Why does it matter?"

"In a few hours, you will open your portal to the magical nexus polluted with demonic energy," said Kal, his body tense with anger. "We have no idea how the nexus reacted to the demonic invasion, but one thing I am certain about. Every moment you spend there will be a literal torture to your senses. You're going to feel like you are standing on top of Everest—cold and deprived of oxygen.

"There won't be enough elemental Fire for you to channel and the only way either of you will be able to use magic is by channeling the energy you have within. You will be weakened magically and vulnerable to injuries physically as you won't be able to revert and heal yourself.

"Your mental state of constant self-flagellation and all-consuming guilt will weaken you even further, to the point where you won't be able to make the right decision." Kal paused and shrugged, turning away. "It's not like you're making the right decisions now, anyway. Why didn't you tell me about your nightmares? Why didn't you tell me Zmey had you on a short leash?"

"Father, you don't understand," mumbled Gunz, everything inside him twisting into a pulsing knot of raw pain. "I don't know why I didn't tell anyone! I wish I could let go of this guilt and stop feeling this way, but I have no idea how!"

"By forgiving yourself," said a deep voice somewhere on his left.

Gunz lifted his head and saw the Ancient Master of Power

standing in the doorway. Mrak Delar made his way inside the room and halted in front of him, a sad smile on his face.

"Trust me, I wrote millions of scrolls on the subject of *'royal fuck-ups and self-forgiveness'*. Kal can attest to it," Mrak said, reaching into his pocket.

He produced a small box and opened it, showing its contents to Gunz. A silver ring lay on the dark red silk inside the box. Two stones, red and gray, were embedded into the silver, creating a design similar to the yin-yang symbol but without small round inclusions. A faint mist of magical energy permeated the air around it. Gunz observed the ring with interest and his lips stretched in a lopsided grin.

"Are you proposing, Master?" he asked and immediately received a slap on the back of his head from his mentor.

"I was considering," replied Mrak Delar without blinking an eye, "but I'm married already, and my wife is a lot prettier than you."

"Here you go," muttered Kal, rolling his eyes, "let the duel of wits commence. I'll let you two talk." He got up heavily, straightening his pants and turned to Gunz, putting his hand on Gunz's shoulder. "I will see you in the morning, my boy."

The Great Salamander stilled as if he was going to add something, but then just shook his head and walked out the door. Mrak Delar sat down on the edge of the bed where Kal had been sitting just a moment ago and carefully took the ring out of the box.

"It took two Masters of Power to create this ring for you, my friend," he said quietly, placing it in the palm of Gunz's hand.

As soon as the ring touched his skin, Gunz felt the sharp ping of its magical energy rushing through his body. He held his breath and frowned, bringing it closer to his eyes.

"How does it work?" he asked, touching the stones with his finger.

"You are not going to like it," warned Mrak Delar, his fingers playing with the empty box, opening it and shutting it closed, "but this was the only thing I could come up with on such short notice. I wish you told me everything earlier, but oh well… We created a complex enchantment and placed it on these two stones.

"The ring will stop Zmey, or anyone else for that matter, from entering your mind when you're asleep or unconscious, but unfortunately it will also block your fire and magic, similar to the way the gray stone jewelry does. You'll be weak and physically vulnerable, so don't put this ring on your finger unless you're ready to sleep. On top of that, the ring will block the psychic bond Aidan created, and possibly your blood bond with Yaroslav will also get affected."

"I understand," said Gunz. The idea of losing his magic and his ability to communicate with his friends was troubling him, but the idea of the Lord of Chaos entering his mind again was a lot more terrifying.

"I spoke with Yaroslav and Aidan," continued Mrak Delar. "One of them will always be awake when you're sleeping. Just in case."

Gunz bowed his head. "I can't believe this is happening," he whispered, barely audible.

"Could be worse." Mrak Delar flicked his eyebrow, smirking humorlessly. "Big friggin' deal—you need a babysitter while you're sleeping."

Gunz chuckled, throwing a quick glance at his friend. "How about Peyton? Have you spoken with her too?"

"No," replied Mrak Delar quietly. "I have no idea what this young witch is up to. She's like two people in one—one is sweet and kind, and the other is angry and stupid. The way she behaved was like she had a death wish. Both Akira and Yaroslav could kill her faster than any of us could make a move. It's like she was trying to provoke them both."

Gunz nodded, thinking back to the first time he had met

Peyton, back at *Missi's Kitchen*. Mrak's observation was right on the money—two different personalities. But to be fair, he had never seen her communicate with Yaroslav or any other employee of Akira's company. The way her apartment was guarded against vampires raised more than one red flag in his mind. There had to be a reason for that.

"I know what you think," said Mrak Delar, interrupting his train of thoughts. "Right now you are searching high and low for some kind of reasonable explanation for all that. Don't bother. Only time will tell. Just be careful around Peyton. You can't trust her."

"Then why is she going with us? This trip to the nexus doesn't strike me like a walk in the park and I prefer to have people I can trust next to me," said Gunz, rubbing his shoulder tiredly. "Jim kind of pushed her on us and then Yaroslav stepped in, always the knight in shining armor." He fell back on the bed, placing his arm over his eyes. "I think my brain is fried and I'm too tired to think about things like that. I feel like those giant statues on Easter Island—all head and no body."

Mrak Delar looked heavenwards and the corners of his mouth quirked up. "Yeah, you do remind me of the Easter Island statues, but the bottom part of them, not the head."

"Ahh, shut up, jackass." Gunz smiled faintly, folding his arms under his head.

Mrak laughed, rising. He pulled a chair closer to the bed and sat down, facing Gunz. "To answer your question about why Peyton is going with you. When I was in Kendral, I talked to the Destiny Keeper. His answer was as evasive as ever. He said her place on the Destiny Board is with you and your team, and he refused to give any other information."

"Well, that is the worst thing he could say," mumbled Gunz closing his eyes. "She can't stand Yaroslav... or maybe just vampires in general. I think every time he touches her, she is ready to throw up."

"Yes, and there is that," murmured Mrak Delar. "Why don't you put this ring on and try to get some sleep. It's late and we're all tired."

Gunz nodded and carefully slipped the ring on his finger. He expected the ring to suppress his fire, but what happened was a lot worse than any of his wildest expectations. As soon as the silver wrapped around his finger, his fire was gone. He clutched his chest, gasping for air. As his body tensed and his muscles locked, he stared at Mrak wide-eyed, unable to say a word. Everything around him spun and his stomach clenched.

Mrak Delar pushed on his shoulders, forcing him to lie down. "Hush, Gunz, it should be over in a moment. It's the gray stone in the ring," he said softly. "Just close your eyes and try to breathe."

Gunz closed his eyes, but even with his eyes shut, he felt like he was on a boat during a storm. When he finally was able to fill his lungs with oxygen, he moaned and carefully cracked his eyelids open.

"Is it going to be like this every time I put this goddamn ring on?" he mumbled. He lifted his arm up and noticed that his hand was shaking.

"Yes, and probably even worse when you are in the nexus," replied Mrak Delar. "I'm sorry, but I'm not sorry. It's a lesson to you, my friend. If I had known earlier, I would have had more time to come up with a better solution."

"With all due respect, Master," muttered Gunz, dropping his arm powerlessly, "you are a one-of-a-kind evil bastard."

Mrak Delar laughed open-heartedly, throwing his head back. "That I am. But I am also a one-of-a-kind evil bastard who will keep the Lord of Chaos out of your stubborn head. Now, try to get some sleep. I'll stay in your room this night and observe you. Just to make sure that the ring does its job." He folded his arms over his chest and stretched his legs, trying to find a better position in the uncomfortable chair.

"It better..." Gunz exhaled. "Hey, Mrak?"

"Uh-huh?"

"The City of Gold scares you shitless, Master. Why is that?" asked Gunz, fighting the haze of weakness and sleepiness.

"I have a history with King Alexander, the ruler of the City of Gold. I can never go back to this place," replied the Ancient Master flatly. "If you can help it, stay as far away from this man as possible."

"Something tells me it's not going to be possible, since this is where I have to go—the City of Gold, the demons' stronghold..."

"Well, make sure that before you walk through the gates of the City of Gold, you explore the situation in the Land of Dreams," said Mrak Delar quietly. "Visit a village or a town. Talk to people. You may find out something that could help you with your mission. You know the City of Gold is a trap, so don't jump into it blindly. King Alexander is..." He trailed off and massaged his temples with his fingers as if the conversation was giving him a headache. "Fire and ice... out of all the places in the nexus, it has to be this cursed City!"

"It always is, Mrak." Gunz chuckled mirthlessly and closed his eyes.

Slowly the exhaustion took over, and he finally fell asleep.

CHAPTER 13

~ ZANE BURNS, A.K.A. GUNZ ~

Just as Mrak Delar had promised, his sleep was peaceful, undisturbed by nightmares or dreams and when he woke up, he felt refreshed and rested. But when he opened his eyes, he didn't find the Ancient Master in the armchair next to his bed. Instead, Kal was sitting there with his legs outstretched and his arms folded over his chest.

"Good morning," murmured Kal, his eyes crinkling at the corners. "Did you rest well, my child?"

Gunz nodded, sitting up, and rubbed his face with his hands, wiping off the leftovers of sleep. Then he lowered his hands and pulled the ring off his finger. A short electric shock made him yelp and squeeze his hands into fists, but it was gone almost immediately. Elemental power and magic rushed through his body like a tidal wave and his eyes lit up with a red glow. For a moment, he held his breath, enjoying the feeling of his power returning to him.

"Put the ring here," said Kal, offering Gunz a small box. "Master Mrak Delar said it will protect you from the effects of the gray stone magic."

Gunz took the box, placed the ring inside and closed it.

"Where is Mrak?" he asked, setting the box on the bed next to him.

"I replaced him half way through the night. He needed rest just as much as you did, if not more," replied Kal dryly. "I don't know if you noticed, but after everything Mrak did yesterday, he was drained, almost on the verge of shutting down."

"Dammit," cursed Gunz quietly, wondering how he could have missed the signs.

All Masters of Power were extremely powerful, their abilities and powers bordering with those of a god. Nevertheless, their bodies were still human and the more they used their power and magic the faster they were getting drained. After excessive use of their magic, they had to allow themselves to rest and recharge or their bodies would shut down of their own accord.

"Is he okay?" asked Gunz, staring at the picture of a terrified lizard on his pants, his scalp prickling with guilt. "Where is he?"

"He's fine, don't worry. It's amazing how fast you find a reason to blame yourself for everything that happens around you," replied Kal, sarcastic twinkles dancing in his eyes. "He's downstairs with Gwyn and the others."

Gunz made a move to get up, but Kal leaned forward, placing his heavy hand on his shoulder and forced him to sit back down.

"Before I let you go, there is something I need to tell you, Gunz," said the Great Salamander, his expression hardened.

Gunz sat down, bracing himself for bad news. "I'm listening," he said, his fingers squeezing the silk sheets.

"It's been a few years since I first laid my eyes upon you, Gunz," started Kal, his voice unusually flat and void of emotions. "Since that time, you have grown as a Fire Salamander and as a man. But one thing you've never learned, and no matter how hard I try teaching you, when it comes to asking for help, you are hopeless. You never learned how to ask for help when you need it."

"Father—," started Gunz, but cut himself off and bit his lip.

"I know, your heart is in the right place," continued Kal calmly. "You're always trying to protect those you love, and I appreciate it. This is why we're having this conversation now."

"I don't understand," mumbled Gunz. "What's going on, Kal, just tell me straight."

"It is me telling you straight," huffed Kal, fire igniting in his eyes. "In a few minutes, you are going to open your portal into the polluted nexus. Even though you're not going there alone, none of you know what to expect. No planning, no strategizing, no way to get ready. You're going to be walking into a location full of unknowns where anything is possible."

"Isn't it always like that?" asked Gunz with a shrug. "Any time I end up in the Land of Dreams, I receive the same advice —expect the unexpected."

"Yes, but this time is different," growled Kal without even trying to hide his aggravation. "You never ask for help, but I noticed that when you're pushed into a corner, you chose to summon Mrak Delar. Not this time. If you find yourself in a situation where you need help, you will not call the Ancient Master. Do you understand me?"

"No, I don't!" yelled Gunz, slamming his fist on the bed. The box with the ring jumped up and fell on the floor with a loud thud. "What are you saying, Kal? I thought with the nexus sealed, no one can travel in or out except you and me? Why would I summon Mrak if I know he can't get there!"

"But he can! That's the problem," hissed Kal, leaning forward, his burning eyes just inches away from Gunz's face. "And I bet you anything, before you leave, he will tell you that. And I am telling you... No, I'm ordering you not to summon Mrak Delar no matter what. If you find yourself in desperate need of help, you will summon me. Am I clear, young Salamander?"

"Yes, sir," replied Gunz, cold fingers of fear squeezing his heart. But then he jumped to his feet, throwing his hands up. "Kal, I always comply with all your orders, but I still want to understand why."

"I thought you knew." Kal measured him with his steady gaze, his thin lips set in a grim line. "There is one more way to travel into a sealed nexus or to any world for that matter."

"How?" asked Gunz. His voice faltered as he knew the answer before Kal said anything.

"By ripping through the fabric of reality. As far as I know, there are only three people in all the worlds who are powerful enough to attempt that. Master Mrak Delar is one of them." Kal leaned back in his armchair and took a short pause before continuing, "You know that mutilating the fabric of reality is a serious offense and the Destiny Council prosecutes anyone who dares to do that."

"I know," replied Gunz quietly as understanding washed over him, wiping out his frustration.

"Good. I see you're finally grasping the reality," said Kal with a sigh. "Mrak Delar is not favored by the Destiny Council. Don't get him in more trouble than he already is. You don't want to see him sporting the Destiny Cuffs."

Gunz nodded, rubbing his knuckles with his thumb, his nerves on edge.

"This is not all," Kal continued. "A few years ago, Mrak was held captive by the king of the City of Gold. It was a dark time in the Ancient Master's life and if he never told you about that, it's not my place to disclose his secrets. But to make a long story short—what King Alexander did to him was beyond cruel. I was the one whom Mrak called for help and when I saw his condition..." Kal shuddered and fell silent. "Anyway, by summoning

Mrak to the City of Gold, you may give King Alexander a chance to finish what he started."

"I understand," said Gunz rising. "It's not like I was planning to put any of my friends in danger anyway, but for as long as I am in the nexus, I swear I will not summon Mrak Delar. I'm not going to call you either, Father. I trust that between a god of the Otherworld, the Great Fire Salamander and an old vampire, we'll be able to deal with whatever comes our way."

"Ugh, there you go again," muttered Kal. He got up and before Gunz could react, he seized his hair, pulling his head back. "A mix of pride and stupidity is a sure recipe for disaster, young Salamander, and you're overflowing with both. Nothing is a lesson to you. Just put it through your thick skull—*you do not know!*"

He let go of Gunz's hair and pushed him in his chest. Gunz fell back on the bed, a lopsided smirk on his lips, as he gazed up at his mentor. Kal rolled his eyes and chuckled.

"Go change." He tapped lightly on Gunz's leg and headed toward the door. "Gwyn has way too much fun with his closets' magic."

Gunz watched Kal exit the room, carefully closing the door, and a wave of dread spread through him. Until now, he had no time to sit down and think. With them being chased through the world, everything was progressing too fast. He had no doubt that his decision to infiltrate the nexus was the right one and he was the right man for the job. Actually, he was the only man for the job.

He also knew that this mission was not going to be easy. But only now, as he watched Kal exit his room with his shoulders slumped and a vibe of despair lingering over him like a stormy cloud, did he realize how truly important and dangerous his mission was.

The Great Salamander didn't like getting involved into the affairs of human realms. It had been ages since he stopped controlling his elemental power and that made his presence anywhere next to people who weren't touched by the World of Magic impossible. Usually, he allowed Gunz to take care of his own problems, getting involved only if there was no other choice, and he never showed any signs of concern or fear.

Never, until now...

CHAPTER 14

~ ZANE BURNS, A.K.A. GUNZ ~

Gunz halted by the door and looked back, surveying the bedroom one last time to make sure he didn't forget anything. He found everything he needed in Gwyn's closet. Now the Swiss army knife was resting comfortably in the pocket of his military cargo pants and as far as weapons, there was nothing else he needed.

He wasn't sure why he had chosen military cargo pants and combat boots as opposed to his usual jeans and sneakers, but for some reason it felt right for this mission. Nevertheless, it reminded him of the way he used to dress when he fought in the Underground Supernatural pits, and he shivered as if the temperature in the room dropped a few degrees.

The ring Mrak Delar had built for him was securely locked in the box in his other pocket. All he had to do was push the door open and walk out. Yet something was holding him back, making his skin crawl with dread. Possibly it was his last conversation with Kal that didn't sit well with him.

"What are you staring at?" Gunz muttered to the terrified lizard with large round eyes on the pajama pants that were lying on the bed. Then he sighed and walked out of the bedroom, forcing his nervousness and unwanted thoughts under control.

The depressed atmosphere in Gwyn's living room didn't help Gunz with his internal turmoil. Aidan stood at the other end of the room, conversing with Yaroslav in a soft whisper. Gwyn ap Nudd, Mrak Delar and Kal sat around the coffee table, silent and grim. Peyton had curled up in Gwyn's giant armchair. With her knees bent and her arms wrapped around her legs, she looked grim and a little scared.

As soon as Gunz walked in, everyone turned toward him. Mrak Delar got up, his every move unusually heavy and stiff.

"Ready?" he asked, brushing loose strands of his hair off his face. He threw a quick glance at Aidan and Yaroslav and switched his attention back to Gunz.

Gunz nodded.

"Where are you opening your portal to?" asked Kal. Compared to the way he had looked just an hour ago, he appeared calm and collected now.

"Isle Buyan," replied Gunz. "I hope around the World Tree the demonic presence is not going to be as heavy as in other places of the nexus. I'm not in a rush to jump into enemy territory without any intel. I want to see if I can gather some information from Sirin and Alkonost before we decide what to do next."

"Good choice," muttered Gwyn ap Nudd, rising.

As Aidan headed toward Gunz, Gwyn seized his arm to stop him and frowned, his usual lighthearted cheerfulness gone.

"Be careful. We don't know how the nexus has reacted to the pollution and what to expect when you get there," he said to Aidan, his already pale face almost translucent with worry. He glanced around, his cat-eyes darting from his son to Gunz, then to Yaroslav and finally settling on Peyton. "All of you… Peyton, now is a good time to put away your animosity toward vampires and start working with Yaroslav. Stand together with the three of them or die alone. These are your choices, witch. None of us know what you are going to find there. This is the first time in my life I have no information whatsoever…" His voice faded away and he dropped his arms.

Aidan nodded, ready to leave, but Gwyn pulled him into a quick embrace, giving him a light tap on the back. Gunz's skin prickled with unease as he observed his friends, and the feeling of dread that he had been feeling since he woke up intensified tenfold.

"Young Salamander, I need to have a word with you before you go," said Mrak Delar, gesturing toward the kitchen.

Young Salamander? Since when is Mrak using my title? Gunz glanced at Kal and saw his mentor shaking his head no, a silent warning in his burning eyes.

Gunz followed Mrak Delar into the kitchen and closed the door as he walked in. The Master of Power was leaning against the counter, his hands squeezing the cold marble countertop so hard, his knuckles were white.

"Mrak, I know what you are about to say," started Gunz, leaning against the counter across from his friend, "and I'm asking you not to. I'm going to be fine. We all are going to be fine."

"Gunz, listen. If any of you need—"

"I won't."

"You don't know what I was—"

"I do know."

"Gunz!"

"Mrak, I said no," said Gunz firmly, guilt shredding his insides. "You're right. I have no idea what we're about to walk into, but no matter what happens, I am not going to call you. If I need help, I'll call Kal."

"No, you won't," objected Mrak Delar dryly, folding his arms over his chest, his cold gaze drilling through Gunz. "We both know that."

"No, I won't," agreed Gunz, silently cursing at how well Mrak knew him. "The demons want a Salamander. It is enough that I'm taking a chance crossing over to their territory. I am not going to bring the second Salamander into the mix."

"It leaves only me," said Mrak Delar through his clenched teeth. "I am the only one who can enter the nexus in case the four of you need help. You will summon me. Am I clear, Young Salamander!"

"No."

"Obviously you still don't understand how important your mission is," growled Mrak Delar, the energy field spiking furiously around him, and the walls of Gwyn's glass house trembled. "It is more important than your life or mine, or anyone's for that matter. The future of magic itself depends on it. The Land of Dreams must be recovered, purified, and unsealed. So, if the four of you need help, you *will* summon me. It's an order!"

"An order? Screw you!" hissed Gunz, slamming his hand on the counter, but then rubbed his face, forcing his anger under control. "Goddamnit, Master… Don't you think I know all that? I know everything and still, I'm not going to summon you… I will not put your name on the Destiny Council's 'most-wanted' list! And most certainly, I am not going to let King Alexander get anywhere near you. No matter what happens there, I'll figure it out. I always do!" He pushed himself off the counter, his chest shuddering with angry breaths. "I appreciate the offer, Ancient Master, but I have to respectfully decline."

He bowed to Mrak Delar sharply and walked out of the kitchen.

Gunz crossed the living room, deliberately not meeting Kal's eyes and nodded at Gwyn ap Nudd. The King of the Otherworld muttered a short spell and everything around them lit up with a soft white glow.

"I removed the wards," said Gwyn. "Do it quickly."

Gunz waved his hand, unfolding the flaming curtain of the

Fire Salamander portal. He allowed Aidan to go through first and then carried Peyton through the fire. When he came back, Mrak Delar was sitting next to Kal, looking as calm as usual.

Gunz said his goodbyes to Kal and Gwyn and then approached Mrak Delar. "Take care of yourself and my world, Master," he said, offering his hand to him. "Jim will need your help here more than I out there."

The Master of Power nodded and got up heavily. He took Gunz's hand and Gunz felt a sharp ping of Mrak's magic surging through him. He pulled his hand away, frowning.

"What did you do?" he whispered so only Mrak could hear him.

"Gave you a little energy boost before you cross over," replied Mrak with a hardly noticeable smile on his calm face. "A parting gift to my friend."

Gunz nodded to him and turned toward his flaming curtain. He placed a protection shield over Yaroslav and carried him through the portal.

* * *

As soon as Gunz stepped outside the portal, he lost his breath as if someone had punched him in his gut. He doubled over, pressing his hand to his chest, gasping for air with his mouth open. Weak and disoriented, he dropped to his knees, bending down to the ground. Forcing his heartbeat to slow down, he sat back on his heels.

Aidan was lying on the ground, breathing laboriously, and Peyton was sitting next to him, holding his hand. Her other hand was pressed to her chest, and she was taking sharp breaths, struggling to fill her lungs with air.

The only person who seemingly was unaffected by the new, demonically challenged magical nexus was Yaroslav. The vampire leaned forward slightly, offering Gunz his hand. Gunz took it and got up.

"Kal was right," he mumbled, rubbing his forehead. "It does feel like standing on top of Everest—thin air and cold. The initial effect is quite jarring."

"There is hardly any magical energy and the elemental powers are suppressed to a minimum," said Aidan, scrambling to his feet with effort. "And whatever magic and power is still here, it's infected with some kind of demonic energy. It's rather sickening."

Gunz surveyed the area, searching for the World Tree. He was positive that he was in the right place, but he could hardly recognize the once beautiful isle in this gray cold land. There were no flower fields and fresh greenery. The ground was covered in patches of brown dead grass and thick gray fog was slithering over the land, obscuring his vision. As insignificant as it was, he sensed a slight stench of demonic essence intertwined with the heavy odor of decaying foliage and wet dirt.

It was unusually quiet—no chirping birds or buzzing insects, no noise of rolling waves. The silence, thick and heavy, pressed on Gunz's nerves with the feeling of upcoming danger. He narrowed his eyes, straining his vision to see through the gray veil of fog but couldn't see farther than ten feet away from him.

"The World Tree is right there," said Yaroslav, pointing to his right.

"You can see through the fog?" asked Aidan.

"Not clearly, but I can see the outlines." Yaroslav shrugged. "And why wouldn't I? I'm a vampire, certain perks come with the territory."

"Exactly," huffed Peyton, shoving her hands in the pockets of her pants. "He's a goddamn demon. Why would he be affected by the demonic pollution?"

"Well, thank God for small favors then," grumbled Aidan. "At least one of us can see and hear inside this milk carton, so we're not completely deaf and blind."

"Let's go," said Gunz grimly, starting on his way toward the Tree.

The closer they got to the World Tree, the easier it became to breathe. The density of the fog dropped and only the disgusting dirty mist hung in the air, sticking to their exposed skin in large round droplets. It was also slightly warmer and lighter here. Gunz approached the Alatyr Stone and halted staring up at the World Tree, his chest tightened with anxiety.

The Tree no longer looked the way he remembered it. Even though there was still a separation between the dayside and the night side of it, the border was faded, barely noticeable. The moon and the stars were gone from the nightside, and the sky was veiled with dirty stormy clouds. On the dayside, there was no sun and only a slightly brighter spot of light lingered in the evenly gray sky, shining weakly through the mist.

The heavy green foliage that used to weigh down the giant branches was gone and only a few yellow and brown leaves still hung limply, ready to fall with the first gust of wind. Gunz placed his hand on the massive root of the Tree that was wrapped around the Alatyr Stone, disappearing under the ground. The bark felt dry and rough under his touch.

He sent some of his fire energy through the roots, summoning Sirin and Alkonost. A moment later, two large birds descended from the top of the tree, landing on the bottom branches. Both birds were the size of an ostrich, their bodies covered in rich plumage, but their heads weren't the heads of birds but rather that of beautiful young women.

Alkonost, the bird on the sunny-side of the tree, had gorgeous silvery-white feathers and her shiny tail feathers were as long as the tail of a peacock. She smiled warmly at them, but her large blue eyes remained sad.

Sirin, the bird on the moon-side of the tree, was just as beautiful and large, but her plumage was black with added shades of electric-blue. Her face was identical to the face of the other bird, but deep sadness seemed to be etched permanently on her tender features as large tears kept sliding from her aquamarine eyes.

"Hello, my dear friends," said the white bird, her smile growing a notch happier. "You didn't forget about us in this time of troubles."

"Yeah, right," replied the dark bird immediately with a giant roll of her eyes that elicited more tears, "they didn't forget about us. As if they care. They need something from us, otherwise they wouldn't be here."

"Aw, sister, don't be such a Debbie Downer. They do care about us," purred Alkonost, spreading her beautiful white wings. "Look, the cute Young Salamander and the god of the Otherworld are here to help us, and they brought this absolutely gorgeous royal vampire with them... Just looking at him makes me feel better."

"The only thing they care about is the fact that they lost their favorite toy—magic. Otherwise they wouldn't be here," huffed Sirin. Her tear-filled eyes halted on Peyton and she laughed. It wasn't a real laugh but more like a dark chuckle, and coming from the prophet of doom, it was terrifying. "Oh, my dear gods... and who else did they bring with them? This is truly hilarious!"

"What are you talking about?" asked Aidan, taking a step closer to the tree.

"Ignore her, handsome young god," purred Alkonost. "Sirin loves to play on other people's nerves. That's all she's good for."

"Young? For gods' sake, sister, raise your standards! In which century was he young? He's nearly twenty-five hundred years old!" yelled Sirin, folding her wings on her back.

"That's quite enough," muttered Gunz.

He sent more of his fire energy through the roots of the tree and whispered a spell Kal taught him a while ago. The birds shifted closer, meeting at the border of day and night. They opened their wings, embracing each other and stared down at Gunz without blinking.

"What would you like to know, Great Fire Salamander?" they asked in unison, their musical voices intertwining into a beautiful harmony.

"What's going on here?" asked Gunz, staring heavily at the birds. "Who took over the nexus and how can we stop them?"

The birds exchanged a heavy look and turned back to him before starting to sing in flat, emotionless voices.

"When the light is retreating in fear, and the night is here to stay...

"Your powers and magic are useless... even fire cannot save the day...

"When the dark becomes light, and the light becomes darkness...

"When the predator gives its life for its prey...

"You can find the path in absolute darkness...

"But only if you are willing to pay..."

Both birds flinched and stopped talking. They exchanged another heavy look and Sirin cried out, like she was in infinite pain. Horror-stricken, Gunz watched as large tears rolled down the tender cheeks of both Alkonost and Sirin. Without saying anything else, both birds rose in the air and melted into the dark clouds at the top of the World Tree.

"Well, that was one giant waste of time and poor poetry," mumbled Aidan. "We already knew that our power and magic were useless."

"When the dark becomes light? Is that even possible?" Yaroslav shook his head.

"Yeah, how about a predator giving its life to save its prey?" asked Peyton, wrapping her arms around herself as a gust of chilly wind rushed through the isle. "I don't see that happening any time soon."

A path in absolute darkness... pay what?

Gunz shuddered, remembering his first encounter with Sirin and Alkonost. The last time they had also predicted that the price of victory would be high. Too high. And now he knew what they had meant at the time. He had lost the woman he loved... in the worst possible way. The price had been too high, at least for him. So, what could he pay now? He had nothing left but his life. If it was his life the birds were chirping about, he would give it willingly, but he would not sacrifice the people he cared about.

Never again.

Gunz turned to Aidan but had no time to say anything. A large black portal opened up at the base of the Alatyr Stone. It was swirling lazily in a counter-clock motion, freezing winds howling inside it. He recognized the portal, and the fear, which he couldn't control, assailed him. He staggered back from it but couldn't fight its overwhelming dark pull.

Before the sinister darkness took hold of him, he saw Aidan jumping headfirst into the portal.

CHAPTER 15

~ ZANE BURNS, A.K.A. GUNZ ~

Gunz opened his eyes, staring into the blinding darkness, and sucked in a sharp breath, his heart thundering in his chest. He jolted to his feet, but his knees buckled, and he fell back, an overwhelming weakness spreading through him. He groaned, feeling a pair of strong hands seizing his shoulders, pulling him up into a sitting position.

"Zane, relax. Everything is okay." He heard Yaroslav's voice and then Aidan's as the god of the Otherworld muttered a spell, conjuring some light.

A few glowing orbs rose in the air, illuminating a spacious room with a shimmering blue light. Gunz looked around, taking in his surroundings. He was sitting on a low sofa with Yaroslav standing next to him, his hand still resting on his shoulder. Aidan was standing by a cold fireplace with his elbow resting atop a marble shelf. Peyton stood next to Aidan, her arms wrapped around her body, her lips purplish-blue from the cold.

Everything inside the room breathed with luxury, yet it wasn't overly exuberant and whoever had furnished this space had exceptional taste, decorating it with comfort in mind. Gunz didn't recognize the place, but the feeling of weakness and cold was all too familiar and the memories associated with it weren't good ones.

The tall door opened and Gunz exhaled with relief, leaning forward. "Voron... what the hell, man?"

"Hell?" Voron approached him, offering his hand to him. "You're not that lucky. Welcome to the Dark Nav, Mr. Burns." A wide smile split the old warrior's face as Gunz rose to his feet and squeezed his hand in a handshake.

"What are we doing here?" asked Gunz, lowering back to the sofa as the next wave of weakness enveloped him. "Ugh... The Nav is killing me. There is absolutely no elemental energy here."

"Behold your King, the Lord of the Nav, the mighty god of Destruction, Chernobog," replied Voron, a one-sided smirk curving his lips.

Gunz cringed inwardly, listening to the introduction that brought forth the painful memory of his first meeting with Chernobog.

Voron bowed in the direction of the door as it opened again, and a tall man walked inside. Everything about him was dark. He had long black hair and beard. The light of the orbs reflected on the folds of his black silk shirt that was tucked into his tight black pants. His hand, gloved in black leather, rested on the obsidian pommel of his sword, sheathed in a black scabbard attached to his belt. Darkness itself wasn't as dark as this man.

Gunz slid down to the floor, taking one knee and inclined his head, struggling to keep his position while the floor swayed under him.

"My lord," he said calmly, greeting the ancient deity. His last visit to the Dark Nav hadn't been pleasant and even though he had worked on the same side with Chernobog before, the Slavic god of Destruction never gave him a feeling of comfort.

"Young Salamander," said Chernobog, slightly inclining his head, "you may rise. Out of all of you, the Dark Nav affects you the most, so I don't mind you sitting in my presence." Then he turned to Aidan and gave him a hardly visible nod. "Aodh mac Lir. Prince Yaroslav Potemkin, you may rise."

Just now Gunz noticed that Yaroslav was kneeling by his side. As the vampire got up, Chernobog's eyes halted on Peyton and the corners of his mouth twitched in a hardly visible smile, partially concealed by his thick facial hair. Peyton paled under his steady gaze and curtsied awkwardly.

"And who is this lovely young—um—witch?" asked Chernobog, his eyes twinkling with sarcasm as he turned to Yaroslav for some reason. "Would you kindly make the introduction, Prince?"

"My name is Peyton, my lord," replied Peyton, stepping forward before Yaroslav could say anything, notes of annoyance clear in her voice.

"Peyton. Charmed. You and the vampire prince," said Chernobog heavily rolling his R's and then laughed slapping his hands on his thighs. "You four just made my day. I didn't think that considering the current situation in the nexus and on the Isle Buyan, anything would make me laugh." He stopped laughing, but humor remained in his black eyes as he glanced back at Yaroslav and slightly shook his head. "Anyway, there is a reason I brought all of you here, so let's get to business."

The god of Destruction headed to a large armchair and lowered himself down, crossing his legs at the knee. His eyes grew colder as he observed everyone in the room once more, slowly stroking his thick black beard with his long fingers decorated by multiple rings.

"What were you planning to do, Mr. Burns?" he asked after a short pause.

"Our initial goal was to investigate the situation in the nexus and find out who is behind this mess," replied Gunz calmly. "So, we were going—"

"No," said Chernobog, interrupting him and the iron tones

in his voice didn't leave a space for discussion. "As soon as Voron takes you back to the Yav, you are all going to go straight to the City of Gold where you will leave your friends outside the wall and give yourself up to King Alexander. Period. There must be no mistakes and failure this time. I must know their plans. And you Mr. Burns are going to do whatever it takes to make it happen. And if you must submit yourself to slavery or betray your friends, you will do that. Am I clear, Mr. Burns?"

"But, my lord, I don't think we should do it," Gunz objected calmly. "It's obvious that the City of Gold is a trap and I can't allow myself to be captured. I will go to the City, but not before I gather some information and get—"

Chernobog leaned forward, his hand clasping at the arm of the chair. "Don't you dare disobey me, boy!" he hissed, pinning Gunz with a furious stare, and the walls of the room trembled. "I believe they gave you ten days. So, by arguing with your god's orders, you're wasting your time." He smirked frostily, straightening up. "And your breath."

"Zane, don't," said Yaroslav using their physic connection, and squeezed Gunz's shoulder with his fingers.

"Yes, Zane, listen to your undead friend," said Chernobog, leaning back in his armchair, raking Yaroslav with a mocking gaze.

Voron stepped next to Chernobog, raising his hand warningly. "Mr. Burns, you'll do well to comply with my lord Chernobog's command."

"My apologies," muttered Gunz inclining his head. "Please continue."

"On the surface it seems like King Alexander is running this demonic show," continued Chernobog, "but it's just an illusion. He's nothing but a dangerous and ruthless maniac—a puppet in someone's capable hands."

Chernobog got up and started pacing the room silently,

darkness following in his wake. Aidan threw a pointed stare at Gunz and shook his head no.

"Unfortunately, little pawns can get out of hand sometimes," continued Chernobog dryly. "He began to annoy me, and I started to believe that it was time to deal with him. I was just about to send Voron to summon you, Young Salamander, when I overheard the king's conversation with the Otherworld."

"My lord, if I may ask," peeped Peyton, raising her hand like a first grader during a lesson. Chernobog nodded, and she continued, "You're the god of Destruction—all powerful and dangerous. Why can't you just smite this evil king together with his demonic empire?"

Voron and Chernobog exchanged a quick look and burst out laughing. Even Aidan smirked, shaking his head slightly.

"She is so sweet when she is not deadly, is she not?" asked Chernobog, sobering up. "Knowing what you are, witch, I'll forgive your ignorance and try to explain why it is not an option."

"Yes, please... I would greatly appreciate it, my lord," exhaled Peyton, her eyes widened with fear.

"You see, I am a god and the Lord of the Dark Nav," started Chernobog as he halted next to the fireplace, leaning against the wall. "My power is here, in the Nav, but in the Yav, I have no authority and since King Alexander is alive and technically a human, there is nothing I can do to stop him.

"My twin brother, Belobog, who resides in his palace in Prav, has the power over the Yav, but him and I rarely see eye to eye... I am the darkness and he is the light. He is good and I am evil, blah-blah-blah. Our father never loved me as much as he loved him... But never mind that... The gods of Prav don't care that the human realm is deprived of magic and the nexus is—"

Chernobog rolled his eyes, waving his hand in a gesture that plainly expressed his true feeling toward his brother.

"Anyway, Mr. Burns, I believe it is in your best interest to listen to me carefully," he said, raking Gunz with his black eyes. "A little while ago, while you three"—he pointed at Gunz, Aidan and Yaroslav—"were fighting the dark soul of Rasputin, your good friend Master Mrak Delar failed his mission. He failed to bring to light Rasputin's true purpose and reveal the plans of the followers of Chaos. Now we all are suffering the consequences of his failure."

Gunz nodded and bowed his head, already realizing where all this was headed.

"So, since I can't do much myself and you're clearly showing your unwillingness to cooperate, I have only one option—I have to summon someone who is close to a god in his power to do my bidding," continued the god of Destruction, a cold smirk lingering on his face. "Mrak Delar perhaps? I think it's a good opportunity for him to redeem himself by completing the mission he failed before. I'm sure King Alexander will be only too happy to extend his hospitality to the Ancient Master as they were closely acquainted previously. Or should I say, Mrak's back was closely acquainted with the king's whip? What do you think, Mr. Burns?"

A pained, crooked smirk curved Gunz's lips before he could stop it. He looked from Aidan to Yaroslav and then his reproachful gaze stopped on Voron. For a moment an expression of sympathy crossed the old warrior's hardened face, but it disappeared quickly as Voron averted his eyes.

"Leave Mrak Delar out of all this. Please, my lord. I wasn't arguing with you. All I was asking for was a few days before I have to give myself up to King Alexander," said Gunz calmly. With a deep sigh he lowered down to his knee heavily and pulled his knife out of his pocket, turning it into a sword. He placed the tip of the blade on the floor, resting both his hands on the pommel and raised his eyes at Chernobog. "Your wish— my sword. I'll do as you command, my lord."

For a moment, Chernobog stared down at Gunz, his face

cold and expressionless. Then he approached him and tapped on his shoulder. "Much better, Young Salamander," he said evenly, underlying tones of superiority and sarcasm in his every word. "At least Kal managed to instill some manners in you... When you get to the City of Gold, here is what I need you to do..."

Chernobog quickly outlined his plan without going deeper into details. His explanation was presented in a form of a strict order that must be taken probatum and once he was done, he snapped his fingers and vanished before any of them could ask any questions. Voron remained in the room as he was the one who was supposed to escort them out of the Dark Nav.

"I hate dealing with gods. Sneaky, slippery bastards. You can't trust them," muttered Gunz, but then threw a quick glance at Aidan and added, "No offense, Aidan." He leaned heavily on his sword as he got up to his feet. All through the short conversation, or rather monologue, Chernobog had kept him on his knees.

"None taken," replied Aidan, waving his hand dismissively.

"Gods can't deal like normal people, can they?" asked Gunz, falling back on the sofa. "It's their way or the highway. What he forces me to do is reckless and stupid!" He rubbed his face tiredly as irritation spiraled through him.

"Of course, you can't trust them! This is why they are gods, Young Salamander. They know things we do not, and their ways are not always obvious to us," huffed Voron with a shrug. "You already angered him, so if you don't want to visit Chernobog's dungeons again, I suggest, you stop talking and get moving."

Giant black wings opened up behind Voron's back as he started to chant, and a large black portal opened up in front of him.

"After you," he said, gesturing at the rotating darkness, and smiled.

CHAPTER 16

~ ZANE BURNS, A.K.A. GUNZ ~

Gunz walked out of the portal and took a deep breath. Even though on the surface, the flow of magical energy and elemental powers was diminished by the demonic pollution, it was still better than down below. He remembered the initial effect of the polluted nexus on his senses and smirked. After spending an hour in the Dark Nav, it no longer felt as depowering and overwhelming.

"Doesn't feel as bad, does it?" asked Voron, echoing his thoughts and tapped Gunz on his shoulder.

"No, it doesn't," replied Gunz. He glanced at Peyton and Aidan, noticing that they didn't look as sick as before either, even though Peyton was shivering violently, her arms wrapped around herself.

"A little gift Chernobog bestowed upon you before you managed to piss him off. He couldn't completely eliminate the influence of dark magic on you, but he managed to give you at least some immunity," explained Voron, fully serious. "It took him a few hours."

"A few hours?" repeated Aidan, pulling Peyton closer as he

wrapped his arm around her shoulders to warm her up. "I thought we spent no more than an hour in the Nav."

Voron smirked, pointing at the fading sun, slowly inclining toward the horizon. "Time moves differently in absolute darkness."

"I'm just curious," said Gunz, narrowing his eyes at Voron, "how did you open a portal out of the Dark Nav? I thought only Chernobog could do it."

"Things have changed since the fight for Mount Karasova," replied the old warrior, staring into the white nothingness over Gunz's head. "My lord Chernobog had to endow me with some extra powers. Now I can do it too. Anyway, look around, Zane. Here is a parting gift from me." He waved his hand.

They were no longer on the Isle Buyan, standing in the middle of a winter wonderland. An endless field, covered in a deep layer of snow, was sparkling with the reflected colors of the setting sun. Far on the horizon, an uneven shape of a forest rose like a dark sinister wall.

The air was crisp, the way it could be only in the winter frost, and even though the slight odor of demonic essence was still present, it wasn't as jarring as it was before. Gunz exhaled, watching the small white cloud of his breath lingering in the air. He could feel the cold, but it didn't bother him. However, the snow around him was quickly melting, threatening to soak his clothes with icy water and that was a problem.

Aidan wasn't enjoying the weather either, his stiff shoulders and pale lips betraying the fact that the god of the Otherworld wasn't entirely immune to cold either. But Peyton was the one who truly suffered the freezing weather, clutching to Aidan for dear life, and even though he pulled her closer to share his body heat, she still looked like a human-sized icicle. The only person who remained completely unaffected by both cold and demonic energy was Yaroslav.

Gunz stepped out of a small frosty puddle before the water got through his combat boots and glared at Voron.

"What exactly was your gift?" he muttered grumpily. "You threw us literally in the middle of a frozen wasteland and you call it a gift?"

Voron gazed heavenward and sighed.

"Salamanders—like father like son—always hot under the collar. Let me explain," he said patiently as if he were talking to a schoolboy, but his eyes darkened and Gunz could see that this fake calmness wasn't coming easy to the old warrior. "Chernobog is the god of the Dark Nav. He is not famous for his kindness and patience. Don't you get it? You cannot argue with him!

"Yes, you were right! Yes, you should investigate the situation in the nexus. And no, you shouldn't give yourself up to the enemy! I agree with you! But who cares? Who wants to be right and dead, Zane?"

Voron stopped talking for a moment, breathing hard. He looked up at the gray sky, veiled by the heavy white feathers of falling snowflakes, and groaned, shaking his head.

"You infuriated the god of friggin' Destruction, Zane, and you can't do it without suffering the consequences," continued Voron. "As much as Chernobog wanted you in the City of Gold at once, now he wants to punish you even more. And he got me to do it. To punish you, he ordered me to open the portal next to the City of Silver. If I did that, it would place you at least seven days of a walk away from the City of Gold. Walking in these weather conditions would be a torture to you, Zane, and I couldn't do it to you. It's enough that you'll have to submit to King Alexander..."

His voice faded into the emptiness, and two deep vertical lines between his eyebrows got deeper. He cleared his throat before continuing as if every word he had to say was hurting him.

"You have three days. That's how long it takes to walk from here to the city walls." He waved his arm toward the forest. "Travel north and in a few hours, you should reach a small village. Talk to people there, see what you can find out. I pray to all the gods you learn something useful to help you cleanse the Land of Dreams of this pestilence."

"Thanks," muttered Gunz, shaking his head. The prospect of giving himself up to the evil king was making his blood run cold.

"Voron, why is it so cold?" Peyton managed to say through her chattering teeth. "I thought the nexus was supposed to be an everlasting summer."

"It used to be, my lady," Voron said as he took his fur-adorned cloak off and wrapped Peyton into it. "In case you don't know, the nexus is a living, breathing magical entity, and this is the way it reacts to the demonic invasion. And the closer you're going to get to the epicenter of it, the colder it'll become. I expect the City of Gold to be the City of Ice by now. Something like this happened a few years ago and I must tell you, it wasn't pretty."

For a moment, he fell silent, his eyes fogged by the memories of those days. Then he turned to Aidan. "My lord, it's time for me to go. Take care of our fiery friend… if you can," he said with a light bow.

"I don't think it's possible," said Aidan chuckling and hopped aside belatedly as a large snowball propelled by Gunz's hand hit him square in his chest, sending sparkling snow dust in the air.

Voron just rolled his eyes and approached Yaroslav. "Yaroslav, be careful," he said so softly that Gunz, who stood just a step away, could barely hear him. "Demons are the danger you know. Beware of the danger you don't know, Prince." He threw a glance at Gunz. "The Young Salamander gave up a lot to keep you alive. Don't disappoint him."

Gunz seized Voron's elbow, squeezing it hard. "What are you talking about, Voron? Speak plainly."

Voron's eyes moved down, halting on Gunz's hand.

"I told you as much as I could without getting myself flogged and thrown into the dungeons," he said firmly, his jaw set. "I wish I could drop you off a little closer to the village, so you wouldn't have to struggle through the snow-covered land, but unfortunately, there are only a few places in the entire nexus where Chernobog wouldn't spot me opening the portal. This field is one of them. By opening the portal here instead of the City of Silver, I disobeyed the direct order of my master and I don't expect him to reward me for doing that."

Gunz dropped his hand and bit his lip, rubbing his forehead with his fingers. "I'm sorry, Voron, that was uncalled for. You're right, I'm a little hot under the collar. Your master blackmailed me into submission, holding my friend's life over my head, and on top of that he decided to punish me. But nothing of this is your fault. Thank you for everything you've done for us today."

"Take care of yourself and your friends, Salamander," said Voron with a sad smile on his weather-beaten face. "I'm sure the demons already know that you are inside the nexus and that despite their order, you are not alone. Godspeed."

He chanted softly to open the portal and then walked through it, disappearing on the other side.

* * *

BY THE TIME THEY REACHED THE BORDER WITH THE FOREST, THE sun was gone, and the chilling eyes of darkness stared at them from every corner, hiding behind the thick trunks of leafless trees. Aidan muttered a spell, conjuring the light orbs, and sent them up. The shimmering blue light reflected from the deadly white layer of snow, making it sparkle like tiny diamonds under their feet.

Even if there was a path through the woods, it wasn't visible, and the sky, veiled by thick dark clouds, had no stars to show them the direction. Luckily, Yaroslav with his heightened vampiric senses intuitively knew where North was and they kept following him, sinking knee-deep into the snow.

With the shortage of magical energy, even insignificant spells were coming with an effort and Gunz didn't expect Aidan to keep the light orbs active for much longer. God or not, Aidan still needed magical energy and even with Chernobog's help, he was getting more and more tired with every moment he had to keep up his spell. Using the other sight too often was draining them just as much as casting spells or channeling elemental energy.

Gunz wasn't sure how long they had been walking. Voron was right when he said that in the darkness time flowed differently. They moved slowly, silently following Yaroslav, and the squeaking of the snow under their feet was the loudest sound in the frozen forest.

Despite the low temperature, the snow was wet and sticky, which made their journey so much harder and more exhausting, and every next step came with more effort than the previous. Gunz stared at Yaroslav's and Aidan's backs, noticing that Aidan also started to slow down his pace, and only Yaroslav stayed as light on his feet as he was a few hours ago.

I wonder how Peyton is managing to keep up. She's just a witch, more human than any of us, wondered Gunz. All through their journey, she remained silent, stoically fighting through the frozen thickets. He glanced back just in time to see Peyton falling with a loud yelp.

"Peyton!" he yelled, closing the distance between them as quick as he could. He pushed his arm under her shoulders and tried to get her up to her feet, but she groaned and dropped back into the snow.

"Zane, my leg... I caught something under the snow... it

really hurts," she moaned, breathing hard, and lowered her eyes, staring away from him. "I'm sorry. I know you didn't want me with you, and you were right. I am holding you back."

Gunz looked at her, feeling a little ping of guilt for the way he treated her earlier. "Let's see if Yaroslav can tell us where we are," he suggested. "Let's find out how far away we are from leaving this godforsaken place. I don't particularly want to stop for the night in the middle of the forest with no fire."

"A Fire Salamander without fire." Peyton giggled and Gunz couldn't help but smile back at her.

He bent down and lifted her with a strained grunt, holding her close to his chest. She gasped but didn't object, wrapping her arms around his neck.

"I'm sorry," she whispered into his ear.

"Hey, Slavik," he called using their psychic connection, *"how much longer do we need to walk before we're out of the forest? We need to stop. Peyton hurt her leg, and to be honest, I am dead on my feet."*

"Give me a moment," replied Yaroslav and disappeared into the darkness.

He came back a minute later with Aidan in tow. "It's still a long way to go until we reach the edge of the forest," he said, "but about a mile ahead, there is an opening where we could camp out and take a break."

"Another mile?" asked Peyton her voice barely above whisper. "I'll try..." She trailed off and squirmed uncomfortably in Gunz's arms.

Yaroslav exchanged a quick look with Aidan and Gunz and then turned to Peyton. "My lady," he started softly, and Peyton raised her head, a mix of emotions reflected on her weary face. "I would like to offer my help. Please allow me to carry you until we reach the clearing. I wouldn't dare to offer something like this to you, but both Zane and Aidan are too tired, so I'm the only one who can."

"You would do it... for me?" she asked after a moment,

staring down at her hands, her fingers fumbling with her ring.

"Yes, my lady, of course," replied Yaroslav softly. "If my touch doesn't offend you, that is."

She looked up at the vampire and bit her lip, bitter tears gathering in her eyes. "Thank you," she mumbled.

Yaroslav approached Gunz and took Peyton from his arms. She moved his long hair back and settled in his arms, placing her head on his shoulder.

"You are colder than snow," she murmured into his neck.

Yaroslav's lips stretched into a wide grin. "I'm a cold-blooded, bloodsucking leech," he purred, not without a fair load of sarcasm in his voice, "what did you expect?"

Peyton didn't say anything, but her cheeks flashed hot red and she hid her face into Yaroslav's shoulder.

Even though Yaroslav had to carry the extra weight, it didn't slow him down, but both Aidan and Gunz were getting too worn out, and it took them almost an hour to reach the small clearing Yaroslav was talking about. The vampire lowered Peyton down, helping her rest her back against a tree and wrapped Voron's cloak tightly around her. Without saying anything he disappeared into the woods. He came back a few minutes later, carrying a few branches and unloaded them on the snow.

"I'm not sure building a fire is a good idea," pointed out Aidan, staring at the branches with doubt. "A beacon for demons to find us."

"There are wild animals here," said Gunz, waving his hand at the dark forest.

"Not here. There were a few wolves following us earlier, but now they're gone," replied Yaroslav with a shrug as he pulled out his katana. "One of us has to be up while you're sleeping anyway, Zane. So, I'll stay with you and keep an eye on wild beast, demons, or anything else that dares come this way. You, Aidan and Peyton can get some rest."

The vampire took his leather coat off and placed it on the ground, motioning Gunz to lie down. Gunz looked at the coat and cringed inwardly, shame coiling within him. He hated with a passion the fact that his friends had to babysit him while he was sleeping, feeling like a burden.

"If you lie down on the snow, you'll get soaked with icy water and I don't think you'll enjoy the experience," said Aidan dryly, interrupting his thoughts. "So, put your ring on and lie down on Yaroslav's coat. Not necessarily in that order."

Gunz sat down on the coat and reached into his pocket. He brought the box with the ring out and opened it, shuddering inside. Staring at the piece of jewelry, he silently cursed himself, Skiper-Zmey and everything that brought him to this moment in his life. Then he clenched his jaws so hard, his teeth squeaked, and put the ring on.

Everything happened exactly as he expected. His muscles contracted, twisting his body into a giant ball of pain. He grunted, his teeth clenched, and fell on his side. His stomach heaved and his eyes watered, making the forest around him shaky and blurry. He felt Yaroslav's hands on his shoulders, holding him down just the way Mrak Delar had done when he tried the ring on the first time.

A few minutes later, it was over, and Gunz turned to his back, staring into the dark sky absently. He folded his arms over his stomach, feeling fatigued and vulnerable. Guilt and shame surged through him with new strength as he met Yaroslav's and Aidan's concerned gazes, and he closed his eyes.

"We know how you feel." He heard Aidan's voice in his head. *"You have nothing to be ashamed of. That's what friends are for. We take care of each other."*

Gunz nodded, still unable to face them. A moment later, the snow squeaked under the weight of Aidan's body as he lay down next to him. Gradually, exhaustion took over, and he didn't notice when he fell asleep.

CHAPTER 17

~ YAROSLAV ~

For a while, Yaroslav slowly paced around the perimeter of the clearing, making sure that no one—demons or wild animals—could come anywhere near them unnoticed. With his heightened senses, he could detect anyone approaching their makeshift camp before they could do any damage, but it was the unnatural thick silence of the forest that made him restless, pressing on his nerves.

Being nervous wasn't a natural state of mind for him. As a vampire backed with many years, he had learned to deal with things as they came, and not to worry about stuff he couldn't control. Nevertheless, since Voron had escorted them out of the Dark Nav, a nagging sensation of upcoming trouble had not left him for a single moment. And right now, in the silence of this winter forest, it increased tenfold.

He stopped pacing and his eyes settled on Peyton. He sighed, rubbing his arms as if suddenly he could feel the cold. The young woman hated him with a passion even though she'd never exchanged a word with him before. He couldn't blame her. He was old enough to have witnessed countless massacres where vampires destroyed entire villages in a matter of a few hours without much care whom they killed or how old their victims were. Pregnant women, children, elderly—for vampires all that made no difference. The only thing they saw was blood. The only thing they cared about was the all-consuming thirst.

For all he knew, someone in Peyton's family had been killed by a vamp or an upir. He recalled the way her apartment looked —filled with anti-vampire artifacts and silver. She was a witch, touched by the World of Magic, so if she saw a vampire feeding on a human, she had no illusions—she understood exactly what was going on.

That would surely explain her fervent hatred of him. In her eyes he was nothing but a repulsive representative of his kind and if that was the case, there was no way around it. The only thing he hoped for was that her attitude toward him wouldn't jeopardize their mission.

Yaroslav kneeled next to Gunz, carefully probing his mind through their psychic link but didn't notice anything alarming and sat down on the snow next to him. Being so close to Gunz, he could hear the blood rushing through his veins and the even beat of his heart. The thirst spiked through him, and he felt his fangs starting to expand. He jumped to his feet, covering his mouth with his hand and staggered back, almost stepping on Peyton's outstretched legs.

"Hey!"

He heard Peyton's voice and spun around. She wasn't screaming, but to him her angry whisper sounded louder than a gunshot.

"I'm sorry," he mumbled, carefully stepping away from her. Just now he realized that she didn't call him a disgusting vamp and even though she didn't use his name either, it was definitely a step in the right direction.

Peyton bent her knees, pulling her legs to her chest, but immediately hissed in pain and leaned forward. Rubbing her leg below her knee gently, she cursed quietly under her breath.

"How bad is it?" asked Yaroslav. He didn't need to ask as he could detect the light scent of blood coming from her. He swallowed, suppressing the desire to sink his teeth into her neck and looked away so she wouldn't notice the hungry red glow.

For a moment her narrowed eyes lingered on him as if she were searching for some kind of clue, but then she shrugged and leaned back against the tree. "I don't know," she replied. "I didn't bother looking, but it hurts even when I don't move."

"Would you mind if I take a look, my lady?" he asked, hoping that he sounded friendly enough for her to trust him—if it was even possible. Due to the weather conditions, they were moving slower than they planned, and Peyton's injury could slow them down even further.

"Knock yourself out," she muttered indifferently with a small shrug. "You're not going to make it worse than it already is."

Yaroslav lowered down to his knees next to her and gently pulled her pants up to her knee. A couple of inches above her ankle, he saw a large swelling with a jagged welt cutting across it. It wasn't deep, but it was still bleeding. He swallowed hard at the sight and smell of her blood and turned away for a moment.

"Thirsty?" she asked snidely.

A painful sting twisted his insides, but he didn't reply and just lowered his head allowing his long hair to fall over his face so she couldn't see how deeply her words affected him. Yaroslav brought his arm to his lips and bit into his own wrist. Dark streams of blood spilled from under his fangs, permeating the air with its metallic scent.

"Whoa… hold it right there, cowboy," hissed Peyton, pushing his hand away. "I will not touch this stuff, you disg—" She cut herself off, staring furiously at him.

"Disgusting vamp?" offered Yaroslav. "I know, you don't have to remind me."

Completely ignoring her, he seized her injured leg to stop her from moving and positioned his bleeding wrist over her wound.

He let a few drops of his blood fall into the welt, ignoring her desperate attempts to push him away. Gently running his fingers over her skin, he made sure his blood coated the entire affected area and sat back on his heels. A few seconds later, the edges of the welt started to close up, and the swelling subsided.

Peyton took a deep breath as she watched the healing process with widened eyes. Yaroslav got up and bowed lightly before returning to the center of the clearing where Gunz and Aidan were sleeping.

"Hey—um—Yaroslav…"

Yaroslav turned around, his eyebrows climbing up. "Yes, my lady?" he asked with a light bow.

"I wanted…" She cleared her throat and looked to the side, her fingers playing with a small twig uncomfortably. "I wanted to say—you know—thank you. For your help that is."

"No gratitude required, my lady," replied Yaroslav, sounding a touch colder than he intended. "I'm sure those words don't come easy for you."

He turned away and headed toward Gunz. Holding his hand over his chest, Yaroslav quickly scanned his mind through their connection and once sure that his friend's sleep was undisturbed, he sat down next to him, bending his knees, and stared into the darkness without blinking.

EVEN SUNRISE IN THE DEMON-POSSESSED LAND OF DREAMS wasn't normal. The darkness gradually got replaced by a dim gray light as the sun slowly creeped up over the horizon, its rays still concealed by the thick dirty layer of fog. The air remained as frosty as it was before and all together there wasn't much difference between day and night.

Yaroslav shook Aidan awake and then turned to Gunz. As

soon as his hand came in contact with Gunz's shoulder, Gunz opened his eyes but didn't move, his jaw set.

"It's okay, Gunz," said Yaroslav quietly as he got up and offered his hand to his friend, feeling the hot touch of the Fire Salamander's fingers on his skin as he took it. "Time to go. Take your ring off."

Gunz sat up heavily, rubbing his face with his hands and then carefully took the ring off his finger. A shudder ran through his body and he grunted, squeezing the piece of jewelry in his fist.

"I hate it," he muttered, placing the ring into the box, and shoved the box into the pocket of his cargo pants.

He got up and grabbed the leather coat, giving it back to Yaroslav. The coat was wet as the snow had melted under the Salamander's hot body, and Yaroslav shook it a few times to get rid of the water before putting it on. A large puddle remained in place where Gunz had lain just a moment ago, and now the water slowly started to freeze, a thin layer of ice spreading over it.

"We should get going," said Aidan, shaking the snow off his pants and jacket. "I don't know about Peyton and Gunz, but I'm starving, and I don't think there is any game in this frozen wasteland. Let's find that village Voron told us about."

Yaroslav cringed inwardly, thinking that getting food for his companions would be a lot easier than finding the nourishment he needed. While the thirst was bothering him already, so far he could keep it under control. Aidan was right though—he needed to get something to satisfy his need for blood. Unfortunately, he couldn't sense any animals in this godforsaken forest, and he knew that sooner or later, his thirst would become a serious issue.

"I can scout ahead," suggested Yaroslav, running his fingers over the grip of his katana to make sure it was sheathed securely under his coat. He turned around, ready to take off, but Gunz grabbed his elbow stopping him.

"How about Peyton?" he asked, a guilty lopsided smile on his face. "It's easier for you to carry her than for Aidan or me. Do you mind?"

"She can walk on her own," replied Yaroslav. "I healed her while you were sleeping."

Aidan and Gunz exchanged a bewildered look and stared at Peyton with shock and a touch of mockery. She blushed furiously and turned away from them.

"Yaroslav, is north this way?" she asked, waving her hand ahead, her voice a little hoarse.

"Yaroslav? Hey, man, she called you by your name," whispered Gunz, his gray eyes sparkling with suppressed laughter. "You moved a level up from disgusting vamp."

Yaroslav sent a heavy look his way, slightly shaking his head and replied to Peyton, "Yes, my lady, you're walking in the right direction."

* * *

ONCE YAROSLAV SAW HIS FRIENDS HEADING NORTH, HE TOOK OFF at full speed. He wasn't worried about them getting lost in the dark forest. With his velocity, he could cover quite a few miles before they would walk a few yards—and that with the deep snow slowing him down.

He found the village in no time. Just like Voron had said, it was located a few miles away from the edge of the forest. Moving fast and soundless, he surveyed every street—luckily there weren't many of them. It was still early, and the village stood dark, empty and motionless. Everything around—the fences, the houses and the land—was covered by a thick icy blanket. The snow looked white and untouched, and it seemed like the villagers had never left their houses since the winter started.

Just like everywhere in the nexus, Yaroslav detected the presence of dark magical energy and demonic essence, but it wasn't heavier than usual, and it was safe to assume that in this village, they would be as safe as anywhere else. His thoughts traveled back to the frozen forest where he had left his friends and worry slithered through him. This weather wasn't kind to the Fire Salamander, and Gunz was having a hard time. He was sure his friend was in a lot of pain, but as usual, he refused to show it or ask for help.

Somewhere on the opposite side of the village, a dog howled, probably sensing his presence, and immediately a cacophony of howls rose in the air. Snow squeaked as a door opened with a loud bang somewhere to his left, and a low male voice shouted at a dog, cursing the noisy animals, merciless weather, and his wasted life.

Time to leave, thought Yaroslav, heading back toward the forest to find his friends.

He noticed Gunz, Aidan and Peyton from far away. They were just nearing the border with the field lying between the woods and the village. Aidan was walking first, using some of his magic to clear the path ahead, and knowing that any use of magical energy came at a price, Yaroslav had to wonder why the god of the Otherworld was exhausting himself. Peyton was following Aidan and Gunz concluded the procession, which was probably a good idea since the snow was melting beneath his feet, creating frosty puddles.

A few seconds later, Yaroslav reached Aidan, showering him with a fountain of snow as he came to a sharp halt. Aidan cursed, shaking the snow off his hair and jacket irritably.

"You're flying fine, Slavik." He chuckled. "It's your landing that needs some work."

"Did you find the village?" asked Gunz, catching up with

them. His face looked tense, more tense than usual, and he was fidgeting with his pants, soaked with water.

Yaroslav took in his friend's appearance, and he no longer wondered why Aidan was using his magic to clear their path.

"About ten miles north," replied Yaroslav, gesturing toward the village.

"Ten miles?" Gunz threw a desperate glance at Aidan.

"I can do it," replied the god of the Otherworld with a dismissive wave of his hand, but the strained expression on his face suggested otherwise.

Yaroslav fell in step with Aidan, moving silently by his side. There was nothing he could do to help either of his friends and for a while they walked in silence. The scenery remained deadly white and boring, and the ten miles seemed like a hundred.

The sun was in zenith, but it didn't mean it got any warmer. On the contrary, it felt colder than before as the wind picked up and it started snowing, adding to the overall misery. Aidan's face was paler than the snowstorm around them and his stiff shoulders showed just how hard it was for him to use his magic in these conditions. Gunz also began to slow down, his face contorted with pain. Peyton wrapped herself into Voron's cloak, only her eyes visible between the furs.

Yaroslav stopped, waiting for Gunz to catch up to him and then offered him his shoulder for support. To his shock, Gunz didn't object, leaning heavily on him and his silent compliance was scarier than his fury.

At this pace, we're not going to reach the village before sunset. If we reach it at all... Dammit, thought Yaroslav, wondering how long it would take for Gunz in his condition to kill him, if he attempted to carry him the rest of the way.

"Hey, Gunz," started Yaroslav from far away, "we're not even half-way through and it's already past noon."

Gunz glowered at him. "Don't you dare, Slavik. I'll survive."

"You're in pain."

"And?"

"You don't have to be."

"I said no," replied Gunz flatly.

"Aidan is getting drained."

"Slavik—," yelled Gunz, throwing his hands in the air and suddenly fell silent, staring around, an expression of concern changing his face. "Where is Peyton, Slavik? A second ago she was walking in front of us."

Yaroslav spun around but couldn't see the young witch anywhere. "Peyton!" he yelled, but there was no answer. The snow got heavier than before, and visibility was close to zero even with his sharp vision. He called Aidan, asking if he could see Peyton. A second later, the god of the Otherworld popped out of the white veil next to them and the troubled expression on his face answered Yaroslav's question.

"Dammit," muttered Gunz, and the fire energy spiked around him.

His body emitted a wave of heat and Yaroslav jumped aside, shying away from the elemental fire. A moment later Gunz swayed, almost falling into the frosty puddle he was standing in, but somehow managed to remain on his feet.

"She is right there," he said, breathing laboriously, and pointed to the left. "I can sense her magical signature. She's not alone, Slavik. Be careful."

"Who is she with?" asked Aidan, channeling more of his magic, and his eyes shone brighter. "I don't sense anyone."

"Anything," said Gunz quietly. "I don't know what it is. It's not a demon, and it's not a human either. I can't recognize the energy signature."

Yaroslav turned in the direction Gunz pointed, ready to go, but Aidan grabbed his coat, stopping him.

"We're going together, and you will slow down to my level," said Aidan. "Just in case."

As soon as they stepped off their path, the snowstorm intensified. The wind howled, mercilessly beating into their faces, and Yaroslav had to lean forward, fighting the pressure of the gale. There was no way to run. At this point, he was happy he could move at all. In a matter of a few seconds, his eyelashes and hair got covered in a sticky layer of snow. He glanced to the side, noticing Aidan battling the storm next to him.

The farther they walked, the heavier the storm became. Every step was taking a significant effort and Yaroslav wasn't sure they would ever find Peyton at all. *What if we don't find her in time?* He didn't even know who she was with. Voron said the cold weather was the reaction of the nexus to evil presence and judging by the quickly deteriorating conditions, whatever Peyton was with couldn't be good.

Yaroslav brought his hand up to protect his eyes and sharpened his vision, struggling to see through the milky-white curtain of swirling snowflakes. At first, he couldn't see anything, but a few minutes later he noticed a dark silhouette. He wasn't sure if it was Peyton, but the next gust of wind brought a familiar scent removing all doubts.

"I think I see her." He waved his hand to attract Aidan's attention, gesturing toward the general area where he noticed Peyton.

"I see nothing," replied Aidan. *"Who's she with?"*

"Can't see..."

Yaroslav took two more laborious steps forward and stilled as all of a sudden everything went quiet. It was as if he had crossed an invisible barrier into the eye of a storm. On his left and on his right, he saw a rotating wall of snow, but in front of him everything was clear and peaceful.

In the center of a small circular area isolated by the storm, he saw Peyton. She sat next to an old woman who was lying sprawled on a bed of snow. Her face was crossed by a web of deep wrinkles and one of her eyes was covered by a filthy patch. With her matted gray hair and disheveled clothes, she looked weak and frail, and while her appearance was that of a human, he could sense darkness in her the likes of which he had never sensed before.

Yaroslav stared at the crone, unable to take another step. The small hairs on the back of his neck rose and a chilling shiver ran down his body as he finally recognized who she was. Like in slow motion, he watched Peyton leaning forward to help the old woman to her feet. Something snapped inside him, ripping him out of a trance.

"Peyton! No!" he shouted, sprinting toward her.

CHAPTER 18

~ YAROSLAV ~

The world blurred around him as he took off at the highest speed he could muster. But as fast as he was, he was too late. With horror Yaroslav watched Peyton placing her hand on the old woman's shoulder. As soon as she touched her, time stopped—at least it stopped for him. He froze in midair, unable to move. All sounds disappeared and the constantly rotating wall of snow halted, large snowflakes lingering in the air.

He struggled to break the magic that held him imprisoned in a sort of time bubble, but he couldn't. By his side, he saw Aidan going through the same pointless battle. The woman got up, standing next to Peyton. She was skinny and tall—at least seven feet in height if not more. Her dark disheveled clothes wrapped around her bony body and as she spread her arms wide to yawn and stretch, she looked like a giant scarecrow.

Her skin resembled old parchment paper, crumpled many times over, its unhealthy yellowish color clashing with the whiteness of her surroundings. The greasy strands of her gray hair hung limply along her triangle skull-like face. The eyepatch was gone and Yaroslav saw one large eye, glowing with a sinister yellow light, in the center of the woman's forehead. As she wrapped her arms around Peyton, her lipless mouth stretched into a terrifying semblance of a smile, exposing her rotten, brown teeth.

"*Aidan! Do something!*" Yaroslav yelled, desperately pushing against the restraints of magic that held him in place.

"*Trying...*" Aidan growled, his face strained, a pulsing blue vein crossing his forehead.

The white aura of his magical energy lit up around him, and his eyes shone brighter, as the god of the Otherworld pushed through the time bubble. With a thunderous bang, the dark magic gave in and the time resumed its flow.

Too late…

The old woman's body shimmered, starting to lose its density, looking more like a ghost now. Her fading arms wrapped around Peyton tighter, and with horror, Yaroslav saw her climbing onto the young witch's shoulders. He made an attempt to grab her and pull her down, but his fingers slipped through the monster. With a loud cackle, the woman completely faded away.

Once she was gone, the storm resumed, but it lost its intensity and wasn't nearly as powerful as before. Yaroslav turned around and about a hundred yards away he saw Gunz. He was still where they left him, and Yaroslav wondered how much time had truly passed from the moment he ran after Peyton to the moment the monster faded away.

Gunz probably noticed him too because he waved his hand.

"*Slavik, what was it?*" asked the Fire Salamander, a deep worry in his voice carried through their psychic connection.

"*Trouble, Zane. Big trouble,*" replied Yaroslav, dropping his arms powerlessly. "*God save us all… I have no idea what to do to help her now.*"

"*Does this old hag have a name?*" asked Aidan, carefully approaching Peyton. His steps, slow and heavy, demonstrated just how much the use of his magic cost him.

"Likho Odnoglazoe," replied Yaroslav, stating the Russian name of the monster as he followed Aidan.

"One-eyed Likho! Fire Almighty!" yelled Gunz, throwing his arms in the air. "Bring Peyton here. I wonder if my purifying Fire can cleanse her off this vile creature."

"I doubt it," replied Yaroslav, shaking his head, "but it's worth trying."

He approached Peyton, halting next to Aidan. She stood in the same pose, staring into space.

"Peyton," called Aidan, tentatively touching her shoulder.

She raised her eyes at him, and a weak smile appeared on her face. "Aidan... I don't feel so good," she whispered weakly, reaching for his arm as she collapsed.

Aidan bent down and helped her sit up. Looking dazed and confused, she got up to her feet with Aidan's assistance and stood swaying. Then her foggy gaze fell on Yaroslav and she shrunk back, away from him, her eyes overflowing with fear.

"Vampire," she hissed, pointing at him with her trembling hand. "Disgusting, bloodthirsty vamp! Stay away from me!"

Peyton channeled her magic and snow flurries rose around her, lingering in the air. She held out her hand and a blob of dark energy materialized in her palm.

"Peyton," yelled Aidan, stepping between her and the vampire. "This is Yaroslav! Don't you recognize him?"

"Move away!" the witch yelled, pushing him to the side with unexpected strength.

Aidan, weakened by the use of magic, lost his balance and dropped to one knee. The dark swirling energy in Peyton's hand grew larger, and she brought her arm up, ready to send it flying.

"No, you don't," growled Yaroslav.

In one fluid motion, he closed the distance between them, squeezed Peyton's wrist with one hand and punched her in the face with the other—a short jab that seemed to be light to him, but in reality could knock a horse out. Peyton dropped into the snow, unconscious. Two dark bruises spread under her eyes and the bridge of her nose started to swell, dark blood streaming down her chin. He lifted her, placing her limp body over his shoulder, and offered his hand to Aidan, helping him up.

"That was one hell of a jab." Aidan smirked faintly, starting on his way back to where they left Gunz. "I think you broke her nose."

"I'll ask for forgiveness later. Let's see if Zane can cleanse her first," murmured Yaroslav, regret and shame rolling through him.

Now that the snowstorm had dwindled down, the walk back took just a few minutes. Yaroslav passed Peyton over to Gunz and took his leather coat off, placing it on the ground. Gunz lowered Peyton on top of it and channeled just a little of his elemental power.

"Fire Almighty," he mumbled as he scanned the witch with his other sight. "I've never seen anything like this." He gathered as much elemental energy as he could and weak flames sprung up to life in the depth of his eyes, coloring them red. "Aidan, can you protect Yaroslav?"

Aidan nodded and muttered a spell, wrapping a dense protective shield around Yaroslav. "Do it quick, Zane," he said, his voice shaking with strain. "I'm too exhausted to hold it too much longer."

Gunz spread his arms, unleashing his element. His energy rushed through Peyton unobstructed and if she was possessed by a common demon, it would have been gone. But unfortunately, it wasn't the case.

Even through Aidan's shield, Yaroslav felt the touch of the purifying Fire. He cried out, feeling like he was being burned from the inside. Aidan's hand grabbed his arm, jerking him closer and this tiny movement just added to his anguish, blurring his vision. The god of the Otherworld muttered another spell, wrapping an additional layer of protective magic around him. As the shield did its job, the pain subsided, and he could see clearly again.

A few seconds later, Gunz let go and dropped his arms, biting his lip. "Didn't work," he said quietly.

"I didn't think it would," said Yaroslav. "It's the One-eyed Likho we're dealing with. There are no known ways to get rid of it, as far as I remember." He stood for a moment, shuffling through his memory hoping to find any information that could help, but then shook his head and lifted Peyton again. "Let's get going. We should try to reach the village before sunset."

* * *

YAROSLAV COULDN'T SAY HOW LONG THEY HAD BEEN TRAVELING. Both Aidan and Gunz had drained themselves when they used their magic trying to fight the Likho. As slowly as they walked, it was visible that for Gunz every step came with considerable pain.

A few minutes after they started on their way, Peyton regained consciousness. This time she recognized Yaroslav but didn't attempt to kill him. However, her eyes widened with fear, and he felt her body stiffened in his arms. She didn't say anything, just quietly sobbed. Tears ran down her cheeks, freezing almost immediately.

Yaroslav shifted her position, moving her weight to his left arm, and wrapped Voron's cloak tighter around her. She didn't object, but her sobs became louder.

"Why is she so scared of you all of a sudden?" asked Aidan, falling into step with him. "She used to hate you, but she was never afraid of you or any vampire for that matter."

"It's not her. It's Likho talking," replied Yaroslav with a sigh. "Did you see that blob of dark energy she manifested earlier? That wasn't Peyton's magic. It was Likho's."

"What the hell is this Likho and how does it work?" asked Aidan, staring at Peyton with concern. "The purifying Fire works on anything that is not pure in nature. Why didn't it work this time?"

"Because Likho is not a demon or a vampire," chimed in Gunz. "It's—um—evil fate? A spirit of misfortune? I don't even know how to explain. She blocks all the good and happy memories a person has, allowing sorrow and fears to take over."

"Here is my main concern," continued Yaroslav. "Once Likho takes over someone, it doesn't stop until the person is dead. Most victims take their own life, and something tells me Peyton has the kind of past Likho loves to feed on. I'm afraid, in the conditions we're in and with an overabundance of dark energy around, Likho's magic will work on her extremely fast. If we don't figure out what to do quickly, Peyton has a few hours left at most. Let's get to the village and see if we can do something to help her."

At his words, Peyton's sobs turned into loud crying. She pushed against Yaroslav's chest, struggling to get away, but he squeezed her tighter and after a few seconds she gave in.

"Just kill me!" she wailed, staring at Aidan angrily. "Why are you torturing me by allowing this unholy beast to touch me?"

For the next few minutes, she cried without stop while cursing Yaroslav and calling him names that made both Gunz and Aidan blush. Yaroslav ignored her words, but her constant fighting and trashing started to slow him down. Finally, Aidan gave up, and as tired as he was, he took over. Once she settled in Aidan's arms, she stopped cursing, muttering something under her breath about her pointless, miserable existence.

The faded sun was slowly lowering down when the barely visible silhouette of the village materialized on the horizon. For some reason, at the sight of the village Peyton got more agitated. She cried, squeezing Aidan's neck with her arms, muttering something about the danger ahead, and when Aidan ignored her, she started fighting him.

"You can't force me! I'm not going there!" she wailed hysterically, aiming to strike Aidan in his face.

Aidan grunted, pressing her tighter to his chest. Something cracked and a yelp of pain escaped her lips, but it did the trick and she fell silent, angry tears streaming down her half-frozen face. Aidan released his hold just a little, allowing her to breathe. Even though he looked like he was at the end of his rope, Aidan kept walking, hardly moving his feet.

"Aidan, I think you had enough," said Yaroslav, "let me take her over."

Aidan shook his head no, frowning. "I don't think it's a good idea," he replied, his voice hoarse. "She's so terrified of you now, it may increase Likho's influence on her. We're almost there." He jerked his chin toward the village growing on the horizon. "I'll make it there... somehow."

Yaroslav didn't object, finding truth in Aidan's words, and just continued on his way in silence, a wave of unease spreading over him every time he laid his eyes on Peyton. He didn't know how he missed it—perhaps it was the unchanging, endless whiteness around them or the deafening silence that dampened his senses—but one second Aidan was walking next to him, and the next second, he was down on the ground with a dagger in his shoulder.

Yaroslav dropped to his knees next to Aidan, exploring his wound. Despite the extreme situation, his thirst intensified at the sight of blood, streaming from the wound on Aidan's shoulder. His fang expanded, and he turned away pressing his hand over his mouth.

"Slavik—Peyton!"

He heard Gunz's voice and looked back to see Peyton standing just a few feet away from them. Dirty swirls of dark magical energy encapsulated her as she wielded her magic tainted by that of Likho. She pointed down and struck the ground with a black lightning bolt.

A sickening crack split the silence and a large hole materialized in front of her, quickly filling up with water. Long fractures slithered away from it in all directions and with shock Yaroslav realized that all this time they had been traveling over a giant frozen lake. Peyton turned her back to the gaping hole in the ice and looked at him, a sinister smirk playing on her lips.

"I should be taking you with me, filthy vamp," she hissed, "but at this point I just want for all this to be over." Her eyes darted to Gunz and a cloud of sadness shadowed her features. "Tell Aidan, I'm sorry."

Before anyone could stop her, she spread her arms and fell backward, quickly sinking into the icy darkness.

Yaroslav threw one more glance at his friends, a sad smile touching his lips. He had to save Peyton—it wasn't a choice. She wouldn't be in this situation if she hadn't gotten involved to help him. And he was the only one who could do it... Aidan was wounded, and Zane had an extreme intolerance to water, especially cold water. It must be him.

"Save the nexus, Zane... Restore magic... I'll find you as soon as I can," he promised and dove headfirst into the dark water of the frozen lake.

CHAPTER 19

~ ZANE BURNS, A.K.A. GUNZ ~

The walk to the village seemed to be endless. Aidan's bleeding had stopped, but between the blood loss and magical exhaustion, he could hardly move. Gunz tried to give him as much support as he could, but he wasn't in much better shape. The snow kept melting around him, soaking his clothes all the way through with icy water, and the constant burning pain was driving him crazy.

When they finally approached the first house, the sun was gone and a cold wind was howling through the empty street, banging the open window shutters and gates. The entire village gave the vibe of a ghost town and Gunz thought he wouldn't be surprised if he saw a real ghost lurking in the shadows.

"Do you think there is anyone alive in this place?" Aidan stopped, his arm pressing heavily on Gunz's shoulders.

"There is only one way to find out," replied Gunz, pointing at the dark house nearest to them.

They walked through the open gate and quickly crossed the tiny yard. Gunz halted in front of the entrance and raised his hand, ready to knock. But before his knuckles touched the wood, the door cracked open and a middle-aged man stuck his head outside. He pushed Gunz aside and surveyed the street behind him warily. Then he seized Gunz's shoulder and silently ushered him and Aidan into his home.

Once everyone was inside, the man locked the door and turned around. His attentive gray eyes moved up and down as he checked Gunz and then darted to Aidan, lingering on him a few seconds too long. His forehead furrowed and his jaw tightened as his gaze halted upon the dark brown stain on Aidan's shirt.

"Help him sit down," he said, motioning at a large oak table.

Gunz pulled one of the heavy oak chairs out and carefully lowered Aidan onto the seat. The man walked out of the room and came back a few minutes later, sporting a bottle with clear liquid inside, three goblets and a few clean rags. He tore the rags into strips, creating makeshift bandages and placed them on the table. Once done, he opened the bottle and the harsh odor of alcohol wafted through the small semi-dark room. He poured some liquid into each glass, handing one goblet to Gunz and one to Aidan.

"Drink," he said, his voice rasp as if he had a cold.

Gunz took the drink from the man's hands, held his breath and downed its contents in one gulp. Lowering the mug down, he exhaled and closed his eyes as the burning liquid rushed down his throat, warming him from the inside. The man nodded at him approvingly, a light smirk touching the corners of his mouth. Then he got up and left again. He came back a moment later with a linen shirt and pants hanging over his arm. He threw the clothes into Gunz's hands and jerked his thumb at the door on his left.

"You are a Child of Fire," he said, and it wasn't a question. He simply stated the fact. "With these wet clothes on, you are probably in pain. Go change while I take care of your friend, who is, if I'm not mistaken"—he squinted his eyes, staring at Aidan—"a deity of some type, but not a Slavic one. And don't look at me so shocked. Both of you are too tired to conceal your energy signatures and I can read them loud and clear, even without my magic."

Gunz exchanged a quick look with Aidan and went into the room to change. The bedroom was a tiny windowless box with one narrow bed taking up most of the space. With a sigh of relief, he shed the wet clothes and quickly got dressed. While he was hanging all his wet stuff on the footboard of the bed to dry, he glanced at this heavy combat boots. *No way they'll get dry by tomorrow,* he thought with a sigh. He looked at his bare feet and smirked—standing on the icy-cold floor wasn't pleasant, but at least he wasn't in pain.

When he came back into the living room, he found Aidan sitting in the same chair with his shirt off, his hand squeezing the edge of the table frantically as their host was cleaning the cut on his shoulder with alcohol.

"A flesh wound," the man muttered more to himself than to Aidan or Gunz as he continued his work. "The blade went through the trapezius muscle..." He glanced at his patient and smirked. "You're a god. You'll be back to normal by dawn."

He finished applying the dressing, fixing it over Aidan's shoulder and sat down, arching his brow at Gunz.

"So, how is it that the two of you ended up here and with your magic more or less intact?" he asked, folding his arms over his chest.

"What do you mean?" asked Gunz.

"Well, I used to be a wizard, until the nexus was taken over by the dark forces," the man replied with a shrug. "Now, I have no magic."

"But how—," Gunz started to ask, but the man sighed heavily, shaking his head.

"I'm not sure how," he responded, his fingers fumbling with the empty goblet. "It feels like the entire nexus is locked within a circle of God's snare. I'm sure this is not it—a God's snare of this size is impossible to conjure or maintain, but it sure feels like it. Besides, all things that go bump in the night are functioning just fine... And then there are the two of you, who somehow managed to retain some of your magic and power."

"Do you know anything about King Alexander?" asked Aidan, probing his wounded shoulder with his fingers gingerly.

The man stared at Aidan for a moment, his expression blank. "Please tell me you are not going to the City of Gold," he said. A dark shadow of fear crossed his features, but quickly disappeared, leaving his face calm and slightly sad.

"We are," replied Gunz, leaning back in his chair. "Is there anything you can tell us?"

The man chuckled humorlessly. "Yeah, there is only one thing I can tell you—if you value your life, stay away from King Alexander and his cursed city."

"So I've been told," Gunz mumbled as Mrak Delar's words flashed through his mind.

The man lowered his eyes, rubbing his knuckles with his thumb and it became so quiet in the room that Gunz could hear the wind whistling through the empty street outside the house.

"Are you saying every magical being inside the Land of Dreams lost their magic?" asked Aidan, breaking the prolonged pause.

"Pretty much," replied the man with a shrug. "The gods are locked in the Prav. Even Chernobog doesn't leave his hellhole. And did you see the World Tree? It's dying..." His voice, filled with sadness, trailed away and he lowered his eyes, staring at his hands absently. "Morena rules the nexus now. She turned it into her personal Kingdom of Ice and from what I see, she's here to stay."

"Morena? That's weird," Gunz said, exchanging a heavy look with Aidan.

The goddess of Winter and Death was supposed to be locked in Chernobog's dungeons. That had been the deal the god of

Destruction had made with Veles after the battle for Mount Karasova. The other thing that Gunz found strange was that both Voron and Chernobog retained their power and magic. Were they immune to whatever blocked the magic in the nexus?

"I thought the freezing weather was the nexus' reaction to the demonic pollution," said Aidan.

"Possibly it is. I can't be sure," the man agreed, "but everything that's going on here lately, sure looks like Morena's handiwork." He got up, grabbed the empty goblets from the table, and pointed to the door of the bedroom which Gunz used earlier to change. "Why don't you go and get some sleep. There is only one bed in that room, but that's all I can offer."

* * *

Gunz helped Aidan lie down, placing a couple of pillows under his shoulders, and then sat at the other end of the bed, stretching his legs. Some things their host said didn't sit well with him and his mind was racing a hundred miles per hour, trying to find an explanation that would make sense.

"Don't hurt yourself, Salamander," said Aidan, chuckling. "You are thinking so loud that I can hear your brain crackling."

"Do you trust Chernobog? Or Voron for that matter?" asked Gunz, finally voicing the question which troubled him the most.

"Chernobog?" Aidan shrugged and winced, pressing his hand to his shoulder. "You can't trust any gods. Especially the gods of the deathly realms."

"You're a god of the Otherworld," Gunz said, arching his brow at him. "Are you saying I shouldn't trust you either?"

"Ahh, come on, Zane," grumbled Aidan, looking heavenward, "you know what I mean. Gods are flaky and they always have some ulterior motives. You can never trust them a hundred percent. Having said that, I don't believe Chernobog is our enemy."

"You've heard what the man said—icy kingdom and all," said Gunz. "Morena should be locked up in Chernobog's dungeons, not creating her personal playgrounds. And how is it that Voron still has his magic while everyone else lost it?"

For a moment Aidan remained silent but then sighed and shook his head stubbornly. "I can never trust Chernobog, but Voron is not a god, and he is a warrior of the old code. I trust him. I'm sure there is a reasonable explanation to all that."

Gunz nodded as he lowered his feet on the cold floor and got up. He grabbed a skimpy-looking blanket and covered Aidan with it.

"Why don't you get some sleep," he said. "I'll be right outside your door."

"Wake me up in two-three hours," murmured Aidan, his eyes half-closed already. "You need to get some shuteye too, and I have to be awake for that."

Gunz nodded and walked out the door. For the first time since they arrived here, he had a moment to observe the house. The living room wasn't large, no more than ten feet by ten feet. A single window had neither curtains nor shutters and with frosty designs on the glass, it looked cold and empty. Out of furniture, there was only the heavy oak table with four chairs around it and a wooden coat rack next to the entrance.

At the other end of the room, he noticed a cold fireplace and headed toward it. Squatting in front of it, he gathered a little of his magical energy and whispered, *"Ignius."*

Even this tiny bit of magic came with an effort, but a few seconds later, a bright flame manifested on top of the firewood, dancing and crackling happily. Gunz smiled at it as if it were his best friend and sat down on the floor, pulling his knees to his chest. For a few minutes, he just stared at the cheerful flame, squinting his eyes at it like an oversized feline. A presence of his own element—even a tiny one—made him feel better, calming his ragged nerves.

"*Yaroslav...*" he called tentatively, searching for the connection with his friend. "*Slavik?*"

There was no answer. Either their psychic link was severed or... Gunz stopped himself from finishing this thought. He just couldn't allow himself to drown in sorrow, and the mere notion of losing his friend would do just that—plummet him into the endless vortex of pain and grief.

A light touch to his shoulder made him flinch and Gunz looked up to find their host standing next to him. The corners of the man's mouth lifted just a little and crow's feet bunched up around his gray eyes as he raked his hand through the thick mop of his salt-and-pepper hair.

"Do you mind if I join you?" he asked, pointing at the floor next to Gunz.

"On the floor?" asked Gunz and a lopsided grin split his face. "Please, be my guest. Oh, wait... It's the other way around—I am *your* guest."

The man sat down and for a few long minutes they sat in silence. Then he turned his head, staring at Gunz thoughtfully.

"What's your name, son?" he asked finally. "I never got a chance to get either of your names or introduce myself."

"Zane," replied Gunz, extending his hand to the man. "Zane Burns. And my friend's name is Aidan."

"Artem," the man introduced himself, returning the handshake. "Your hand is hot. I was right. You are a Child of Fire."

Gunz nodded but didn't reveal his true nature, and Artem didn't press the issue.

"What troubles you, Zane?" he asked instead.

Gunz raised his eyebrows, staring at Artem with surprise, but then leaned forward, placing his hand over the fire and closed his eyes. His fingers played with the fire mechanically, making a tiny flame run from his pinky to his thumb and back.

"Everything," he replied a moment later. "Everything I have

seen in the nexus on the way here... and everything you said earlier."

Artem nodded as if he was agreeing with him, but then shook his head no. "Yeah, I'm sure the situation in the Land of Dreams is enough to give a mighty headache to anyone." He smirked faintly. "But I daresay, this is not what truly troubles you, Zane."

Gunz glanced at him, nibbling on his lip. The man was more perceptive than he expected. He was never comfortable talking about his feelings and right now it wasn't something he needed.

"I'm just worried about my friend," he replied flatly after a short pause.

"Aidan is a god. He'll survive." Artem chuckled, giving him a quick tap on his back.

"Not Aidan. There were four of us when we crossed into the nexus." Gunz sighed, massaging his aching shoulder. After supporting Aidan's weight for a few hours while they made their way to the village, his muscles were sore and stiff, and for the first time in his life he wished he was a little taller.

Artem threw a quick glance at him but didn't say anything, and Gunz appreciated his silence more than he would any words of encouragement. There was nothing anyone could say that would make him feel better.

"It's my fault," he said quietly, a tightness in his chest making it hard to breathe. "All of it. I should have never allowed them to come with me."

"You seriously think you had a choice in that matter?"

Gunz ran his hand over the fire, placing the flame down on a piece of wood and exhaled slowly. Then he got up, fully intending to go back to check on Aidan, but the man seized his arm, stopping him.

"Hold on a second, young man," he said sternly, getting up to his feet, and waved at the table. "I think we should talk."

"Young man?" asked Gunz with a shrug, meeting Artem's

eyes. "I could be older than you, for all you know. Aidan is over two thousand years old, but he doesn't look a day over thirty."

Artem chuckled, scratching the back of his head. "You got me there."

He pulled the chair out and sat down, pointing at an empty one across from him. Gunz sighed but took a seat, folding his arms on top of the table.

"So, Zane, why do you think *everything* is your fault?" asked Artem, leaning back in his chair. Sparkles of sarcasm lit up in his eyes as he cocked his head, staring at Gunz.

"I don't want to talk about it," muttered Gunz dryly, making a move to leave, but Artem raised his hand, stopping him again.

"I'm sorry, Zane, you're right—it's none of my business," he said peacefully. "I'm just an old wizard who lost his magic. What do I know? But there is one thing I wanted to mention before you go to check on your friend. I don't know your purpose, but something tells me you didn't break into the magically sealed nexus for a midnight stroll over a frozen lake. Am I right?"

"Something like that," replied Gunz unwillingly.

"If you are here to get rid of this demonic scum and restore the flow of magical energy, then I can guarantee—you're going to fail," declared Artem, as calm as a summer morning.

"And why is that?" asked Gunz, his throat suddenly dry.

"Unfortunately, there isn't much I can tell you about the person who stands behind this demonic mess," continued Artem, "but one thing I know for sure—the king of the City of Gold is as evil as it gets and whoever he's working with is exceeding him in wickedness. If you don't believe me—take a walk around the nexus. See what happened to the City of Silver and the City of Copper and talk to those who are still within the walls of the fallen kingdoms. These people are ruthless and cold, and they will do anything to achieve their goals. They have no weaknesses, no remorse."

"Tell me something I don't know." Gunz smirked, hiding his

face in his hands, fatigue making his every move torturously slow.

"Zane, wake up," growled Artem, leaning forward. "Your debilitating guilt and self-flagellation are your greatest weaknesses, son! Have no doubt—King Alexander and his evil master will exploit every weakness you have. They will feed on your guilt and sorrow, and if you try to fight them, they will do anything it takes to kill you!"

"I'm a goddamn immortal Fire Salamander!" roared Gunz, slamming his hand on the table, anger spiking through him. "I can't die! Dammit! Sometimes I wish I could! That would make everything so much easier and people around me would stop getting hurt!"

"This is exactly what I'm talking about!" shouted Artem, rising. "This is the kind of mindset that will get you to fail your mission. You're here for a reason, so get your nerves under control and stop blaming yourself for things you have no control over. Remember, your mission is the only thing that matters!"

"You must stop blaming yourself. You have no choice, or you will become an easy prey to the first demon you meet in the nexus." Kal's parting words surfaced in Gunz's mind and he sat back powerlessly, his anger simmering down. He rested his forehead atop his folded arms and closed his eyes. He heard the sound of a chair being moved and then a soft touch to his shoulder, but he remained motionless, his limbs filled with lead.

"I'll be right back." Artem's voice came through muffled and distant.

A few seconds later, he heard the shuffling steps as the wizard returned to the room. With an effort, Gunz lifted his head and found Artem standing next to him with two goblets in his hands. He offered one of them to Gunz and lowered himself heavily onto a chair. Then he raised his goblet and downed its contents without saying a word.

Gunz followed suit and then placed the empty cup on the table. He rubbed his face tiredly, feeling slightly dizzy as the alcohol did its job, dampening down his turmoiled emotions. The dizziness was gone almost immediately, leaving his mind clear and alert.

"Thank you," he said hoarsely. "I needed it."

"What? A drink?" Artem chuckled, his gray eyes narrowed yet filled with humor.

"No. A wake up call."

CHAPTER 20

~ ZANE BURNS, A.K.A. GUNZ ~

Gunz sat on the floor with his back rested against the wall. Aidan was still asleep, and he didn't want to wake him up, letting his friend heal and restore at least some of his strength. In his head he kept going over the latest events, including his conversation with Artem. The same questions still bothered him as his exhausted mind was trying to process the information.

After a while, he caught himself on the verge of falling asleep and forced himself to get up. Sleeping without the ring on his finger wasn't an option. Using the ring without Aidan on guard wasn't an option either. He pressed his hands to his eyes and then massaged his temples with his fingers as he slowly exhaled.

Throwing one more glance at Aidan, he headed toward the door, careful not to produce any noise as he stepped on the squeaky wooden floor.

"Where do you think you are going, Fire Gecko?"

Aidan's voice made him stop in his tracks and turn around. The god of the Otherworld sat on the bed, gently removing the bandages off his shoulder. In the few hours that had passed, the laceration had healed and only a fresh pink scar remained on his skin as a reminder of what had happened at the frozen lake.

"How are you feeling?" asked Gunz, lowering himself down next to him. Just sitting on the bed made his body ache with weariness.

"Better than you, judging by the way you look." Aidan got up, gingerly flexed his shoulders and winced, rubbing the affected area. "Now, lie down and put your ring on. We're not going anywhere until you get at least a few hours' rest."

Too worn out to object, Gunz lay down on his side and reached for his pocket. He pulled the box with the ring out and cringed, cold sweat beading his forehead from the mere thought of putting it on.

"I'll try without it," he suggested tentatively, placing the box back into his pocket.

"Not a chance," objected Aidan taking a stand with his arms crossed over his chest.

Gunz sighed, realizing that his friend wasn't about to give in. He grabbed the ring out of the box and turned onto his back, taking a few deep breaths like before a dive. Slowly, he put it on his finger and as his entire existence collapsed into a twisting vortex of pain, he felt Aidan's hands on his shoulders, holding him down.

Once the last aftershocks were gone, Gunz entwined his fingers over his stomach and stilled, his chest rising and falling with ragged breaths. He was sore and weak before he put this torture device on. Now he was barely alive, not sure he could move a finger even if his life depended on it.

"Try to get some sleep, Zane," said Aidan, settling down on the floor by the wall. "I'm not going anywhere."

Gunz closed his eyes and everything around him disappeared.

* * *

THERE WAS NOTHING...

No dreams, no visions. Absolutely nothing. A thick darkness surrounded him. It was so dense, he could almost feel it touching his skin, caressing him like a passionate lover. And he wanted it. It was the restful oblivion he had desired for such a long time. Nothing was hurting physically. Nothing tormented his soul. No one was trying to kill him or his friends. He was at peace. He was happy... Even if all that was nothing but an illusion created by the magic of the ring, he didn't care.

Gunz didn't know how long it lasted, but suddenly, he caught a slight movement in his peripheral vision. In the absolute darkness, a tiny flare of light seemed foreign and unwanted. But it was so quick—almost undetectable—that he wasn't sure if he saw something or if it was just an illusion. He relaxed again, positive it was nothing, just to see the movement again.

I am sleeping... It's a dream... Wait... I can't have any dreams with the ring on...

The flickering light became more persistent, and now he could see that it wasn't just a light. It was a person, their entire body shining with a warm golden glow of a human soul. He got up and walked toward the light while clearly realizing that he was still asleep. Soon, he ran into an invisible barrier. The person stood on the other side of the barrier, banging frantically with both fists against it.

Gunz put his hands against the barrier and sharpened his senses. The sound of banging was coming through muffled, but besides that, he could also hear the person screaming something. Despite the situation, he didn't feel threatened. On the contrary, whoever this person was, they made him feel safe.

"*I can't hear...*" he mumbled. Then he punched the invisible wall with his fist. "*Goddamnit! I can't understand.*"

He leaned forward, resting his forehead against the barrier and pressed his hands to it. The person on the other side stopped banging and placed their hands against his.

"Zane..."

He heard the voice as light as a wisp of morning fog and everything inside him crashed.

"Angie..."

"Zane!"

She screamed his name over and over while he kept punching the barrier separating them until his knuckles started bleeding. He wasn't sure what changed, but now he could hear her better. Her voice was still muffled, but he could understand her every word.

"*My love, it's me,*" she pleaded with him. "*Take this barrier off. It's me, I swear. I have a few minutes and I want to spend them with you... please... Zane... wake up...*"

* * *

"Zane, wake up! Gunz! GUNZ!"

The sound of Aidan's voice—too loud for his overextended senses—ripped him out of the semiconscious state he was in. He jolted up, cold sweat running down his tense face, and grabbed Aidan's arms with his shaking, bleeding hands.

"Aidan, I need to take this ring off," he managed to say. His teeth were clenched and for some reason he couldn't unclench them. He felt like he was running a high fever, his thoughts in disarray, his body not responding to the commands of his frantic brain. "Aidan, Aidan... please... I must..."

He grabbed the ring, struggling to pull it off, but he couldn't. He had no strength even for such a minute task.

"Aidan, I'm begging you," he moaned, fighting the overpowering weakness. "Help..."

Aidan grunted, doubt written all over his tense face as his eyes fell on Gunz's bleeding knuckles. Nevertheless, he grabbed his hand and pulled the ring off. A short electric shock pierced Gunz's body, and he fell back, breathing laboriously.

"I'm with you," Aidan said firmly as he sat down on the edge of the bed, "do what you need to do."

"Thank you," murmured Gunz, slowly drifting to sleep.

* * *

THERE WAS NO DARKNESS. HE WAS BACK IN HIS HOUSE IN CORAL Springs, the bright morning sun beating through the open window. Gunz sat up and searched the room, but there was no one else here.

"*Angie?*" he called tentatively, his heart beating frantically in his chest.

He felt a soft touch to his shoulder but didn't move, afraid of what he could find there.

"*Zane...*"

Slowly he got up and turned around. Angelique was sitting on the bed, gazing up at him. There was so much love and longing in her absolutely normal human eyes that he had no doubt—it was her, his Angie, not Zmey pretending to be her. She extended her hand, reaching for his, and he took it, his fingers trembling under her touch.

"*Zane, my love... my beautiful strong boy,*" she whispered, tears shining in her eyes. "*We have just a few minutes before Zmey comes for me.*"

He sat down on the bed next to her and pulled her closer, encircling her shoulders with his arms. She cupped his face with her hands, gingerly forcing him down. He gave in and his lips touched hers for a brief moment before he pulled away. He had to see her, just to make sure it wasn't another illusion Zmey created to torture him.

"*I love you.*"

His voice sounded like a low growl, but he didn't care. He kissed her again, a deep scorching kiss, infused with all the passion, longing, and pain he had in him. For a moment time stopped for them, and there was nothing he wanted more than for the time to stay still forever.

When she finally pulled away, the absence of her lips on his felt jarring, painful, unwanted. He searched her face, trying to take in every detail so he could return to it later.

"But how?" he asked after a moment, taking her hands into his.

"Zmey can't break through into your mind anymore and he's seething with rage," she replied, lowering her eyes. "He wanted me to deliver you a message, so he gave me ten minutes with you on one condition—I'm not to talk to you about anything else."

"I see," he muttered. A tidal wave of pain enveloped him at her words, and he got up, stepping away from her involuntarily. "What is the message?"

"I hate to be his messenger and to deliver these words to you," she whispered, gazing up at him with remorse. "He said to tell you that you can keep playing your little games, but no matter what you do, you can't escape what's coming. Your position on the Board of Destiny was locked and your destiny was set in motion. He will see you perish in black flames, but before you die, you will witness the death of all those you hold dear. Starting with the Master of Power who created that ring."

For a moment he stared down at her, processing everything she just told him. A fear tightened his chest, but he made an effort to suppress it and laughed—a short, dry sound that he couldn't recognize as his own laughter.

"Screw him. I've heard all this before," he growled and leaned forward, pulling her back into his arms. He kissed her hard, feeling her lips parting obediently under his. With surprise he noticed that there wasn't a familiar wave of fire within him, and for a split-second, he wondered if it was because of the situation in the nexus or because it was a dream.

He let go of this thought immediately, because at the moment, it wasn't important. Nothing was. Nothing except her.

Except the sound of her heart beating in unison with his. Except the salty taste of her tears on his lips. Less than ten minutes—that was all he had.

He let go and watched her as she touched her slightly swollen lips with her fingers, swallowing the tears.

"Angie, what did you mean when you said a while ago that I made a terrible mistake?" he asked, his voice hoarse.

She shook her head and looked away. "We can't talk about that..."

"Then what can we talk about?" he asked, throwing his hands in the air.

"Nothing... don't talk at all... All I need is you by my side," she replied as she got hold of his hand, pulling him closer.

He sat down on the floor, placed his head on her lap, and wrapped his arms around her legs. There was so much he wanted to tell her, but he couldn't say anything. And not because of Zmey's orders, but because everything inside him was twisted in unbearable agony and he didn't want the scream of his tormented soul to break free to the surface.

Angie was right. They shouldn't be talking. He wasn't sure if Zmey could hear or even see them, so the less they said the better. He felt her fingers slowly threading through his hair, caressing the rough stubble on his unshaved cheek and closed his eyes, enjoying her touch.

"Zane, remember that one evening when you sang for me?" she asked all of a sudden.

The corners of his mouth quirked up a little, and he caught her hand, planting a soft kiss to her palm. "How can I forget that?" he replied with a sad chuckle. "Weren't you afraid that your neighbors would call 911 if I didn't stop?"

"Sing for me," she said, ignoring his question.

"What? Now?" Shocked by her request, he raised his head and stared at her for a brief moment.

"Now is all we have..."

He lowered his head back onto her lap and started singing. He didn't know why he picked this song—it just came to his mind and he went for it. No song could make his singing voice sound better, anyway.

As soon as the first words of the Queen song escaped his lips, he felt a few large cold drops falling on his cheek. Angie's hand moved down and halted on his shoulder, squeezing it. He continued singing without looking at her, afraid that if he caught sight of her face, her tears, he'd fall apart.

His voice broke, and he stopped singing. He moved into a kneeling position before her and pressed his hands to his burning eyes as flaming tears trickled down from under his fingers.

"I can't do it, Angie," he breathed out. There was nothing left in him—no anger, no will to fight. He felt as if he was suffocating, choking on his own anguish and despair. *"I can't live forever knowing—"*

She sighed and gently pushed his hands down, exposing his face. *"Yes, you can, and you will. For both of us,"* she replied. *"I love Queen's music, but you picked the wrong song, my love."*

As her voice trailed off, she leaned forward and kissed him, burying her fingers into his hair. He moaned, rising up on his knees to be closer to her, to prolong this moment, which could have been their last moment together.

Suddenly something had changed. Her kiss became harsh and demanding, and her hand pulled on his hair, yanking his head back. He let go and a heavy shudder rattled his body as he saw Angelique's eyes—yellow with dark-red vertical pupils.

"Zmey," he growled pushing her away, wiping his lips with the back of his hand. *"I got your message, now get the hell out of my head."*

Angelique's image began to change, morphing into a figure of a tall bald man. His lips stretched into a cold smile and the forked tongue of a serpent flickered in and out of his mouth.

Gunz jerked trying to get up, but his body didn't obey him, locked by Zmey's magic.

"Now, now, little Salamander," said Zmey, wagging his finger at him, "stay on your knees. Your position satisfies me. I'm here to offer you help, actually."

"Help?" Gunz laughed bitterly. "Sure, you can help me by finally dying and staying dead. Forever."

"Forever... how sweet," Zmey murmured, staring at him with mockery. "I thought I heard you sing to your little girlfriend that you didn't want to live forever. And may I say—your singing voice is more terrifying than your purifying Fire power? No wonder sweet Angie chose to stay with me."

"Screw you," Gunz growled, pushing against the restraints of Zmey's magic as a scorching blast of anger surged through him, "and thank you. Now I know how to get rid of you—all I have to do is sing."

Zmey barked laughing as if Gunz just told him the funniest joke he'd ever heard, but then cut his laughter off abruptly and folded his arms over his chest, staring down at him icily.

"Listen to me, boy, because I am not going to offer something like this again," he seethed. He leaned forward and seized his throat, forcing his chin up. "Your girlfriend is dead. Her spirit lives only in connection with mine. So, whether you live forever or you die, you can never be with her again."

With sudden clarity, Gunz realized that Zmey told him the truth. For a moment, the room spun around him and he felt like he was submerged under water, unable to breathe in. He grunted, suppressing the nausea, and raised his eyes, meeting Zmey's derisive stare.

"Wonderful, we're finally on the same page," Zmey jeered, letting go of his throat. He rubbed his hands together, delighted, and continued, "So, here is my offer, Salamander. I can give you what you want—an eternity with Angelique. I swear that if you do what I want, I will release her soul into any deathly realm of your choice. And after *that, I'll help you die and reunite with her behind the veil."* He stared down at Gunz, a crooked smirk distorting his lipless mouth. *"After all, no one wants to live forever, right?"*

Gunz nodded, dropping his head. *"What do you want me to do, Zmey?"* he asked, his jaw set, his voice no more than whisper.

"You'll find out very soon. Come to the City of Gold alone and be ready to follow every instruction of my loyal servant. You do your part and I'll do as I promised." Zmey cackled throwing his head back and vanished.

As soon as he was gone, Gunz fell flat on the floor, just now realizing that if it hadn't been for the restraints Zmey placed on him, he probably would have collapsed a long time ago. A terrible howl, filled with anguish and despair beyond anything a normal person could handle, escaped his lips as he slammed his fist into the floor.

CHAPTER 21

~ ZANE BURNS, A.K.A. GUNZ ~

"Zane, wake up!" He heard the voice in his mind, but he couldn't identify it. Someone was shaking him vigorously and a light slap across his face followed shortly after. He gasped and finally was able to crack his eyelids open.

Aidan...

The god of the Otherworld was standing over him, his eyes filled with concern, his fingers squeezing Gunz's shoulders. The fog in his mind slowly started to dissipate, leaving him with gut-wrenching memories and debilitating grief.

"Aidan, stop shaking me," he said, raising his hand. His lips moved forming words, but no sound came out from his dry throat.

"Dammit," muttered Aidan, letting him go. "I knew I shouldn't have let you take this ring off."

Gunz sat up, scratching his unshaved chin and sighed. "Aidan," he started to say, but cut himself off and cleared his throat before continuing. "Did you hear? I was trying to keep our connection open."

"Yes."

"Everything?"

Aidan nodded. "What are you going to do?"

Gunz got up and swayed on his feet as a wave of weakness overwhelmed him. He grabbed the headboard to steady himself and chuckled darkly.

"What do you think I am going to do?" he asked, cringing inwardly at how cold and emotionless he sounded. He ground his jaw and hissed through his gritted teeth, "I am going to kill them all, Aidan. They will die screaming. I swear on my goddamn power."

As he growled his last words, his eyes lit up with the red glow of his element.

"Zane—," Aidan began, but Gunz threw one scorching gaze at him and he fell silent.

Gunz took off the linen pants and shirt that Artem had given him yesterday, his every move sharp and jerky. Then he threw everything on the bed and grabbed his own clothes. The pants were still damp, but he ignored it and quickly got dressed. As the cold fabric of the shirt touched his skin, he grunted, rolling his shoulders uncomfortably. Then he sat down on the bed and pulled his boots on, his unbending fingers fumbling with the laces.

"Dammit!" he growled, dropping the laces and stared at his trembling hands with annoyance. He slapped his hand over his tattoo and snarled, "Mishka, I need you."

Mishka materialized in the room with a light pop. His glowing red eyes brushed over Aidan and halted on Gunz. He lowered down to his level, hovering in front of his face.

"Boss," he said in a high-pitched voice, "what happened to you? Seems like the Fire Salamander has left the building?"

Gunz stared at the wyvern, feeling empty inside. "Zmey drained me... I need fire," he said quietly. "A lot of it. As much as you can give me."

"What makes you think I have any?" yelped Mishka, his

golden wings flapping nervously. "Did you forget? We are inside the nexus two-point-o, demonic edition—elemental powers are not included with your subscription."

Gunz caught Aidan's laughing eyes and chuckled, his anger simmering down.

"Mishka, your eyes are glowing red and your wings are golden," he said, extending his arm for the wyvern to land on. "Besides, since you are not bitching up a storm, you have the fire. So, cut the crap and share."

Mishka huffed, expelling a small cloud of white smoke, but landed on his forearm. Gunz lifted the wyvern up, allowing him to move to his shoulder.

"Come on, Mishka, sharing is good," he purred to the wyvern, stroking his wings.

"I hate sharing," muttered Mishka, pouting like a little kindergarten girl.

"Sharing is caring," offered Aidan. He tried to suppress his laughter, but it came out in a loud snort which made it worse.

Mishka rolled his flaming eyes at him, muttering something under his breath that sounded awfully like "it's great to be a god".

"Fine," he said grouchy, waving his wing at the bed, "lie down. I'll share, but don't ask again. There isn't much elemental energy here and I need it for myself."

The small fire boost Mishka gave him was enough for Gunz to restore some of his strength and, most importantly, calm his nerves. Perhaps it wasn't only the energy boost, but Mishka's usual shenanigans—slightly naïve but always kindhearted—partially brought him back from a state of emotional turmoil.

Once Mishka camouflaged himself in his tattoo, Gunz laced his boots and walked out the door with Aidan following him. Artem was in the living room, sitting next to the table which was already served for breakfast. A light smell of hot herbal tea and fresh bread spread through the room, making the cold house feel warmer and homier. As soon as Gunz and Aidan appeared in the living room, he got up and waved at the table.

"Good morning. I hope you both are feeling a little better," he said, his eyes halting on Aidan's shoulder. "Sorry, but this is all I have to offer—tea, bread and goat cheese."

"Thank you," said Gunz as his stomach spasmed painfully. The last time he had anything to eat was when they were in the Otherworld.

They ate quickly and in silence. Once they were done, Artem leaned forward, his fingers playing with the empty cup nervously as a troubled expression clouded his face. Gunz glanced at Aidan and made a move to get up, but Artem straightened, raising his hand.

"Before you go, let me give you at least some directions," he said slowly, as if he was struggling to find the right words.

"Thank you," said Gunz, sitting back down. "We have very little information, so anything you can tell us will help."

Artem nodded and swallowed with effort. "Keep going north. There shouldn't be any villages or towns on your way," he started, looking somewhere over Gunz's shoulder. "Considering the weather conditions and assuming nothing or no one will slow you down, you should reach the City of Gold by tomorrow night. It's about one and a half days of walking."

Gunz nodded, staring at his skinned knuckles.

Nothing or no one? Zmey wants me in the City of Gold as soon as possible, but I'm not sure Aidan is welcome there, he thought biting his lip. He glanced at his friend and read the reflection of his thoughts in his eyes.

"The closer you will get to the City of Gold, the colder it will become," continued Artem, glancing out the partially frozen window where the dim morning light was reflected in the dead-white layer of snow. "And you Zane, as a Fire Salamander, are vulnerable to this weather, but there is nothing I can give you to protect you from the melting snow. Just be careful if you can… both of you…" His voice trailed away, and he shook his head.

Artem got up heavily and started clearing the table, but then dropped the empty plates back down with a loud clatter and stood motionless with his arms dangling powerlessly alongside his body. After a moment he raised his eyes and gestured toward the exit. He walked Gunz and Aidan to the door and halted. The somber expression on his face made him look like he aged at least twenty years overnight.

"Thank you, for everything you've done for us, Artem," said Gunz, offering his hand for a handshake. The wizard shook his and Aidan's hands and opened the door for them.

"Just one more thing before you go," he said. "The City of Copper and the City of Silver have fallen and have been taken over by demons a while ago. People of both kingdoms are suffering in slavery. I don't know if there is anything you can do for them… I can't believe I am saying this, but you two are the only hope the Land of Dreams have left. Since Lady Gatekeeper sealed the nexus, I had no idea that anyone could get here from the outside world. Besides, I don't think anyone else is brave enough to come here and try to do anything to stop this invasion."

"Or stupid enough," murmured Gunz mostly to himself, but Aidan heard him and poked him in the ribs.

Artem smirked, watching them and then pulled Gunz into a quick hug with a short tap on his back. "Stupid or brave or both… either way. Just remember what we talked about yesterday."

He nodded at them one more time and disappeared into the house.

CHAPTER 22

~ ZANE BURNS, A.K.A. GUNZ ~

The following few hours proved Artem was right. As they kept progressing north, the weather deteriorated rapidly, and every next step was taking more and more effort. While they were still moving along the deadly white desert that seemed to have no end, the wind started to pick up, driving the swarms of snow flurries into their faces.

A few times, they noticed dark forms of villages far on the horizon, but just like Artem had said, they were away from their path, so they kept walking forward. At first, Aidan tried to use his magic to shelter both of them from the heavy assault of winter, but soon Gunz had to stop him as even the light use of his magical energy was draining Aidan physically faster than he expected.

Gunz gritted his teeth, ignoring the constant pain, his mind focused on one thought only—where was the trap? After the conversation with Zmey, he had no doubt that what happened to Yaroslav and Peyton wasn't coincidental. It was a trap set with one purpose—to get rid of his friends and leave him alone by the time he needed to face the big-bad. After all, it had always been Zmey's goal, from the moment they were attacked back in his own world.

Now, every minute he was expecting the other shoe to drop, and he had no idea where it would drop and when. His eyes fell on Aidan's back and he swallowed hard, guilt rearing its ugly head again.

Aidan slowed down and fell in step with him. "Stop thinking out loud," he said, shielding his face with his arm. "Your thoughts are giving me a migraine."

"Don't tell me you disagree," muttered Gunz. He pulled the jacket collar up and wrapped it tighter around his face, but that didn't help. The snow was beating him in the face, melting at the touch with his hot skin, and icy rivulets ran down his face and neck, leaving his skin raw and blistered in their wake.

"I didn't say that. What do you think the City of Gold is? An oversized mouse trap for one little Fire Gecko," replied Aidan with a shrug. "It doesn't stop you from going there."

"Do I have a choice?" He wrapped his arms around his body, lowering his head, as the next gust of icy wind hit him. Then he sighed and added, "Someone has to, so why not me. It was either me or Kal and you didn't think I would send the old man in my stead, did you?"

"Old man, huh?" Aidan chuckled, but quickly sobered up. "Listen, there was one thing Zmey said to you that bothers me a lot more than the prospect of an upcoming trap."

"Oh, yeah?" Gunz gave him an arched stare. "Besides everything he said, which particular statement bothered you the most?"

"He said that your destiny was set in motion," replied Aidan, throwing a quick sideways glance at him. "You're young, Zane, and there is a lot you still don't know about the Board of Destiny and how it works."

Gunz stopped in his tracks, grabbing Aidan's arm. "I'm not

in the mood for a lecture about my age, Aidan, so cut your geriatric bullshit and tell me what that means."

Aidan glanced at him and resumed walking. "Keeping in mind freewill and all that, there are only two ways the destiny of a person can be set in motion," he explained. "It's either a celestial event or a decision of the Destiny Council."

What the hell? Gunz blinked at Aidan a few times, once again forgetting to block their connection.

"Exactly," Aidan replied to his thought. "I didn't expect you to know something like that. It takes years to understand all this high-level crap. Anyway, do you know of any celestial event associated with you?"

Gunz shrugged. "I don't think so."

"I didn't think so either, so all this reminds me unpleasantly of the time a few years ago, when the Destiny Council was compromised. You probably remember that too—Mrak Delar and your other friends from Kendral were involved."

"I remember, but didn't Gwyn do some spring cleaning there?" Gunz shivered, thinking of the Destiny Council and their shady ways.

"I wish I could talk to Gwyn," muttered Aidan. "Something is not right."

"You can't. Not from the Land of Dreams."

"I know. You asked me what troubles me and I explained," said Aidan, sounding slightly nervous and irritated. "There is nothing I can do about that until either the nexus is freed, or we return to the Otherworld."

Gunz was about to tell Aidan that he would rather see him going back to the Otherworld than fall into a trap like Yaroslav and Peyton had, when he noticed something on the horizon. He came to a sharp halt and grabbed Aidan's arm to stop him, pointing forward. In the last dim rays of the setting sun, he saw the dark outline of something that looked like a village or a town.

"A town?" Aidan's question confirmed his suspicions.

"I don't remember Artem mentioning any towns or villages on our way," Gunz said. As soon as the words escaped his mouth, his intuition started to raise red flags, waving them like a cheerleader with pompons during a football game. "Aidan, we should go around it."

"You think it is—"

"It's a trap for you," said Gunz, shivering, as if all of a sudden he could feel the freezing temperature.

Aidan frowned, wrapping his jacket tighter but nodded. They swung slightly to the left, heading northwest to go around the town, but the farther they walked, the closer the town seemed to be. By nightfall, they could clearly see the tall wall with heavy gates and no matter how far to the left they went, the gates always remained right in front of them.

"Something tells me, we won't be able to go around it," muttered Gunz.

His stomach knotted, and he stopped, taking in the grim view that unraveled in front of them. They stood no farther than a hundred yards away from a tall dark wall. It was so tall that it completely obscured the town behind it. Silent and sinister, it towered over them with malice. The wind intensified and the snow started to fall heavier—a sure sign of evil ahead.

He expanded his Salamander senses and his skin crawled. This entire area breathed with dark energy, which was demonic in nature yet seemed to be a lot darker than that of a regular demon, and while it felt vaguely familiar, he couldn't quite place it.

"Aidan," he called, his voice tense and hoarse.

"I know. It's hard to miss."

Gunz seized Aidan's arm, turning him so he could face him. "Aidan, you're not going inside this town," he said firmly. "We can't go around it and it's an obvious trap for you. I am going to open a portal back to the Otherworld for you and then I'll go into this town alone."

"Uh-huh," hummed Aidan, narrowing his eyes at Gunz. "Not a chance."

"Aidan, please! Zmey wants me in the City of Gold," said Gunz, desperation making his voice break on the high notes. "He is not going to harm me until he gets what he wants. But you are a different story. He would do anything to get you out of the way."

Aidan smirked warily, staring to the side. "Agreed on all accounts. So, what are you going to do? Dance to Zmey's tune? Roll over like a little puppy? I thought a few years ago, you were the one who expected me to stand and fight, Zane!"

"Aidan, I *will* stand and fight, but I can't—" He cut himself off, muscle twitching in his jaw. "I refuse to watch my friends being taken out one by one. We already lost Yaroslav and Peyton." A low growl rumbled in his chest and he clenched his fists, finding himself unable to voice his greatest fear.

"Look at me, Salamander," hissed Aidan, and his eyes lit up with the white glow of his magic, an indication of anger brewing within him. "Sometimes the only way out is through. In our case—it's literal. We must go through this"—he waved his hand at the dark wall—"whatever it is... a trap? A town filled with every monster from demonology books? I don't friggin' care! Look! At! Me!"

Gunz raised his face, holding his friend's blazing gaze. "Aidan, they *will* destroy you."

"Give me some credit, Zane," said Aidan. "I'm a god of the Otherworld. Not an easy prey to kill."

"I know, you're immortal, but you are not at your full power. They can destroy your physical body and you'll be forced to come back to the Otherworld anyway," objected Gunz, throwing his last card on the table. "And that would be the best case with the worst case being them torturing you until you beg to die."

"Torturing me? After what Mrak Delar did to me, I laugh in the face of torture! They haven't got what it takes to stop me." Aidan laughed, but his laughter sounded strained. "Listen to me, Zane. We are going to go through these gates, and we play it by ear. But no matter what, I am not going to let these assholes take you and deliver you to King Alexander wrapped in chains with a bow on top like a Christmas present. Do you understand?"

Gunz shrugged. "What's the difference? I will end up in the City of Gold one way or the other."

"Here is the difference," said Aidan, sounding more intense than before. "You have no choice but to go to this cursed city and identify whose dark soul runs this freak show. You are the only one who can do it. But you will go there as a free man, meeting with King Alexander when *you* are ready. We're not going to let some demonic assholes bind you in chains and drain whatever magic you have, to throw you on your knees before some evil Zmey flunky."

Gunz nodded, swallowing hard.

"If we get attacked… No, when we get attacked, I'll try to get us both out. But in case I am not strong enough to do it, I'll make sure you escape no matter what. Don't argue with me, Zane," Aidan continued, cutting the icy air with his hand impatiently. "They're not going to kill me or destroy my physical body. I promise, I'll be fine. Complete the mission. It's the only thing that matters now. I'll get Yaroslav and Peyton and we'll find you as soon as we can."

Aidan held out his hand and Gunz locked it in a firm handshake.

"Let's go," muttered Gunz, heading toward the wall. "Let's see what they serve in this hell's kitchen and who's the chef."

* * *

Gunz stared at the heavy oak gates reinforced with iron-forged elements. In the center of each side of the gates, there was a large iron knob that looked like the face of a demon with four massive fangs protruding from its grotesque mouth. A partially rusted ring was hanging from the demon's jaws, held by the fangs. The idea of touching this hideous excuse for a doorbell made Gunz cringe, but he raised his hand and grabbed one of the rings, feeling the coldness of the iron under his fingers.

This was it. And no matter what was awaiting him behind these gates, it was time to face it. He knocked three times and dropped the ring.

A moment later, Gunz heard the sound of commotion behind the gates and they opened up with a mournful screech. Three men—at least they looked like men—stood in front of them. All three were short, no more than five feet tall. They were dressed in identical long red winter coats adorned with red-fox furs. On their heads, they had fluffy fur-hats with fox tails attached to them, which seemed to be too large for their size.

As soon as the gates opened all the way, all three took their hats off and bowed low to Gunz, brushing the snow beneath their feet with the fox tales. Gunz stiffened as he noticed a pair of short curved horns decorating each man's head. They straightened up and their mouths stretched into the semblance of a smile that was meant to be welcoming, but the set of small pointy teeth it exposed ruined the first impression.

"My lord Fire Salamander," said the man in the center, sounding as sweet as honey, "we're pleased to welcome you to our city." He gave Aidan a quick once-over, his beady glowing eyes sliding up and down his body, and then added frostily with an indifferent flick of his hand, "And your friend may come in as well, if he must."

The man bowed again and all three of them stepped aside, allowing Gunz to pass through. But as Aidan walk through the gate, Gunz heard one of them muttering something under his breath and it didn't sound welcoming at all.

Gunz turned around, staring down at the little monsters with unconcealed threat. "What did you say?" he growled.

"Nothing, my sparkling lordship." Their mouths stretched even wider, which made them look so much more revolting. "Nothing at all. We just want to show you and your absurdly tall friend the way to the palace of our Lord and Master. Please follow us."

Gunz glanced at his watch, registering that it was only six o'clock, but since the sun had gone down already, the entire area was submerged into darkness. Nevertheless, with his sharp Salamander vision, he could see clearly enough, and he quickly surveyed the area, committing to memory every small detail on their way.

The town wasn't really a town, but more like a one-street village. The continuous snowstorm buried everything under a white untouched blanket, but even this incredible amount of snow couldn't conceal the fact that the houses on both sides of the street were abandoned and partially demolished. Windows had no glass, and the doorways stood absent of doors. The fences were destroyed, and the leftover posts were still sticking out of the ground among piles of broken pickets and splinters of wood.

"Who the hell are these creatures?" asked Aidan, using their psychic connection.

"Not sure," replied Gunz.

He threw another glance at the three men walking ahead of them and his heart skipped a beat. With a gust of wind, the vent on the back of one of the man's coat separated, and he noticed a long red tail with a thick brush at the end which resembled that of a donkey.

"*Oh, shit,*" muttered Gunz, staring at the tracks in the snow the men were leaving behind—the heart-shaped, two-toed footprints of a goat. "*Oh, shit... oh, shit... I think I know what they are.*"

"*I think one 'oh, shit' would be enough to give me the heebie-jeebies.*" Aidan gave him an arched stare. "*What are they?*"

"*Nothing good.*" Gunz shivered. "*Biesy... er... Bieses... Bies... Ugh... I don't even know how to say it in English. They are a demonic entity in their natural state. Evil to the bone and as malevolent as they come. You can expect pretty much anything.*"

"*Can hardly wait...*" Aidan rolled his eyes.

"*Aidan, this is really bad.*" Gunz frowned, biting his lip.

"*How so?*"

"*Remember what I told you about possible torture?*" He looked at his friend, silently pleading him to stop. "*Skip the word 'possible' and magnify it tenfold.*"

"*It changes nothing.*"

The street seemed to be endless, and the snowflakes swirled around them like a swarm of angry bees. Gunz surveyed the area, with shock noticing that the snow was a lot heavier around him and Aidan, following their every step, as if a storm cloud was glued to them, hanging right above their heads.

He raised his arm, shielding his face from the assault of the snowstorm. Far ahead he saw the dark silhouette of a half-demolished building that looked like a large barn. Its roof was gone and only the supporting beams were still hanging in the air, seemingly held by nothing.

Somehow, the darkness was thicker above the barn and as they came closer to the building, Gunz realized why. A black cloud was spinning above it in a constant counter-clock rotation. Unlike a tornado, its motion was silent, and that made it look even more threatening. Purple lightning bolts and electric discharges were flashing continuously inside the cloud, but there was no thunder.

Aidan stilled, staring at the rotating darkness with curiosity. "Is that where we're going?" he asked out loud, pointing at the barn. "I think the structural integrity of this building was compromised a few centuries ago. Are you sure it's safe, my lord?" He pushed Gunz slightly, with a half-frozen wink.

The Bieses snapped around, gawking at Aidan with their glowing red eyes. Then the one in the middle stepped forward and stretched his lips into something that was supposed to be a friendly smile as he bowed again.

"My lord Fire Salamander, I assure you, this building is stable and absolutely safe. Please follow us inside. Our Lord and Master is burning with anticipation to make your acquaintance." He smiled and bowed again. "No pun intended of course, your flaming lordship."

The Bies threw another scorching stare at Aidan, and his smile morphed into a predatory snarl. He turned back to the other two *Bieses* and headed toward the barn. Aidan exchanged a quick look with Gunz, but as soon as he took his first step forward, he fell into the deep snow.

Watching Aidan silently struggling with his body partially covered by snow, Gunz cursed under his breath and went down to his knees to see what the problem was. He leaned forward, grabbed as much snow as he could, and pushed it off of Aidan. But despite his effort, the deadly white veil was growing taller and taller, and within a few seconds, Aidan was completely submerged under it.

"Friggin' *Bieses*," Gunz cursed quietly and placed his hands over Aidan, whispering a warming spell, *"Calidarius..."*

The heatwave expanded beneath his hands. It wasn't nearly as strong as it would normally be, but it did the job, quickly devouring the snow. A heartbeat later, Aidan was lying in the middle of a giant puddle, his entire body bound by some thorny roots and leafless vines. One of the vines cut across his face, gagging him. A few drops of blood spilled from the corner of his mouth.

"What the hell," mumbled Gunz, reaching into his pocket.

He pulled his Swiss army knife out and cut all the roots and vines, helping Aidan to get up. Aidan straightened his pants and wiped his bleeding lips on the sleeve of his jacket.

"This is just the beginning," Gunz said through their psychic link.

"Going to get worse?" asked Aidan, chuckling.

"A lot worse, I suspect," replied Gunz, staring at his friend with curiosity.

"Like an army of demons in their natural form?"

"Yup, something like that..."

"Armed with sharp, pointy objects?"

"Yup."

"Immune to our powers?"

"Most likely."

"Fire away! Hmm... no pun intended, your flaming lordship."

Gunz shook his head at his friend's newly found optimism—or most likely nervous bravado—and kept walking. As they got closer to the barn, he realized that there was no way around it. The street dead-ended into the barn door and just like outside the city where they couldn't avoid walking through the gates, the barn seemed to be stretched all the way in both directions, disappearing into the darkness. The barn door was looming in front of them, and Gunz was positive that if he attempted to walk around the building, the door would keep moving along.

"Looks like the only way out is through."

He heard Aidan's voice in his head and nodded. *"Bring it on?"*

"No, my friend," replied Aidan, and there was so much sadness in his voice that Gunz did a double-take.

Aidan's expression was the best version of a poker face, calm and collected, but his eyes were glowing just a little. Gunz knew

Aidan long enough to know that his friend was getting ready for a deadly fight.

"Aidan—," he started to say, but Aidan shook his head once and his expression hardened.

"Zane, I don't know what is behind that door," he said, staring above Gunz's head at the barn, "but I already can sense its malignant presence. It's powerful and evil... I'm sure you detected it too. So be ready. As soon as we walk inside, Aodh mac Lir will take the center stage. Possibly the demons—whatchamacallit—Bieses will be immune to my magic, but this is not why I am going to take my chance of using so much of my power. I'll use it to break this maze spell and set us free... or at least get you out of here."

"Aidan, you'll be channeling the power from within. It will drain you... You'll be—"

"Not up for discussion," Aidan cut him off. "You do as I say, when I say it. Live today to fight tomorrow. I already told you. I'll be all right. There is nothing they can do to me. I'll find Yaroslav and Peyton and we'll meet you at the City of Gold."

Gunz nodded, his chest tightened with agonizing dread. The main *Bies* turned to him, motioning in the direction of the barn door and his upper lip curved up in a feral snarl while his eyes lit up with a sinister scarlet glow.

"Your burning lordship, please come in. Our master is expecting you."

The other two *Bieses* pushed the door open, folding down into a low bow before him. Gunz glanced at Aidan one more time and stepped into the darkness of the building.

CHAPTER 23

~ AIDAN ~

As soon as the door opened, Aidan drew in a short breath and stilled with his hand at his throat. A poisonous miasma of sulphur invaded his nostrils and a powerful spike of a demonic energy field overwhelmed his senses. Once Gunz crossed the threshold, a downpour of cold water mixed in with icicles fell upon him. It seemed to be pouring from everywhere and there was no place to hide.

Gunz cried out and collapsed, dropping flat on his back. As half-frozen rain kept assailing him, he screamed and his muscles spasmed, making his body arch like a stretched bow. Thin scarlet rivulets ran down his face where the sharp icicles cut through his skin.

Using magic to conjure a shield around Gunz wasn't an option as Aidan was trying to preserve every ounce of energy he had in him to break them both free from this place. So he did the only thing he could to help his friend. He fell on top of him, shielding him with his body.

"Zane, focus on me. Look at me!" He doubted Gunz could see or hear anything. His face was contorted with pain and his pupils were dilated into two black vortexes filled with undiluted agony.

Goddammit! How could I make such a stupid mistake? Aidan thought, as icy water ran down his head and neck, sending uncontrollable shivers through him.

Gunz had been so positive that this place would be a trap for him, he convinced him. Aidan didn't consider for a moment that it could be a trap for a Fire Salamander. He was right when he told Gunz that Zmey wanted him in the City of Gold but not as a free man.

Not if I can help it, he thought making a split-second decision. He had to get Gunz out of here, no matter what price he'd have to pay.

"Hang in there, my friend! I'll make it stop in a minute."

Dripping frozen water, Aidan slowly straightened up while gathering his magic. He tapped into the limited magical energy he had within him, realizing that it wasn't enough to do what he planned originally. *Plan B,* he thought with a bitter smirk. With his limited resources, there wasn't space for a mistake. He had to get everything right the first time.

"Praecidio Amnia," he hissed, covering Gunz with a protective shield.

He heard squeals and screeches of demons as they launched at him. With one wave of his arm, he threw them back and channeled all the magic he had within, transforming into his full godly form.

Holding a large bow in his hand, he was dressed like an ancient hunter, including the quiver with arrows strapped to his back. A black mask flashed over his face but quickly disappeared. Blinding white light exploded around him and the darkness shied away, hiding into the far corners of the barn.

Aidan opened his sight and saw the fabric of the maze spell wrapping around him and flowing through the building. He turned toward North—at least he hoped it was the right direction—and raised his arm, grabbing an arrow from his quiver. Placing it on his bow, he sent it flying. Shining with the white light of his magical energy, the arrow flew across the barn, cutting through the fabric of the maze spell and creating a small opening.

As the floor suddenly became unsteady under his feet, Aidan realized with horror that his power was quickly dwindling down. He wasn't sure he had what it took to get Gunz out, but he had to try while the opening in the maze spell he created was still available.

Aidan dropped to his knees next to Gunz, placing his hand on Gunz's shoulder. "Live today to fight tomorrow. I'll find you, my friend," he whispered, not entirely sure if Gunz could hear him. Using the crack in the fabric of the spell his arrow created, he teleported him out of the barn and outside the town's walls, hoping that he didn't throw him too far off course.

Live today to fight tomorrow...

These were the same words Uri had said to him when he had helped him escape a few days earlier. With pain twisting his heart, Aidan realized that he was slowly losing all the people he cared about, one person at the time. Angel had been gone since they returned from California, and then Svyatobor had gone to Prav to ask about him shortly after. He had no idea what had happened to Uri and there was no way to find out. He just got separated from Yaroslav and Gunz, and even though he made a promise to Gunz that he would find them both, he wasn't sure he could keep it.

But the biggest loss of all was Tessa. From the moment the Archmage of the Guardians Order summoned him to let him know about her disappearance, there wasn't a minute in a day he didn't think about her. He had searched for her in every realm he could think of—the realms of Death and the worlds of the living. There wasn't a trace of her anywhere and he couldn't understand how it was possible.

She was his first thought as soon as he opened his eyes early in the morning and the last thought before he fell asleep at night. And right now, as his body drained by the use of magic finally gave in and he slowly collapsed to the ground, unable to stop the darkness from overpowering him, her name was the only clear thought in his frazzled mind.

Tessa...

* * *

Why is it so dark...?

Aidan blinked a few times as his vision readjusted to the darkness of his surroundings. He found himself on his knees, his arms stretched wide, chained to two poles on either side of him. There was no one watching him, so he pulled on the chains just to realize that he was too weak to fight. The amount of magical energy he had used to break Gunz free completely drained him, magically and physically.

He grunted, dropping his head to his chest, and closed his eyes again, thinking about how he could escape this situation. Using magic was out of the question and that left him with no hope for escape any time soon. He needed rest and food—the two things that weren't anywhere in the foreseeable future.

He felt a sharp pain in his side and jerked into the opposite direction, as much as his restraints would allow him. His movement was followed by a loud snickering and hissing whispers all around him. Aidan squinted his eyes but still couldn't see anything except dark shapeless shadows moving and swaying like a bunch of dirty rags in the wind.

"Show yourselves," he said faintly, "enough with your games."

A dim red glow partially illuminated the area and now Aidan could see that he was still in the same barn, and *Bieses* were circling around him, hopping up and down in some freakish dance. The pesky little creatures had lost their fur coats and had only long red caftans on with red sashes wrapped around their waists. Their exposed legs were covered in thick fur and had hooves instead of feet, which made the bottom part of their bodies look like that of a goat. They all had long tails with a fur-brush at the end and short hooked horns on their heads.

Their continuous movement was making Aidan's stomach churn, adding to his overall miserable situation. Once in a while one of the demons would touch him, and their every touch resonated with pain through his body as though they were digging into his flesh with their sharp claws. Possibly they were, but Aidan was too sick to look down. He closed his eyes, suppressing the nausea, wondering how long they could keep hopping and dancing this disgusting jig when he heard a voice. It was just another screeching voice of a *Bies*, but this time it was filled with authority.

With an effort, he opened his eyes and saw one of the little monsters standing right in front of him, staring at him with unadulterated gluttony in his glowing eyes. The *Bies* cocked his head and a derisive snarl distorted his already revolting features. He raised his arm with sharp hooked claws and the rest of the demons halted, staring at their leader with hungry expectation reflected on their hideous faces.

The leading *Bies* approached Aidan. Rising on the tips of his hooves, he seized Aidan's chin with his fingers, overwhelming his senses with the reek of sulphur. His claws dug into Aidan's skin, drawing blood. The *Bies* cackled, turning Aidan's face from left to right, basking in his defenselessness.

"Are you ready, little man?" the *Bies* asked mockingly and despite his situation, laughter bubbled up in Aidan's chest. Even down on his knees, he was taller than the tallest *Bies* in this giant hellhole.

The *Bies* sauntered away, followed by the dancing crowd of

demons. He halted at the opposite wall and turned around. With a theatrical motion of his skeletal arm, he shouted, "It is time!"

His voice bounced off the barn's walls, disappearing into the soundless rotating darkness above it. The *Bies* observed his audience and smiled at them, his pig-like snout stretching wider. Then he raised his arm and announced with the best manners of a high-class Master of Ceremony, "Let's welcome the one, the only, the Master of Darkness and the Lord of Nefariousness..."

His last words drowned in the voices of the other demons as they started to chant all at once, and Aidan didn't get a chance to find out the name of the glorious nefariousness that was apparently coming for him.

The sound of chanting morphed into a loud even hiss and as much as Aidan sharpened his hearing, he couldn't understand anything they were saying. As they kept their chant, the ground trembled and a large fracture cut across the barn floor. A bright red light erupted from the depths of the earth, blinding Aidan for a moment. He blinked a few times, colorful dots floating in his vision.

The thunder rumbled from beneath and the ground quaked again, aftershocks and tremors rolling through the floor. Aidan grunted as sharp rocks bit into his knees. Unable to make a move, he hung in his restraints helplessly. The bright light dimmed down and at last he could see a dark figure slowly rising from underground. It cast a giant shadow on the walls of the barn, merging seamlessly with the rotating darkness above.

Aidan tensed, involuntarily pulling at the chains restraining him. Abruptly all the demons stopped chanting and bent down in a deep bow. The thunder ceased and the ground stopped shaking. Aidan raised his eyes and swallowed back the bile rising to his throat. A giant monster was standing a few yards away from him, rising at least ten feet above the ground.

For the most part, he was shaped like a man. His long thin

hair, greasy and covered in chunks of mud, was falling over his rounded shoulders and down his back. His shoulders were too narrow compared to the size of his colossal body, wrapped into a long cloak made out of dirt and uneven patches of moss.

But it wasn't his body that made Aidan hold his breath. It was his face. Everything below the man's low forehead was covered by his eyelids. Long and hairy, they were falling in thick folds of skin all the way to his feet, concealing the monster's face and the entire front of his body.

The old man moved his head from left to right as if he was observing the assembly and then extended his arms forward. The skin of his hands was also covered in dirt, and his yellow nails, long and hooked, were the only part of his body that weren't brown or black. The MC-*Bies* rushed to his master, took his hand and helped him move forward.

To Aidan's shock, instead of walking forward, the monster stepped down, as if he was progressing down a ladder. A few steps later, he made it to the ground, rising no more than five feet tall. Led by the *Bies*, the monster came closer to Aidan and halted a few feet away from him.

I feel like Gulliver in the land of Lilliputians, Aidan thought, staring down at the little monster, flabbergasted.

"Where is he?" the monster asked, his voice low and dull, as if it was coming from a grave.

"Right in front of you, Your Devouring Hideousness," replied the MC-*Bies*, bowing three times with a wide snarl cutting his face from ear to ear.

The Devouring Hideousness nodded, making his grotesque eyelids wobble and waved his arm at the *Bies*. "Lift my eyelids," he commanded in his flat voice. "Move it."

"Yes, Your Wicked Impatientness, in a jiffy," mumbled the *Bies*, waving franticly at his subordinates.

The tight circle of *Bieses* separated and two more demons

with heavy iron pitchforks walked inside, halting in front of the old man, waiting for his command.

Blood froze in Aidan's veins as he finally identified the monster in front of him. *Vij,* he thought, feeling the drops of cold sweat sliding down his face. *But how? Why? Vij is a resident of the Dark Nav, Chernobog's loyal servant. He wouldn't do anything without his god's command. Or would he?* A wild stampede of thoughts rushed through his mind. *What if Zane was right? What if Chernobog is playing for the other team?*

Vij waved his hand, ordering the *Bieses* to proceed. They lifted his eyelids and carefully started rolling them up with the iron pitchforks. Aidan observed the process with disgust. For a human, meeting Vij's heavy stare meant immediate death, but it was so much more than just death.

With his eyelids down, Vij couldn't see anything, but once his eyes were open, there was nothing in this world or any other world that could be hidden from him. He was the force behind destruction and death, famine and pestilence, the lord of night terrors.

Aidan shuddered, his fingers wrapping tighter over the chains holding him in place. He was a god and Vij couldn't kill him as he would a human, yet a dreadful feeling spread through him as he watched the *Bieses* at work, making him even weaker and more unsteady than he already was.

With a soft moan, he let go of the chains and dropped his head, leaning slightly forward, supported only by his outstretched arms. There was nothing he could do but wait and see what Vij was planning to do once his eyes were opened.

Luckily he didn't have to wait long. He heard a loud group sigh and immediately, someone seized his hair yanking his head backward. He groaned and jerked his head to the side, freeing his hair, but another *Bies* seized his chin, holding him steady in his grip.

Aidan looked up, meeting Vij's penetrating stare. The

monster's eyes were as large as plates, taking most of the space on his misshapen face. They were glowing with a dim red light, but Aidan could see the sickening yellow gleam rising from the depths of Vij's eyes.

Aidan's skin prickled, and the hair rose on the back of his neck as Vij wrapped him into the suffocating hold of his magic. Everything inside him tightened, and he grunted, clenching his teeth hard in response to the unimaginable agony which sprung to life within him, originating in his head. As the pain grew stronger, he could no longer contain his screams, his entire existence wiped out and replaced by the torment with no end to it.

It was over as abruptly as it started. Vij turned his eyes to the left, breaking their eye contact, and Aidan was left panting, gasping for air. The MC-*Bies* hopped closer to him. He grabbed Aidan's face with both hands, turning his head left and right as if he were trying to access what was wrong with him.

"Why is he not dead, Your Glorious Nauseousness?" he screeched, pointing at Aidan. "Did your vision get worse? Should we get you some reading glasses? Age changes and all…"

Vij huffed, turning his entire body toward the *Bies*. The two little demons who were holding his eyelids quickly shifted with him.

"I do not need glasses, you ignorant fool," growled Vij, turning back to Aidan, forcing the other two *Bieses* to switch their position swiftly. "The reason this man is still alive is that he is not a human. At least not entirely."

The *Bieses* got agitated, shifting around nervously.

"Yes, Your Malevolent Evilness, forgive our ignorance," mumbled the main *Bies*, bowing low before him. "But what kind of beasty is he then if he's not human? A wizard? I saw him using some strange magic."

Vij cackled. His entire body shook, shedding dirt and moss off his clothes and raising clouds of dust in the air. Slowly he lifted his arm and pointed his finger with a hooked nail at Aidan.

"You brought here a god of the Celtic Otherworld, imbeciles, and you had no idea," he said, his hollow voice rolling through the barn.

"A god?" yelped the MC-*Bies*, pressing his hands to his chest in horror. "He doesn't look like a god, but like a disgusting human! Forgive us, oh Mighty Wickedness…"

"Forgive us… forgive us…" The whispers echoed his words, spreading through the barn as every single *Bies* dropped to their knees, lowering their horns to the ground, their tails curling in the air.

Vij rolled his oversized eyes, his movement accompanied by a soft squeaking sound. "I'll deal with him," he hissed, waving at the *Bieses* to rise. "Help me get closer to him."

Aidan chuckled mirthlessly as he watched Vij's slow progress toward him and shook his head. "I don't think so," he objected tiredly, calmly meeting Vij's deadly gaze. "You can't deal with me. No one can."

He moved his fingers, and a smile stretched his lips as he realized that as drained as he was, he still had a tiny spark of magic in him. With a significant effort, he gathered all he had, redirecting the energy toward his right hand and quickly drew a tiny rune in the air, infusing it with his magic. He touched the rune with his index finger and whispered Voron's name, summoning him.

CHAPTER 24

~ AIDAN ~

The rotating dark sky above the barn got darker, if it was possible. It spun faster and a bright lightning bolt sliced through the air, hitting the ground right next to Aidan. He flinched and raised his eyes, staring into the dense darkness above his head.

Vij's drilling eyes bore into Aidan's, eliciting a cry of pain out of him. "Who did you summon, god of the Otherworld?" asked Vij, his dull voice carrying underlying tones of predatory excitement. "You're outside of your domain and your pantheon has no power here."

"You're right," Aidan agreed calmly. "This is why I summoned someone from your pantheon. I hope you'll be happy to see a familiar face."

"From my pantheon, huh?" huffed Vij nonchalantly and slowly started moving his eyes up.

The movement of his enormous eyes was strange and terrifyingly creepy. Gradually, his eyeballs rotated upward under the rolled-up eyelids, supported by the iron pitchforks. Aidan couldn't help but shudder, watching the deadly monster raising his eyes, while his entire body remained completely motionless.

Switching his attention back to the darkness above, Aidan saw Voron slowly descending through the vortex of the portal, his large black wings fully expanded behind his back. Chernobog's righthand man landed softly on the ground next to Aidan and looked around, quickly surveying the area. As his eyes fell on Vij, his normally emotionless face blanched, and his lips parted a little, but he instantly composed himself and turned to Aidan with a light bow.

"You summoned me, my lord." Voron folded his great wings, taking in Aidan's desperate situation. It wasn't a question. He was just stating the fact. Then he turned to Vij, folding his arms over his chest and ordered in a no-nonsense tone, "Vij, you better be dropping those eyelids at once."

The two *Bieses* who were holding Vij's eyelids trembled, their shifty red eyes darting from Voron to Vij and back. They whimpered, dancing in place as if suddenly they had an urgent need for a chamber pot, ready to drop the pitchforks and run for their lives.

Vij lifted his arm a little and wagged his filthy finger at the *Bieses* as he said just one word, "No." Then he pointed at Voron. "You *are not* my master, old crow."

"Excuse me?" hissed Voron, unsheathing his sword.

Vij glowered at him and his lipless mouth moved, forming something that was supposed to be a derisive smirk but looked like a dark crack in his face filled with broken, rotten teeth. A low groan rumbled in Voron's chest as he fought Vij's deadly magic, but he didn't make a move, calmly holding the monster's malignant stare.

"Take him," ordered Vij, pointing at Voron, his voice as hollow as ever.

A loud hissing noise filled the barn as all *Bieses* moved as one, repeating Vij's command over and over. Voron raised his sword, getting ready to fight.

"Voron, no! You can't fight them all alone!" shouted Aidan,

straining to raise his voice over the commotion. "Get us the hell out of here!"

Voron didn't turn around to face Aidan. Instead, he swung his massive sword, in one fluid motion cutting through two iron pitchforks like they were nothing but two toothpicks. Vij yelped as his enormous eyelids unfolded, falling all the way to his feet with a sickening thud. The Bieses squealed like a bunch of pigs and charged Voron.

The ancient warrior laughed diabolically while his sword delivered deadly strikes to any demon who dared to come within his reach, and he looked like he was enjoying himself too much.

"Voron!" Aidan yelled, pulling at his restraints.

Voron glanced at Aidan over his shoulder and grunted. "I was just starting to have some fun," he muttered as he touched the chains that were holding Aidan.

The chains disappeared, and Aidan fell forward on all fours, breathing laboriously. Voron's wings expanded behind his back, lifting him a few feet in the air as he started to chant. The *Bieses* shouted something furiously and charged at them, but for whatever reason they couldn't get closer, running into some kind of invisible wall.

"I truly hope there is a good explanation to all this," whispered Voron. He put his hand on Aidan's shoulder and snapped his fingers.

The barn spun around like a crazy carousel, turning into a continuous foggy blur, and when the fog finally cleared out, Aidan found himself lying in the middle of a white nowhere.

* * *

SNOW WAS FALLING IN SLOW FLUFFY CHUNKS. THE COLORLESS SKY seemed to be seamlessly connected with the untouched whiteness of the ground. And as far as Aidan could see, there was nothing except the frozen desert.

Voron stood in front of him, his wings gone, and with his black clothes and armor, he looked stark and foreign in the surrounding achromatic background. The ancient warrior held out his hand and Aidan took it, rising to his feet with effort. Now that he was outside the cursed town, he felt better, but he was still drained by the excessive use of his magic and he knew it would take him a while to get stronger in these conditions.

"Where are Zane, Yaroslav, and Peyton?" asked Voron without any preamble.

"I don't know," replied Aidan with a sigh. "I intend to find out if you help me a little. But before we continue, I must ask you straight, Voron, and you better tell me the truth."

Voron stiffened, and a muscle twitched in his jaw. "Have I ever lied to you, my lord?" he asked quietly, his fingers squeezing the pommel of his sword, his knuckles white. "What would you like to ask, Aodh mac Lir?"

"There is no easy way to ask something like this," said Aidan, too tired to feel uncomfortable or search for better words. "Have you or your master switched sides?"

Voron's eyes widened, his black eyebrows climbing up. "Excuse me?"

He looked so shocked and lost that Aidan had no doubt this question came as a complete surprise to him. Nevertheless, he needed to be sure.

"You heard me," he replied, sounding a little more forceful than he intended. "Have you or Chernobog switched sides? Are you working with the followers of Chaos?"

For a split-second Voron stiffened, but then dropped his arms powerlessly along his body, shaking his head. "I most certainly have not," he growled. "How dare you suggest something so—"

"Voron!" yelled Aidan, interrupting him. "How about Chernobog? Is there a chance Morena convinced him to free Zmey? Think! It's important."

Voron shook his head. "Impossible. Morena is locked in the dungeons. Chernobog has not visited her since the fight for Mount Karasova. He hates Skiper-Zmey. Think about it! His wife cheated on him with Zmey. She broke his heart…" Voron looked away, his dark eyes staring into the white emptiness. "Why would Chernobog want to help his wife's lover?"

"Good question," Aidan muttered, rubbing his forehead as exhaustion settled somewhere deep in his bones. "And I have a few more good ones for you. Why did Vij hold me captive? Why did he try to capture Zane? He is supposed to be a Chernobog servant. Why has every wizard in the nexus lost their magic, and the gods have locked themselves in Prav, but you and Chernobog are not affected? Why?"

"I don't know either! I have no idea!" Voron looked at him, and Aidan saw how deeply his questions hurt the old warrior. "Chernobog has many servants and he can't keep an eye on every single one of them." He fell silent for a moment and then threw his hands in the air, resentment shadowing his features. "Heaven and earth, Aidan! How could you even think that! I can guarantee you—Chernobog won't be pleased when he finds out about what happened."

In one swift move, Voron unsheathed his sword. Aidan blanched, taking a step back, but Voron thrust his blade into the ground and heavily kneeled before him, resting his both hands on the guard.

"My lord," said Voron, his voice soft but firm, "I swear on my power and I swear on my honor that neither I nor my master Chernobog knew anything about Vij's betrayal. I also swear that we didn't switch sides. As to your question about why I still have my power, I'm sorry, but I can't answer that as I am sworn to secrecy by my master. I already disobeyed him once for Zane. I can't do it again without some serious consequences."

For a moment Aidan just stared down at the kneeling warrior, lost for words. Then he ran his fingers through his hair, throwing snow off the top of his head, and touched Voron's shoulder.

"Please don't kneel before me, Voron," he said. "It's not necessary. With everything that's going on, I feel lost. I'm trying to find a way out and all I can see are dead ends. I think instead of looking for answers, I should look for my friends, starting with Peyton and Yaroslav as I promised Zane. The answers will come later."

"What can I do to help?" asked Voron rising, shaking the snow off his pants.

Aidan quickly recounted all the events of that morning when they lost Peyton and Yaroslav. Voron just shook his head, a troubled look on his face, sending shivers down Aidan's back.

"What do you know, Voron?" he asked, massaging his shoulder, just now noticing a dull ache in the wound that was supposed to be completely healed.

Voron pursed his lips, disappearing into his thoughts for a moment. "Was that the frozen lake which lies past the forest I dropped you at?" he asked, stroking his short beard as a deep frown creased his forehead.

Aidan nodded, a thick lump settling in his throat.

"Not the best place to be," mumbled Voron, "but it could have been worse."

"It can always be worse," muttered Aidan. "Do you think they are still alive?"

Voron averted his gaze, staring at his hands. "Possibly," he said after a while. Then he raised his eyes. "Are you willing to take a swim in a frozen lake, my lord?"

"Of course," replied Aidan. "The only problem is, I can't breathe underwater."

"What would happen if you drown?" asked Voron, looking at him with curiosity.

"My spirit will return to the Otherworld where Gwyn ap Nudd will restore me," explained Aidan with a shrug. "I can't really die, Voron, but that would throw me out of the nexus, and I won't be able to come back. It's not an option for me."

"Then I suggest you hold your breath for as long as possible and don't die, my lord," replied Voron with a light bow. He grabbed Aidan's shoulder and as his obsidian wings opened up, he snapped his fingers.

CHAPTER 25

~ YAROSLAV ~

The sky just started to lighten up with the approaching dawn and the grass was heavy with morning dew. A dense gray fog spread over the land, mixed in with dark smoke rising over the burning houses in dirty swirls. There was nothing moving in the destroyed village as all its residents were no longer among the living. Men, women, children and elderly lay motionless, their bloodied corpses sprawled on the ground, their wide-open eyes staring into the colorless sky with horror.

The copper odor of blood permeated the air and even the heavy stench of smoke and burnt flesh couldn't conceal it. Deeply shocked, Yaroslav stood in the middle of a narrow village road, looking at the piled up bodies. Right before his feet, he noticed a young woman. Her pretty face was splattered with blood, her throat ripped by sharp fangs, blood still trickling down from the terrible wound.

He turned his palms up and gaped at the scarlet stains on his skin. Carefully he ran his tongue over his upper teeth, feeling the sharp tips of his fangs protruding from his mouth. With a trembling hand, he touched his lips, detecting the slippery wetness under his fingers. He brought his hand down and the look of fresh blood on his fingers made his thirst spike up to the next level. He grunted, backing away from the corpse of the young woman.

"No…" he moaned, shaking his head, horrorstricken. "It couldn't have been me… I couldn't have killed all these people…"

He took another step back and tripped over something, falling flat on his back. Hastily, he scrambled up into a sitting position and saw that it was the body of a young boy. He was lying on his stomach, his head turned at an unnatural angle, his open eyes frozen with fear. His throat was shredded to pieces and dark blood soaked his raggedy clothes.

Yaroslav stared at him, frozen in place. The boy couldn't be older than twelve. Slowly, he got up and surveyed the area. He was the only man standing. He couldn't sense the presence of other vampires in the village and every single villager was dead. A terrible realization hit him like freezing water, and he collapsed to his knees. Bending down to the ground, he squeezed his head with his hands, his fingers buried into his long hair.

"No!" he howled, unshed tears burning in his eyes. "No! God help me…"

* * *

"Wake up, vamp!"

A hard slap across his face ripped him out of the terrible nightmare and he jolted up with a start. His vision was uncharacteristically blurry, and he pressed his hands to his eyes, his move accompanied by the loud clanks of chains. He blinked a few times and was finally able to see. However, what he saw didn't give him a warm and fuzzy feeling.

He was in a semi-dark room that looked like a dungeon with a tiny single window crossed by thick iron bars. Behind the bars, he saw another stone wall, and he had to wonder why the iron bars were needed, since there was no way anyone could escape through that window.

Peyton stood over him, her hands on her hips.

"Finally," she grumbled irritably. "I'm sick of hearing you scream and pray and say all sorts of nonsense."

"Sorry," mumbled Yaroslav. "Where am I?"

"Not Miami," she replied mockingly.

Yaroslav pushed himself up into a sitting position and leaned his back against the rough stonework, staring at the silver bands locked around his wrists. He touched his neck and felt the slick surface of a silver collar under his fingers, which was connected to the wall by a short chain. His skin under the silver was raw and bleeding, and the weakness he felt was overwhelming.

He dropped his hands onto his lap and tilted his head back, resting it against the wall. All this unpleasantly reminded him of the time when he was fighting in the Supernatural pits as a captive fighter, and cold shivers ran down his spine.

"Night terrors?" asked Peyton snidely, staring down at him. "The ghosts of your victims haunting your dreams, vamp?"

He raised his eyes at her, feeling like her words were draining the last strength he had and sighed. "Vamp?" he asked, hardly moving his lips. "I thought we were over that—"

"We?" hissed Peyton, squatting in front of him. "There can never be a 'we' when it comes to you and me, *vamp*." She accentuated the word 'vamp', disgust dripping out of her every word.

"Why, Peyton?" he asked, looking down at his shackled, bleeding wrists. "I just want to understand. Did some other vampire hurt you or someone you love? I've never done anything to offend you. I'd never even met you before I joined Aidan's team. You are like two people in one and I don't—"

Before Yaroslav finished his statement, she backhanded him hard across his face. His head jerked to the side and hot white light exploded behind his tightly shut eyelids. He gasped, pressing his hand to his cheek, but then dropped his head to his chest and fell silent. With a low growl, she seized his neck, forcing his face up.

"Not so mighty now, vamp?" she snarled, glaring at him. "I wish I had my stake here." With her other hand, she pulled his shirt down, exposing his chest over his heart.

He smirked mirthlessly, holding her furious stare. "I wish you had it too," he agreed calmly. "That would teach me a lesson... I should've let Likho drown you."

"I didn't ask you to dive after me!" yelled Peyton, raising her hand again.

Yaroslav closed his eyes and turned his head to the side, ready for the strike, but it didn't follow. Instead, he felt her fingers slowly brushing over his cheek where his skin was still prickling from her previous slap. He sensed the heat of her body caressing his face as she leaned closer to him, tucking a strand of his hair behind his ear. He tensed under her touch, not sure what to expect next or how to react to it.

Slowly, he opened his eyes and found her face just a few inches away from his. The arrogant, angry expression was gone, and her azure gaze was filled with curiosity and warmth. The hateful Peyton was no more, replaced by the sweet girl his friends loved and respected.

"Fire and ice," he whispered, unable to take his eyes off of her.

"What did you say?" she asked, and he felt a touch of her warm breath on his face.

Yaroslav just shook his head slightly, afraid to say something that could trigger the personality change in her. Now that she was so close to him, he could sense the ominous presence hovering over her—the Likho hadn't let go of her even when she tried to commit suicide by falling into the frozen lake.

He remembered diving into the lake after her. In the dark waters he had barely been able to see her body slowly sinking down, her copper hair lingering around her face like a soft reddish cloud. She hadn't struggled, hadn't tried to swim up, as though the instinct of self-preservation was completely extinguished in her dying body.

Yaroslav reached her a minute later. As he pulled her limp body to his chest, he realized that they were too deep, and worry swirled through him. He wasn't sure if it was the coldness of the water or Likho's malignant magic, but his own movements were slow and lethargic, and if he tried to bring Payton up, she would be dead before he could reach the surface, anyway.

He stared down, sharpening all his senses, and far at the bottom of the lake, he noticed a black hole that looked like an opening into a cave. He swam there as fast as he could, hoping that the cave had at least a small air pocket. As he moved through the opening, he felt the resistance of some strange magical energy, but he had no time to wonder about it. As he stepped on hard ground, he sighed with relief. The cave was dry and filled with air, completely water-free.

He kneeled and placed Peyton on the floor, leaning over her. She wasn't breathing. Yaroslav swallowed hard, realizing with horror that he had no breath, and mouth-to-mouth CPR wasn't an option. He just pushed this thought away and started with the chest compressions, praying to all the gods he knew that it would be enough to bring her back. A moment later, she coughed, and he turned her to her side as water spilled from her mouth. The last thing he remembered was a sharp pain on the back of his head.

And now, he was sitting shackled to the wall, weak and hurt, and this strange young woman who had been ready to kill him just a moment ago, now was gazing at him as if he were the centerpiece of her entire existence. He had no idea what to do, what to say or how to behave with her. But most of all, he had no idea how to help her get rid of Likho's deadly influence.

"Yaroslav..." she whispered his name, placing her hand against his cheek. "I'm sorry. I shouldn't have hit you. I have no idea why I did that."

He nodded silently. She gently threaded her fingers through his long hair, brushing it off his face, and tucked it behind his ear again.

"You have such a strange but beautiful name," she continued, ignoring his silence, her bright blue eyes fixed on his. "I hate it when Zane and Aidan call you Slavik... Your full name has mystery and power to it, and this shortened version is just not right."

Peyton fixed his face between her hands and leaned down until her lips touched his cheek. He froze, afraid to make a move. He wasn't sure what made him feel more uncomfortable—her hate and resentment toward him, or her affections.

"Yaroslav Potemkin," she exhaled. "I hate you..." Her lips found his, and she kissed him hard, forcing his lips apart.

He didn't fight her, realizing with shock that his body responded to her kiss with more eagerness than he expected in the given situation. She let go a moment later and pulled away sitting back on her heels next to him, a conflict reflected on her troubled face.

"I hate you," she repeated, tears gathering in her eyes. "I'm supposed to hate you... I must... but since I laid my eyes on you, I could never—"

She stopped talking and averted her gaze. He didn't say anything, but his hand went up automatically, covering his lips. The chains clinked, and he winced as the silver cuffs slid down slightly, causing him more pain. She gasped as her eyes settled on his raw wrists and took his hand into hers, gently stroking his knuckles with her thumb.

"I don't understand... nothing fits," she mumbled, a swift shadow of vulnerability crossing her face. "It's not supposed to be like this. Yaroslav, say something. Please!"

Yaroslav swallowed the thick lump in his throat. "I don't know what to say, Peyton," he responded, his voice hoarse. "I'm trying to understand you and I can't."

"Nothing fits," she repeated airily, shaking her head. Her copper eyebrows rose like she was ready to cry, and her lips quivered. Then she brought his hand to her face and placed her flushed cheek against his cold palm. "Nothing makes sense. I shouldn't…" Her voice wavered and she hid her face in his hand.

Yaroslav shrugged. "Peyton, I'm not sure what you're talking about," he said softly, his thumb gently caressing her cheek, "but sometimes life throws things at us that are completely unexpected and make no sense, and we're supposed to work to make them fit. No matter how impossible this task seems to be."

"You don't understand." She pulled away, releasing his hand, a tortured smile appearing on her face for a brief moment. "You're the one who doesn't fit," she said, and her voice shook with suppressed emotions. "You're like that proverbial square peg… and I can never fit you in any round—" She cut herself off suddenly, blinking furiously at him and then added with a lot more force in her voice. "Don't you dare say something smartassy, Yaroslav Potemkin!"

"I wasn't going to," he said innocently, raising his hands up as he bit his lip to stop himself from laughing.

"Ugh," she growled, "you're so not a gentleman, vamp."

Yaroslav laughed and threw the hoop of his shackled arms around her, pulling her onto his lap. "I never claimed that I was." He lowered his face slightly and saw her lips parting. Her long copper eyelashes fluttered as she closed her eyes. He smiled over her lips and murmured, "Let me show you how a non-gentleman vamp can kiss, my lady."

His kiss was soft and tender, and she moaned, leaning into him. He deepened his kiss, his fingers buried into her hair. As his body throbbed with desire, he forced himself to let go. With his lips still touching hers he whispered, a mischievous laughter bubbling within him, "Do you still believe I can't fit a peg into a hole, my lady?"

She gasped and pushed against his chest but couldn't get away, held in place by his shackled arms. He chuckled, watching her squirm. She was finally able to lift his arms and free herself when a hollow sound of slow clapping filled the dungeon.

Yaroslav snapped his head in the direction of the sound and saw a short, balding man with a large wobbly belly standing at the other end of the room. He was barefoot, dressed in linen pants and a shirt that showed a few patches of curly gray hair on his chest. Two beautiful young women were standing on either side of him. Their long dark gowns seemed to be out of place in this dark cell and their presence in the company of this old unremarkable man felt off.

"Tsk, tsk, tsk," the old man clacked his tongue, staring at them mockingly. "The predator decided to screw around with the prey. Rather fascinating."

"What are you talking about, old man," growled Yaroslav, pushing Peyton behind him. "I'm not a predator."

The man snickered, arrogance unmistakable in his voice.

"No, you are not, vampire. At least, not today. Today, you're a helpless prey. Actually, I was referring to her." He pointed his beefy finger at Peyton and added, "Hey, girl, didn't your mother ever teach you not to play with your prey?"

CHAPTER 26

~ YAROSLAV ~

"What are you talking about?" growled Yaroslav, rising to his feet. The man smirked an all-knowing smile and his women tittered, covering their mouths with their well-manicured hands. Yaroslav stared heavily at Peyton. "What is he talking about, Peyton?"

"Yaroslav, I can—," she started, but then averted her eyes, a vibe of guilt almost palpable around her.

He stared down at her, everything inside him tight like a wound-up spring. Then he clenched his jaw as he turned back to the man, looking askance at him.

"I saw her apartment," he said hoarsely. "It's equipped to withstand a year-long siege by an army of vampires. So what? She is a witch, and she is familiar with the things that go bump in the night—"

"Aw, how sweet," the man sang mockingly. He cocked his head, staring at Yaroslav with narrowed eyes. "Are you really that dumb, Prince Potemkin? Or are you just turning a blind eye to everything she does, to her attitude toward you, to her behavior."

The man waved his hand at the women. They nodded

silently and moved toward Peyton. Their movement was hard to describe as walking. They were gliding, seemingly not touching the floor with their feet as there was no sound accompanying their progress, nor an up and down motion in their steps. Peyton watched them, her eyes glassy, her mouth opened a little.

They approached her and put their hands on her shoulders, staring directly into her eyes. Yaroslav could feel the magical energy around them spike and it was a strange feeling. As a vampire, he wasn't that sensitive to the fluctuation of the magical energy field, but theirs was so powerful that he felt it with his skin.

Peyton stared back at their large eyes—the color of a lake on a sunny day, enthralled by whatever magic they were wielding. After a moment, both women turned around and inclined their heads at the man.

"She's ready, master," they said in unison, their voices musical and just as magical as their appearance.

The man walked up to Peyton and stopped, giving Yaroslav an arched stare. More than anything, Yaroslav wanted to rip this man apart with his bare hands, but he recognized that while wrapped in silver he was too weak, and his short chain would keep him in place. Besides, a tiny voice in the back of his mind was already whispering all the answers to the riddle which Peyton's behavior had been all this time.

He knew it…

He had always known it, but for some reason he refused to see what was right in front of his eyes.

Since Yaroslav didn't say anything, the man seized Peyton's shoulder and turned her around. She didn't resist, her arms hanging limply along her body. The man wrapped her long bushy hair over his wrist and forced her head down. On the back of her neck, right under the hairline was a small tattoo—an

Ankh symbol stylized to look like a sword with a winged serpent circling around it.

"Sisterhood of the Sun," whispered Yaroslav.

"That's right, Prince," agreed the man snidely, letting go of Peyton's hair. "Your girlfriend is a vampire slayer. Not just any hunter. She belongs to one of the most ancient organizations that hunts and destroys your kind."

Yaroslav stared at the man, unable to take his eyes off of him. *Sisterhood of the Sun...* The ancient order, created centuries ago when the first vampire walked the land, dedicated to one purpose only—kill vampires, wipe their entire race off the face of this world. Not every woman could become a member of this order and being touched by the World of Magic wasn't enough to be accepted.

The order accepted only female candidates and the selection process was harsh and vigorous. The young women were supposed to possess certain traits as humans and as witches. Once accepted, they were trained physically and psychologically, becoming nothing short of merciless killing machines. When it came to vampires, nothing could stop a member of the Sisterhood from achieving her goal.

"But wait," continued the man, pulling the collar of Peyton's shirt down. "Take a look at this beauty. Do you know what this one does?"

Yaroslav stared at a small rune tattooed on Peyton's back, weakness spreading over him. He knew what it was. "This rune protects her from a vampire's influence," he managed to say. "I couldn't glamour her even if I wanted." He rubbed his forehead, chains clinking heavily with his every move. "Who are you? Why am I here?"

"Please tell me you are not in love with her, Prince?" asked the man, amusement twinkling in his eyes. "Hold on, let's change that. Please tell me you *are* in love with her. That would make this game so much more entertaining."

"Who are you??" shouted Yaroslav, taking a few steps toward the man, until his chain stretched to the limit.

"Me?" asked the man, an over-exaggerated surprise on his face. "I'm no one. I'm just doing my job."

"Which is?" growled Yaroslav as rage flashed through him.

"Which is keeping you imprisoned and on a short leash for the next few months," replied the man nonchalantly and then added with a light flick of his hand. "I also have permission to kill you if you are not obedient enough. So, tread lightly... Your Highness."

Suppressing all his emotions, Yaroslav remained still. "Who are you?" he repeated his question frostily.

"Haven't you heard, Prince? Curiosity killed the bat. Oops, I meant—cat. Come to think of it... Can you turn into a bat?" The man cackled, his large belly wobbling like jelly.

Yaroslav didn't reply.

"Fine, I'll indulge your curiosity," said the man with a dismissive wave of his hand. "Allow me to introduce myself, Your Highness. I am Vodyanoy and these two lovelies are my loyal Rusalkas."

His appearance started to change and a moment later, a tall man with bulging round eyes and a large belly was standing before him. His hair and beard were green, covered with a disgusting layer of algae and muck, and his hands looked like webbed paws, shining darkly with fish scales.

Vodyanoy—a water demon, Lord of the Underwater kingdom. I can't fight him. In his own domain, he's unstoppable, thought Yaroslav, forcing himself to remain calm and motionless.

Vodyanoy's greenish lips quirked up in a smile as he arched his bushy eyebrows at the Rusalkas. Both women approached Yaroslav. They sauntered around him swaying their hips seductively, their hands shamelessly exploring his body and their every touch sent a jolt of desire through him. He grunted, suppressing the primal need their magic awakened in him and caught their hands, squeezing their wrists.

"Hands off if you want to keep them," he growled through gritted teeth. He pushed them away and turned to Vodyanoy. "Keep your water-bitches away from me, if you know what's best for you."

Vodyanoy frowned, drilling Yaroslav with his bulging eyes. "I was trying to be nice to you," he hissed. "But if that's how you want to play, so be it." He nodded at the Rusalkas, jerking his thumb toward Peyton and then turned back to Yaroslav. "Remember, I don't have to keep you alive, Prince Potemkin. I just need to keep you away from the surface. By any means necessary that is. So, let's make it entertaining. Let the predator become the prey."

He held out his arm, muttering something under his breath, and a sharp wooden stake materialized in the palm of his hand. He threw it at Peyton's feet. Then he pointed at Yaroslav and a cloud of Vodyanoy's magical energy enveloped him. For a moment, the room spun around him and Yaroslav swayed, struggling to stay on his feet.

When the strange sensation was gone, Yaroslav noticed that the silver cuffs and collar had disappeared, replaced by regular reinforced steel, and his chain became slightly longer. Absent silver, his skin started to heal right away, and he rolled his shoulders, enjoying his quickly restoring strength.

"Aw, how nice," Vodyanoy purred, rubbing his hands. "This is exactly what I wanted to see—the infamous Vampire Prince at his full strength. Well, almost at his full strength. You're still limited by the length of your chain and just to spare you worthless labor—this chain is enchanted. Even with your vampire strength, you can't break it."

Vodyanoy headed to Peyton and halted in front of her. With his foot, he pushed the stake closer to her. "Pick it up," he ordered, staring down at her with disdain.

Peyton pressed her lips in a stubborn straight line and didn't move. Her eyes darted to Yaroslav, and he saw the pained expression on her face. She no longer was under the Rusalka's trance, but despite her origins, she had no desire to fight him.

"Pick it up!" roared Vodyanoy and when she remained still, he seized her arm and with one quick move slashed her wrist with his sharp nails. Dark blood gushed from the cut and Peyton hissed in pain, jerking her arm back.

The heavy metallic odor of blood invaded Yaroslav nostrils, and he sucked in a sharp breath as thirst sprung to life within him. His eyes lit up with a hungry scarlet light and his fangs expanded. Struggling to control his need for blood, he pressed his hands to his mouth and staggered away from her until his back hit the wall.

Vodyanoy draped his arm wrapped in algae over Peyton's shoulders and whispered into her ear, knowing perfectly well that Yaroslav could hear every word he was saying. "Look at him, Peyton. He is just another vampire, driven by his unstoppable bloodlust. For him, you are nothing more than a walking-talking all-you-can-eat buffet. Come on, girl! You are a hunter of the Sisterhood. Do your duty! Pick up this stake and kill him!"

"No," Peyton whispered without taking her eyes off Yaroslav.

"Well, this is interesting," murmured Vodyanoy, stepping away from Peyton. "As a member of the Sisterhood, you are aware that the thirst is not something vampires can control. The longer he spends without feeding, the thirstier he'll become. Soon, the thin layer of humanity he still has will be gone and the only thing you'll be left with is a feral beast, controlled by the thirst." He bent down and picked up the stake, thrusting it into Peyton's hands. "When it happens, you'll need it."

He moved closer to Yaroslav, but not close enough for the vampire to reach him. "Prince, when the thirst will wipe out who you are, you will fight her, and if I know anything about the Sisterhood of the Sun, she will reduce you to ashes. And I'll be watching when it happens." He turned back to Peyton and waved his hand in her direction. "Likho, make it so, sweetheart."

Vodyanoy cackled loudly, throwing his head back, shedding chunks of algae to the floor. Then he opened the door, letting the Rusalkas exit first and followed them.

* * *

The sound of the lock made Yaroslav flinch. He slid down to the floor, hugging his knees with his arms and rested his head atop his knees. But no matter what he did, he couldn't control the rising thirst. His throat felt dry, like someone filled it with hot sand and the only thing he could think of was blood. Peyton's blood. He could smell it in the air, he could hear her heart pumping it through her body, and no matter what he tried, he couldn't suppress his instinct to kill and feed.

"Yaroslav?" she called him tentatively, her voice soft.

He raised his face and saw her recoil. He knew what she saw —scarlet eyes and long fangs. "Vodyanoy was right," he said, hardly recognizing his own voice as it came out raspy and low. "I have a hard time controlling the thirst. You should stay as far away from me as you can. The chains are strong enough to hold me down… I hope…"

"I don't think I will."

Shocked by the change in her voice, Yaroslav looked at her again and shuddered. The Peyton who had been kissing him just a few minutes ago was gone, replaced by the hunter of the Sisterhood. In her hand she was holding the stake Vodyanoy gave her, tapping it on the open palm of her other hand.

He got up to his feet, pressing his back to the wall, and met her icy gaze calmly. As he mentally started to get ready for what was coming, he saw it—Likho's semi-translucent image was hanging over Peyton like an ominous spirit. The monster's skinny arms wrapped around her, her bony fingers disappearing into Peyton's flesh. Likho's head was rising above Peyton's, her single eye shining with a sinister yellow glow.

But there was something else there, something Yaroslav hadn't noticed before, and it made him do a double take. His eyes caught a bright green flare of light on Peyton's chest. He sharpened his vision and saw a small pendant hanging on a delicate chain. As much as he recalled, the young witch had never worn any jewelry. Now he also understood why—she was a hunter, a well-trained fighter who knew that any jewelry could be a problem during hand-to-hand combat.

An icy smile curved Yaroslav's lips as he realized what it was. He ripped his shirt exposing his chest and placed his hand over his silent heart.

"Come get me, hunter," he said, his every word accompanied by a low hiss. "Here is my heart." He drew a circle on his chest with his finger.

Peyton screamed, her face contorted with blind rage. Raising the stake, she charged at him like a crazed bull. Likho spread her bony arms, her dark raggedy clothes flying around her like a war banner. She was feeding on Peyton's anger and her entire being glowed in sinister exultation.

Yaroslav bent his knees slightly, ready to spring into action as he watched Peyton's approach. He remembered Peyton's fighting style—forceful, but calculated and cold-minded. Now she was burning with hatred, her mind far from clear and he knew it wasn't her, it was Likho driving her insane.

As she approached, swinging her hand with the stake, he moved aside and lightly pushed her into the wall. As light as his shove was, she hit the stone with her face and blacked out for a split-second. The stake fell on the floor with a loud clatter, landing next to her feet. This quick moment was enough for him to seize her shoulder and spin her around. His other hand reached for the pendant and ripped the chain off her neck as he lowered her to the floor.

The moment the pendant was off Peyton's neck, Likho became corporeal again, now easily visible even in the poor light of the dungeon. The old hog squealed and charged Yaroslav from atop, spreading her arms wide, aiming at his face with her sharp claws. He ducked to the side as far as his short chain allowed him, avoiding Likho's assault.

His move just infuriated the monster. She squealed again and turned toward him breathing hard, her gray greasy hair fanning around her skull-like face in thin dirty strands. Yaroslav didn't wait for her to attack him again. He swung his arm with the pendant and crushed the green stone against the wall.

The pendant blew up with a thunderous bang and a blast wave spread through the dungeon, knocking him off his feet. He fell on his back, skidded on the floor and came to a sharp stop once he reached the full extent of the chain. He cried out as the metal collar dug into his throat, drawing blood with its sharp edges.

Likho recovered faster than he expected and pounced on him, landing on his chest. She wrapped her crooked bony fingers around his throat, squeezing it. Yaroslav reached to the side and grabbed the stake that was lying next to Peyton who was still unconscious on the floor. As Likho kept squeezing his throat, he laughed darkly.

"I'm a vampire, bitch," he croaked. "You can't suffocate someone who doesn't breathe."

He drew his arm back and plunged the stake into Likho's only eye. The monster howled, clasping her hands to her face as thick greenish-black goo spilled from under the stake. She rose in the air above him, spinning like a tornado and howling just as loud.

Yaroslav pushed himself up on his elbows, staring at the monster, transfixed. A heartbeat later, the old hog halted, her face turned up toward the ceiling while her hand pointed down at Yaroslav, and she cackled as she pulled the stake out of her eye socket and threw it forcefully in his general direction.

Yaroslav rolled to his side, but the stake still grazed his shoulder, eliciting a cry of pain out of him. Likho hollered something incoherent and with a loud bang exploded into a cloud of dust. Clasping his bleeding shoulder, he fell on his back and closed his eyes with a low groan.

It was over.

Likho was gone. He knew that he hadn't killed the monster —Likho couldn't be killed, but at this moment, it was no longer his concern. He had a bigger problem on his hands—while Peyton was free from Likho's influence, she still belonged to the Sisterhood of the Sun. It meant since early childhood she was taught to hate vampires, to slay them without a thought, without mercy. She was the hunter, the mortal enemy of every vampire out there, and being so close to her, for the first time in his life, he felt like prey.

"Yaroslav?"

He heard Peyton's trembling voice, but he didn't move. He wasn't sure he wanted to see her or hear her.

"Yaroslav!" she yelled, her voice ringing with fear.

The next moment, he felt her trembling hands touching his face, brushing his hair off. He cracked his eyelids open and saw her blue eyes right in front of his, her face transformed by fear.

"Oh God," she moaned, leaning down, pressing her wet cheek to his, "I thought the monster killed you…"

"I would be a pile of ash if she did, wouldn't I?" Yaroslav asked and then added dryly, "I'm sure as a member of the Sisterhood of the Sun you know how a dead vampire looks."

Peyton straightened up, sitting on her heels and gazed down at him, tears overflowing her blue eyes.

"Shut up, you Royal Pain," she muttered. "Just shut your mouth… if you can, with these blades protruding…" She touched the tip of his fang with her finger and giggled, wiping the tears off her eyes. "I feel so much better now. What was this monster?"

"One-eyed Likho," replied Yaroslav, pushing himself up on his elbows.

"That doesn't tell me much," mumbled Peyton, staring at the deep cut on her arm. "But I don't care. I'm just happy she's gone."

He glanced down at her bleeding arm and turned away, lying back down. The smell of her blood was increasing his thirst and he had a hard time controlling his instincts.

"Maybe you should go to the opposite end of this room," he said hoarsely, "where I can't reach you."

"Thirsty?" she asked. He nodded, ashamed to look at her. "Is that why your fangs…"

"Vodyanoy was right, you know?" he said quietly, folding his hands on his stomach. "At some point I won't be able to control the thirst anymore. Please go, Peyton. I'll never forgive myself if I hurt you."

Yaroslav felt Peyton's fingers wrap around his arm above the cuff but didn't open his eyes and turned his face away from her. He hated the idea of her seeing his fangs and his glowing red eyes.

"Open your eyes, Yaroslav," Peyton demanded, squeezing his arm.

He sighed but opened his eyes and looked at her.

"I'm not going anywhere. You didn't abandon me, despite the way I treated you… I'm not leaving you. Period," she said. "I'm a hunter of the Sisterhood. I know how to handle a feral vamp without killing him. Besides, we still need to figure out how to get out of this shithole and I'm not leaving you behind."

Before he knew it, she leaned down and kissed him. Shy and tender at first, her kiss deepened, her tongue gently touching his fangs as she explored his mouth. She broke the kiss a moment later and gazed down at him, a sensual smile curving her slightly swollen lips. With her untidy bright hair falling around her round face, she looked like a little sunshine.

Yaroslav gazed up at her, his every cell craving her touch, and his lips parted as desire electrified him. "Beautiful..." he exhaled, before he could stop himself.

Peyton grabbed his shackled arms and moved them above his head as she straddled him. She let go of his arms, leaned forward, and for a moment lingered just an inch above his face before kissing him again.

As soon as her lips touched his, the floor trembled and the door into the dungeon flew open with an earsplitting bang. With vampire speed, Yaroslav lowered the hoop of his arms, pressing Peyton to his chest and rose to his feet, his back to the door as he endeavored to shield her with his body.

"And here I thought you needed my help. What you truly needed was a room!"

The sound of familiar laughter filled the cell and Yaroslav released Peyton, turning around with a sigh of relief.

"Aidan."

CHAPTER 27

~ ZANE BURNS, A.K.A. GUNZ ~

Gunz wasn't sure how long he had been walking. It had to have been over twelve hours. It had been past midnight when Aidan teleported him out of the hell-town, and since that, the sky had gotten a little lighter indicating sunrise. But thereafter, it remained the same dull shade of gray. The snow picked up, and the air became so cold, even he started to feel the effects of the freezing weather.

He wasn't sure how far Aidan threw him off course. Relying on his Salamander senses, he kept moving North—or at least he hoped it was the right direction. At first, he crossed a wide empty field and entered another frozen forest. After a while the forest opened up into a valley that was mainly rolling hills.

The upward and downward motion made his walk even harder. He climbed the top of the next hill and halted there, breathing hard. As soon as he stopped, snow started to melt around him, soaking his already wet clothes with freezing water, but he ignored the pain and focused on observing the area.

From his elevated position, he could see a narrow dark line

of a forest. He placed his hand over his eyes to protect them from the snowstorm which seemingly was getting heavier and squinted. Just past the forest, he noticed a soft golden gleam. The city wasn't visible yet, but the light that reflected off its golden domes was coloring the horizon in a weak yellowish shade.

"City of Gold," Gunz murmured and shivered. "I'm not ready... God knows I'm not ready..."

With remorse he thought of his friends whom he had left behind, each of them in a desperate, dangerous situation, and he cursed himself and this mission that brought him to this point. He always knew that he would have to face whatever unspeakable evil was hiding behind the walls of this cursed city alone, and he also knew that this mission wouldn't be a walk in the park. Yet he had never expected to stand before the enemy's stronghold, feeling so lonely and miserable.

His friends sacrificed themselves to get him to this point. He couldn't stop now. *"Aidan? Yaroslav?"* he called through their psychic link. There was no answer. *What if—*

"No what ifs," he commanded to himself and started on his way downhill.

After a while, he crossed the valley and entered the forest. The trees stood covered in ice, long thick icicles dangling from their skeletal branches. As a gust of arctic wind rushed through the forest, the icicles jingled like some freakish wind chimes. A few of them broke off and fell down, almost striking him.

"Dammit!" he swore, jumping aside. "Well, that could present a problem."

He wrapped his jacket tighter around himself, raising the collar to protect his face from the icy wind and moved forward as fast as he could muster in the knee-deep melting snow. But no matter how fast he was moving, it wasn't fast enough. Every next gust of wind broke off icicles, sending them flying down as sharp and as fast as any spear. Soon his face and hands were covered in blood and his skin was raw everywhere where the icicles touched him.

Gunz pushed through the forest, counting the moments he had to spend in this icy inferno, when he heard a noise, which sounded unnatural and alarming in the silence of this dead forest. He stilled, sharpening his senses. Now that the snow wasn't squeaking under his feet, he could hear it better.

It was the voice of a woman. She was crying and sobbing as if someone had torn her heart out. Gunz searched the area around but could see nothing, so he moved in the direction of the sound, almost running, if one could call his struggling through the banks of snow a run. Soon, he noticed a dark figure curled up on the top of a tall, snowy hill and sped up toward her.

He halted a few feet below and carefully peeked over the top. The woman didn't appear to be dangerous, but in the Land of Dreams, he couldn't trust his eyes alone. He probed the area around but didn't notice anyone else. She was emitting a light magical energy, but it didn't seem to have a dark signature to it. Even though there was nothing alarming about her, he decided to err on the side of caution. He stepped back to the foot of the hill and placed his hand to his arm over his tattoo.

"Mishka," Gunz called quietly, keeping his eyes on the area where the woman was.

"Why are we whispering?"

A high-pitch whisper, sounding somewhere behind his back, made him flinch and twirl around. His move raised a wave of snow in the air, for a moment obscuring his vision with a sparkling veil. When the snow lowered down, he saw Mishka the wyvern hovering in front of his face, fire dancing in his narrowed eyes.

"Mishka!" he hissed, throwing his hands in the air. "You scared me shitless! You can't creep up on me like that!"

"We, mighty wyverns, don't creep," huffed the wyvern, spitting a tiny fireball at him. "We manifest in a calm and majestic manner."

"Well, maybe mighty wyverns don't creep around, but you do it all the time." Gunz chuckled, shaking his head.

"Prove it!" Mishka whispered hotly. "When did I creep around the last time?"

"Well, let me see," started Gunz, despite the situation he wanted to laugh. "How about that time when you—"

"Enough, enough!" hissed Mishka waving his wings at him vigorously. "You got me this time. You're right!"

"I'm always right."

"Except when you are wrong, which is most of the time." Mishka stuck his tongue out at him, landing on his shoulder, and Gunz had a hard time not to burst out laughing.

"Fine, my friend, I need you to do something for me," he whispered, gently stroking the wyvern's hot wings.

"But of course you do," grumbled Mishka lifting his wings in a shrug. "You never call me for something fun. When it is something fun, you call Aidan or that royal vamp of yours. For me, it is always hard physical labor."

"Sorry, Mishka, I promise, when all this is over, I'll call you for something fun." He winked at the wyvern.

"Volcano diving?"

"Volcano huh?" Gunz stared at the wyvern with his jaw dropped, but this conversation was taking too long and he needed to get things moving. "You got it. Sounds like a blast!"

"I'll believe it when I see it!" Mishka folded his wings on his back and demonstratively turned away from him. But a moment later, he turned back and slapped him on the back of his head with his wing affectionately. "Fine, fine... What do you want?"

"On the top of this hill, there is a woman. Possibly in distress."

"I hear her crying," Mishka murmured into Gunz's ear. "Do you need me to calm her down? Dealing with emotional women is my forte."

"Mishka no," whispered Gunz, impatience boiling up within him. "I need you to do what you do best. Manifest in the calm and majestic manner above her like a mighty wyvern you are—way above her—and let me know what you see. I need you to be my eyes."

Mishka flew off his shoulder, hovering right before his face, staring directly into his eyes. Then he waved his wings and cocked his head. "Are you blind?"

"No, why? Ahh, Mishka, why are you taking everything so literally?" hissed Gunz, rolling his eyes. "It's a figure of speech! Just do it already, would yah?"

Mishka huffed, emitting a small cloud of smoke and vanished. He came back a few seconds later and landed on Gunz's shoulder.

"What a beautiful foxy lady she is. She has a little magic of her own, but it doesn't seem to be dark. I would say, she is absolutely safe to approach," he whispered into his ear. "Since when are you afraid of women, boss?"

"What? I'm not afraid of—"

"Oh, I know," whispered Mishka, a wide dragon-like grin on his face. "It's the fear of rejection, right? Am I right?"

"What? Ahh Mishka, no!" muttered Gunz. "Okay, I got to go and see if I can help her."

"Sure you do," purred Mishka with a sly wink. "Go get her, tiger—um—Salamander."

Gunz was about to respond, but then decided that the safest course of action was to ignore the chatty wyvern and get to business. He turned around and headed uphill.

"Ignoring me, I see?" Mishka whispered into his ear, flying next to his head.

Gunz didn't reply and just shot a burning gaze at the wyvern.

"Jupiter, you are angry, therefor you're wrong!" Mishka concluded triumphantly and a moment later he felt a burning in his tattoo as the wyvern camouflaged himself there.

Fire Almighty, this crazy wyvern is quoting Dostoevsky, thought Gunz as he stepped on top of the hill.

"We, mighty wyverns, are highly educated." He heard Mishka's voice in his head and silently rolled his eyes, leaving his last remark without a response.

Mighty wyvern my ass, thought Gunz and immediately felt an electric shock surging through his body.

He grunted, halting for a moment to deal with the pain. But even this insignificant noise alerted the woman. She gasped, wrapping her arms around her head protectively and her sobs became louder. Gunz approached her and lowered down to one knee.

"My lady, I'm sorry I scared you," he said, trying to sound as friendly as he could muster. "I mean you no harm. I heard you crying, and I wanted to make sure you were okay."

Slowly she lowered her arms, exposing her face. She looked young—no more than twenty years old. She had a pure snow-white complexion, untouched by freckles or blemishes, but what really stood out on her face were her eyes. They had a beautiful golden color, slightly lifted at the outer corners, and they peered at Gunz with curiosity even though a shadow of fear was still imprinted on her tender features.

She wore a large fur hat, made of red fox fur, and with interest, Gunz noticed that the fox's ears were still intact, topping it. Perky flaming-orange curls escaped from under her hat, falling to her chest. She tucked the loose strands of hair under her hat and the corners of her full, coral lips lifted a little in a tentative smile.

Gunz couldn't help but smile back at her. "Hi there... What's your name?" he asked.

"Alisa," she whispered, lowering her eyes, her bright red eyelashes fluttering like the wings of a butterfly, throwing long shadows on her pale cheeks.

"Are you okay, Alisa? Can I help you?"

"I think I may need your help to get home," she replied, sounding hopeful.

"Are you lost?" asked Gunz. They were surrounded by an icy forest and as far as he could see there weren't any populated areas anywhere around.

She looked up and shook her head, a cloud of snowflakes flying off her furry hat. "Oh, no, kind stranger," she said, her eyes getting wider as she spoke. "I'm not lost, but I can't walk. I live just at the edge of this forest, not far from the City of Gold."

She waved her hand in the general direction of the City. Then she pulled her long fur coat apart, demonstrating her small feet adorned in soft fur boots. One of her boots was torn and stained with dark-brown spots of blood.

"I don't even know how it happened," she mumbled, averting her gaze as shame colored her white cheeks in a tender shade of pink. "One moment I was walking home and the next moment, I was down with my foot bleeding." A heavy sob shuddered her shoulders. "Now, I can't make it home and it's getting colder and colder."

Gunz looked in the direction of the City, but from where he stood, he couldn't see the end of the forest.

"How far away is your house from here?" he asked, wondering if he had enough strength to carry her. She seemed to be petite, but he was already at the end of his rope. And between his wet clothes and the constantly falling icicles, which seemed to always find their way under his jacket or to the exposed parts of his skin, the persistent nagging pain was driving him insane.

"Not far at all, my lord," she said, looking back in the direction of her home. "In this weather conditions, maybe"—she gazed heavenward like a person who was calculating something —"less than an hour's walk? Forty minutes?"

An hour... I hope I don't collapse together with her, Gunz thought miserably, offering her his hands.

She took his hand and got up, standing on one foot. Her eyes fell on the cuts and burns on his skin and she gasped, covering her mouth with her other hand. "But you're hurt yourself, my lord!" she exclaimed. "I can't—"

"Yeah, you can," muttered Gunz, lifting her easily. She was smaller than he expected, no more than five feet tall and her fur coat was probably heavier than her body. "It's just small cuts and scrapes. I'll survive." *I hope...*

"Thank you," she said, wrapping her arms around his neck.

Gunz couldn't say how long he'd been walking through the frozen forest, but it felt a lot longer than forty minutes or even an hour. He could hardly move his legs and Alisa didn't seem that light anymore.

"When you said that your house was within a forty minutes' walk, was it a cautiously optimistic estimate?" he muttered, a wave of irritation rising within him as his strength was quickly dwindling down.

She giggled and pointed forward. "We're almost there." The forest ahead was getting lighter and the soft golden glow of the City of Gold was breaking through the veil of snow.

Gunz sighed and forced himself to keep moving, staring at the lighter part of the woods ahead like it was the proverbial light at the end of the tunnel. A little while later, he noticed the dark outline of a house and Alisa murmured into his ear that it was her home. This news gave him a small boost of strength and he headed in the direction of the house, counting the moments when he would be able to relax and take some rest.

With his mind blank and his vision unfocused, he kept walking, listening to the sound of the snow under his feet. After a short while, he noticed that Alisa was humming softly, her voice entwining with the whistling of the wind. She was actually singing, her voice melodious and insinuating, and he sharpened his ears to hear the words of her song. When he was finally able to make out her words, he froze in place, flabbergasted.

"The beaten one is carrying the unbeaten one," she purred, her fingers playing with the hair on the back of his head. "The beaten one is carrying the unbeaten one."

"Are you kidding me!" Gunz yelled, dumping Alisa into the bank of snow. She yelped, struggling to get up but just sunk deeper into the snow, her arms and legs dangling in the air. "All this time I thought you were hurt, but you're nothing but a sneaky, deceiving…" His voice faltered for a split-second as anger took his breath away and he shouted, throwing his hands up, "You are a friggin' fox! Alisa? Lisa Alisa? I hate goddamn Russian fairy tales!"

Mishka snickered in his mind. *"I warned you. I told you she was a FOXY lady,"* he said snidely, making an accent on the word 'foxy'.

"You couldn't have been clearer?" growled Gunz.

"I could," Mishka agreed, tittering, *"but where is the fun in that?"*

"I'll deal with you later, flying rat!"

"Firetwat!"

He grabbed Alisa by the collar of her fur coat and yanked her up to her feet. Fury spiked through him, rising to a precarious level, and despite the lack of elemental energy in the nexus, a weak fire ignited on his shoulders. She watched the flames slowly moving up and down his arms breathlessly and a wide grin split her sly face.

"Yes, I am a fox, a werefox to be precise. And no, I am not

hurt," she purred, her grin getting wider, displaying a set of small sharp teeth. "But I am also a fox who will give food and shelter to the little Fire Salamander who is highly wanted by King Alexander. And I am the only fox who can help you get in and out of the City of Gold unnoticed."

CHAPTER 28

~ ZANE BURNS, A.K.A. GUNZ ~

After the argument with Alisa, Gunz barely made it to the house even though it was within view. The constant pain which the opposing element inflicted upon him drained the remains of his physical strength and he could barely breathe, let alone move. With a guilty look on her face, Alisa provided him with some support, helping him all the way until they reached her home. Possibly she was remorseful about tricking him into carrying her for such a long time, but he doubted that was the case. After all she was a sly, sneaky fox.

As soon as they crossed the threshold and she locked the door, she helped him to sit down at the table and headed into a side room. She came back a few minutes later and offered him a pair of pants and a shirt, telling him some confusing story about her boyfriend. He blinked at her a few times, hardly comprehending what she was saying, not sure that he had enough strength to change. She threw the clothes into his hands and left. Or maybe she was still in the room, but he could no longer see her.

A moment later, he felt her tugging at his shirt, and he had no strength to object. Feeling drowsy and lethargic, Gunz moved his arms, allowing her to take the shirt off and put a dry one on. Like through a veil of fog, he saw Alisa kneeling before him, pulling his boots off. He didn't feel comfortable with that, but he didn't think he could even move, let alone stop her from doing it. But when she got up and leaned forward to take his pants off, he grabbed her hands. With shock he realized that he was so weak that he couldn't wrap his fingers around her wrists.

"Alisa, please," he mumbled faintly. "This is something I should do myself."

She giggled, covering her mouth like a young innocent girl, and waved her hand dismissively. "Go on. Don't let me stop you." Then she put her hands on her hips and stared at him, mischievous twinkles playing in her gold eyes.

"Privacy? Please?" asked Gunz, heat creeping up his cheeks under her unwavering gaze.

She laughed but turned around and disappeared behind one of the side doors. With unbending fingers, Gunz unbuttoned his cargo pants and moved the zipper down. The cold, wet fabric seemed to be glued to his legs and as he pulled it off, he felt as if he was pealing his skin off. Once he finally changed, he moved the Swiss army knife and the box with the ring into the pocket of his new pants.

"Are you hungry?"

Gunz heard Alisa's voice from behind the door and shook his head no. He didn't feel hungry, too tired to think about anything except sleep. He dropped onto the chair and folded his arms on the table, resting his forehead atop his arms.

"By the way, I can't hear you shaking your head while I am in the other room," said Alisa, gently nudging him on his shoulder. "You have to speak up, dear."

"Then how did you know that I shook my head?" asked Gunz as he sat up, a tired lopsided grin making a quick appearance on his face.

"Well, you can't blame a girl for wanting to have a little entertainment," she replied, giggling, her sly eyes crinkling at the corners. "Besides, you do have something to show, so no reason to be so shy." She wagged her eyebrows at him, suggestively.

Gunz grunted, his ears burning, and that made Alisa laugh out loud. "Okay, my savior, let me show you to your bed."

"Please tell me you have more than one bed in your house," said Gunz, shifting uncomfortably, squeezing his wet clothes in his hands.

"Why?" she asked, a suppressed laughter ringing in her voice. "Are you afraid that I'm going to take advantage of your vulnerable state?"

"Something like that," muttered Gunz.

She chuckled, shaking her head. "I don't think you can perform in your condition, sweetie, and I don't accept half-assmanship in bed." She winked at him and pointed at the open door on his right. "Your virginity is safe with me. Sweet dreams, loverboy."

* * *

Gunz lay down on the bed and inhaled the scent of freshly washed linen. His eyes started to close of their own accord, but he forced himself to remain awake for another few minutes.

"Mishka..." he called, tapping on his tattoo. "I need—"

"You need my help. Tell me something I didn't know," grumbled the wyvern, materializing above him.

"Mishka, please..." Gunz whispered with an exasperated sigh. "I have no strength for another verbal duel with you. I need to get some sleep and to do it, I must put Mrak's ring on. Can you stay with me while I am asleep?"

"Are you afraid of the dark, little Salamander?" asked

Mishka, making large round eyes at him. "Is there a monster in your closet?"

"The only monster in my closet is you, my friend," muttered Gunz with a faint smile. "I don't cheat on you with other monsters."

He pulled the ring out of the box and slipped it on his finger. The room spun around him, his body convulsed, and he almost fell off the narrow bed. He choked, unable to breathe in, and clutched at his throat, tears of pain in his bloodshot eyes. Once the aftershocks were over, he turned on his back, folded his hands on his stomach, and finally relaxed.

Like through a veil, he felt Mishka landing on his chest and sighed with relief as the wyvern shared some of his elemental fire with him. "Thank you, my friend," he whispered—or he thought he did—allowing the peaceful oblivion to embrace him.

* * *

Gunz woke up from the sound of laughter and sat up on the bed, trying to recall everything that happened yesterday. His memory obediently presented him with the grim recount of his current situation, and the atmosphere of amusement in the other room felt painfully inappropriate.

"Aidan? Yaroslav?" he called in his mind and bowed his head hopelessly when he received no answer.

Rubbing his unshaved cheeks with his hands, he glanced at the window, adorned with pretty light curtains. It was probably morning, but he couldn't be sure since the dull gray sky outside looked pretty much the same every hour of the day. He stared down at the ring on his finger and pulled it off, squeezing the metal headboard of the bed to stop himself from screaming.

Gunz placed the ring in the box and put it in his pocket, just now noticing that his own clothes were gone. He got up, wondering if the werefox managed to sneak into his room while he was asleep and what Mishka had been doing when it happened.

But once he walked into the living room, his question was answered. Alisa was setting the table up with Mishka riding on her shoulder, holding a piece of toast in his paw. Gunz halted by the door and cleared his throat. Alisa twirled around and the corners of her mouth lifted just a little.

"Good morning, dear," she said, gesturing at an empty chair, inviting him to sit down. "I pray you slept well?"

"Yes, thank you," he answered uncomfortably, sitting down.

"That's good," murmured Alisa, placing a plate with a couple of sandwiches in front of him. "Then eat quickly. It's already past noon, and I believe you still want to visit the City of Gold today, am I right?"

"Past noon?" asked Gunz flabbergasted. She was talking about going to the City of Gold like it was an afternoon stroll on the beach.

Alisa nodded, moving a glass with water closer to him. "Yesterday you looked slightly off, so I didn't want to wake you up," she explained.

"Slightly," huffed Mishka, almost choking on his toast.

"Traitor," muttered Gunz, biting into his sandwich.

By the time he finished his meal, Alisa came back with his clothes. Everything was clean and dry, and he noticed that she even patched his shirt in a few places where it was torn.

"Here you go," she said, placing everything on the chair next to him, "but if you don't want to be spotted by the king's guards as soon as you pass the gates, I suggest you wear something else."

"What do you propose I wear?" asked Gunz dryly. "Sorry, but my luggage didn't make it through the portal."

Alisa rolled her eyes and petted Mishka's back. "How do you live with this asshat, Mishka?" she asked.

Mishka tittered, waving his wing at Gunz, but then flew up

and landed on his shoulder, pressing his hot head to Gunz's cheek. "Yeah, he is a firetwat, most of the time, but he is my firetwat," he said affectionately. "Besides, Kal woulds kill me if I let anything happen to him."

Gunz sat at the table, listening to Alisa and Mishka cracking jokes on him, and smiled absentmindedly, his thoughts far removed from here. In this tiny house, hidden in the icy forest, it felt as though there was no demonic invasion or a brewing war. Everything was calm and peaceful. Yet inside, he was stretched to the limit, all the unknowns coiling within him like a bunch of snakes, poisoning his mind with dread and fear.

* * *

When they made it to the City of Gold, the sun had already gone down, submerging everything under the heavy cloak of darkness. The temperature dropped significantly, and the city walls were glistening with a thin layer of ice. Despite the cold weather, the snow kept falling without stop, adding to the already large snowbanks by the wall.

Gunz looked up at the white walls disappearing into the dark sky, wondering how Alisa was planning to get him inside this fortress unnoticed. There was only one entry—the main gates—and from where they were, he counted at least four guards standing there.

"Now what?" he asked quietly.

She arched her eyebrow at him, smiling with superiority. "Leave it to me, dear. Am I a fox or not?" She winked at him and added, "All you have to do is keep your mouth shut and your energy signature under control."

She adjusted her foxy hat and swayed her way toward the gates. With his heart thundering in his chest, Gunz followed her. Just as they reached the entrance, two guards stepped forward, blocking their way in. Both were tall and massive, and

Gunz had no doubt that both had considerable bulk hidden under their winter coats.

Carefully suppressing his own energy signature, he scanned the guards with his Salamander senses. He wasn't surprised to find out that all the guards were something other than human, but with his magic suppressed to a minimum, it was hard to figure out what they were exactly.

"Hello, boys," purred Alisa, fluttering her long eyelashes at them. "What are you doing here so late and in such despicable weather? Don't you have some warm bed waiting for you at home?"

"Hi Alisa," said one of the guards, stepping forward to give her a hug that lasted a touch too long to be appropriate. "King Alexander is getting a little paranoid. He's expecting some Fire Salamander to show up here any day, and he wants all guards at the highest alert." He huffed, shaking the snow off his shoulders. "I didn't know there was a Fire Salamander other than Kal, and I don't see the Fire Elemental wandering around this kingdom of snow and ice. From what I've heard, all Children of Fire are intolerant to this kind of weather."

"True that," confirmed Alisa, nodding her head. "Why does he need this Salamander, anyway?"

"Hell if I know... or care," said the guard with a shrug. "Our orders are simple—if this Salamander shows up here, we're to deliver him straight to the king himself. Restrained, if possible."

"Yeah, whatever," replied Alisa with a blazing smile. "I just want to visit my grandma."

The guard nodded, his eyes darting to Gunz and then back to the fox. "And who is this fellow with you? I don't recall seeing him before."

"Who? Him?" asked Alisa, slipping a quick glance back at Gunz. "Oh, he's nothing to worry about. He's my new—you know..." She winked at the guard suggestively and giggled, her cheeks flushed.

The guards stared at Gunz with narrowed eyes and he smiled at them sheepishly, inwardly thanking Alisa for giving him a giant fur hat, gloves and a long coat to wear. If not for these heavy winter clothes, every little snowflake would leave a red spot on his skin, putting on display the reaction he has to cold water.

"This one seems a little smaller than the previous one," muttered the guard. "Are you lowering your standards, Alisa?"

"No, I am not," Alisa objected, her hands on her hips. "The height is not the most important measurement when it comes to a man." She arched her eyebrow at the guard and grabbed Gunz's hand, pulling him inside the city. "Sorry, boys, but my grandma is expecting me. I'll stop by on the way out."

Followed by laugher and the slimy jokes of the guards, they passed through the gates and walked away, following the main city street. Wide and well-lit by multiple torches, it led toward a giant palace. Even from this distance, Gunz could see the massive golden domes topping the towers, a chain of tall columns upfront, and large stained-glass windows.

Alisa took a side road, avoiding the palace, and once they were far enough, she halted and glanced around. The street was empty, but it didn't mean that one of the king's loyal subjects wasn't hiding behind curtains in one of the houses. Grabbing Gunz's arms, she turned him to face her and placed her hands on his shoulders.

"Where did you want to go, dear?" she asked, gazing up at him.

"I don't know," he answered after a short pause. "I have no idea, Alisa. I just know that I can't allow myself to be captured and I still have no information about what exactly is going on in this place."

"I see," she murmured softly, all humor gone from her golden eyes. "I think we should visit my grandma after all. Who knows? She may have some information for us."

"Is she also a fox?" asked Gunz.

"A werefox, thank you very much," replied Alisa.

"Okay, I guess we're going to see your grandma, Little Red Riding Hood," he agreed with a smirk.

She chuckled, rising on her tiptoes. "What big eyes you have," she purred. Then she grabbed the sides of his fur hat, pulling him down, and pressed her lips against his.

Gunz stiffened, his arms dangling along his body, not sure what to do. Luckily, she let go of him quickly and a slightly drunken smile appeared on her face. "Yum, not bad for a little firetwat," she said, showing him the tip of her tongue.

"What was that?" Gunz growled, brushing his hand over his lips.

"That was a free show to all the king's spies that were watching us through these windows." She waved her hand at the dark houses and headed down the street.

Definitely a Russian fairy tale—the farther I go, the scarier it becomes... he thought as he followed the fox to her grandmother's house.

CHAPTER 29

~ ZANE BURNS, A.K.A. GUNZ ~

Alisa's grandma opened the door and ushered them in without saying a word. Once they were inside, the elderly lady peeked outside and locked it. She turned around, tucking a strand of her long gray hair behind her ear and gave Gunz a quick once-over, pursing her lips. Her perceptive eyes explored him from head to toe and she sighed, switching attention to her granddaughter.

"I should have known," she said with reproach. "As soon as the king announced the manhunt... I should have known that the Fire Salamander would end up on my doorstep with you, Alisa."

"Come on, Grandma," Alisa whined, but then giggled and threw her arms around her neck. A second later she pulled away and addressed Gunz, "This is my grandmother, Elizaveta."

A warm smile graced Elizaveta's face as the older fox embraced her granddaughter. Gunz observed them, noticing the family resemblance. She looked like an older version of Alisa and even though her long hair was no longer copper, and her golden eyes had paled with time, she still managed to keep this playful, happy-go-lucky vibe about her that reminded him of Alisa so much.

"Well, I guess I'm stuck with you, boy," she said to Gunz, patting him on his shoulder. "What's your real name, Salamander?"

"Gunz," he replied, just now realizing that he had never given his name to Alisa. "I'm sorry for the intrusion. I was just wondering if you knew anything about—"

"You wish to know why the king wants you," Grandma finished his sentence. "Of course you do." She walked inside a small room and sat down on an old sofa, motioning at the two chairs in front of her. "I hope my granddaughter at least fed you, Salamander. Or did she toss you into her bed as soon as you crossed her threshold?"

"No, my lady," replied Gunz with a light bow. "Your granddaughter has been quite hospitable."

"Sure, she is." The old lady stared at him for a moment and giggled not unlike Alisa. "How old are, boy? You still remember how to blush and get shy."

Gunz didn't reply but a shy lopsided smile tugged at his lips as his hand went up to his flushed cheek automatically.

"To be fair, Grandma, when I found him in the forest behind my house, he wasn't much of a lover," said Alisa, flopping into a chair. "A bloody mess—that's what he was."

Elizaveta shook her head slightly, frowning. "I can imagine. A Child of Fire in this kind of weather? You got to be in constant pain, Gunz, are you not?"

"Yes, my lady," Gunz replied, shifting in his chair under her exploring gaze.

"Uh-huh," mumbled the old fox. She picked up her yarn and knitting needles and started knitting as if her granddaughter and Gunz weren't in the room.

Gunz glanced at Alisa and she just gave him a half-shrug.

"Grandma," called Alisa. She leaned forward and tapped the old lady on her knee. "Is there anything you want to tell us?"

The grandmother kept knitting without taking her eyes off her work.

"There isn't much I can tell you, Gunz," she said at length. "But there was one thing I overheard when the king's personal guards were gossiping in the tavern. Drunk bastards. One guard said the king needs the Fire Salamander to retrieve something for him." She made a meaningful pause, raising her eyes to see the reaction her words produced on her listener. Then she gave Gunz an arched stare and continued, "That's right. The guard said that whatever this object is, only the Fire Salamander can survive the quest and deliver it to the king."

"Must be something related to fire," Gunz mused, nibbling on his lip as he shuffled all possible explanations in his mind. "I can't think of anything else."

The old fox stopped knitting, putting the yarn and needles on the couch next to her. "Like I said, you're just a boy, Gunz. Brave and selfless, but still just a boy—inexperienced in the way of the darkness. Whereas King Alexander speaks 'evil' fluently. You should stay as far away from him as possible."

"So I've heard," Gunz muttered, rubbing his forehead tiredly as his chest tightened with worry. "What could it be? Outside being able to control the fire, what can a Fire Salamander do that any powerful wizard cannot?"

Elizaveta smiled at him, tiredness imprinted in the deep wrinkles around her eyes, and got up. Gently, she patted him on his cheek and sighed.

"You can survive, child," she said. "You're an immortal Fire Salamander. *Immortal* is the keyword here. No matter how perilous this quest is, you can't die."

"Who wants to live forever," whispered Gunz, rubbing his knuckles with his thumb. He cringed inwardly as his memory presented his last conversation with Zmey. "Even if I can retrieve whatever it is he wants, how can he guarantee that I'll deliver it to him? I am not stupid—"

He cut himself off as the words of Rasputin's letter materialized in his mind. *"You good folks are all so predictable. It is your desire to always do the right thing that makes you predictable in the first place. It makes you weak and vulnerable to those who are willing to go the extra mile and explore other opportunities, outside the boundaries of the so called good and evil."*

"No..." Gunz whispered, perspiration beading his forehead.

"I see you're grasping the reality," said the old fox. "I don't know what it is, so don't bother asking, but I am sure our good king has a surprise for you. And not the kind you're going to like."

"I'm sure he does," agreed Gunz, suddenly feeling the winter chill inside the cozy house, warmed up by the fire in a small fireplace.

Grandma got up and walked to the window. Lifting the curtain, she peeked outside and turned around. "Alisa, I think you both should go back to your house now," she said. "As much as your friend is trying to suppress his energy signature, I can read it bright and clear."

Gunz raised his eyebrows, throwing a guilty look at the old fox, and shrugged. There was nothing he could do aside of what he was doing already. His magic and elemental powers were limited, and constantly suppressing his powerful energy signature was taking a lot of work and strength.

"I understand," continued Grandma with a light wave of her hand. "Not your fault. But if I can sense it with ease, so can the king's wizards. You shouldn't stay within the city walls, if you don't want to be discovered that is."

Both Gunz and Alisa got up and headed toward the door, but as they were ready to step outside, the old lady stopped them.

"Alisa," she said in a hushed voice, "don't use the main gates.

Go around the palace and use the small exit by the creek. The guard who stands by the door knows both of us well." She gave Alisa a small package neatly wrapped into yellow parchment. "Give this package to him and he'll let you out of the city quietly."

Elizaveta turned to Gunz, both hope and fear gleaming in her pale eyes.

"Child of Fire," she whispered, her wrinkled hand caressing his shoulder, "you truly are our only hope. Magic is dying, and I don't think anyone else is coming to help." She glanced at the empty street over his shoulder and sighed. "Be careful, boy…" She took a deep breath and added in a low growl as anger transformed her kind features, "Do what comes natural to you. Burn them to ashes, Salamander!"

Gunz nodded, unable to say anything as a thick lump stuck in his throat. Alisa gave a quick hug to her grandmother and they both walked outside.

Following the old lady's advice, they walked toward the palace. Alisa knew the city well, so they were weaving in and out of small streets, avoiding the main, well-lit road and unwanted attention. Soon they circled around the building, following the tiny path barely visible under the blanket of snow.

The grandeur and glory of the palace was slightly diminished by the thick white layer that partially concealed some details of architecture as well as golden embellishments and ornaments. But for some unexplainable reason, its golden domes and cupolas remained uncovered, shining dimly with a soft yellow-orange glow.

As they approached the last tower, the weak presence of a familiar energy signature touched Gunz's sharp senses. Putting his hand on Alisa's shoulder, he came to a sharp halt and surveyed the area. As he closed his eyes and focused on the sensation, a deep shudder ran through him, making him squeeze Alisa's shoulder tighter. The energy signature—the perfect blend of darkness and light, the mix of heavenly power with underworldly strength—he knew it well, but he hadn't sensed it for such a long time.

"Alisa," he whispered, his voice hoarse and shaky, "what is this tower?"

She glanced up at the golden dome and shrugged, her eyes widened. "I don't know," she mumbled. "Just another wing of this shit-palace—" Suddenly she fell silent as understanding dawned on her. Her little mouth shaped the letter 'O' and her eyes widened. "It's not the tower. It's what's under it—the dungeons."

"The dungeons," echoed Gunz, "of course, it makes sense. At least some of it."

"What are you talking about?" asked Alisa, pulling Gunz forward. "Gunz, we can't just stand here. We should keep moving."

"Yes, let's go," he muttered under his breath absently. *Tessa, oh God... this is why Aidan couldn't find you anywhere. But he should have sensed you before the nexus was sealed... I don't understand. And how did you end up imprisoned in this city in the first place?*

With his thoughts on Tessa's mysterious situation, Gunz didn't notice how they reached a small door in the wall surrounding the city. Alisa gave the package to a young guard, chatting animatedly with him. Then she hugged him, kissing him on his cheek, and he let them out of the city without asking any questions.

As they left the City of Gold behind, the snow intensified even more, but luckily their walk to Alisa's house wasn't long enough for Gunz to start feeling the assault of the opposing elements. Walking inside, he took his coat and hat off, hanging everything on the coat rack, and dropped onto the chair, stretching his legs in front of him.

His thoughts circled back to the city dungeons. He was positive that it was Tessa's energy signature, but he had no idea what to do to help her. Alisa's grandma was right—King Alexander had a surprise for him. The evil monarch wouldn't hesitate to blackmail him, holding Tessa's life over his head, to ensure his compliance and fast return with the mysterious item he needed Gunz to retrieve.

He didn't know what this item was, but it couldn't be anything good. How could it, if an evil king and a dark spirit desired it so much that they went through all this trouble just to force him into the position he was in right now. He thought back to the night in the Otherworld when all of them had gathered to discuss the situation. The main mission hadn't changed —he still had to find out who stood behind this demonic invasion and eliminate them, but now it had also become deeply personal for him.

Chernobog held Mrak's safety in his hands, forcing Gunz to go to the City of Gold. And what bothered him the most was that the god of Destruction wanted him to meet with the king immediately, without giving him any time to learn anything about the king's intentions and get ready. The Slavic deity didn't care if Gunz would be enslaved by the king as long as he went there.

Now, the situation had gotten worse tenfold. Cornered by Chernobog on one side and by King Alexander on the other, he wasn't sure how to proceed. But one thing was clear to him though—he couldn't let the king harm Tessa and he couldn't deliver the magical artifact to him either. And most of all, he couldn't allow himself to get enslaved. Never again.

On top of it, he had disobeyed Chernobog's command and now he didn't know how that would affect Mrak and him for that matter. Gunz threw his head back, squeezing it with his hands and a painful growl escaped his lips.

"Aidan, I wish you were here," he whispered, lowering his arms as exhaustion settled in his muscles. *"I found your Tessa, my friend... Where are you?"* His mind subconsciously reached out to his friend through their psychic link.

"Zane..." He heard Aidan's voice in his mind and almost fell off the chair.

CHAPTER 30

~ ZANE BURNS, A.K.A. GUNZ ~

"Aidan!" Gunz yelled and jolted to his feet, knocking the chair down.

For a moment he forgot that Aidan couldn't hear him unless he used their psychic link. Alisa rushed into the living room and froze in the doorway, staring at him puzzled.

"It's okay, sorry," he mumbled, raising his hand to stop her from asking any questions. He picked up the chair and sat down, closing his eyes and focusing on his connection with his friend.

"Aidan, you're alive... and still in the nexus," he said, happiness warming him up from inside.

"Of course I'm alive. I'm a god after all," replied Aidan with a light chuckle. *"You said something about Tessa?"*

Gunz noticed the fluctuation in his friend's voice, concern and anticipation overshadowing everything else. He frowned, slamming his hand on the table, fully realizing how Aidan must have felt when he mentioned Tessa's name.

"Aidan—," Gunz started but cut himself off, not sure how to deliver the news.

"Spill it, Salamander," Aidan's voice growled in his mind. "Stop squirming and tell me straight. What's going on?"

In a few words Gunz told Aidan everything that had happened to him from the moment they got separated and everything that he learned from Alisa's grandmother. He also shared his concerns about the possible intentions of the king. For a few long seconds, Aidan remained silent.

"So—" Aidan paused as if he needed to take a breath and then continued. "So, what are you planning to do?"

"What do you think I am going to do?" asked Gunz calmly, making an effort to keep his emotions under control.

When Aidan didn't reply, Gunz rested his elbows on the table and hid his face in his hands, his mind blank. There was nothing to think about—he had to get Tessa out of the City of Gold and back to safety. He would never wish for anyone to suffer the pain he'd been going through since he lost Angelique. He wouldn't wish that kind of torture on his enemy, let alone his friend. Besides that, he couldn't allow King Alexander to push him into a corner, using Tessa as leverage.

"I am going to save Tessa, man. What did you think? I'll do whatever it takes to get her back to you."

He lowered his arms and saw Alisa standing in front of him, her narrowed eyes burning holes in him. He raised his finger to his lips, silently asking for a few more minutes. She pulled a chair out and sat down across from him, folding her hands on her lap.

"Zane, I can't ask this of you. Too dangerous," said Aidan, but their psychic link carried through the wave of fear and despair he felt.

Without saying it, his friend was pleading for the safety of the woman he loved, and Gunz couldn't blame him.

"I didn't hear you asking anything of me." Gunz raised his eyes at Alisa, thousands of thoughts flashing through his mind, and clenched his jaw. "I will get Tessa to safety, Aidan," he said, fury blazing through him. *"And then I will kill them all. I'll wipe them off the face of this Earth. I swear on my goddamn power!"*

"Whoa! Hold your horses. Both of you." Gunz heard Yaroslav's voice and couldn't help but smile, feeling relieved. *"Zane, you are not going anywhere alone. Tell us where you are, and we'll be there as soon as we can. And all this 'kill them all' business... It's not you, my friend. Your anger is talking, and to deal with someone like King Alexander and whoever is behind him, you must have a cold mind."*

"We, Fire Salamanders, don't do well with cold."

Gunz chuckled, but then leaned back in his chair, folding his arms over his chest, and bit his lip. Yaroslav was right. He was angry. No, what he felt right now was far beyond anger or even fury. But he didn't believe that the anger was clouding his judgement. On the contrary, his mind was clear and alert.

"Listen, Slavik—," he started to say and fell silent.

A sharp pain struck him, making him stiffen. He opened his mouth, struggling to breathe in, and his arms went up of their own accord. He squeezed his head with his hands and fell to the side, crashing to the floor. His body curved into a ball and he screamed, no longer able to tolerate the pain.

Alisa was next to him almost immediately. He saw her terrified eyes, her lips moving, but couldn't hear anything as the pain in his head intensified. Somewhere in the back of his mind, he heard Aidan and Yaroslav asking him if he was okay, and he focused on the sound of their voices.

A moment later, the pain subsided, turning into a continuous pulling sensation in his head, and he finally recognized what it was.

"A summoning call," he breathed out, turning to his back. "Someone is summoning me, and they're not gentle about it." He dropped his arms alongside his body and a pained uneven smirk curved his lips.

"Zane? Are you okay?" A wave of concern Aidan experienced engulfed him through their connection.

"*Alive,*" replied Gunz.

"Who's summoning you?" asked Alisa, mortified.

"Not sure," croaked Gunz, struggling to sit up. "But I might have an idea."

"I hope you do!" A loud voice boomed through the house and Alisa flinched, hopping to her feet, staring around frantically.

"You broke our agreement, Salamander," the Voice thundered, and the walls of Alisa's house trembled.

"I don't remember us agreeing on anything, dumbass," muttered Gunz, rising with a low grunt.

"Allow me to refresh your memory," said the Voice snidely.

A strike of pain crippled Gunz. He wrapped his arms around his head and dropped to his knees, bending forward. "Stop... the summoning call..." he panted, tears of pain gathering in his bloodshot eyes.

"You were supposed to come to the City of Gold within ten days," the Voice shouted, but the summoning call softened. Gunz still had a terrible headache, but at least he could breathe again.

"I believe I have four days left," replied Gunz, sitting up.

"No, you do not," objected the voice icily. "The deal was—you come to me alone and I will spare your world. ALONE! You disobeyed me by coming here with a god, an old vampire and a witch. Now, our original deal is no more, but there is something I wanted to show you. A little motivational message, so to speak."

"Show me how?" asked Gunz, but before the question escaped his lips, he already knew the answer.

"Open your mind, Salamander," ordered the Voice.

Gunz cringed inwardly at the memory of this very same command he received just a few weeks ago from a man who held him captive back in California. Feeling a light touch to his mind from the outside, he suppressed the desire to fight it and sat down on the floor, closing his eyes. Somewhere in the back of his mind, his friends were shouting something, worried about him. They couldn't hear the Voice, but they could feel his emotions. *"It's that demonic jackass, and he wants to show me a vision,"* he told them before forcing their voices out of his mind, and whispered, "Go ahead..."

A blinding light exploded in his head, adding to the nagging pain of the summoning call. His fingers clenched into tight fists and with a low guttural growl, he threw his head back, opening his mind to his enemy.

As the light dwindled down, he found himself falling into an endless vortex. His fall, slow at the beginning, gradually increased in speed and even though he knew it was just a vision, his chest tightened with fear and perspiration covered his forehead. He forced himself to calm down and keep his mind open. *It's just a vision.*

His fall stopped as abruptly as it began, and Gunz exhaled, taking in his surroundings. As his eyes adjusted to the darkness, he realized that he was standing in the middle of a cell or a dungeon—a tiny space with no windows. He twirled around and froze, horror chilling his blood. At the other end of the room, in a corner, he saw Tessa.

She sat on a concrete floor, with her eyes closed and her head tilted to the side slightly, seemingly asleep. Her long dark hair fell over her colorless face in long matted strands. Her hands, covered in multiple layers of dirt, rested in her lap, and her clothes were torn and disgustingly filthy.

She didn't have any restraints on her, but when Gunz lifted his eyes, he gasped and staggered back, his steps unsteady. The ceiling of the room was decorated by a half-faded pentagram and a large gray stone was embedded into each point of the star. This size gray stones could drain anyone with magic to a nearly comatose condition.

This is why Aidan couldn't sense you...

In this matchbox of a cell, helpless and miserable, she looked smaller than he remembered her. Anger and pain swirled through Gunz at seeing her like this, making him tremble from head to toe.

"Tessa," he moaned, his hands balling into fists. Forgetting that it was just a vision, he rushed to her and raised his arm to brush her hair off her face, but his fingers slid through the image. *Tessa, oh God... What did they do to you? Please look at me, say something...*

Gunz didn't hear Aidan's scream, but he sensed his pain with every fiber of his being. A raw anguish the likes of which he had never felt before enveloped him, sending his own world into a swirling tornado of pain so severe that he almost blacked out. He grunted, falling to all fours, breathing strenuously, and his stomach clenched as he realized that he projected his last words through their psychic link and Aidan heard everything he thought.

A split-second later, the vision was gone, and he found Alisa sitting next to him, gently stroking his back. He lowered his face into his hands, almost touching the floor with his forehead and moaned softly.

"I see you enjoyed my little presentation." The Voice cackled with malice. "Do you feel yourself properly motivated to renegotiate our deal?"

"Zane, what did you see? Tessa... is she..." said Aidan, sounding barely above a whisper. *"Please tell me she is alive... Please tell me you—"*

"She's alive, Aidan," replied Gunz, trying to pull himself together, but with Aidan projecting his turmoiled emotions, he couldn't do it. His power responded to his condition and a weak wave of elemental fire slowly rose within him. *"Please try to calm down. I need to be able to think clearly... and your—well, I need you to calm down."*

He got up to his feet and clasped his hands behind his back

to stop them from shaking. Taking a deep breath, he suppressed the elemental fire within him, regaining his composure.

"What the hell do you want from me?" Gunz growled, addressing the Voice.

"You will leave right now and go to the City of Gold," commanded the Voice with the authority worthy of a king. "You will go through the main gates where my guards are expecting you already. You will allow them to restrain you and deliver you to the Throne room of my palace. The rest you will find out when you get there."

"Your palace?" Gunz smirked humorously. "I assume I am speaking with King Alexander?"

The king grunted, probably realizing his mistake. "It doesn't matter," he replied arrogantly. "You will do as I command, Salamander."

"I will come to the City of Gold as you requested, that's fine," Gunz replied calmly, slightly shaking his head. "But there will be no restraints of any kind."

The king cackled. "You are not in a position to bargain, Salamander. You will obey me, or your little friend will suffer the consequences."

Gunz folded his arms over his chest and cocked his head. "No, she will not," he objected firmly. "You touch one hair on her head, and I will destroy you."

A heavy silence enveloped the room and Gunz could hear the wind howling outside the house.

"I admire your resolve and courage, Salamander," a different voice replied after a while with tones of respect. This voice was a lot deeper and sounded stronger, and Gunz wondered if it belonged to the main person behind this demonic mess. "But you truly are not in the position to bargain. My one word can send your entire world back into the stone age, consumed by chaos. Your friends from Kendral and the Otherworld can't stop me. You know it's not a bluff.

You are the only one who can save Therasia and save your world."

Gunz propped his hands on the table, leaning forward, and bowed his head to his chest. His thoughts went back to his world, and he wondered if Jim, Akira and Mrak were able to keep the chaos from rising.

Save Therasia, save the world, he thought angrily. There was no saving the world if this evil incarnate would get his hands on a powerful magical artifact.

Feeling cornered, he slammed his hand on the table and straightened. "I will come to the City of Gold," he said quietly. "You don't need to restrain me. I will comply with your demands willingly."

"Fine," replied the second voice and the ease with which he agreed set Gunz on edge more than if he would keep arguing. "Come immediately and you'll continue the conversation with King Alexander in person. His guards will escort you to the Throne room."

The headache disappeared and Gunz collapsed into a chair, cold sweat running down his face and back.

"Zane, what happened?" asked Aidan.

"I'm going to the City of Gold now," he replied flatly. "I can't wait for you and Yaroslav to arrive. Tessa's life is at stake. I can't..." He trailed off and got up, wiping the sweat off his forehead with the back of his head. *"Don't worry, I'll take care of Tessa. Where are you now, do you know?"*

"At the other end of the nexus," replied Yaroslav. "A small village next to the City of Copper."

"Good," said Gunz. "Stay there. Don't come here. I'll find you when it's all over."

"But, Zane, you'll be alone," started Yaroslav. "I'm a powerful vampire, Aidan is a god, and Peyton is a witch. We could help—"

"No," Gunz cut him off. "Chernobog and King Alexander are already blackmailing me, and I don't need your wellbeing used against *me on top of that. Stay where you are. I'll get in touch as soon as I can."*

He closed his eyes and focused on the psychic link, blocking their connection. He needed a few minutes of peace to get his thoughts in order. As he opened his eyes again, he saw Alisa. She was sitting across the table from him, patiently waiting for him to say something.

He smiled at her tiredly. "Alisa, I have to leave now." She tried to say something, but Gunz shook his head stopping her. "You've heard the demon. I have no choice. But I was wondering if you could help me with something."

"Anything," she whispered, tears gathering in her golden eyes.

As Gunz started explaining what he wanted her to do, she was staring at him with her mouth open, shock imprinted on her pretty face, but once he finished, she just nodded.

"I'll do everything I can," she promised, walking him to the door. "Be careful, Gunz. Like my grandma said, you're our last hope."

Yeah, right... How am I supposed to fight with my hands tied behind my back?

CHAPTER 31

~ ZANE BURNS, A.K.A. GUNZ ~

The dull gray sky got slightly lighter, a sure indication of sunrise in the demonic Land of Dreams, when Gunz stopped at the top of a hill, a short distance away from the city wall, observing the gates. From his position, he counted at least ten guards as opposed to the four he had seen earlier this night. King Alexander wasn't taking any chances. But neither was he.

He walked down the slope and headed toward the back side of the palace. Stopping in the shadows beneath the wall, he placed his arm over the tattoo.

"Mishka," he called in a soft whisper.

The wyvern materialized in front of him with a light pop. He looked around and landed on Gunz's shoulder.

"Let me guess," he whispered, rubbing his head against Gunz's cheek like a regular house cat. "You are planning to do something dangerous and stupid and you want me to leave."

Gunz leaned his back against the rough stones of the wall and smiled. "You know me well, my friend."

"I wish I could say the same about you," huffed the wyvern with an exaggerated roll of his flaming eyes. "I'm not going anywhere, doofus. If I leave you, who is going to think? Between the two of us, I've got all the best parts—the looks and the brains."

Gunz pressed his hand over his mouth to stop himself from laughing. "Oh really? And what exactly do I have then?"

"Hmm," Mishka hummed, rising in the air, and gave Gunz a quick once-over. "It is a tough question... I don't even know... not much here... or there..." He moved his wings as if he was measuring him. "Well, you definitely have a great personality. But you shouldn't be asking me. Ask women. They seem to like you—I have no idea what they find in you."

"Um, thank you?" muttered Gunz, smirking, but then sobered up. "Mishka, I am about to walk into a trap and there is no way I can avoid whatever is coming. So I have no choice, but you do."

"No, I don't," replied Mishka and Gunz did a double-take. He had never seen the wyvern so serious before. "Didn't you get it by now, Salamander? I'm with you, no matter what." Then he winked at him, a dragon-like grin spreading on his face, and added, "You're hopeless without me, firetwat."

Before Gunz could say anything, the wyvern disappeared, and he felt a light burning in his arm as Mishka morphed back into his tattoo. Swallowing the thick lump in his throat, Gunz channeled some of his fire energy. As the bright flames ignited at the bottom of his eyes, he turned toward the wall and knocked on the small hidden door. The guard opened almost immediately and stilled, gaping at Gunz with his mouth open.

"King Alexander is expecting me," said Gunz, observing the young guard's reaction with a light smirk. "Please show me the way to the Throne room."

"You are—," mumbled the guard, struggling for words.

"The Fire Salamander," Gunz supplied helpfully, his smile growing wider as the guard's eyes grew rounder. "I believe I'm highly wanted by your king, am I not?"

"Yes, my lord," replied the guard, gradually coming back to

his senses. "But His Majesty ordered—" The young man cut himself off, staring awkwardly at his hands in thick winter gloves.

"To have me restrained," Gunz finished the statement without hiding the sarcasm in his voice. "Yeah... no. Not gonna happen."

"But my lord—," mumbled the guard, shifting from foot to foot.

Gunz gazed heavenward, pursing his lips. "Just take me to your king, would yah?" he said peacefully. "You seem to be a nice man, so please don't put me in a position where I'll be forced to hurt you." He redirected his fire to his hand and a weak flame ignited on the tip of his thumb. The guard gasped, cowering back.

Gunz smirked, giving him an arched stare. "So, what is it going to be, soldier?"

The guard gaped at him for a moment, a chain of emotions flashing through his pale face, but then bowed and stepped aside. "Please follow me, my lord."

"Smart choice," murmured Gunz, following the guard along the side wall of the palace. The young man was so terrified of him that he didn't say a word and didn't slow down until they turned the corner. He halted at the bottom of the wide steps partially covered by snow, staring at Gunz pleadingly.

"Now what?" asked Gunz with a sigh.

"There are more guards at the door," explained the young man, not meeting his eyes. "They will subdue and bind you, my lord. You can't fight 'em all. There are just too many of them."

"I'm sure they will try," muttered Gunz, heading up the slippery marble steps.

With sudden clarity, he realized that all the suffering he and his friends had endured in the last few days, the stress, the unknown and unpredictable—all that, led to this very moment. Good or bad, at least some of his questions were going to be answered in that Throne room, and a bunch of guards in medieval armor weren't going to bring him down to his knees.

Fire rose within him, but he didn't bother suppressing it, even though he knew that the use of his elemental power was draining him physically. He made it to the entrance and halted, facing six large men who blocked his way. Carefully he scanned them with his Salamander senses and stifled a sigh—all six of them had magic, but their magical energy was polluted by the yellow glow of the energy of Chaos.

"Stop!" commanded a guard, unsheathing his sword and the rest of the guards followed.

"Your King is expecting me," Gunz growled, his hand moving down to his pocket with the Swiss army knife. "You can let me in peacefully, or I'll make my way in. Straight through you."

The guards exchanged a look and burst out laughing. Their reaction wasn't something new to him. He got used to men who were a lot taller than him reacting this way. And normally he found it amusing, since in most of the cases he was the one who laughed last while delivering their sorry asses to them. But today, even though he wasn't afraid of these overgrown jackasses, he also wasn't in a mood to tolerate their bullshit.

In one swift motion, he pulled out the Swiss army knife, manifesting his sword, and allowed his fire energy to consume it. The guards gasped, backing away from the smoldering heat, but quickly recovered and raised their blades, holding them at the ready.

"Fine, we'll do it your way," hissed Gunz, assuming a fighting stance.

In his peripheral vision, he noticed the young guard who escorted him here, standing by his side with a sword in his hands, ready to fight his comrades. Gunz didn't get a chance to get surprised as the door into the palace flew open, raising a sparkling snow dust in the air, and a short, stout man ran outside. He stopped, separating him from the king's guards and raised his arms up.

Breathing heavily like a person who hasn't done any exercises or physical work in years, he pressed his hand to his chest, struggling to catch his breath. Leaning forward slightly, he nodded at the guards, waving his other hand at them. They exchanged bewildered looks but lowered their weapons.

"No... fighting..." he panted, sweat glistening on his crimson-colored face despite the cold weather.

Gunz extinguished his fire but held the blade at his shoulder while observing the newcomer with interest. The man finally straightened up and turned to Gunz, making an abnormally high count of his chins wobble with his every move. It seemed like his chins seamlessly merged into his chest in a few uneven folds. With his thick waist and large bulging eyes, he reminded Gunz of an old, fat frog.

Gunz arched his eyebrows at the stranger silently, not sure he wouldn't burst out laughing if he unlocked his lips. The man bowed ceremoniously to him, folding his thick body with unexpected agility, and his fat lips stretched into a broad, fake smile, which completed his resemblance to a frog.

"My lord," he said, his voice an insinuating purr that didn't fit well with the icy gleam in his eyes. "The Fire Salamander. I'm the royal counsellor Isidor. His Majesty, King Alexander, is expecting you. Please kindly follow me."

He turned around and headed toward the entrance without looking back to make sure Gunz was following him. Gunz lowered his sword but didn't turn it back into the knife and sped up to catch up with counsellor "Frog".

Inside, the palace was dark and cold. The air seemed to be just as frosty as it was outside as if winter extended its icy domain into the building. Despite the darkness, the grandeur and over-exuberant luxury of this place was clearly visible in every golden ornament, heavy crystal chandeliers and expensive tapestries.

Gunz had no time to look around as counsellor Isidor was moving with unexpected speed for a man whose size horizontally was larger than vertically. He made his way to the top floor and halted in a spacious lobby, breathing laboriously. Gunz glanced at him, wondering how many flights of stairs away from a heart attack he was. The man recovered quickly and headed toward a door on his right. Opening it, he gestured at Gunz to come in.

"Your chambers, my lord," he said with a bow, but a carnivorous smile on his round face predicted nothing good.

I wonder if that's how a mouse feels, standing in front of a mousetrap, thought Gunz but walked inside, and since there was no one there, he turned the sword into a knife and placed it back into his pocket.

He stopped in the middle of the room, quickly surveying his surroundings, wondering why he was escorted here and not to the Throne room as he expected. Just like everything in the palace, it was furnished in a pretentious, tasteless manner to show off the degree of opulence and wealth of the king. A large four poster bed was situated in the far end of the room, surrounded by a dark, heavy canopy with gold trimming. Next to it, there was a small table on short, curved legs and two massive armchairs with tall backs, decorated by golden ornaments.

To Gunz's surprise, a single large window wasn't locked by bars or metal lattice. He expanded his Salamander senses and probed the area. As soon as he did that, he held his breath and froze in place, forgetting about Isidor's presence next to him.

The room was encapsulated in a spell which was supposed to block any magic—incoming or outgoing. It wasn't the God's snare and normally, it wouldn't present a problem for him should he decide to escape. But with the limited magical energy he had at his disposal in the demonic nexus, he wasn't sure he could break free without draining himself into a coma.

Nevertheless, it wasn't the blocking spell that made his skin crawl, sending a wave of dread through him, twisting his stomach into a knot. A hardly visible trace of some other magical energy was lingering in the air. It wasn't fresh, more like a leftover residue of magic, but he still sensed it clearly. He knew this magical signature well and could recognize it with his eyes closed.

"Mrak..." he exhaled, cold perspiration glistening on his forehead.

"That's right. Master Mrak Delar had the pleasure of enjoying this very accommodation for a short while a few years ago."

Gunz heard an unfamiliar voice and spun around. A tall man stood in the doorway, staring at him with an arrogant expression on his long face. He was slender, bordering on skinny, but his rich velvety jacket and a white shirt with large lacy cuffs and collar were masking his poor physique well. Despite his natural height, he wore leather boots with heels, which were a little too high for a man. A heavy gold necklace was weighing down on his skinny neck and a number of gold rings with large gemstones decorated his fingers.

He wasn't handsome, his face too long and his features pinched too close together. His shifty pale eyes, thin lips and flared nostrils suggested a proclivity to evil and uncontrollable anger outbursts.

"His Majesty, King Alexander," announced Isidor with a deep bow.

The man stared at the counsellor and then waved at him dismissively. "You may leave us, Isidor," he said. "I'll call you if I need you."

Gunz lowered down to one knee and bowed his head slightly, keeping his eyes on the king through his eyelashes, hoping that the king would touch him. One handshake or a pat on the shoulder would be enough for him to send an energy sample to Chernobog. But King Alexander stared down at him for a few long seconds and then flicked his wrist, motioning him to get up as he proceeded toward the window.

"Yes, like I said," he continued so softly that Gunz could barely hear him, "the Ancient Master of Power, stayed here, in this very room." He waved his hand around absently as if he were reminiscing with a friend about a time long gone. "Once someone told me that the Fire Salamanders have extremely sharp senses. They were right, weren't they? You could sense your friend's magical energy signature even though a few years have passed since he was here the last time."

King Alexander stared out the window and flicked his wrist, inviting Gunz to join him. Gunz approached and looked out. The room had a view of the large city square. Even though everything was covered with a thick layer of snow, Gunz could see a tall wooden platform situated in the center of the square. Two tall posts were erected on each side of the platform, manacles attached to the top of each pole.

"Beautiful view. Is it not?" asked the king, his shifty eyes settling on Gunz. "Come closer, Salamander, I want you to look carefully at this platform. This was the place where your friend spent a few weeks hanging in chains for the amusement of the good citizens of my city."

Gunz swallowed hard as Kal's words about Mrak's previous encounter with the king flashed through his mind. Without intending, he shrunk back, his hands closing into fists, and the fire energy spiked around him.

The king cackled loudly and walked to a large armchair, lowering himself down. He leaned back and crossed his legs at his knees. Gunz turned toward him, resting his shoulder against the wall next to the window, and took a few cleansing breaths, getting his anger under control.

"Now, let's get to business," the king announced loudly. "The reason you are here is that I need you to retrieve something for me and deliver it here, into my palace. It's nothing special. Just a book."

"A book? Really? Amazon doesn't deliver to the Land of Dreams?" asked Gunz snidely.

"I already have a court jester and your insolence will get you nothing but trouble, Salamander," said the king, regarding him with an icy stare. "I suggest you listen to me carefully and don't interrupt, if you don't want to change the view from your window. Don't forget, your friend is still in my dungeon and I can have her sprung up between those two posts faster than you can say 'Fire'."

Gunz clenched his jaw but didn't say anything. Everything inside him twisted with uncontrollable anger and it took a serious effort to control his desire to strangle this man with his bare hands. Killing the king would do nothing since it wasn't him who truly ran this show. Besides, Chernobog was right about one thing—they must know what the followers of Chaos were after and why. He had failed to learn it back in California. He couldn't fail again.

The king nodded, disdain twisting his lips into the semblance of a snarl. "Now that I have your attention, Salamander, here is what you are going to do," he continued dryly. "In a few minutes, my wizard will arrive here and open a portal for you. My loyal servants will meet you on the other side, and they will instruct you on what needs to be done."

"Hmm," hummed Gunz, shoving his hands into the pockets of his pants. "All this sounds very mysterious, but no. Not going to happen. Until I meet with your master and discuss this mission with him, I'm going nowhere."

The king jolted up, his nostrils flaring angrily. "How dare you!" he yelled, slashing the air with his arm. "I am the king. There is no one above me and you'll do well to remember that!"

Gunz ignored the king's angry outburst and for a few long seconds a tense silence ruled the room. Suddenly King Alexander closed his eyes and took a deep breath. A moment later he laughed and waved his hand dismissively, sitting back into the armchair.

"You are partially right, Salamander," he said, baring his yellow teeth in a fake smile. "I do have a partner in all this. He is not my master, just like I am not his sovereign. We stand equals. And even though you cannot meet with him right now, he promised that once you come back and deliver the book to us, he will meet with you personally. You have the word of a king." He raised his hand up.

The word of a king. Right. Judging by the king's behavior, he was communicating with his "partner" telepathically. And even though Gunz couldn't trust them as far as he could throw them, he didn't want to anger the king's partner, recognizing that in the demonically infused nexus, he had the upper hand.

He plastered a smile and nodded, lowering his tensed shoulders. "That's fine. I can wait, but can you give me at least some details? What book is it? Where do I have to go to get it? I don't want to go on a dangerous quest completely blind, you know?"

"Blind?" King Alexander cackled but then pursed his lips irritably, tapping his fingers on the arms of his chair. "You will learn one step at the time. As you go. Am I clear, Salamander? Do not try my patience, boy, because your every little misstep will reflect on the back of that little girl who is already in poor condition from what I hear. If you want to see her alive, you will obey." He slammed his hand on the armrest, making his point.

Gunz stiffened, feeling all the blood draining from his face. A fire rose within him and he could no longer control it. Small flames materialized on his shoulders, leisurely moving up and down his arms. The king slowly got up to his feet, staring at him with widened eyes, but Gunz made an effort, extinguishing the fire and raised his hand up.

"Your Majesty, I will do as you wish," he said quietly, "but would you do something for me before I leave?"

The king peered at him with narrowed eyes, disbelief reflected on his pinched features as if he was expecting Gunz to set him on fire, but then squared his shoulders, assuming a regal stance and folded his arms over his chest.

"Depends," he said dryly. "What do you want, Salamander?"

"Can I have a short meeting with Tessa?" Gunz asked, his shoulders slumped like in resignation. He sounded pleadingly, but everything inside him was burning with suppressed rage and he had to lower his eyes so the king wouldn't see the angry flames dancing there. "I promise, I'll do your bidding, if you allow me to see her for a few minutes and talk to her. I'll leave right after."

"You will? Really?" asked the king mockingly, moving closer to him.

"You have my word," he said, staring down at his clenched hands.

The king seized Gunz's chin, forcing his face up, his long nails cutting into his skin.

"Look into my eyes and address me properly," King Alexander growled, crushing his chin with his skinny fingers. "Give me your word that you will do as I wish and come back here with the book, and I will allow you a short visit with your girl."

Gunz slowly raised his eyes and couldn't help it as the corners of his mouth quirked up. He pressed his hand to the rune on his rib and sent some of the king's energy through it to Chernobog. "Your Majesty, you have my word. I'll do as you wish," he said calmly, his gaze cold and steady. *Be careful what you wish for, asshole, because I'll make sure you get everything you deserve...*

The king cackled, letting go of his chin. "Fine, I'll ask my guards to escort you into the dungeon, so you can meet with your little friend."

He raised his hands, ready to clap to summon the guards, but Gunz shook his head stopping him.

"Your Majesty, please, you can't send me to her cell," he said, fidgeting in place, trying to sound as uncomfortable as he could muster. "In the vision you showed me, I saw a massive gray stones pentagram built into the ceiling of her cell. If I spend just a few minutes there, the gray stones magic will drain me, and I won't be able to go anywhere."

The king measured him with his devious eyes and frowned. "You're right." He glanced around the room and shrugged his shoulders. "Well, this wonderful room is magic-proof. If it held a Master of Power imprisoned, it'll hold a little Fire Lizard too. I think I can allow you to meet with your friend here."

He raised his arms and clapped three times, summoning the guards.

CHAPTER 32

~ ZANE BURNS, A.K.A. GUNZ ~

Gunz sat down in the armchair the king had been using just a few minutes ago. Leaning forward, he propped his elbows on his knees and lowered his face into his hands. *Voron, I sent you a sample of the king's energy,* he thought, rocking back and forth slightly. *Please tell me he is possessed by a dark soul so I can deal with this evil bastard...*

He didn't expect Voron to answer his question, recalling that the last time, the ancient warrior showed up in person to deliver Chernobog's message. But this room was magically blocked, and he didn't think Voron could break through this spell. He shook his head, leaning back in the armchair and stretched his legs. A dull headache originated somewhere behind his eyes. It wasn't strong, but it was persistent, and he brought his hands up, massaging his forehead with his fingers above the eyebrows. Nothing helped, and as if to add to his misery, a soft hissing noise joined the headache.

"What the hell?" Gunz muttered, rising, and walked to the window. He pressed his forehead to the icy glass and stared outside. His eyes fell on the platform and he shuddered, his imagination presenting a picture of Mrak Delar sprung up between two posts. He held his breath and staggered back, away from the window.

Looking at his watch, he realized that the king sent his guards to bring Tessa about fifteen minutes ago and it was taking longer than he expected. He started pacing the room, dealing with the constant noise in his head. It was getting louder and the pressure behind his eyes was building up to such a degree that he could no longer handle it.

He dropped to his knees, squeezing his head with his hands. "What's going on..." he mumbled, his eyes watering.

"Zane..." Breaking through the constant background noise, Voron's voice materialized in his mind.

"Voron," moaned Gunz, "you're melting my brain."

"Sorry, this was the only way I could deliver the message from Chernobog," continued Voron in a quick whisper. *"You need to keep going. King Alexander is human. Chernobog wants the energy sample from whoever stands behind the king."*

The noise in his head subsided, taking the headache with it. Gunz scrambled to his feet, shaking his head. "Human? Barely. Only in his anatomy," he muttered, returning to the armchair.

Just as he sat down, the door opened up, hitting the wall with a loud bang as if someone kicked it in. Gunz jolted to his feet just in time to see two of the king's guards entering the room, dragging Tessa between them. She wasn't walking on her own, hanging limply like a raggedy doll in their arms.

The guards let go of her and she fell to the floor in a heap of dirty rags. Gunz crossed the distance between them, going down to his knees, and gently lifted her head, placing it on his lap. Her eyes were closed, and she was taking short, uneven breaths.

"You have ten minutes, Salamander," announced the guard, and they both left, shutting the door behind them.

Gunz heard a click as they locked it and switched his attention to Tessa. He lifted her gently, cringing at how light she was and how fragile her thin body felt. She placed her head on his chest and her eyelashes fluttered as she opened her eyes.

"Zane," she whispered, looking up at him, "is it really you? Not another illusion?"

"No, Tessa," he replied, his voice hoarse, pain twisting his insides. "It's really me. You should start feeling better in a few minutes as the effect of gray stone magic wears off."

He pressed his lips to her forehead and carefully lowered her onto the armchair. Then he took one knee before her, taking her hand into his.

"Please tell me Aidan didn't exchange you for me again," she croaked, looking down at him.

"No, Tessa, I'm here of my own accord, but I am going to get you out," he whispered, his thumbs caressing the dry skin of her hands covered in layers of dirt. "Aidan will find you soon."

She smiled faintly and shook her head. "How are you going to do it?" she asked. With a visible effort, she raised her arm and placed her trembling hand on his head, softly stroking his hair. "Even in my condition I can sense that this room is magic-proofed."

"I am a Great Fire Salamander, Tessa," he said with a confident smile, but inwardly he felt anything but confident. Then he sighed and added, repeating Kal's favorite statement, "I'm the Fire. I'm everywhere and I know everything."

"Fire my ass, you moron…" Tessa chuckled, and her large brown eyes, surrounded by deep dark circles, lit up with humor. "Kal friggin' junior," she murmured, seizing a handful of his hair and yanking weakly at it.

He glanced at his watch and cringed. "Listen, Tessa," he whispered, rising. "I am going to open my portal, and you will have to step through it on your own. Can you do it?"

She nodded, but there was no usual self-assurance in her eyes. "Are you coming with me?"

"No, Tessa," he replied, carefully channeling the fire energy from within, directing it to his hands. "I don't think I have enough power to break through and send you outside the sealed nexus, but I will send you somewhere safe, and Aidan will find you soon."

"Zane, I'm not going without—"

"You are, Tessa," he objected as fire lit up at the bottom of his eyes. "Your presence here makes everything a lot more dangerous. I can't allow King Alexander to push me into a corner and as long as he holds you, I'm not free to make my own choices."

"I understand, but—"

"I don't have enough power in me to go with you through the portal while sustaining it," he continued urgently. "You must go alone. Besides, my work here is not done."

Tessa lowered her face and nodded, tears sliding down her dirty cheeks, leaving glistening trails in their wake. He helped her get up and carefully let go to make sure she could hold her own weight. She swayed on her feet but managed to keep her balance.

"Ready?" Gunz asked. He glanced down at his watch and added, "We must rush. The guards should be back here in less than five minutes."

She nodded, and he waved his hand to unfold the fire curtain of his portal. A light flare of fire followed his motion, and nothing happened. He growled, straining as he channeled more of his elemental fire. Flowing with bright red flames, a portal unfolded before him.

Since Tessa was the daughter of Perun, Slavic god of Thunder, he knew his elemental fire couldn't hurt her, but in her weakened condition he couldn't take a chance. He touched Tessa's arm and muttered a protection spell through his clenched teeth.

Tessa stepped closer to the portal and gasped as the smoldering heat enveloped her. She halted for a moment and turned her head, looking at Gunz over her shoulder.

"Zane, Angel is in trouble," she said, barely above a whisper. "The Reaper part of me senses his distress."

"Is he also here? In the City of Gold," asked Gunz.

"No, I don't think so... I can't sense where he is, but I know that something is terribly wrong."

"Tessa, you must go..." he exhaled, struggling to sustain the portal. "Tell everything... to Aidan..."

Tessa nodded and stepped through the portal, disappearing on the other side.

Opening the portal within a magically sealed room took a lot of energy, and between sustaining it and keeping the protective shield around Tessa, he was completely drained.

Magically and physically, he thought faintly as his legs gave in and he collapsed to the floor. Like in a nightmare, he saw the door open and men walk inside. He was so drained that he couldn't look up. All he saw was a pair of polished black boots with abnormally tall heels. He watched one of the boots pull back and slam him in his stomach.

Gunz grunted, losing his breath, and curled into a ball, gasping for air, while the king kept kicking him without watching where his kicks were landing. He could barely hear anything through an even buzz in his ears and his vision was growing blurrier and darker with each second.

He felt the pain of each strike, but he couldn't scream. As the next kick landed on his face, the metallic taste of blood filled his mouth. Curling tighter, he managed to bring his arms up to cover his head. Through the buzz, he heard a new voice shouting something, and the pain stopped.

He felt someone lift him off the floor and he moaned as every move reverberated with pain in his drained body. The last thing he felt before he passed out was the softness of the bed under his back.

CHAPTER 33

~ ZANE BURNS, A.K.A. GUNZ ~

A downpour of half-frozen water on his face ripped him out of his oblivion and Gunz jerked up, gasping for air. With no strength to keep an upright position, he fell back on the wet bed with a low grunt. His body was one entangled aching mass and his face was swollen to such a degree that he could barely open his eyes. If pain could have been converted into music, each of his cells would have its own tune, all together creating a massive, earsplitting discord.

"He is still too weak, Your Majesty," said a familiar voice somewhere above him.

"You did a number on him yesterday, Alex," another voice, deeper and stronger, growled above him, the sound of it bringing unwanted memories. "That was stupid. Stupid and reckless! If he can't function, we can't get what we need."

Where did I hear this voice?

"Oh, yeah?" replied King Alexander, his voice shaking with fury. "He disobeyed me! He had it coming."

"He disobeyed *you*?" The second voice snickered sarcastically and clapped his hands. "Well, that is priceless. What bothers you more, Alex? The fact that this young Salamander had done something no one expected was possible or that your little prisoner escaped, and you no longer can coerce him?"

Oh, yeah... In Alisa's house... He was the second voice summoning me...

Gunz cracked his eyes open and squinted at the bright light in the room. He blinked a few times, readjusting his vision, and noticed a dark shadow quickly vanishing from sight. King Alexander was standing next to his bed with two guards positioned on either side of him.

One more man stood by the door with his arms folded, leaning his back against the wall. He had long white hair and a bushy gray mustache which made it impossible to guess his age. His face, while not ugly, had an inscrutable expression of a man who got used to seeing the pain and suffering of others without flinching.

The King glowered at Gunz, his thin lips set in a straight line, his nostrils flaring. An irritable growl escaped his lips as he yanked a tight leather glove off his hand, his moves sharp and jerky. Bending down slightly, he slapped Gunz with it across his face and then turned toward his guards.

"Get him to his feet," he ordered, putting the glove back on his skinny hand.

One of the guards approached Gunz and carefully pulled him up into a sitting position. He moaned, pressing his hand to his burning cheek as every square inch of his body responded with a nagging pain.

"Try to get up," the guard whispered into his ear so no one else could hear, providing him with some support, and just now Gunz recognized him. It was the same young man who escorted him to the palace from the backdoor and was ready to fight the others to help him.

Gunz nodded, lowering his feet on the floor, wincing from the stabbing pain in his ribs. Bearing heavily on the young guard's shoulder, he got up and stood swaying slightly in front of his enemy, calmly holding his angry gaze. The king stared at him for a moment and then waved at the older man who still stood by the entrance, seemingly indifferent to everything the king was doing.

The man approached him and bowed. Then he cocked his head, staring at Gunz, and a hardly noticeable grim smirk touched his lips beneath his mustache. Gunz tensed, feeling the rude invasion of the other man's magical energy as he scanned him. He couldn't protect himself from the dark sorcerer's assault, still drained magically and severely hurt physically.

"Stop. If you want to know something about me, just ask," he croaked, fighting to break their eye contact to no avail. This powerful magical intrusion was more than he could handle in his condition. The room spun around him and the floor slipped from under his feet, sending him into a downward spiral. He probably would have fallen if the young guard hadn't held on to him.

The sorcerer snickered and wagged his finger at Gunz. "There is nothing you can tell me that I don't already know." Then he turned to King Alexander and bowed. "Your Majesty, are you sure you want to send him out now? Magically speaking, he is useless without his fire energy, and"—he slipped a sarcastic glance at Gunz—"there is no place on his body that isn't bruised. Twelve hours wasn't enough for him to regain his strength. There isn't enough elemental fire in the nexus."

"He is going at once," objected the king, stamping his foot on the floor like a toddler ready to throw a tantrum. "Open your portal, sorcerer!"

"As you wish," the man murmured with a sinister smirk. Reaching into his pocket, he pulled out a piece of chalk and a small vial. Then he walked to the wall next to the entrance and started to draw a man-sized pentagram.

"How much longer, sorcerer?" asked the King, tapping with his foot, impatiently.

"Ready, Your Majesty," replied the older man, turning around. He gave Gunz another derisive once-over and waved his hand. "Come closer, Salamander. If you can, that is."

Gunz let go of the guard and took one unsteady step forward. This small motion was enough to send him spiraling over the proverbial pain threshold, and he collapsed to one knee, bracing himself with his arms against the floor. Feeling the coldness of the slippery marble tiles under his hands, he lifted his strained face and looked at the king, sweat running down his forehead and neck.

"This is unacceptable!" squealed King Alexander, pacing in front of Gunz, once in a while throwing a scorching look at him. Suddenly, he came to a sharp halt and gave Gunz an arched stare, his upper lip curved up in disgust. "Someone needs to help him through the portal. Once this creature of Fire is on the other side, he'll regain his strength quickly."

The young guard grabbed Gunz's arm, helping him up, and turned to the King. "I'll go with him."

It took them a little while to make it to the wall with the pentagram on it. The sorcerer shook his head slightly, doubt written all over his face, but the king frowned, glowering at the old man with unconcealed threat, and he raised his hands up showing him a small vial with a dark potion inside.

"Do it already!" the king shouted, his voice bouncing off the walls, sending shivers down Gunz's spine.

The sorcerer spun around and smashed the vial against the pentagram. Gunz had seen potions for opening portals before, but never had he seen anything like this. A heavy odor of sulphur permeated the air as dark muddy liquid spilled on the wall, dripping down to the floor in heavy sticky drops. The floor trembled and a thin crack appeared on the wall, following the outer shape of the pentagram.

As the fracture kept growing, a dark portal opened in place of the pentacle, spinning in a counter clock direction. Purple lightning bolts flashed in the revolving darkness and the cold winds howled within it. The sorcerer looked tensed, his both arms outstretched toward the wall, sweat running down his strained face and it was obvious that sustaining this monstrosity open was taking all the magic and strength he had.

Gunz had never seen a portal like this. Even the portal into the Dark Nav didn't feel as cold and sinister as this rotating atrocity. Adrenaline spiked through him, making his heart thunder desperately against his ribcage, and his fingers grasped at the guard's shoulder involuntarily.

The king noticed his reaction and snickered, waving his hand at the portal. "Don't worry, Salamander. It feels a lot worse than it looks. You see, since that old tramp, whom you know as the Gatekeeper, sealed the nexus, opening a portal into the human realm presents a problem. This portal is not your vanilla gateway, but rather a tear in the fabric of reality infused with the energy of Dark Nav. A sorcerer cannot tear a fabric of reality, as you are probably well aware, but the essence of Nav does the trick. I am sure, as a creature of the elements, you will enjoy the journey through it immensely."

A tear in the fabric of reality? Gunz thought, small hairs rising on his neck. *Where is the Destiny Council Enforcers when you need them? Or are they like the highway patrol—showing up only when you're speeding... And how did they get the energy of Nav bypassing Chernobog?*

The King approached Gunz, patting him on his cheek and snickered as Gunz jerked his head to the side to avoid his touch. Then he flicked his wrist at the guard who was supporting Gunz and said with an ominous snarl on his face, "Off you go. I'll see you back soon."

As Gunz came closer to the portal, he sensed its dark energy and shuddered. "Together…" the guard whispered, and they dove into the rotating blackness headfirst.

* * *

When Gunz jumped into the portal, he knew it was going to be bad. He just didn't realize how truly bad it was going to be. With his throat constricted, he felt like he was deep underwater, and he couldn't expand his chest to breathe in. He twisted in the air, clutching at his throat with both hands and suddenly hit the ground with the back of his head.

He wasn't sure how long he was out, but the first thing he felt when he came back was someone yanking him roughly to his feet. He cried out and jerked just to discover that he was held by a few pairs of strong hands.

The surrounding air was cold, but not winter-cold and a heavy smell of damp foliage lingered in the air, mixed in with the revolting reek of mold and decay. Water was dripping somewhere in close proximity and the constant bangs of drops seemed to be too loud in the ambient silence.

It was so dark that even his sharp Salamander vision couldn't help him discover where he was. One thing was for sure though—he was back in the human realm. Despite the shortage of magical energy and elemental powers here, it was a lot better than back in the nexus polluted by Chaos. He exhaled and focused on channeling the energy of fire, trying to give himself a little boost to restore his strength.

"He is back, guys," said an unfamiliar male voice with a heavy Russian accent. "And his skin is getting hotter. We need to get moving."

"Roman, turn the light on," yelled another voice. "I can see nothing in this shithole!"

A moment later, Gunz heard the soft click of a button and an electric lantern lit up on his right, illuminating the area with bright white light. He was standing inside of a small room with dirty concrete walls, a single tiny window crossed by rusty iron bars and a metal door. The window had no glass and the soft rustling of the wind playing with tree branches suggested that the building was located either in a forest or somewhere in a city park.

Besides him, there were five men in the room—four of them were total strangers whom he had never seen before, and the fifth was the young guard who had jumped through the portal with him. Two men were holding him, which he was glad they did as he wasn't sure he could stand on his own yet. The other two were standing in front of him with their arms folded.

All four men were tall and muscled with short haircuts and stylishly trimmed stubbles on their chiseled faces. Dressed in dark jeans and black leather jackets with *MP-443 Grach* tucked into their waistbands, they were picture-perfect Russian thugs. For whatever reason, they chose to speak in English and their heavy accents identified their nationality without leaving any doubts.

"What does he need to do to heal?" asked one of them, addressing the guard while pinning Gunz with a scornful stare. "He can barely stand on his own and the master said that he must be in his full power to complete the mission."

"He is a Fire Salamander," replied the guard quietly. "He needs fire, I guess."

Morons, thought Gunz, expending his Salamander senses. All four men were humans, but the purity of their souls was tinted with the yellow glow of Chaos. *They are humans, working for demons. Sold for thirty pieces of silver...*

Since Gunz had met the young guard at the backdoor into the City of Gold, he had never checked his magical signature and now, as soon as his Salamander senses touched him, he knew that he wasn't human. He wasn't a wizard like most of the King's guards either. He was a pureblood werewolf and his energy signature was loud and clear.

Gunz cringed inwardly, not sure if it was a good thing or a bad one. Werewolves weren't famous for being friendly or patient. In the human realm, they didn't like to get involved into the affairs of other magical beings, staying within the boundaries of their packs and obeying only their pack master.

However, this young werewolf was from the Land of Dreams, not from the realm of humans, and he wasn't sure if the same rules applied to him. Besides, so far he had been nothing but helpful, sometimes risking his own safety.

One of the men stepped closer, bending his knees slightly to be on the same level with him and smirked. "Hey, Salamander, what's your name?"

Gunz met his mocking gaze and a cold smile appeared on his face before he could stop it. "Gunz," he replied. "And to answer your previous question, to heal myself, I need to revert into my natural state."

"Uh-huh," hummed the man. He looked at his friends, but they just shrugged their shoulders. "Well, go for it then. Don't let me stop you."

Gunz rolled his eyes. There was enough elemental fire here for him to revert, and for a split-second he considered doing it, burning these four ignorant thugs to ashes. But as much as he wished he could wipe their derisive smirks off their faces, he couldn't destroy them. He still had no idea where he was supposed to be going and how to retrieve the magical artifact, and these four arrogant fools were the only people who could tell him.

"I can't do it with the five of you in the room, morons," he grumbled through his gritted teeth. "You'll die the instant I revert." He looked around the room, his eyes slowly moving from one goon to the next, finding no sign of any intelligent thoughts on their faces. "Also, I need to know where I am. If there are any humans within a mile radius, they are all going to die, too."

"The Master told us that we were immune to your fire, Salamander," replied the second thug nonchalantly. "You can't hurt us."

"Are you willing to bet your life on it?" asked Gunz, raising his eyebrows.

"Roman?" asked the second thug, gaping at the man in charge. Then all four of them turned around, for some reason staring quizzically at the werewolf.

"He is telling the truth," confirmed the young guard with a shrug. "Immune or not, we need to leave and walk away from this place as far as we can."

"Are you saying that this—whatchamacallit—natural state generates a blast wave like—"

"An atomic bomb? Yeah, that's right," Gunz interrupted him with a dismissive wave of his hand, "I am a living, breathing weapon of mass destruction."

The four thugs stared at the guard again.

"I already told you. He is telling you the truth," said the young man, sounding slightly annoyed, heading toward the door. "We should leave."

The two men who held Gunz let go off him and backed away as if he were a leper. Gunz swayed but managed to stay on his feet. All four of them huddled by the door, ready to run.

"Hey, assholes, you didn't answer my question. Where am I?" he shouted after them, throwing his hands in the air. "Am I in the middle of a populated area?"

Roman turned around and his eyes darted from Gunz to the werewolf as a tightlipped smile stretched his mouth. "Well, you're in the middle of a forest, miles away from any city," he said, cocking his head a little as he stared down at him. "Give us fifteen minutes to put some distance and you can do your thing. No one will die." He glanced at his friends and snickered. "Well... Almost no one."

He pushed the young guard toward Gunz. The werewolf didn't expect it and tripped, falling at Gunz's feet, looking up at him with an expression of horror imprinted on his face. "Please," he mouthed soundlessly, tears brimming in his widened eyes.

Gunz glowered coldly at the thug and shrugged indifferently. "You'll be killing one of your own," he said dryly. "King Alexander sent his personal guard to keep an eye on me. So, yeah, go ahead and kill him. I don't give a damn."

"Why?" whispered the wolf.

Gunz ignored him, staring coldly at the four stooges by the door.

"We don't know him, and neither the king nor our Master had informed us that they were sending a guard with you. You were supposed to come alone," replied Roman, his hand slowly gliding down toward his gun as though he was expecting Gunz to retaliate. But since Gunz said nothing and didn't move, they turned around and walked out the door.

He heard a few metallic clicks as they locked it and a moment later, the roar of an engine announced that they were gone. Gunz glanced down at the guard and sighed.

"Get up, wolf," he said, shaking his head. "You're not going to die. At least not by my hand. Besides, if you're serving the king, you're probably immune to my power, anyway."

"You know I'm a werewolf?" The young man scrambled to his feet and scratched the back of his head, making his short hair spike up. For the first time, Gunz noticed how truly young he was. With his dark hair and golden-yellow eyes, he looked no more than twenty. "But how are you going to heal yourself?"

"Of course I know you are a werewolf. I can sense it." Gunz sighed. "What's your name? I don't like calling you wolf or a guard."

"Nikita," replied the young man. "You can call me Nik."

"Okay, Nik," continued Gunz. "I need you to go all the way to the door and sit down there. Sit tight and no matter what you see, do not move. Do you understand me?"

Nik blanched but nodded and sat down on the floor, cowering in the corner. Gunz regarded him with suspicion, wondering why this young wolf was helping him. Not fully trusting him, he decided to wait for the right moment to ask this question and headed to the opposite end of the room. Lowering down to the floor, Gunz closed his eyes and channeled his elemental fire and magic at the same time. As his element surged through him, he exhaled, his breath coming out like a soft moan, and opened his eyes.

Never did he think that one day he would enjoy the limited amount of magic and power available in the human realm. Since he had discovered the Fire, he always thought that compared to Kendral and the Land of Dreams, the human realm was deprived of magic. But after spending time in the Dark Nav and the polluted nexus, he changed his mind.

He rolled his shoulders, enjoying the feeling of his power returning to him and let the fire take over. As the small flames started to rush up and down his arms, he got up and walked closer to Nik. The wolf whimpered softly, wrapping his arms around his head, shying away from the sweltering heat he was emitting.

"Look at me, Nikita," Gunz growled, extending his hand engulfed in fire to him. The young man lowered his arms and met Gunz's flaming gaze. "Why are you helping me? You were the king's guard, but you were ready to fight your own to help me. Why? Tell me the truth and I will spare your life."

"My lord," moaned the wolf, "please, I swear I mean you no harm. It's about Alisa and her grandmother. My mother is not well, and Elizaveta is the best healer in the City. She's keeping my mother alive." He fell silent for a moment, staring at Gunz with a haunted look in his eyes. "And"—he stuttered and exhaled—"and I'm in love with Alisa, my lord. Please forgive me, but I'm helping you because you are her friend."

Gunz peered at the young man, something inside him

crashing and burning as the thought of Angelique flashed in his mind. What would he do to be with her again? What wouldn't he do...

"Hang in there, Nik," he said, his voice hoarse. "It's about to become very hot and probably scary. But you have to trust me that I'll do everything I can to get you back to your mother and Alisa."

Gunz moved his hand over Nik's head in a circular motion. *"Praecidio Amnia,"* he whispered and once he saw the soft glow of his protection spell enveloping the wolf, he added a second layer of protection, *"Praecidio Amnia Circula Archni."*

He moved as far away from Nik as the limited space of the room allowed and closed his eyes, silently asking Kal for help. Gunz knew that Kal wasn't a god and the Fire Elemental couldn't hear his prayer, but every time when he was in a tough spot, in his mind, Kal was the only god he prayed to.

Channeling as much power as he could gather, Gunz let go, partially reverting into the natural state of the Fire Salamander. His body dissolved into flames and he screamed, spreading his arms wide, stopping himself from reverting all the way. Through the rush of fire, he heard Nik scream, and as much as he enjoyed his current state, he suppressed it, assuming his human form.

Gunz flexed his muscles, making sure that the pain and soreness were gone and glanced at the wolf. The young man lay on the floor, curved into a ball with his arms over his head, and his entire body was trembling from head to toe. Otherwise, he appeared unharmed and Gunz chuckled. With one wave of his hand, he removed the protection spell and touched Nik's shoulder.

"You can get up now," he said. "It's over."

The werewolf sat up and pulled his legs to his chest, resting his arms atop his bent knees. He eyes traveled up and down Gunz's body as if measuring him before he averted his gaze.

"You're so powerful. I've never seen anything like that," he said with a slight shake of his head. "Why are you tolerating all this abuse? These four idiots... You could have killed them with one touch of your fingers."

Gunz sighed, lowering to the floor next to him. "There was nothing more I wanted to do than end their miserable existence," he growled, his hands clenching into fists, "but I can't."

"Why not?" asked Nik, raising his eyes at him. "I don't understand. You are the Fire Salamander. You could have killed them and opened your portal to any place in any world. Why wouldn't you run? Leave this place and the cursed king behind. You don't have to return to the City of Gold."

"I wish it was that simple." Gunz smiled, but his smile didn't reach his sad eyes. "I can't run, my friend. It wouldn't solve the bigger problem."

"What are you talking about? What bigger problem?"

"If I run, who is going to find a way to cleanse the nexus and restore the flow of magic?" asked Gunz. "The Land of Dreams and Kendral are still sealed and until the demonic invasion is stopped and the nexus is purified, they will remain locked. That leaves the world of humans vulnerable to any evil asshole who dreams of a chance at world domination. I'm the only one who can do it. And I'm not even talking about the king's threat to destroy this realm if I disobey him."

Gunz fell silent, staring down at his hands. A moment later, he huffed and shook his head, feeling tired and resigned.

"Besides, Chernobog made it crystal clear to me that he wanted to know who was leading the followers of Chaos now, and I know for a fact that he won't stop until he's learned it," he continued quietly. "And if I don't do what he ordered me to do, I have no doubt that he will fulfill his threat and summon Mrak Delar. And that would be a death warrant for my friend. I can't have it, Nik."

"I'm sorry..."

"Yeah, not as sorry as I am." Gunz chuckled bitterly. "So, you understand now? Killing these thugs isn't an option. At least not yet. I need them to tell me how to get the book, so I can return to the City of Gold and identify the king's partner. It's the only way. I have no choice but to do it."

"But you do have a choice!" Nik yelled, slamming his hand on the rough concrete floor. "Refuse to look for this book. Let this stupid artifact rot wherever it is now. The king lost his leverage over you. He can't force you anymore."

"Yeah, this thought crossed my mind. Not once." Gunz rubbed his face, hopelessness settling in his every cell. "But the reality is, these people, or demons, or whatever the hell they are… they will never stop until they have this book. If not me, they'll find someone else who can deliver it to them. So, I prefer to find this book first and make sure that these evil bastards will never put their hands on it."

For a while, they sat in complete silence, each deep in their own thoughts. Then Nik got up and offered his hand to Gunz. "I will help you if I can," he said as Gunz got up and squeezed his hand in a handshake. "You can count on me."

Interrupting their conversation, the lock clicked again, and the same four men walked inside. Roman pointed at his wristwatch and showed Gunz handcuffs, dangling from his index finger.

"It's time, Salamander," he said. "Let's see if our master is right and you really can do it."

"Do what exactly?" asked Gunz icily, carefully gathering his fire magic in his hands.

"You'll find out when we get there," replied the thug with an evil smirk on his face. "Turn around. Hands behind your back."

Gunz turned around slowly, crossing his hands. "Is it really necessary? If I wanted to run, I could have done it while you were gone." He thought for a moment and added, "Actually, I could have done it even with you four idiots being here. You don't have what it takes to stop me."

"Master gave us exact instructions on what to do and how to handle you," replied Roman, locking the handcuff on Gunz's wrists. "Step by step."

Before Gunz could react, Roman seized his hair, forcing his head to the side, and he felt a sharp twinge of pain as a needle penetrated his neck. He groaned, struggling to turn around, but the room swam around him making his stomach churn and a moment later, darkness devoured him.

CHAPTER 34

~ ZANE BURNS, A.K.A. GUNZ ~

The sharp odor of ammonium salts did its job, yanking Gunz out of oblivion and bringing him back into the unfriendly world complete with cold water and a sharp pain of an injection administered to his neck. He winced, jerking away from the atrocious smell, and took in his surroundings, clasping his hand to his neck.

He was sitting on a tiled floor, his back resting against a wall, the restraints gone. The room was dark and empty, and the strange odor of some chemicals was lingering in the air. A few plastic shelves stuffed with different bottles, toilet paper and cleaning supplies were pushed against one of the walls. A plethora of brooms, mops and dust brushes hung on the other.

The four thugs stood by the door, staring down at him with derisive smirks on their faces. Nik sat next to him, his wrists handcuffed, a large bruise decorating his left eye. Gunz wiped the water off his face with the sleeve of his jacket and turned to the werewolf.

"Nik, are you okay?" he asked quietly. The guard nodded silently. His eyes flashed to the thugs, and he dropped his head.

"Gunz?" asked Roman mockingly, stepping forward. "Is that your real name?"

"As real as you can get," growled Gunz, rising, noticing with relief that despite the sedative the thugs gave him earlier, he felt strong and powerful. "Where are we?"

"Well, Gunz, you are back home, in the capital of your motherland—Moscow," announced the thug, sarcasm in his every word.

"I'm from Belarus, dumbass," huffed Gunz. "What am I doing here?"

"Straight to business then? No guided tours?" Roman guffawed, winking at his friends. "I like dealing with people who don't need small talk. You are right next to the Kremlin, Gunz. In the Mausoleum to be precise, the employees' side of it, of course." Roman jerked his thumb at the door behind him.

"What am I doing here and why?" asked Gunz dryly, slowly gathering fire energy and redirecting it to his hands.

Roman approached him and put his hand on his shoulder as if he was his best buddy. "I wish I could tell you, my friend," he whispered into his ear. "But our master is extremely careful. This information is on a need to know basis only, and I guess I don't need to know. We get paid enough not to ask questions."

"So, what *do* you know?" asked Gunz, throwing Roman's hand off his shoulder.

"Our job was to deliver you here, Salamander, and stay with you until the portal was opened," explained the thug. "The rest you'll learn on the other side."

Just as Roman finished talking, the air next to him shimmered like a mirage and a large portal opened up, shimmering with a rotating blue light. There was nothing dark or strange about this portal, but the look of it set Gunz's nerves on edge.

Roman flinched and hopped to the side, cursing, but quickly recovered and pointed at the portal.

"Your cue," he muttered. "Off you go."

"I am going with him," said Nik in a no-nonsense tone, getting up to his feet. "My king ordered me to stay with him no matter where he was going."

"Knock yourself out, guard." Roman laughed, tapping Nik on his shoulder, and the other three thugs echoed his laughter. He grabbed Nik's arm and took the cuffs off. "I doubt you'll be coming back."

Nik ignored the thugs. Coming closer to Gunz, he motioned at the rotating portal. "Together?"

Gunz nodded and jumped through the shimmering spinning air.

* * *

WALKING OUT OF THE PORTAL, HE FOUND HIMSELF IN A LARGE poorly lit room with a low ceiling and two arched doorways, leading into the darkness. The air was stuffy and fetid, and the white stonework of the walls was covered in patches of black mold and dirt.

"Where are we?" whispered Nik, staring around with widened eyes.

"I'm kind of getting tired of asking this question," mumbled Gunz and held out his hand, manifesting a few light orbs in his palm.

He threw the orbs up and the shimmering bluish light illuminated the area. Expanding his Salamander senses, he explored the room and frowned.

"These walls are infused with some strange protective magic," he murmured, running his fingers over the rough surface of the stones. "It's not really wards… and it is weak here…" He pointed at the doorway on his right. "Seems to get stronger over there."

A short man in a dark trench coat separated from the shadows and approached them. He halted in front of Gunz, staring up at him and his lips stretched into a smile which could have been called kind if only it touched his small brown eyes. He ran his hand with short sausage-like fingers over his bald head, slicking over the remaining few strands of hair.

"Hello, Child of Fire," he said dryly, pulling closer the lapels of his coat, which refused to close over his sizable belly. "I see you brought a lapdog with you?"

Nik took a step forward, a feral growl rumbling in his throat, and his eyes lit up with the bright orange light of a werewolf on the verge of transformation. Gunz put his hand on the wolf's shoulder, squeezing it. The man in front of them was exuding a vibe of a dark magical energy and starting a brawl with him wasn't the right move. At least not right now.

"I assume I am talking to some expendable Zmey's lackey?" asked Gunz coldly.

"Lackey, eh?" The man cackled, his stomach jiggling up and down and his thick nose stretching wider together with his mouth. He stopped laughing abruptly, his cold shifty eyes boring into Gunz. "The entertainment hour is over, Child of Fire. Now, you are going to follow my orders and do as you're told. Am I clear?"

"Crystal," growled Gunz, glowering down at the dark wizard, suppressing the desire to set him on fire.

The man reached into the inside pocket of his coat and produced a notebook page, folded twice. Gunz took the paper from his hand and unfolded it. A map of passages and corridors was drawn on it with a single thick red line marking the way.

"Child of Fire," started the man, shoving his hands into the pockets of his coat, "you're standing in the ancient labyrinth under the Kremlin. It had been locked many years ago, but the main secret of it was never discovered."

"A secret?" asked Gunz, feeling the hairs slowly rising on his arms as a vibe of unease spread through him.

"Yes, the legendary Golden Library of Tsar Ivan the Terrible," replied the man, his eyes lighting up with a predatory hunger. "Today, you'll have the honor of opening the door into one of the most mysterious and powerful collection of ancient books."

Gunz had heard before about this mythical library, but according to the legend, it had been lost for centuries and no one has ever been able to prove that it was real.

Since Gunz remained silent, the man continued. "As you follow the map, you'll come across a few wards—dangerous, high-level magic. Trust me, these wards cannot be broken. I tried. But as a Fire Salamander, your portal can burn through the invisible walls these wards erected. Since the walls are see-through, you should have no problems doing it." He stopped talking, expecting questions.

"Go on," said Gunz, arching his eyebrow at the man. "Assuming, you are right, and my portal can burn through this protective magic, what should I do when I get into the library?"

"There are hundreds of books, scrolls and manuscripts in the Golden Library, but you will take only one," said the man, crossing his hands behind his back. "You'll find it on top of a large oak table, and it is the only book that will be opened. The name of the book is the *Dark Codex*. Don't touch anything else. Take the book and get back here as soon as you can, following the same path."

"The Dark Codex?" Gunz huffed with a half-shrug. "This name promotes the feeling of comfort and security. What happens once I bring the book here?"

The wizard cackled. "I guess you'll find out when you come back." He gave Gunz an arched stare filled with mockery and added, "If you come back, that is. I suggest you leave your pet here if you value his life."

Gunz looked at Nik, but the werewolf just shook his head. "Together," he said with a hardly visible nod.

"I'll see you here in about thirty minutes," said the wizard, walking away toward the passage on his left.

* * *

FOLLOWING THE MAP, GUNZ CAREFULLY MOVED THROUGH THE narrow dark corridors, running his fingers over the rough surface of the white stonework. The first time Kremlin's oak walls had been rebuilt using the white limestone was during the reign of Grand Prince Dmitri Donskoi around 1366, and Gunz assumed that this chain of corridors was dated to that time period. Possibly it was even older, and when the Kremlin was rebuilt into stone, these passages were reinforced too.

Only in the second part of the fifteenth century, the Kremlin had been reconstructed using the red stones, but by the looks of these passages, Ivan the Great didn't bother rebuilding the labyrinth underneath. Neither did Ivan the Terrible. They were old and untouched for many years, and Gunz couldn't help but think about all the mysteries this ancient place was hiding.

As he turned the corner, he came to a sharp halt, holding his hand back to stop Nik. The corridor ran into a dead-end. A white stone wall blocked their path and there was no way around it. Gunz approached the wall and touched it, scanning it with his Salamander senses. Not satisfied, he opened his other sight and chuckled.

"Clever," he muttered under his breath. Then he turned to Nik and pointed at the barrier. "I've never seen such a clever protection spell. You see this wall?"

Nik nodded. "It has to be one of those wards the wizard told you about," he said. "But didn't he say it was see-through?"

"But it is," replied Gunz, staring at the magical obstacle in awe. "The secret of this magic is that there is no wall. Look through it, Nik. Don't let your eyes tell you otherwise."

"Mighty Veles," mumbled Nik, narrowing his eyes at the fake

wall. "There is absolutely nothing there. Just a continuation of the passage."

"This spell is incredibly powerful," whispered Gunz, more to himself than to Nik. "Well, let's see if the wizard was right and the Fire Salamander can burn through it—"

"Mr. Burns, stop!"

Gunz spun around and stiffened. Two men stood in front of him, blocking the corridor. Dressed in medieval armor—knight's chainmail covered by long white surcoat and a hooded cloak—they stood motionless with their long swords unsheathed.

"What the hell?" mumbled Gunz, his hands lowering to the pocket of his pants where he had his Swiss army knife.

"Mr. Burns, you need to stop what you are doing and leave," said one of the knights with a heavy French accent, taking a step forward while lowering his hood. "Please, *mon ami*."

"Raoul," Gunz exhaled, relief warming up his chest as he recognized the Warden, "what are you doing here?"

"Zane, please, listen to me," the Warden said urgently, putting his hand on Gunz's shoulders. "You can't go any farther. The Wardens Order sent us here to protect what lies beneath this wall. We can't let you through, even if it means fighting you."

Gunz bit his lip, nodding his head slightly. "Raoul, I must do it," he said quietly, having a hard time keeping his emotions and his power in check. "I have no choice and a lot depends on it, including the safety of the human realm. But I swear to you that whatever I retrieve from the Golden Library will never fall into the hands of evil. Would you take my word for it?"

"Who is this man, Brother Raoul?" The second Warden approached them, staring down at Gunz warily. His French accent was even heavier than Raoul's and a vibe of animosity was lingering around him. "Why are you still reasoning with him instead of restraining him?"

"Brother Luc, please," hissed Raoul. "Let me figure this out."

"Luc de la Crosse, I presume?" asked Gunz, holding out his hand. "My name is Zane Burns. It's nice meeting you, sir."

The Warden glanced down at Gunz's hand but then took it and squeezed it slightly. "Your hand is hot," he whispered, his animosity replaced by dismay in a heartbeat. "You are—"

"The Fire Salamander, sir," Gunz finished his statement.

"God save us all," mumbled Luc, crossing himself. "They truly did it… demons and the followers of Chaos… they got a Fire Salamander to do their bidding." He turned to Raoul, his expression that of hopeless desperation. "We can't stop him… we can't fight him—"

"Whoa, Luc, no!" Gunz raised both his hands in a peaceful gesture. "First, I am not going to fight any of you. We work on the same side." He sighed, dropping his hands. "Second, I am not working for demons or the followers of Chaos."

"Oh, yeah?" hissed Luc, taking a step closer to him. "Then what are you doing here, trying to break into a warded library? The very same library demons have been trying to break into for the last few weeks. Eh?"

"Well, what can I tell you? Broward County Library ran out of books of spells, so I had to look elsewhere," replied Gunz, blinking at the Warden with an innocent expression.

"Zane…" Raoul sighed. "I'm afraid you have to give us a better explanation."

"Yes, of course." Gunz lowered his head. "I don't work for demons, Raoul," he said, but then pressed his hand over his eyes, a deep wrinkle creasing his forehead. "I work for someone who is a lot scarier than demons, I'm afraid. I work for Chernobog, the Slavic god of Destruction. And he is not the type you can say no to and live to see another day."

Raoul blanched and pulled away, fear clearly reflected on his handsome face. "No, Zane… Chernobog should never have anything from this library. And come on... he can't kill you. No one can—"

"No, he can't kill me," agreed Gunz, "but he can torture me for all eternity, if that makes it any better." He fell silent, his throat clenched. "But I don't care if he does, Raoul. He can kill me, torture me, do whatever he wants with me. I don't give a damn!" Gunz punched the air as anger spiked through him, bringing flames to life in his eyes. "It's not about me. It's about the Ancient Master. You know that as powerful as Mrak is, he is not immortal and Chernobog holds his life in his hands."

"Master Mrak Delar is a great man, but he has a shady past," pointed out Luc de la Cross, standing behind Raoul. "Nevertheless, even his life is not worth the lives of millions if demons or Chernobog put their hands on some books from this library. *Monsieur* Burns, you cannot proceed." He raised his sword, placing its sharp tip to Gunz's chest, drawing a few drops of blood.

Gunz seized the blade with his hand, pushing it deeper into his chest.

"Kill me, Luc, and you'll be killing all of you here, leaving my path to the library free. So, please, go ahead," he said, his voice shaking with unsuppressed anger. "Try to stop me, and the mortal realm will crumble under the assault of the followers of Chaos. With the three out of four magical realms sealed, this world is bleeding out its magic every day. I can sense it, can you? Do you want to be responsible for the death of magic and the destruction of the human realm, Luc? Do you want to be liable for the death of one of the greatest men who has ever walked this world?" He stepped forward, forcing the blade deeper into his chest, blood streaming from under it, soaking his shirt, and yelled, "Tell me, Luc!"

Luc de la Crosse blanched, stepping away from Gunz, and lowered his sword.

"I didn't think so," muttered Gunz, touching the bleeding cut on his chest with his fingers. He turned to Raoul, dropping his hand. "Raoul, I'm known for making reckless decisions, even stupid sometimes, but this is not one of them. I don't know how to say it or what to say so you would trust me."

"Zane—," Raoul started, but Gunz raised his hand, stopping him.

"Kal always told me that I must trust the Fire Salamander in me, and this is exactly what I'm doing right now," he continued. "The book will be safe with me. I will not give it to Chernobog or to the followers of Chaos. I swear, I will protect it with my life and when all this magical mayhem is over, I will deliver it to the Wardens Order myself."

"Do you swear, Zane Burns?" asked the Warden quietly.

"I do," replied Gunz tiredly. "Do you need me to kneel and swear on my blade?"

For a few long seconds, Raoul remained silent, staring down at his feet. Finally, he looked up, a cloud of uncertainty shadowing his features. "Zane, I'll let you go through," he said, his voice hoarse. "But I must warn you—the library is cursed. I don't know what the nature of this curse is, but I suspect it's deadly. Otherwise, why would the demons need a Fire Salamander? You cannot die."

Gunz shook his head no. "I don't think it's the reason they wanted a Fire Salamander to complete this mission," he objected. "There are other immortal beings out there who are a lot more powerful than I am. Possibly, it is because of the nature of the Fire Salamander portal. I can burn through these wards without the need to break them. I guess, we'll find out soon."

"Maybe," Raoul echoed him. "Just a suggestion—leave your werewolf friend here. He may not survive the curse."

Gunz glanced at the guard, but Nik stubbornly shook his head no.

"Together?" he asked, throwing a cold glance at the Wardens.

"Not this time," Gunz objected firmly. "I don't know what

this curse is all about and I can't risk your life. Besides, I may need your help when I come back here." Then he switched his attention to Raoul. "Raoul, I think it would be better if you and Luc left. As members of the Wardens Order, you can't be a part of this."

Luc huffed, a sad smirk on his face. "If you fail to deliver the book to us when it is all over, Brother Raoul and I will be facing serious consequences. My brother places a lot of faith in you, *Monsieur* Burns. Don't let him down."

Raoul approached Gunz and they exchanged a quick handshake. "Be careful my friend," said the Warden, his dark eyebrows gathering over his striking blue eyes. "God save you."

* * *

ONCE THE WARDENS WERE GONE, GUNZ TURNED TO THE WALL and got in touch with the elemental fire. Then he narrowed his eyes, looking through the spell into the empty, dark space on the other side of the wall and waved his hand. The flaming curtain of his portal opened up in front of him, and the protective spell responded with a loud buzz, making the ancient walls of the passage tremble.

"I'll be right back," he said without looking at Nik and stepped through the portal.

Gunz walked out on the other side of the barrier and glanced back at the werewolf. He sat next to the wall, his legs outstretched in front of him, his eyes closed. Gunz sighed, focusing on the mission ahead, and proceeded into the darkness of the corridor.

Once again, he conjured the light orbs and sent them flying over his head. He walked for a while until the passage ran into a dead-end again. Approaching a solid white wall, Gunz placed his hand on it, checking it with his Salamander senses and his other sight.

The wall was real, but there was also a layer of illusion stretched over it. Besides that, he sensed a powerful protective magic and wards that weren't familiar to him. He focused on the illusion and muttered, *"Ostendium."*

A thin layer of magic unfolded in front of him, exposing what was hidden by the illusion—a heavy oak door. Gunz outstretched his hand through the layer of his magic and touched the door handle. As soon as he did it, a surge of magical energy rushed through him and he pulled away before he could stop himself. A strange sensation spread over him scrambling his mind, leaving only one clear thought—run away.

"A turn-away spell," muttered Gunz, channeling more of the fire energy, allowing the purifying fire to circulate through his system. But as much as he wanted to make himself believe that it was just a basic turn-away spell, he knew that this wasn't the case. There was something so sinister, so threatening in the magical footprint of this spell, that his blood froze in his veins and fear splintered his heart.

He swallowed and took a deep breath to calm his nerves. "I can't see through this wall," he said out loud. The sound of his own voice seemed to have a calming effect. "If I find myself embedded into a table or a shelf, I'll deal with it then."

Gunz waved his hand again, once more unfolding the fire curtain of his portal and stepped through it. For the first time since he learned how to use Fire Salamander portals, he felt a strange resistance as he walked through it, as if an invisible rubber band was stretching, slowing him down, pulling him back. He screamed, fueling his portal with more elemental power, and pushed against the spell with all his strength. The spell gave in and he fell through to the other side, running into a large table.

Straightening up, he looked around, surveying his surroundings. The room wasn't large and the few shelves, overflowing with all sorts of books, scrolls and tomes was making it appear even smaller. A large oak table was taking most of the space and a single book lay on top of it, partially covered by an unrolled scroll.

He expected to see everything buried under a thick layer of dust, but to his amazement, the room was as clean as though it had been visited by a cleaning crew just yesterday. Careful not to damage an ancient scroll, he moved it out of the way, exposing the book underneath.

It had a heavy leather binding, and its yellow pages were covered in tiny black writing. Some writing looked familiar and he recognized the Dragon tongue. But some paragraphs were written in strange hieroglyphs he had never seen before. He had no time to wonder about it. The walls of the room were infused with protective magic and it was pressing on his nerves.

He grunted, bracing himself with his arms against the table and for a moment lowered his head, trying to clear his mind. Then he straightened and closed the book. It had no title. Neither the cover nor the spine had any writing, but as soon as he closed it, a thick leather strap on its side came to life, wrapping around it and a small golden lock materialized on the top, locking the book shut.

"Works for me," he muttered under his breath and lifted the book.

Holding it on the palm of his left hand, he placed his right hand over it and started to chant, channeling more and more of his magic into the spell he was casting. Slowly, the book started to shrink, becoming smaller with every next word he said and finally disappeared entirely.

Gunz moaned, slowly leaning over the table, and looked at his trembling hands. The skin of his palms looked like it was damaged by icy water—all red and covered in blisters. Gathering his remaining strength, he turned around and laughed bitterly. The room around him swum in continuous nauseating motion, his vision blurry, and a burning pain originated behind his eyes.

With a wave of his hand, he opened his blazing portal and was about to walk through it when a lightning bolt struck through the air, throwing him back at the table. He hit his back on the edge and fell to the floor, gasping for air.

"*Praecidio Amnia,*" he whispered, wrapping himself into protective magic and scrambled to his feet. Slowly moving his feet, he moved closer to the portal. Another lightning zig-zagged through the air, hitting him in his chest, pushing him a step back, but the protective shield held.

With everything he had, he threw himself through the portal. The fire wrapped around him, returning some of his strength, and he pushed through the resistance of the protective magic. The pain behind his eyes intensified and by the time he walked out of the portal, it became unbearable.

He dropped to his knees, pressing his hands to his eyes, and a moment later, the pain subsided leaving a strange hollow feeling in his head. Gunz lowered his hands and stared into the absolute darkness.

"*Ignius,*" he whispered and felt the weak rush of the fire energy through his body as a tiny flame warmed up his palm, but the darkness remained impenetrable.

"I can't see," he whispered, his heart pounding heavily in his tight throat. He turned his head from left to right and screamed, horror ringing in his voice.

I'm blind...

CHAPTER 35

~ MASTER MRAK DELAR ~

A shouting, angry mob pushed down the street, blocking traffic, crashing the windows of the stores and vandalizing everything on its way. Police sirens howled over the screams of the crowd as the local police department struggled to control the situation. Someone threw a stone and with a loud crash, the last streetlight got shattered. University Boulevard deepened into the night.

The darkness didn't feel normal either. It was heavy and toxic, rising from somewhere down below, slithering over the roads and plazas like a virulent fog, igniting the mass hysteria and chaos.

Tear gas and electric tasers seemed to have no effect on the raging mob, driven by the energy of Chaos, and the lines of police seemed to be pushed farther and farther back. The crowd was growing with each passing minute as more and more people with glowing yellow eyes joined the riot.

More police cars arrived, illuminating the wide street with colorful flares of light, followed by the SWAT team. Silent like the night shadows, Akira's vampires stood side by side with the law enforcement officers. Per Jim's request, they kept their swords sheathed and used only rubber batons, which wasn't making them any less dangerous. Their strict order was not to kill infected humans but to deal without mercy with the demons who fueled this chaos with their malignant energy.

Mrak Delar stood in the shadow of a building, his arms dangling tiredly at his sides as he watched the shouting mob progressing down the street. It had been five days of this mayhem. The riots were flaring here and there, each one of them more dangerous than the previous one and the local law enforcement agencies gathered all their available resources to no avail.

In the course of the last five days, Mrak hardly got any sleep, and was pulled in every direction. With magical energy dwindling down in the human realm, it was obvious that stopping the Chaos from spreading was more than he could do alone. Even with Akira's help, he knew it wasn't possible.

"Mrak…"

He heard Jim's voice and snapped around. The FBI Agent stood next to him, sweat trickling down his face. He pressed his hand to his chest, bracing himself against the tree, and took a deep breath, trying to equalize his erratic breathing.

"Mrak," he said, when he could finally speak again, "I'm sorry. I know you're tired, but I need you to step in, Master. Please. Police officers are getting hurt."

For a brief moment, he stared at the FBI Agent, a heavy load settling in his soul. Then he nodded. "Yes, of course," he said, his voice hoarse. "Let me try to slow them down, so your warriors can take care of the rest. Please tell them to pull back."

Mrak saw Jim grabbing a small plastic box and shouting a few orders into it, but he didn't listen. With effort, he channeled whatever elemental power and magical energy he could gather. His eyes flooded with the darkness of power and he rose in the air, a light night breeze playing with his long obsidian hair.

As he watched the police retreating, he extended both hands

toward the mob and a powerful blast of air escaped his palms, hitting the destructive crowd. They screamed as considerable winds pushed them back but didn't stop, quickly recovering. Mrak tried to channel more power but didn't find enough for what he needed to do and tapped into his internal resources.

"*Ignius,*" he hissed, drawing a circle with his hand and a wide ring of fire ignited around the crazed mob.

Mrak Delar lowered down, throwing an indifferent glance at the gaping people in police uniforms. He would have to deal with their memories later. Connecting with the power of Fire, he walked through the smoldering flames and stepped inside the circle. The mob was no longer screaming. They didn't try to attack him either, but their faces were void of emotions and their eyes glowed with the malignant light of chaos.

"*Praecidio Amnia,*" he whispered, encapsulating everything inside the burning circle into a protective dome.

"He is alone!" shouted someone in the crowd, and the entire mob took a step closer to Mrak. "Kill him!"

And the crowd echoed their leader, thoughtless and deadly. "Kill him... kill him... kill him..."

"Yeah... go right ahead," murmured Mrak Delar, channeling the purifying Fire energy. His eyes lit up scarlet and he laughed, rising a few inches off the ground.

Not enough, he thought, gathering the power he had within. He rose higher in the air and his body arched as he threw his head back and spread his arms wide, his jet-black hair fanning around his tense face.

An undiluted wave of purifying Fire energy spread around him, confined within his protection spell. Since he wasn't a Fire Salamander, the blast wasn't strong enough to kill the humans, but it was enough to clear their infected minds. As the energy wave rushed through the mob, they stilled, and their screams died down. People looked at each other, confused expressions on their faces, and huddled closer together, away from the smoldering heat of the fire.

He whispered a quick spell to wipe their memories and waved his hand, ordering the fire to cease. As soon as the flames went down, terrified people ran away, throwing back haunted looks at the police and the vandalized street.

Slowly, Mrak Delar turned in the air, looking down at the police officers and the SWAT team. Jim waved his arm from the sideline, attracting Mrak's attention and nodded at him. The Ancient Master sighed, once more connecting with his magic. He waved his hand, casting a few more spells to modify the memories of the humans, and then lowered down to the ground. He fell to one knee, his chest rising and falling with heavy breaths, and lowered his head.

Jim ran to him and placed his hand on Mrak's shoulder, bending down a little to see his face.

"Master, are you okay?" he asked, his voice thick with worry.

Mrak Delar lifted his head, throwing his hair off his face. "I am fine, Agent Andrews," he replied, slowly rising to his feet.

"You're anything but fine, Ancient Master," said Akira, approaching them. She halted next to Mrak Delar, staring up at him as she barely reached his chest. "You can barely keep an upright position, let alone fight."

"Akira, my lady—," started Mrak Delar, but she raised her hand and cocked her head just a little, pursing her puffy lips into a tiny bow.

Then she moved her impassive gaze to the FBI agent and the thin black arches of her eyebrows lowered over her narrow eyes. "Agent Andrews, your Master of Power is drained. If he doesn't get a full night's rest, he will shut down for a considerable amount of time. With everything that has been going on in the last five days, he overused his power."

Jim looked at Mrak, his expression hardened. "Mrak, is that true?"

"Does it matter?" Mrak Delar shook his head, a faint smile touching his lips. "Gunz is not here. Aidan and his team are gone. Even Yaroslav is not here. Who else is going to help you? Human warriors cannot deal with the followers of Chaos and demons. I am the only one who can."

He looked around the empty street with destroyed stores and broken lights and rubbed his forehead tiredly. Akira was right. He needed at least a few hours of uninterrupted rest, but every time he tried to get some sleep, he had been summoned via an annoying mundane device, cell phone, because a new riot had erupted somewhere in the city.

"Mrak, listen—," started Jim, guilt almost palpable around him, but an unusual sound drew his attention and he fell silent, staring at something behind Mrak's back.

Mrak Delar spun around and saw two horsemen approaching them. Dressed in chainmail with long white hooded cloaks and surcoats over them, they looked foreign passing by parked cars and modern buildings.

"Wardens," he mumbled, taking a shaky step back, running into Jim.

"What the hell? Templars?" murmured Jim, reaching for his gun. "Who are these Renaissance Fair castaways now?"

"They are not Templars," replied Akira, unsheathing her katana in one fluid motion. "Well, to be fair, some of them are… were. They're the Wardens, which could be bad news, all things considered."

The Wardens stopped in front of Mrak Delar and dismounted, bowing low to him.

"Master Mrak Delar, greetings," said one of them with a heavy French accent.

"Brother Wardens," replied Mrak Delar instead of hello, arching his eyebrow at the man, "to what do I owe this pleasure? I believe I'm not favored by the Wardens Order."

"To Mr. Zane Burns, Master." The Warden lowered his hood, exposing his worn-out face. "My name is Raoul de Beaumont."

"I know you," whispered Mrak Delar, unease making his shoulders tense. "Gunz spent an endless number of hours in the Wardens' library with you a while ago. He had told me about you. What did he do now that made you look for me?"

"It's not about what he did, Master. Even though—" The Warden cut himself off and cleared his throat, his fingers squeezing the pommel of his sword. "You know how Zane is. His self-preservation level is always below zero, and he would do anything to protect those he loves without much care of what would happen to him. I think it's his personal codex, his own creed. It's about how far he would go to do it and what he would sacrifice personally."

Mrak Delar's hands went up of their own accord, his fingers grasping at the mane of his hair, and he shook his head. "No," he breathed out, color draining from his face. "Please tell me he is not trying to protect me."

"Yes, my lord," said Raoul. "Chernobog forced him to break into the Golden Library, threatening your safety."

"The Golden Library?" Mrak Delar tensed, chills rushing through him. "That place is cursed. He can't die..." A thousand thoughts went through his mind at once, but none of them were of any use. "What would happen to him?"

"I don't know," replied Raoul, bowing his head. "I was trying to stop him. The book he needed to retrieve from the library is extremely dangerous. He swore to me that he would protect it. But at this moment, he is protecting you, Master. I don't know what Chernobog can do to a powerful Master of Power such as yourself, but he found something to blackmail Zane with."

Mrak Delar smirked and a painful laughter escaped his lips. "I know exactly what the god of Destruction holds over Zane." He grunted, a muscle twitching in his tightly pressed jaw. "The only way to deal with any blackmail is by taking away the leverage."

He spread his arms, connecting with all four elemental powers at the same time, and rose a few inches above the ground. Jim seized his arm, pulling him down.

"What are you planning to do, Master?" he asked, squeezing his arm. "This boy is sacrificing his own safety and God knows what else to keep you safe."

Mrak Delar looked down at the FBI Agent, his eyes swirling with all the colors of power, and shook his head. "If I let it go on, who knows what else Chernobog will demand of him," he said, and his deep voice echoed through the empty street. "I have to stop it before it goes too far. Besides, I know that the curse which was placed on the Golden Library is something terrible and if Zane got affected… He will need all the help he can get."

"Master, you're nearly drained," said Akira, softly placing her small hand on Mrak's arm. "What are you planning to do? Can your mortal body handle it?"

"My mortal body be damned," growled Mrak Delar, his hands balling into sizable fists. "And the Destiny Council! I am about to live up to my name and my reputation." He frowned, swallowing hard, and a pained expression transformed his face. "I will wield the darkest, most forbidden magic. Brother Wardens, I don't think you want to witness this, so I'll give you a few minutes to leave."

"Good luck, Ancient Master," said Raoul, bowing to him. "I'll pray for your safety."

Both Wardens mounted their horses and rushed away, the horses' hooves clicking loudly through the silence of the empty street.

"You may want to leave or at least move back," said Mrak Delar, without looking at Akira and Jim.

He gathered as much elemental power and magic as he could

and started to chant. His voice soft in the beginning got louder as he proceeded. The winds picked up, and the lightning forked through the cloudless night sky. As the ground trembled beneath their feet, making both the Scarlet Queen and the FBI agent check their balance, he struck the space in front of him. His hand went through the air as if it were a solid object and when he pulled his hand out, a bright white light erupted from the fracture that was seemingly hanging in midair.

"Oh Mrak, what did you do?" Akira moaned, thick red tears sliding down her face. "The Destiny Council will have your head for it."

"I know, my lady," replied Mrak Delar calmly, turning to the Scarlet Queen. "But this is the only way. I'm sure my situation with the Destiny Council is one of the things Chernobog holds over Gunz and I just removed it. I'll deal with the Destiny Council when the time comes."

He turned away and channeled all the power he could, including the power he had within, and forced his both hands into the fracture. The muscles on his arms bulged and he screamed, making the tear in the fabric of reality bigger.

Without looking back, he jumped through the blinding white light and disappeared to the other side.

CHAPTER 36

~ ZANE BURNS, A.K.A. GUNZ ~

Gunz slid to the floor, his back pressed against the rough wall of the passage and hid his face in his palms. His throat constricted and he couldn't inhale or exhale, his chest shuddering with short breaths, his hands shaking uncontrollably. The only thing he could hear was his own blood pumping in his ears, his heart beating desperately against his ribcage.

Through the mayhem the fear and panic created in his mind, one clear thought emerged, making him lower his arms and lift his face.

I need to revert...

Supporting himself against the wall, he slowly scrambled to his feet and was finally able to take a few deep breaths, calming down his erratic heartbeat. He channeled as much power as he could gather and let go of his control, allowing the Fire Salamander to take over. As he did, an electric shock pierced his body, and he cried out as every muscle contracted, sending him falling to the floor.

A thought, scary and dismal, made his world crash around him. *I can't revert. The protective magic of this goddamn place stops me from doing it. I can't heal... Can the curse be healed anyway?*

I'm blind...

He forced himself to sit up, resting his back against the wall again, and pulled his knees to his chest. He felt small and lonely, insignificant compared to the overpowering darkness surrounding him. He touched his face, feeling the wetness of his skin—tears and sweat. Somewhere far away, he detected a soft sound—someone's breathing. No one could have been here. It was just his feverish mind playing tricks on him.

Stop feeling sorry for yourself, he commanded, wiping his wet face with the sleeve of his jacket. *Get your fireless ass moving. You'll figure it out later. If there is a curse, there is always a way to break it.*

Gunz got up and stilled, helpless and disoriented, not sure in which direction to go. He took a few steps forward, moving his fingers along the wall and ran into the door of the library with his forehead. *Wrong way.* He turned around and moved into the opposite direction, but as his fingers fell into the emptiness of a side passage, he stopped again. Without the map, he couldn't find his way out of this labyrinth. Without his vision, he couldn't see the map.

"Dammit!" he yelled, slamming his hand on the wall, and his voice echoed through the darkness he was living in. *Think... think... don't panic... you can always panic later when you're out of here...*

"*Yaroslav? Aidan?*" he called in his mind, but there was no answer. They were still in the sealed nexus and they couldn't hear him. For a moment, he considered summoning Kal, but quickly abandoned this idea. He didn't know how the magic of this deadly place would affect the Great Salamander and jeopardizing the safety of the only man in his life he considered his father wasn't something he was willing to take a chance with.

"Mishka?" he called tentatively. "Are you with me?"

He didn't see the wyvern, but he heard a light pop somewhere in front of him and felt his fire energy signature. It was sharp and overwhelming. He had never sensed it as clear before.

"Mishka..." He stretched his hand forward searching for the wyvern through the air, just now realizing that his head was upturned and lowered it down. "Can you see?"

"Of course, I can see," replied the wyvern. "What are you doing? Why are you behaving like..."

Mishka's high-pitched voice trailed into silence and his energy field spiked up. Gunz heard the wyvern's wings cutting through the air and the sound of his breathing as he exhaled a small puff of smoke. He couldn't see it, but he detected a light scent of burnt wood and he knew right away what it was.

"Mishka, I can't see," he whispered, afraid of his own words. "It's the curse... I'm blind." Saying it out loud made it more real, and the fear he was fighting to suppress reared its ugly head again, making his stomach churn. "Can you be my eyes? Can you help me get the hell out of this goddamn place?"

Gunz felt the wyvern land on his shoulder, his hot scaly head pressed against his cheek. He could hear the tiny sound of the scales on his chest rubbing against each other.

"Boss," said the wyvern, his voice softer than usual, "your eyes can no longer see the light. It doesn't mean you can't."

"I don't understand—"

"Use the Force, Luke," Mishka interrupted him, but then giggled and added, "Use your *other* sight, ignoramus. Stop being the miserable self-pitying human you are and become the Great Fire Salamander you should be. Use your Salamander senses."

Gunz exhaled, just now realizing that the Salamander senses were taking over for his lost vision and it was happening quickly. This was why the smallest noise sounded like thunder; the tiniest fluctuation in the magical energy field felt like the blast wave of a bomb. This was why he could detect the lightest of scents. The distant sound of breathing... he could still hear it.

And now he knew what it was. As far away as he was, he could hear Nik's breathing.

"I love you, Mishka," said Gunz as hope rose within him.

"Aw, boss, you're making me cry," whined the wyvern, and Gunz felt the hot touch of the wyvern's wings on his skin as Mishka hugged him. "I thought you'd never say those words to me. But you know, a relationship born in extreme circumstances never lasts."

Gunz chuckled, shaking his head. Mishka's usual shenanigans somehow made him feel better. "I don't think our particular relationship is in any immediate danger."

He channeled his power and opened his other sight. Without his normal vision, the other sight worked differently. He looked around in awe. The walls of the corridor were breathing with magical energy. It was powerful but not dark and it allowed him to see the outlines of the corridors.

Gunz glanced to the side and saw Mishka, sitting on his shoulder, enveloped in a red glow of fire energy. He looked down at his hands and saw the red outline of his own magical energy. While he was surrounded by a scarlet light just like Mishka, his glow was mixed with the brilliant white light of his human soul. He put his hand into his pocket and brought up the map. Since the paper was a mundane object, he still couldn't see anything on it.

He sighed, closing his magical sight. "Mishka, I can't see the map with my other sight," Gunz said quietly, feeling despair creeping up into his soul again. "Besides, keeping my other sight open for longer than a minute is draining me. Can you read the map, my friend?"

"Listen, boss, I can lend you my vision for a short time," said the wyvern, shifting uncomfortably on his shoulder, "but you're not going to like the way it feels."

"Do it, Mishka. I don't care if it will turn me inside out," said Gunz, squeezing the piece of paper with the map in his fist. "I need to find my way out, but if I stay blind, I'll be lost in this labyrinth of corridors forever."

"Fine," snapped Mishka, "but don't run complaining to Kal later, telling him that a big scary wyvern hurt your little fire-deprived ass."

As soon as the wyvern vanished, Gunz cried out, wrapping his arms around his head and bent forward, breathing laboriously. A debilitating pain exploded behind his eyes, surging down through his neck and spreading over his shoulder.

"Mishka, bad idea," he moaned. "I can't... ahh..."

"Open your eyes, boss, and start moving," yelled Mishka in his head. *"It'll get a little better when you open your eyes."*

With a low growl, Gunz cracked his eyelids open, bracing himself against the wall. The world around him was glowing red as if it were set on fire. The pain subsided a little, but it was still more than he could handle for a long period of time. Clenching his teeth, he glanced down, every movement of his eyeballs producing a jarring spike of pain.

"Yes!" he hissed, excitement making him forget about the pain for a moment. "I can see the map."

Following directions, Gunz walked through the dark passages. With Mishka's vision, he didn't need any additional light, but he also knew that he wouldn't be able to handle the painful burning in his head that was melting his brain for much longer. He switched to a run and didn't stop until he reached the last barrier.

Focusing on the magical wall, he saw Nik standing on the other side, his head bowed down, his hands crossed behind his back. This was it. All he needed to do was open his portal.

"Mishka," he whispered, committing to memory the area on the other side of the barrier. "Thank you, my friend. You can let go."

He sighed with relief as Mishka's presence vanished from his head, even though the darkness enveloped him once again.

Channeling the fire energy, he waved his hand and opened his fiery portal. Following the presence of the fire, he walked through it and quickly emerged on the other side, almost stepping on Nik.

Nik yelped, pushing him in the shoulder. "Gunz, what are you doing? You nearly burned me to ashes!"

"I'm sorry." Gunz extended his hand forward, finding Nik's arm, and squeezed it. "But—"

"He is blind." A cold, sinister voice interrupted him and Gunz spun in the direction of the sound. "It's the curse, Child of Fire. The one who breaks into the library will lose their sight. Blind and disoriented, they shall wander the labyrinth driven by fear. A man or a monster, they shall be imprisoned here forever with no way to escape."

"You knew it," Gunz huffed, a pained lopsided smirk quirking up his lips.

"Of course I knew it." The wizard cackled joyfully, his foul breath overwhelming Gunz's heightened senses. "But please tell me, Child of Fire, if I had told you that you'd go blind, would it have changed anything?"

Gunz dropped his arms, suddenly feeling too weak to stand. His knees buckled and before he knew it, he was flat on the floor, the darkness waving and spinning, pulling him into its endless sickening motion. An ominous dark energy slammed into him like a hammer, pinning him to the cold concrete.

"I know you have the Codex, Child of Fire," yelled the wizard as the pressure on Gunz's chest intensified. "Otherwise you wouldn't be blind. So, it's time for you to go. My master can't wait to see you back in the City of Gold."

"I'm glad I'm blind then," growled Gunz, pushing against the restraints of the dark magic. "I sure don't want to see your master."

The wizard guffawed, and his heavily layered body shook, spreading waves of bodily odor around him, clearly indicating poor hygiene. Gunz grunted, turning his face away. His sharpened sense of smell was driving him crazy, making his stomach twist.

"Hey, wolf," ordered the wizard. "Pick him up. With your muscles and height, you should have no problem carrying him."

Gunz felt a pair of strong arms lifting him. "Why am I so weak?" he asked in a soft whisper.

"The effect is temporary," explained the wizard, his voice coming from somewhere on Gunz's left and if he could speak any colder, the winter blizzard would rush through the labyrinth. "My magic is draining you. Although I must admit, you were already drained thanks to your attempts to revert and then using your other sight."

Gunz felt an influx of dark magical energy as though it tripled in a heartbeat. He jerked in Nik's arms, but helplessly fell back, drained to a degree where he couldn't hold his head up.

"Nik, it's the king's portal, right?" he asked, wishing he was wrong.

"Yes," replied the werewolf.

"Let's get it over with," muttered Gunz.

He felt Nik moving and the dark, sinister magic of the portal surrounded him with its deadly embrace.

CHAPTER 37

~ ZANE BURNS, A.K.A. GUNZ ~

"Put him down!"

King Alexander's voice cut through Gunz's ears like a dull knife, and he cringed as Nik gently lowered him to the floor. The wizard's dark spell was no longer affecting him, but it didn't make him feel any better. The effect of the polluted nexus slammed into him with its full might, and he assumed that the spell Chernobog had placed on him earlier to ease up the impact of demonic infection on his senses was gone after he travelled back to the realm of humans.

Weak and disoriented, he lay sprawled on the floor, staring into blackness, all his senses stretched to maximum. He felt Nik's presence by his side and that gave him a little reassurance, which was removed with the next screeching order from the king.

"You may go, guard."

He sensed Nik's wolfish energy getting lighter as he listened to the sounds of his steps moving away and then the thud of the door being slammed shut.

A kick into his side came unexpected and the fact that he couldn't see it coming made it so much more painful. Gunz cried out, his hand clasping his ribs, unable to turn to his side or to protect himself from the next assault. He lay, breathing hard, his body trembling with rage boiling within him.

A soft thud announced that the king kneeled next to him, overwhelming his sense of smell with his cologne. Gunz felt the king's bony fingers wrap around his neck, squeezing it. The lack of elemental energy was making it hard for him to breathe as it was, and the king's hand crushing his windpipe just added to his misery. His mouth opened as he struggled to fill his lungs with oxygen, every breath coming out with a low groan.

"Where is the book, boy," screeched the king, applying extra pressure to Gunz's neck. "Give it to me."

Gunz's lips stretched into a cold smirk. "I have it," he croaked. "Not… giving it… to you… asshole."

A bright white light exploded in his head as the king connected his fist with Gunz's jaw and the metallic taste of his own blood filled his mouth. He choked and coughed as blood trickled down his throat.

"Give me the book, boy!" the king yelled, punching him in the stomach.

Gunz gasped and curled into a ball, finally able to turn to his side, gasping for air, blood running down his cheek. "No," he wheezed, "only to your… partner. Never… to you."

The king's hands wrapped around his neck again as he lifted Gunz slightly off the floor and slammed his head against it. All his senses went blank as he passed out. He came back when the king threw a glass of cold water into his face. Gunz moaned, bringing his arms up to protect his head, expecting a kick or a punch at any moment.

It didn't happen. Instead, he heard another voice, and he recognized it as the voice of King Alexander's mysterious partner.

"What are you doing, Alex?" the man asked calmly.

Gunz expanded his senses, carefully probing him. There was

no doubt—this man didn't belong here. He carried a distinct stench of the Dark Nav's energy like a war banner. He wasn't even trying to conceal it. He was the one and he wanted Gunz to know it.

"He has the Dark Codex!" yelled the king, poking Gunz on his bruised ribs with his leather boot. "But he refuses to give it to me."

A short silence followed and then a deep sigh. "You are hopeless, Alex," said the man. "You will never become a great king. Now leave us."

The man gave the order to the king with such calm authority that Gunz wished he could see his face at this moment.

"Fine! But you better get what we need from this abomination," grumbled the king and the sound of a harshly slammed door followed his exit.

Gunz stilled, afraid to breathe, his wide-open eyes staring blindly into the darkness. He heard a chair being moved and then complete silence enveloped the room, accompanied by a touch of magical energy to his senses. After a moment, he noticed that the effect of the demonic nexus started to subside and disappeared shortly after. He inhaled, enjoying the clear air and some elemental energy that became available to him.

"Can you get up now, Child of Fire?" asked the man. There was no animosity or anger in his voice. If anything, he sounded tired.

"Yes, sir... my lord," replied Gunz, scrambling into a kneeling position first and then to his feet, clutching his ribs with his hand as he did. It wasn't only the pain in his bruised ribs that made him do it. He was hoping that he could get close enough to this secretive and dangerous man to send a sample of his energy to Chernobog.

"I'm sorry for the way King Alexander treated you," said the man after a pause. "Do you feel better now?"

Gunz nodded. *Good cop, bad cop?*

"Catch," the man said with a low chuckle, and Gunz heard the soft hiss of a projectile flying through the air.

His Salamander senses, already amplified, stretched to the next level and time slowed down. In one fluid motion, he grabbed the Swiss army knife out of his pocket and manifested his sword. The blade whistled as he sliced the object in half. He stood, holding his sword down, with his head slightly turned to the left as he listened intently.

"You are blind, are you not?" asked the man, sounding so close to him that Gunz took a step back involuntarily.

Gunz nodded. Feeling a light movement of the air near his face, he assumed that the man waved his hand in front of his eyes, checking if he was truly blind.

"My apologies," the man mumbled again and with shock, Gunz recognized sincere tones of regret in his voice. "It was *my* curse that robbed you of your vision, child, and for that I am deeply sorry. I placed it on my Golden Library centuries ago. Unfortunately, I have no idea how to break it. I cannot help you, but perhaps the book you took from my library can... If you ever learn how to use it that is."

"You're Tsar Ivan Vasilyevich. Ivan the Terrible..." whispered Gunz, chills running down his spine, raising goosebumps on his arms.

"The Terrible." The man huffed and by the motion of the air and the slight rustling of his clothes, Gunz was positive that he shook his head. "I prefer *Grozny*, the Russian version of my name, you know? You, as a Slavic man, should understand the difference."

"I do." Gunz nodded and smirked. "Nice chatting with you, Ivan Vasilyevich," he said with a tiny bow, "but I will not give you the book."

He heard a light squeak as Ivan the Terrible lowered himself onto a chair. "I do not remember asking you to do so, Salamander." There was a touch a mockery in his voice.

Gunz shrugged. "If you aren't after the Dark Codex, then what do you want? Why are you here, Tsar? You're dead, for Fire's sake. Why is all these"—Gunz waved his arm around—"demonic invasions? Attacks on Kendral and the Otherworld. Destruction of the Land of Dreams. You're the one who is behind this chaos. King Alexander is nothing. So why?"

"Ahh," exhaled Ivan the Terrible, "it is so much more complicated, young Salamander." He silenced for a moment. "And it is a lot more dangerous than you can imagine. I do want the Dark Codex, but not for the reasons you think."

"Feel free to uncomplicate it, Tsar," growled Gunz, placing the tip of his sword to the floor so he could lean on it. "Until you explain yourself, you are not getting anywhere near the Dark Codex."

He heard the soft squeak of the chair and then steps as Ivan the Terrible got up and walked around him. Gunz lowered his head, sharpening his hearing. Getting punched without seeing it coming wasn't something he wanted to experience ever again. He twirled around, following the direction of the sounds, and stretched his arm out into the darkness.

"Relax, Child of Fire. I'm not going to hurt you."

Gunz felt a touch to his hand and instinctively pulled away. The connection wasn't long enough for him to do what needed to be done.

"I was just going to offer you a chair," said the Tsar, sounding slightly reproachful.

"Thank you. Can you help me? Please?" muttered Gunz, lifting his arm as if searching for the chair. "I've never had royalty taking care of me before."

"Oh, no, Salamander." The Tsar chuckled. "I am not going to let you touch me. Not just yet."

Gunz felt a push under his knees and fell back into a chair.

"Now that you are comfortable… more or less, I think we need to have a word," said Ivan the Terrible, and a chair screeched across the floor as he pulled it closer. He sat down with a soft groan. "Can I get you anything before we start?"

Gunz smirked tiredly. "Yeah... My freedom," he said quietly. "Get back to the Dark Nav where you belong and take your demons with you. That's all I want."

"I hate to disappoint you, Salamander, but the demons are not mine," said the Tsar, and the chair moaned as he leaned against its back. "While I was the one who polluted the nexus with demonic energy, it was the followers of Chaos who orchestrated this demonic invasion as well as the attacks on Kendral and the realm of humans.

"Unfortunately, I still have no idea who stands behind them, but whoever it is, they work with the king directly. Nevertheless, I had to make the situation even worse to get you here and then threw a few obstacles your way to make sure you got here alone. I couldn't have a powerful vampire and a Celtic god messing with my plans. I'm sure Chernobog is not going to appreciate me raising Vij from the Dark Nav without his consent..." He sighed.

Gunz stiffened, shock spreading weakness through his tortured body. All this time he thought all he had to do to stop the demonic invasion and clear the nexus was to find out which dark soul worked with King Alexander. Until a moment ago, he was positive that Ivan the Terrible was the perfect candidate for a dark soul running Morena's errands. Now he wasn't so sure. Even though he couldn't trust the Tsar, his intuition was whispering somewhere in the back of his mind, telling him that Ivan wasn't lying.

"I see it comes as a shock to you," continued Ivan the Terrible, "and I am also glad to see that you do not consider me a liar."

"No, Tsar," replied Gunz. "I don't think you are lying to me... But nothing makes sense. If you are not behind this mess, then what are you doing here?"

"Let's talk about the Dark Nav, child," said Ivan, ignoring his questions. "The reason I do not want you to touch me is because I know about the rune burnt into your ribs, and while I do want you to summon Chernobog and get all this farce over with, I am not ready. Not yet. First, we must clear a few points."

"You want to summon Chernobog," repeated Gunz incredulously, wishing he could see the Tsar's face right now.

"Yes. If you still didn't figure it out, I work for the god of Destruction. I don't know if you noticed that, but he is the only Slavic deity who is not affected by the demonic pollution. Him and his righthand man Voron. That's because as a part of our deal, I kept the two of them safe. Anyway, we are not going to summon him just yet," said the Tsar. "Not before we take care of the Dark Codex."

"You work for Chernobog, right," Gunz repeated, as he lifted his sword, placing it across his lap. "Forget it. I will not give the book to you or anyone else for that matter."

"Are you going to fight me, Child of Fire?" Humor was ringing in the Tsar's voice now. "Blind? Weakened? Surrounded by enemies? I admire your bravery... or your stupidity."

"You'll be surprised what a Fire Salamander can do," growled Gunz, gripping his sword tighter.

"Let's not find out," replied the Tsar peacefully and gently touched his knee. "What are you planning to do with the Codex?"

"Give it back to the Wardens," replied Gunz calmly.

"Then we are on the same page, young man," said Ivan the Terrible.

"You want to give the Dark Codex to the Wardens Order?" echoed Gunz, his eyebrows rising.

"Please stop repeating everything I say. Yes, I want to give the Codex to the Wardens Order. I had wanted to do it centuries ago, but I could not do so at the time. Anyway, now both Chernobog and the followers of Chaos want to have it.

Neither of them should. Do you understand me, Child of Fire? You cannot give this book to Chernobog. The consequences of that will be terrible."

Gunz heard the chair being moved again and the sound of steps as Ivan started to pace in front of him.

"Do you think it was easy for me to get you here?" asked the Tsar, stopping his pacing. "I had to manipulate this insufferable evil fool, King Alexander, to make him believe that a Fire Salamander was the only magical being who could go through my wards and retrieve the Codex. Any truly immortal being could have done it! But the Fire Salamander is the only magical being I could use to hide it."

"I am sorry," mumbled Gunz, "hide it?"

"For God's sake, Salamander, do we have an echo here?" hissed Ivan, slamming his fist on the back of Gunz's chair.

Gunz yelped, jolting to his feet, sword in hand, sending the chair flying to the floor.

"I am sorry… I am sorry… I did not mean to frighten you."

Gunz heard the regret in the Tsar's voice and lowered his sword. Ivan put his hand on Gunz's shoulder, gently directing him back to the chair. For a moment, the thought of contacting Chernobog surfaced in his mind, but he pushed it way, giving Ivan a chance to finish his explanation, and sat down, his shoulders tense with the expectation of an invisible assault.

"Child of Fire, I swear I am not going to hurt you," the Tsar said with a sigh, "but I need you to trust me."

Gunz laughed, a short and painful sound. "How do you expect me to trust you? You work for Chernobog, and you partnered with the worst monster in a human form I've ever seen—King Alexander. It was your power that broke into the Otherworld and your summoning call that tortured me. How the hell do you expect me to trust you?"

The Tsar sighed. "Because you have no choice," he replied and added after a short pause, "I swear on my wife's immortal soul, I want the Codex out of the nexus and safe in the secret Wardens' library."

"You swear on Anastasia's soul?" asked Gunz, disbelief making him repeat Ivan's words again.

"You know my wife's name?"

"Yeah, I studied history in school. You were married more than once, but she was the only woman you loved. At least that is what they say in the history books."

A silence enveloped the room, and Gunz wasn't sure if he offended Ivan the Terrible. Everything he learned in school about this man didn't promote a feeling of comfort and he stiffened, not sure what to expect.

"I need you to undo your spell and show me the Codex," said the Tsar, tension material in his voice.

"No."

"I swore on Anastasia's soul. What else can I do to make you trust me?"

"Nothing."

"You do not understand!" yelled Ivan, stamping his foot. "Now that you found me, you have no choice but to summon Chernobog. He will know if you disobeyed him! And you can't tell him you didn't find the Codex. Your blindness will give it away. Please!" Ivan touched his shoulder again. "I am begging you to trust me. No matter what, Chernobog must not have it."

Gunz got up and swayed slightly, still not used to his blindness. He pressed his left hand to his ribs, channeling his fire to have it ready to summon the god of Destruction if push came to shove. Then he put his sword on the floor, extended his right arm forward, and started to chant. As he continued whispering the words of the Dragon tongue, his hand lit up with a golden light and a large book manifested on his palm surrounded by a puff of white smoke.

"Very elaborate spell work," said Ivan, admiration in his

voice. "So, you are not just any Fire Salamander. You are the Great Fire Salamander, second of your kind."

"Yes," replied Gunz, pressing the Codex to his chest.

"Wonderful. It means you possess the other sight," continued the Tsar. "Open it. I want you to be able to see what I am about to do. It is time to hide the Codex from everyone."

Gunz opened his sight and for the first time since he arrived into the sealed nexus, he saw the infamous and most mysterious Russian Tsar. He didn't see him in a normal sense, but he saw his energy—the toxic essence of the Dark Nav. Through the purple-black outline of Ivan's magical energy aura, he could see the faded image of his face—high forehead, slightly hooked nose, drilling bright eyes, long red hair and a thick beard. The Tsar was unexpectedly tall and had broad shoulders—not the way he was depicted in movies, and Gunz couldn't help but stare.

"You cannot keep your other sight open for a long time," Ivan reminded him, a sad smile touching his thin lips. "Let's get to business. I need to touch the book, so hold it with both hands."

Gunz took the Codex, holding it tight, and allowed Ivan to place his hand on top of it. The Tsar's eyes lit up with the dark energy of the Nav as he started to wield his magic. The spell was short, but through his magical sight, Gunz watched an enormous amount of magical energy spread through Ivan's body, moving to his hand.

A moment later, a second book materialized on top of the first, light wisps of dark smoke swirling around it. It looked identical to the Dark Codex. It even had the same energy signature as the original one.

"What did you do?" asked Gunz, staring at both books with horror.

Ivan the Terrible took the fake Codex from Gunz's hand, placing it down on the chair, and explained, "This book is identical to the Dark Codex in everything except its magic. While the spells inside sound real, they have no magical power, and even though it has the energy signature of the original book, it's absolutely useless. This is the book you will give to Chernobog. Until he decides to use it, he'll be none the wiser."

"And when he finds out the book is fake?"

"It's your head, Fire Salamander."

Gunz grunted, biting his lip. "I'm damned if I do and damned if I don't."

"That's right," agreed the Tsar. "But I've heard you are known for doing the right thing most of the time, and this was the other reason I wanted you here and not the Fire Elemental. I bet this entire scheme on you not letting your mentor come here in your stead. I was right about you… Now, let's hide the real Codex."

Ivan placed his right hand on the real Codex and his left hand on Gunz's forehead.

"Sorry, it's not going to be pleasant, so brace yourself. You can scream if you want."

"It never is," mumbled Gunz, readying himself for the pain. "I hate magic…"

Ivan chuckled softly and his magical energy enveloped Gunz. Through his other sight, he could see bright light surrounding the Codex. The light gathered into a soft glowing cloud, lingering above the book. Then it descended back into the book and moved through Gunz's hand into his arm. What he felt while it was happening wasn't just unpleasant. It was an agonizing nightmare. And as the light kept traveling through his body toward his head, it became unbearable.

His blind eyes widened, and he screamed, throwing his head back, unable to comprehend anything going on around him. Fortunately, the pain was gone soon after and Gunz moaned, falling back on his chair, cold sweat running down his face. When he opened his sight, he saw that the Codex was gone and

Ivan the Terrible was leaning over him, gazing at him with concern.

"Where is the Codex?" mumbled Gunz.

"Right here," replied Ivan, touching his forehead. "You *are* the Dark Codex now, child. Be careful. Until you are with the Grand Master of the Wardens Order, you cannot tell anyone about it. He will know how to extract it. Do you understand?"

"Do I still look the same? Is it visible in any way?" asked Gunz, his voice shaking with worry.

"Just as handsome as you were." The Tsar chuckled. "No, child, no one can see it in you. Not even gods. As far as that—you are safe. Unfortunately, you are not safe from what is coming. Neither Chernobog nor King Alex favor you at this time. So get ready to fight for your... Well, if not life then freedom." Ivan the Terrible placed his hand firmly on Gunz's shoulder. "I am ready. Let's summon him."

Gunz nodded, his chest tightening with worry. He was about to summon one of the most dangerous gods of the Slavic pantheon and give him a fake magical artifact. Somewhere not too far from the room he was in, he could hear King Alexander pacing, muttering something angrily under his breath—another deadly enemy who desired to put his hands on the Codex. Outside the palace, he detected the malignant energy of Chaos getting thicker and heavier.

Things were getting better by the moment.

With an uneven smirk on his lips, Gunz pressed his hand to his side, sending a sample of Ivan the Terrible's energy through the rune.

I am the Dark Codex... What could possibly go wrong?

CHAPTER 38

~ ZANE BURNS, A.K.A. GUNZ ~

"Chernobog, I summon thee," whispered Gunz, cringing at how hollow and faint his voice sounded, but as soon as the words escaped his mouth, he sensed the energy of the Dark Nav increasing tenfold.

He spun around, his head down, his hand outstretched in the direction he thought Chernobog would appear. Tensed beyond the craziest of limits, he felt a touch to his shoulder and cried out, jumping aside.

"It's just me," whispered Ivan the Terrible, "but the portal is opened and Chernobog is coming—" He fell silent and Gunz heard a light ruffling sound of clothes as the Tsar bowed. "My lord, Chernobog." Ivan's voice was calm and steady.

A short sharp pain of electric shock debilitated his body and Gunz dropped to his knees leaning forward, bracing himself against the floor with one hand. Breathing laboriously, he raised his other hand up in a futile attempt to shield his face from an invisible strike.

"Kneel before the god of Destruction, fire worm," growled Chernobog, his voice sounding somewhere to Gunz's left. "Do not presume for one moment that you can remain standing in my presence as though you are my equal."

"My lord," said Ivan peacefully, "do not strike an innocent man as he is your loyal servant. He was not trying to disrespect you. His fault is he cannot see you as he is blind. That was the price he paid for obeying your order and delivering the Dark Codex to you."

Gunz felt someone seizing his hair and yanking his head back. He raised his arms up to grab Chernobog's wrist but stopped himself from doing it.

"He is blind as a bat," muttered Chernobog. "Stay down, Salamander, until I am ready to deal with you. And do not think for a moment that because you delivered the Codex you are forgiven. You disobeyed me, and Voron, who had a soft spot for you, defied my orders to assist you. I want you to know that Voron was punished because of you. His pain is on your conscious."

"What did you do to Voron?" asked Gunz, struggling to conceal his anger.

Chernobog's grip on his hair tightened for a moment before he let go. "He is fine," growled Chernobog, "mostly. Too bad you can't see him."

"I am here, Zane."

Gunz heard Voron's voice, and he sounded uncharacteristically weak and strained.

"Silence!" barked Chernobog. "You both will remain on your knees while I finish my deal with his royal majesty here."

Gunz heard a soft thud as Voron kneeled, his chainmail accompanied his move with a light jingle of metal rings. Chernobog's deathly presence started to lighten as the Slavic deity stepped away, while Ivan halted by his side, placing his hand on Gunz's shoulder. All these shifts and moves were driving him crazy, and every moment he expected something terrible to happen. Something he wouldn't see coming. His fingers touched the floor, finding the grip of his sword.

"Ivan, before we get to business, I want to know what you learned about the followers of Chaos," started Chernobog. "How are they planning to do it this time?"

"Not much, my lord," replied Ivan the Terrible calmly. "Here is what I know. King Alexander and his city are the stronghold of the Chaos forces. Their idea was to pollute the nexus with demonic essence and dark energy to make Lady Gatekeeper do her duty and seal it. Now the Land of Dreams is ruled by Chaos. The realm of humans is vulnerable. Kendral is sealed and the Master of Kendral will remain in his world. Just like Gwyn ap Nudd is forced to remain in the Otherworld."

"I know most of it," muttered Chernobog impatiently. "I had no idea that this idiot King Alexander was such an important figure. Human or not, he needs to be dealt with. Swiftly. The Land of Dreams must be purified and recovered."

"I don't think it'll be so easy," replied Ivan, squeezing Gunz's shoulder slightly. "When Rasputin walked the realm of humans, he did some serious damage."

"What damage?" roared Chernobog, stamping his heavy boot, making the floor tremble with the impact. "I thought the Salamander and his team stopped him before he got a chance to finish his plan."

"They did, my lord," replied Ivan, "but according to the king, Rasputin managed to complete some of his tasks. One of them allowed Zmey to communicate with his followers telepathically. I am not sure who has the direct connection with the Lord of Chaos, but this person is the one who stands behind King Alexander, orchestrating all the latest events."

Gunz stiffened, Angelique's words surfacing in his mind. She said the terrible mistake he made allowed Zmey to communicate with his followers. As understanding flashed over him, he felt the darkness around him starting to spin as his stomach gave a painful jolt, and he leaned forward, dealing with a sudden wave of nausea.

It was his mistake and now he knew what it was—the potion Rasputin gave him, which supposedly was going to separate Angie's essence from Zmey's. The dark spirit told him that to activate the potion, he had to spill it over the sacrificial table.

God, please, no... How could I be so stupid!

Like in a horror flick, he saw himself in the cave beneath Mount Karasova—debilitated by the constant anguish in his soul and destroyed by grief. He broke the vial with the potion far away from the sacrificial stone to get rid of the torturous temptation...

In his mind, he saw the liquid mixed with his own blood dripping down, getting absorbed by the sandy floor of the cave —if not right above then close enough to the grave where his Angelique lay entwined with the Lord of Chaos. He had made a terrible mistake. Gunz moaned, grasping his hair with his fingers as horror chilled his soul, paralyzing him.

"What else?" asked Chernobog coldly.

"Whoever this person is, they are extremely powerful," continued Ivan. "They cast a protection spell that makes them immune to Fire magic and some of the Otherworld's powers. So, sending the Fire Salamander to fight them may not be wise."

"I already knew that," yelled Chernobog, impatience and anger prominent in his voice. "What is their plan? How are they going to break Veles' curse and resurrect Zmey? Did you find out? Why did they need the Dark Codex?"

"I do not know that, my lord," replied Ivan, his hand on Gunz's shoulder shaking a little. "I did all I could, but even though King Alexander knew I was one of the dark souls released by Morena, he did not share everything with me—"

"You failed!" boomed Chernobog and the wall of the Palace trembled like it was nothing more but a house of cards, clearly indicating the god's displeasure. "Just like Mrak Delar failed with Rasputin."

"I did not fail," objected Ivan firmly. "I have the Dark Codex and I brought forth the information about the king. You must uphold your side of the deal now and free Anastasia's soul. That was the deal!"

The energy field of the Dark Nav spiked around Chernobog and a low growl rumbled in his chest. "I am a man of my word and I will do as I promised," grumbled the god of Destruction. "Your wife doesn't belong in the Dark Nav. She is innocent in all this, but you are not, Ivan. You are coming back to the Dark Nav with me where I will decide what happens to you next."

"That is fine," said Ivan the Terrible. "As long as Anastasia's soul is free, I do not care what happens to me. I deserve everything coming my way."

"The Codex, please," said Chernobog and a moment later a sigh of satisfaction escaped his lips—a sound filled with pure elation. "Finally. I've been waiting forever for this moment."

Gunz heard the shuffling of footsteps and then Chernobog announced, "Voron, you may rise. I am leaving now and taking you and Ivan with me." Soft metallic clanks of Voron's chainmail followed as the ancient warrior got up.

"My lord," said Gunz quietly. "I can't stay in the City of Gold in this state. Can you at least break the curse and restore my vision?"

A short pause followed, and he sensed Chernobog approaching him.

"No," said the Slavic deity. "I cannot break the curse. I do not think anyone can. But even if I could, I would not do so. You must learn some humility, and something tells me King Alexander will beat it into you. You will stay here. You and your friends still have work to do. Do whatever you must to get rid of the king and purify the nexus. Am I clear, Salamander?"

"Yes, sir," replied Gunz, his jaw set as he gathered every

single ounce of his will to stop himself from doing something as stupid as getting into a fistfight with the god of Destruction.

A few moments later, the energy of the Dark Nav dissipated and Gunz realized he was alone in the room. With a soft moan, he let go and fell to his side, curling into a tight ball with his arms wrapped around his head.

What have I done... Oh God... how can I fix it now?

CHAPTER 39

~ ZANE BURNS, A.K.A. GUNZ ~

Gunz howled into the darkness and slammed his fist on the floor. Cold metal slipped from under his hand, sliding away with a loud clatter. The sound was too jarring for his elevated senses, but it did the job, ripping him out of his state of despair. He touched the marble tiles until his fingers found what he was looking for—his sword.

He grabbed the blade, pulled it closer, found the hilt, and wrapped his hand around the grip. Carefully, he scrambled to his knees and got up. In the darkness, he felt like he was falling. He groaned, struggling to keep his footing, and tried to open his portal. Either he didn't have enough fire power in him, or the protective magic was reinforced after he broke Tessa out, but he could no longer do it. He cursed quietly and opened his other sight. The walls of the room were infused with magic which was supposed to keep him inside.

Because of the amount of magical energy that was used on the blocking enchantment, he could see the outlines with his other sight. Gunz laughed, his laughter cold and sinister as he moved toward the exit. He placed his hands on the door and channeled as much elemental fire as he could gather from within. Rage boiled over setting his entire body ablaze.

He slammed the door with all he had, sending it flying off its hinges, skidding on the marble floor with an ear-splitting clatter. Between the use of his power and his other sight being open, he started to feel lightheaded. Taking a deep breath, he closed his other sight, allowing the darkness to take him over again.

He closed his eyes and lowered his head to his chest, sharpening his other senses. A few people were coming. He could hear their steps, their elevated heartbeats, and the metallic sound of armor. *King's guards.*

He heard them walk inside the lobby he was standing in, spreading before him in a half-circle. He listened intently, counting their heartbeats, registering their positions—five guards. Somewhere farther away, he detected another heartbeat. Expanding his Salamander senses, he scanned the guards in front of him and with satisfaction noted that Nik wasn't among them. A light scent of a cologne touched his nostrils and the corners of his lips quirked up. The distant heartbeat belonged to the king.

He moved his arm, drawing a circle with the tip of his sword, the sound of metal scratching the marble unpleasant to his own ears.

"Who is first?" he asked, not recognizing his own voice.

He didn't need to see the guards moving forward. He felt them approaching with his very skin, the reek of their sweating bodies and their dark magical energy washing over him like muddy water. Raising his sword, he moved forward with speed he didn't expect from himself in his condition and situation. The guards stood no chance and a few seconds later, he was done. Probing the floor before him with the tip of his sword, he stepped over the bloodied corpses and found the entrance into the corridor leading out of the lobby.

Gunz made a few steps forward and halted, slowly moving his head from left to right. There was no mistake—King Alexander stood a few feet away from him, his heartbeat telegraphing his position. A low growl shook his chest, and he brought his blade, dripping with fresh blood, to his shoulder.

"Please, do try to stop me," he hissed, an unmanageable fury making him tremble from head to toe. "Give me the pleasure of ripping you apart with my own hands."

The king laughed, humor ringing in his voice. "Now why would I do that, Salamander?" he asked, snidely. "I value my life too much, and you are not worth it. You chose to give the Dark Codex to Ivan the Terrible, who betrayed you and left you here, blind and weak. Not the smartest choice."

"Just because I'm blind, doesn't mean I can't kill you," Gunz replied, his lips curved in distaste. "Ask your very dead guards."

He heard the king's laughter again and then a sound of steps, moving to his side. "No, Salamander. I don't need you anymore. You are free to go." He took a short pause and added, "Take the first opening on your right. Be careful walking down the stairs."

Gunz didn't reply. He didn't have to be a genius to know that a trap was waiting for him somewhere between here and the gates of the City of Gold. But how could King Alexander be so sure that he wouldn't kill him right here, in this empty corridor? He scanned the area and confirmed that they were alone.

Taking a few steps forward, he halted next to the king. In one swift motion, he seized the king's throat and ran his blade through his black heart.

The king snickered. "Now that you got it off your chest, do you feel better?"

Gunz opened his other sight and groaned, pulling his sword out of the wall. The king wasn't here. The man in front of him was a manifestation of some kind of spell. While it looked, sounded, and even smelled like the king, it was nothing but an illusion. Gunz shook his head. The anger that gave him strength to fight the guards betrayed him, making him miss the obvious.

Carefully, he moved down the stairs, taking one step at the time, holding the railing tight with his hand. As he stepped on the marble floor, he checked the path ahead and didn't notice anything dangerous. He frowned and bit his lip. He could no longer trust his senses. This peaceful emptiness could have been another illusion.

Moving slowly and silently, he reached the exit door. All he had to do was push it open and he would be out of the palace. Yet he couldn't take another step, his Salamander senses screaming bloody murder. Just to be sure, he tried opening his portal again to no avail.

He sighed and reached out to his friends, using their psychic link. *"Aidan? Yaroslav? Where are you?"*

To his surprise, he got the answer almost immediately. *"Next to the city walls,"* replied Aidan. *"Alisa found us and gave us your message. We're ready. Where are you?"*

A sad smile ghosted his face. His friends were so close, just a few yards away.

"Great, listen to me and don't ask any questions," he said urgently. *"Aidan, I am blind. I am going to try, but something tells me I am not leaving this hellhole any time soon. At least not on my own."*

"We'll get you out, Zane," replied Aidan, his voice shaking with anger. *"Just hang in there. I'll level this godforsaken city to the ground."*

"See you on the other side. Here goes," Gunz mumbled and pushed the door open.

* * *

AS SOON AS HE CROSSED THE THRESHOLD, A DOWNPOUR OF HALF-frozen water descended upon him, crushing him down to the snow-covered ground. He screamed as his body twisted in response to the devastating pain. His muscles convulsed, and his fingers unlocked, dropping his sword.

He heard the snow squeaking under someone's heavy steps, but as the water kept falling on him, he could do nothing to defend himself.

"It is a beautiful weapon," said the king, and his voice sliced through Gunz's hearing, adding to his overall torment. "I think I'll keep it. Perfect addition to my collection."

The king took a few steps away, snow announcing the direction of his movement, but then halted.

"What are you waiting for?" he asked his guards, irritation in his voice. "You can take him now. He is in no condition to fight, cowards." He walked away, mumbling under his breath, "I should seriously consider hiring new guards. These friggin' wimps are good for nothing."

Gunz felt a few pairs of hands lifting him, stripping his jacket and shirt off. He couldn't fight. He could barely breathe. He couldn't even scream when the guards dragged him down the steps and threw him half-naked into the snow, splashing him with a bucket of cold water.

For a moment he blacked out, his frazzled mind no longer capable of dealing with the pain he was in. When he regained consciousness, he felt a painful pull in his shoulder joints. Someone's hands, invasive and careless, frisked him, patting his hips, moving down his legs. He jerked weakly, finding that he was immobilized. He felt metal biting into his wrists, guessing that most likely it was handcuffs or manacles. Someone's hand dove into the pocket of his pants and pulled out the box with the ring Mrak Delar gave him.

"Your Majesty, here it is." He heard an unfamiliar voice and grunted, pulling against his restraints.

King Alexander approached him, lifting his chin with his fingers. "Here it is, Salamander," he said softly, his voice calm and even. "The infamous ring Mrak Delar created for you. A stupid toy that gave so much grief to my master." He ran his fingers down Gunz's neck, following the shape of his shoulders and finally up to his wrist. "I know you cannot see, but I hope you guessed where you are. Did you?"

Gunz remained silent. He didn't think he could talk even if he wanted.

The king chuckled. "I am sure you did. This is the same platform where your friend Mrak Delar spent quite some time entertaining the crowd with his screams of pain." He fell silent, his fingers slowly traveling down Gunz's chest and abdominal muscles, and his touch made Gunz's stomach clench. "Now it is your turn. But before my guards get started, I wanted you to know that this very ring your friend created to help you, will now work for my purposes."

The king seized Gunz's hand and slipped the ring on his finger. Gunz didn't remember screaming. Already tormented by the snow and water freezing over his skin, the pain the ring inflicted upon him blended in, but for some reason he couldn't pass out, thrashing helplessly in the chains. When the last aftershock was over, he hung lifelessly between two poles, his head bowed down.

"Well, not sorry about that." The king snickered. "This is just a precaution. Now I know you can't call your friends for help. And yes, I am well aware of your connection with the half-breed and the vampire." Since Gunz didn't react, he continued, "It is time for me to go, but don't worry. You are not going to be alone. My guards will visit you every half an hour and entertain you."

The king wasn't joking. Like clockwork, the guards came back every thirty minutes and delivered five lashes, striking his back without holding back, and then threw a bucket of icy water over the fresh welts. Every time it happened, it was so unexpected that he couldn't control his reaction, screaming and thrashing in his restraints, eliciting wild laughter from the guards.

At some point he figured he passed out or fell asleep, because he felt someone touching his head. He thought it was a bird, but its energy signature was strangely familiar and even though it had a slight demonic tint to it, somehow it felt welcome. He felt the motion of air as the bird flapped its wings rising, and he screamed after it, begging to come back, but no sound came out from his damaged vocal cords.

He moaned, dropping his head again. The ring blocked his magic and power, and unfortunately his connection with Yaroslav and Aidan too. He couldn't ask them for help. He couldn't summon Kal without any fire. He was absolutely alone.

* * *

"Gunz!"

He felt someone slapping him gently on his cheek and jerked bracing himself for the next invisible assault which didn't follow.

"Oh, Gunz, what did they do to you..."

The voice and the energy signature that touched his senses were familiar, but his exhausted mind refused to place them right away.

"Hold on, my friend, almost done," muttered the voice.

He knew this voice. *Oh, God... it has to be a dream. He can't be here...* "Mrak..." Gunz exhaled as the manacles on his wrists got unlocked and he fell into Mrak Delar's arms. "Mrak, are you really here?"

"Yes. It is me," replied the voice of his friend, "but we have no time to talk. I am going to send you to Yaroslav and Aidan. They'll explain everything."

He felt Mrak lowering him down on the platform and wrapping something warm around him—a cloak, adorned with feathers and furs. Voron's cloak. He gave it to Peyton. *She is alive! Yaroslav saved her.* The Master of Power pulled the ring off Gunz's finger and put it in his pocket. The shock went through Gunz's body, but he was too weak and sore to react to it.

"How about you, Mrak?" asked Gunz, hardly able to whisper. "Are you coming with me?"

"No, my friend." Mrak Delar chuckled darkly. "I believe I owe King Alexander. And you know me—I don't like to be in debt. I'll see you soon."

Gunz heard the Ancient Master snapping his fingers, and darkness swirled around him.

CHAPTER 40

~ AIDAN ~

Aidan stood on top of a tall hill, staring at the City of Gold with narrowed eyes. The sunrise was creeping up, slow and monotonous, coloring the dirty gray sky in slightly lighter shades, but as usual the air wasn't getting any warmer. A tall icy dome encapsulated the city, glistening in the dim light of the rising sun.

An army of demons was stationed in a wide valley in front of the city walls. They stood motionless and silent like grotesque black statues, staring without blinking in the general direction of the hills as if they knew he stood there. Aidan opened his other sight and scanned the army. Quite a few of the demons were pureblood abominations from hell, and he knew it wouldn't be easy to fight them while his own powers were depleted by the polluted nexus.

His thought went back to the fight he had had with the pureblood demons back in Rasputin's lab. There had been only a few of them there compared to the amount of demons in front of the city walls. Back then, he had been in his full godly power and now he was not even half of it. He shook his head, frowning. Winning this battle was not going to be easy.

Besides pureblood demons, there were quite a few demonically possessed humans and the city guards—humans, wizards and occasional werewolves. The guards were shifting uncomfortably, stamping their feet and patting their arms in a futile attempt to warm themselves up. Humans and monsters—they were armed to their teeth. The presence of humans outside the city walls in a company of pureblood demons told Aidan that King Alexander knew they were coming, and he wasn't taking any chances, throwing all his resources out there.

He looked to his left, sharpening his vision and expanded his magical sight as far as he could see, but the horizon remained unobstructed. *Yaroslav and Peyton should have been here an hour ago,* he thought, frowning.

"Slavik," he called in his mind, *"how far away are you?"*

"Almost there. Another fifteen minutes of human walk," replied the vampire. *"How is Zane? Did Mrak get him out?"*

"Yes," replied Aidan. *"He is not... He is still... He needs your help. Get here as soon as you can."*

"Understood, make it ten minutes then," said Yaroslav.

Lowering down next to Gunz, Aidan carefully opened up the cloak Mrak Delar had wrapped him into. For a moment he stared at his friend, his eyes filled with horror, shivers running down his spine.

"Oh, Zane," he mumbled, his fingers locking into fists. "What did they do to you?"

"That bad?" asked Gunz with a hollow chuckle, his wide-open eyes staring into the sky, his pupils wide.

Aidan glanced down again and nodded, forgetting that he couldn't see him. Gunz's entire torso and face were covered in blisters, his skin raw and inflamed. As he gently turned him to the side, he saw that his back was crisscrossed with deep bleeding welts. But worst of all, he was blind.

"How did it happen?" Aidan asked through his gritted teeth.

Gunz smirked weakly and told him everything that had

happened to him since the moment he teleported him out of the demonic barn.

For a few seconds, Aidan remained silent, struggling to process all the information, his mind boiling with fury. One thing was clear though. Chernobog—even though he behaved like an asshole by leaving Gunz in his desperate situation—didn't betray them. The reason the god of Destruction was adamant about them going straight to the City of Gold was because he knew that this time, the dark soul was working for him as opposed to against him. *Jackass, he could have just told us that!* He cursed silently, shaking his head.

On the other hand, the Slavic deity had known about the Dark Codex and the curse, yet he hadn't bothered warning them about it either. He had also known that he couldn't break the curse and restore Gunz's vision, but he just didn't care. He was looking at the bigger picture, and for him, purpose justified the means. Aidan shuddered, his mind flashing back to Mrak Delar.

As if hearing his thoughts, Gunz lifted his head. "How did Mrak get into the nexus?" he asked, his voice strained, and dropped his head back down. "Who summoned him?"

"I don't know who summoned him," replied Aidan at length. "I sure didn't, and neither did Yaroslav. He ripped the fabric of reality, Zane."

"Dammit!" Gunz slammed his hand on the ground faintly and closed his eyes. "I was trying to avoid that. Now the Destiny Enforcers are going to be after him, if they are not here yet."

"They are not here." Aidan laughed darkly. "I don't think they'll dare show up in the middle of this mayhem. But Yaroslav and Peyton are coming shortly with reinforcements, and Yaroslav will heal you."

"Yaroslav with Peyton," said Gunz, his eyebrows rising in disbelief. "That's a new one."

"Don't ask," replied Aidan, smirking. "Did you know that Peyton is part of the Sisterhood of the Sun?"

"You're kidding," muttered Gunz. "Buffy and Spike reunited?"

Aidan laughed. "Yeah, something like that. That explains her burning hatred of all vamps and the way her apartment is decked out in anti-vamp toys."

"It also explains her ever-changing mood and attitude toward Slavik. It's hard to like someone you were trained to hate your entire life." He took a short pause. "And what is she planning to do with Yaroslav now? Kill him with her love?" murmured Gunz. "The Sisterhood will have her head if they find out. And his, too. They're not known for their lenience and understanding."

"I don't know, but I'm not getting in the middle of it. Yaroslav is a big boy. He can take care of himself," replied Aidan. "And Peyton is a powerful and skillful witch. I want to have her on our side when we attack the City of Gold."

Gunz pushed himself up on his elbows but couldn't sit up. Aidan propped him up, providing him with some support. Gunz moved his head from left to right and for a short while, he looked like he was looking down the hill at the dark enemy lines.

"Alisa came through. I can sense the werewolves and shifters down in the valley, all around us," whispered Gunz, closing his eyes. "Thank God. We need to tear this city from stone to stone and capture the king. I think Kal and Gwyn would like to have a word with him. He knows a lot. Can be useful."

"Yes, Alisa found us and brought a small army with her," replied Aidan. "Can you imagine my shock when a beautiful tiny fox came running at me and then turned into an absolutely naked young lady?" He smiled at his memories, but his smile faded away quickly. "King Alexander is no longer in control of the City of Copper and the City of Silver. The City of Gold is his last stronghold. Once we destroy it, we are done. We just need to win this battle and figure out how to demolish this icy dome over the city."

"Did you see Tessa yet?" asked Gunz, his hand finding Aidan's and squeezing it. "I didn't know where you were exactly, and I couldn't open my portal to our world or the Otherworld. So, I sent her to Alisa's house."

Aidan chuckled, warmth expanding in his chest at the thought of Tessa. He glanced down at his friend and swallowed hard. No doubt that some of the pain the king inflicted upon him was because he saved Tessa.

"I've seen her," he said, and his voice shook with emotions. He cleared his throat and continued. "She's still in Alisa's house. As much as she wanted to be here with us, she couldn't. She's still too weak and recovering in the polluted nexus is practically impossible. The gray stones have done a number on her. You know how they work—the more powerful a person is, the harder the stone's magic affects them. And Tessa is the daughter of Perun."

"I'm glad she's okay," said Gunz and for the first time since they crossed over into the Land of Dreams, a warm lopsided smile graced his face, dimpling his cheek. Aidan smiled back at him, cherishing this small display of happiness in this depressing situation.

"I am indebted to you, Zane," he said softly, his voice hoarse. "I am indebted to you forever, my friend."

Gunz chuckled, arching his brow. "Does it mean you'll stop kicking my ass during training?"

Aidan laughed and swallowed hard, biting his lip, glad that Gunz couldn't see his face now. "Dream on, Fire Gecko," he said, trying to sound cheerful, which didn't work. "I'll kick your ass twice as hard now. For your own good, of course."

* * *

Yaroslav arrived as unexpected as ever, interrupting their conversation, raising a fountain of snow flurries in the air. The vampire tapped Aidan on his shoulder and lowered down next to Gunz.

"Hello, my friend," he said softly, leaning forward slightly, a waterfall of his golden hair dropping on Gunz's chest.

Aidan put his hand on the vampire's shoulder. He couldn't see Yaroslav's face, but his voice betrayed everything he felt at this moment.

"Just like the old days, right?" Yaroslav bit his wrist and the heavy scent of the vampire's blood infused the air.

Gunz grimaced but moved his hand up, searching for Yaroslav's. The vampire pressed his wrist to Gunz's lips and finally lifted his face, staring at Aidan with a pained expression on his face.

A moment later, Gunz let go and closed his eyes. "Thank you," he said. "I am still blind as a bat—no pun intended, but at least I'm not in pain."

"I don't turn into a bat," Yaroslav purred, helping him sit up. "But I can turn into a giant bird and deal with a tiny lizard." He took his leather coat off and draped it over Gunz's shoulders. "It is still snowing here, and everything is melting around you. I hope it'll help a little."

Gunz nodded, sliding his arms into the sleeves. "How do I look?"

"Like a seven-year-old wearing his father's coat?" offered Aidan with a soft chuckle.

A mighty boom rattled the air, splitting the silence into shreds. Both Aidan and Yaroslav hopped to their feet and Gunz got up slowly, swaying a little. The demonic army moved forward, slowly advancing toward the hills. Halting in the wide valley, they lowered their shields, creating a wall around them as the energy field surrounding them spiked to a new high.

"What's going on?" asked Gunz.

"It's time," replied Aidan without taking his eyes off the enemy lines. "Yaroslav, I need you with Peyton on the left flank. Alisa and her werewolves are already on the right. Just as we discussed, don't attack until I tell you. It's time we put an end to this."

Yaroslav was gone before Aidan finished his speech and he just shook his head, thinking about the vampires and their ways of disappearing without a word. Then he turned to Gunz and put his hand on his friend's shoulder, noticing that he winced at his touch.

"Zane, I need you to sit this one out," he said firmly.

"Why?" asked Gunz, notes of hurt in his voice. "Yaroslav healed me. I can fight."

Aidan cringed. "You can't see. I know that your Salamander senses are taking over, but you are not trained to fight blind."

"I am," objected Gunz quietly. "Kal trained me to fight blindfolded. I can do it, Aidan. I can help. I can sense how powerful the king's army is and you will need all the help you can get. Their army is three times as large as ours and ten times more powerful."

"I know," agreed Aidan. He realized they needed a miracle to win this battle. "But there is a difference between being blindfolded, knowing that you can take the blindfold off at any time you wish, and being blind. I can't take this chance, Zane. And I am sorry to say something like this to you, but I won't be able to fight if I know you're there in your condition. Please, stay here, on top of the hill."

"Being blind doesn't mean I can't see," whispered Gunz but then nodded and stepped back out of his way.

Feeling like a jerk, Aidan closed his eyes and cleared his mind focusing on the battle. Then he channeled as much power as he could and rose in the air. From his elevated position, he saw that the demonic army spread around, slightly curving their lines on the left and on the right, ready to surround his army that was positioned at the foot of the hill on a slightly elevated terrace.

Aidan smirked. *"Yaroslav, ready?"*

The reply came immediately. *"We're in position."*

Aidan teleported down, positioning himself in front of his army. Then he spread his arms and his body lit up with the bright light of his magic. He knew that at this point he was a shiny target for any demon who wanted to engage him. He also knew that Alisa and her wolves could see his signal. He manifested his sword and turned to the group of people standing behind him, waiting for his command.

All these people had followed him from the Copper and Silver Kingdoms. Some of them were wizards, shifters, or werewolves, but most of them were humans. Not the kind of army he would send against pureblood abominations of hell, but that was all he had, and they were willing to die to save the nexus—the land they called their home, the land they loved.

"For the Land of Dreams," he said, watching his not-so-mighty warriors raising their weapons—sword, spears, and pitchforks—and lifting their shields.

He didn't scream, but somehow his words carried through the silence of the gray morning and the demonic army responded with a mighty roar as they ran forward. Their tight formation stretched to the sides to complete a flanking maneuver. He expected that to happen, but his choices were limited.

Two armies converged in the valley by the hill, their shields coming together in a mighty clash. The air, infused with the stench of sulphur and demonic essence, became thick with flying energy balls and strikes of power. The loud clatter of metal on metal filled Aidan's ears, and he descended, throwing himself in the middle of the fight. Clamorous screams and curses, cries of wounded and dying, bangs of colliding shields and earsplitting clinks of clashing swords—everything mixed into a deafening pandemonium.

Letting his army take care of the lesser opponents, he engaged the demons in their pure forms. Wielding the fire, he struck the monsters with its purifying energy, wishing with all his heart that Zane could have been here. His every strike left a puddle of goo in the surrounding whiteness already smeared with the scarlet color of spilled blood. The demonic stench blended with a copper odor, the reek of sweat, and the unbearable stench of demonic goo.

The demons seemed to be surprised by his ability to kill them, as if they hadn't expected that he could wield his power on their territory, and for a split-second they backed away. It gave Aidan a moment to regroup. He sent a power blast, throwing the weaker demons, humans and wizards off their feet, giving his people a little breather and rose in the air to assess the situation.

They weren't surrounded yet, but the opposing army completed their flanking maneuver and were pushing them from both sides, limiting their movement.

"Yaroslav, now!" he yelled. Manifesting a bright energy ball, he threw it high in the air, signaling Alisa to begin.

A loud multi-voiced howl was a response to his signal. He saw the dark formation of Yaroslav's army advancing from the left, pushing the demonic army to the slope of the hill and limiting their ability to maneuver. As he sharpened his vision, he thought he saw Yaroslav's katana swishing through the air, leaving a pile of dead bodies in its wake. Then his eyes fell on Peyton and he couldn't help but smile.

The young witch was fighting alongside Yaroslav, her magic just as dangerous as her sword. She looked beautiful and deadly as she fearlessly made her way forward without much care who she had to face—demonically possessed humans, dark wizards or even demons in their pure form. A sense of pride spiked through Aidan and he swore to himself that if they all survive this battle, he'll get Jim to rehire her and ask her to join his team.

Aidan turned to the right and watched Alisa's army attack the opposing army from the other side. Wolves, foxes, bears, tigers and panthers assaulted their enemies. They ripped them apart—their claws slashing through flesh, their fangs ripping throats.

Even though the animals' attack wasn't a concern for the pure demons, the enemy lines trembled, losing its perfect formation. The humans of the king's army screamed in horror, dropping their weapons and turned to run toward the city walls, chased by tenacious foxes.

The mighty roar of his army was a response to the retreating enemies as they attacked the remaining army, doubling their efforts. Aidan went down and engaged the demons again, channeling fire through his sword and striking them with his power.

Despite adrenalin surging through his system, Aidan was starting to feel weaker. To fight the demons, he had to use his power and magic, channeling it from within, and it was draining him.

Suddenly, a collective sigh of terror rolled through the valley and the sounds of the battle ceased. Expanding his senses, Aidan froze, horror paralyzing him. The amount of demonic energy had increased tenfold despite the fact that he destroyed a lot of them. He looked up and his mouth opened, sweat running down his face.

The air above them was black as a new wave of monstrous abominations was slowly gathering like an ominous storm cloud. The demonic reinforcement touched the ground and now the entire valley between the hills and the city walls got shadowed by the dark forces—every one of the newcomers was a pure demon.

It's over, thought Aidan, desperately watching the black wall, reeking of sulphur, advancing at them. *I can't fight all of them.*

CHAPTER 41

~ ZANE BURNS, A.K.A. GUNZ ~

Gunz stood at the edge of the hill, his overly stretched senses absorbing every sound, every spike of magical or demonic energy and the tiniest smell of the battle below. Once in a while, he opened his other sight just to make sure he could still see Aidan's shiny presence. It was much harder to find Yaroslav as his vampiric energy signature blended with the demonic essence, disappearing in it. But he could hear his and Peyton's voices, and that was enough for him to know they were alive.

A sudden influx of demonic essence overwhelmed his senses, making him cough and lean forward, clutching his stomach. He forced himself to straighten up and opened his other sight. What he saw made his blood run cold. The entire space between Aidan's army and the city wall shimmered with the darkness of the demonic presence, as malignant and ominous as the energy of the Dark Nav.

"Mishka," he hissed, pressing his hand against his tattoo in a split-moment decision.

A light pop announced that the wyvern was here and then he

heard a gasp. "Boss…" mumbled Mishka. "Did you go for a walk in the Dark Nav? Or Hell?"

"Close to that," muttered Gunz. "I don't have to tell you that these are pure demons. It means Aidan cannot fight them with the limited magic and powers he has here. And Yaroslav, as fast and strong as he is, is not a match for these monsters."

"There are just too many of them, boss," mumbled Mishka, landing on Gunz's shoulder, and for the first time since he had met the wyvern, he sensed his fear. "I'm too little to fight them all."

"I know, Mishka," he said softly, finding the wyvern's hot back and patting him fondly. "I am not sending you there alone, my friend. We will fight them together."

"But boss," whispered the wyvern into his ear as if he were telling him the biggest secret, "don't you know? You are blind!"

Gunz chuckled, shaking his head. "It's kinda hard for me to miss, buddy. I need you to do something for me, so please tell me if it isn't possible—"

"It isn't possible," replied Mishka right away, shifting on his shoulder.

"Mishka!" hissed Gunz throwing his hands in the air. "I didn't even tell you—"

"Anything you do is always crazy, or stupid, or reckless, or all of the above," objected Mishka, pouting. "I am not your enabler. You're pathologically addicted to danger. So, no. It's not possible."

"Mishka, remember how you were able to lend me your vision?" asked Gunz with a sigh. "I need to borrow your vision again, but this time I need a little more than just that." He paused, listening intently to the wyvern's heartbeat, but since it remained as even as ever, he continued, "I need your fire. It seems the nexus doesn't affect you as much as it affects me or Aidan, or Peyton. So, here is what I wanted to ask. Can we be one? Is it possible, my friend? Just for a short time. And if that's going to turn me inside out with pain, I don't care. We must save our friends and the Land of Dreams."

The wyvern sighed, exhaling a small puff of smoke, and the scent of burnt wood invaded Gunz's nostrils.

"We can try," said Mishka. "My fire energy is not affected by the nexus, but I don't know what would happen when we merge. Ready?"

"No, but let's do it anyway," replied Gunz, bracing for the pain.

With a light pop, Mishka vanished, and Gunz screamed as a hot, crippling pain expanded in his chest. He felt as though his heart stopped beating, replaced with something entirely different. He opened his eyes, forcing himself to breathe, and saw the world through Mishka's eyes. Slowly, the pain subsided to a level he could handle without screaming.

"The world is on fire," he whispered as everything around him glowed with an outline of red fire energy. "I'm a friggin' Daredevil."

He placed his hand over his chest and smiled as he detected a double heartbeat—Mishka's and his own. *Well, let's see what we can do...*

Gunz rose in the air and looked down. The deadly battle unfolded beneath him in all its horrifying glory—blood, gore and death reigning over the valley that was no longer white but rather red and black. He could still see Aidan's brilliant light and it gave him hope that all was not lost. But no matter how hard he looked, he couldn't see Yaroslav and Peyton, or Alisa and Nik.

He took a deep breath and focused on the elemental fire, separating himself from everything that was going on below. Glancing from left to right, he realized that he was levitating supported by two giant wings of a wyvern. *Well, that doesn't look strange at all...*

He channeled as much of the fire energy as he could,

expanding his combined Salamander-Wyvern senses as far as he could reach. Somewhere on the outskirts of the Land of Dreams, he felt an accumulation of fire and immediately recognized what it was—the wyverns who had been guarding the sacred garden. He reached farther, connecting with all the wyverns at once, feeling their beating hearts within his grip—all twenty-five of them.

We need you at the City of Gold, ordered Gunz, and the wyverns obeyed him. They rose in the air and vanished. A heartbeat later, they reappeared, lingering in the air in front of him, awaiting his next command. He stared at the largest wyvern and it bowed its head, landing to the ground. Gunz lowered himself on the wyvern's back and silently commanded him to move forward.

He flew over the demons, twenty-four wyverns following him, and glanced down. *"Aidan, Yaroslav, I need you both to pull away and command all your people to retreat as far as possible."* Neither of them answered, but he noticed the bright spike of Aidan's magic and two large energy orbs went up in the air.

"Zane, but how..."

He heard Aidan's voice in his mind but didn't bother to answer. Focusing on his control over the wyverns, he waited a few minutes to let Aidan's army retreat. Then he tapped on the wyvern's back and ordered through gritted teeth, "Destroy them all, my brothers. Every single one of them."

As the wyvern spiraled down, showering the king's army with undiluted fire entwined with purifying energy, the demons screamed and cowered away, trying to shield their heads with their grotesque arms. But nothing could save them. The purifying fire energy consumed the valley, filling every nook and cranny, leaving the monsters no place to hide. Their screams and curses filled his ears as the stench of their burnt flesh invaded his nostrils, and he spread his arms and wings wide, a loud growl escaping his tightly pressed lips.

A few minutes later, everything was over, the valley covered in piles of steaming gray ash—all that was left of the king's demonic army. Gunz brought all the wyverns to a soft landing in front of Aidan and dismounted. He commanded them to leave and released his control. As the wyverns vanished, Aidan approached him. He moved his hand over Gunz's wings, staring into his flaming eyes.

"But how?" asked Aidan. "Can you see? I've never witnessed anything like this."

"We can see," replied Gunz, and his voice sounded like two in perfect harmony with Mishka's. "It's temporary. We cannot stay in this condition for much longer."

Aidan was about to say something, but an earsplitting noise swallowed his words. Gunz spun around just in time to see the icy dome encapsulating the city explode with a thunderous bang. Frosty dust and splinters of ice flew through the air like deadly projectiles. Yaroslav was in front of him, shielding him with his body before Gunz had a chance to react. The icicles bombarded the vampire, and even though they penetrated his skin in a few places, he healed almost immediately.

"We are grateful," said Gunz in unison with Mishka.

Yaroslav let go and stepped back, grabbing Peyton's hand and pulling her closer. He quickly checked her for injuries and draped his arm over her shoulders.

"What happened to the ice dome?" asked Aidan, frowning. "Zane, did you do it?"

"We did nothing," replied Gunz.

The ground quacked under his feet and a bright lightning bolt split the dullness of the sky, accompanied by the low rumble of thunder. The city walls collapsed, raising a cloud of dust and debris.

Gunz spun around and stared at the city walls in awe. Mrak Delar was levitating high in the air, holding King Alexander restrained within his spell.

Through the years, Gunz had seen the different sides of the Ancient Master. He had seen him at his best and at his worst. Kind and companionate, ready to sacrifice himself for those he loved, and cold and calculating. But there was nothing of his friend in the man who hovered above the demolished walls now.

Power and anger were palpable around Mrak Delar. His eyes were flooded with darkness, but even those horrifying black eyes couldn't conceal all the pain his soul held. He laughed, throwing his head back, his obsidian hair rising like an ominous cloud, fanning around his face. And the sound of his laughter was filled with so much hatred and loathing, that Gunz shuddered, shivers running down his spine.

"Mrak," he yelled, stretching his flaming hand toward his friend. "Don't… Do not do it!"

He wasn't sure if Mrak even heard him. The Ancient Master rose higher in the air pulling the terrified king with him.

"Look around, King Alexander," he roared, and his voice boomed through the sky. "Your kingdom of evil is gone. Never again will you dare put your hands on me or anyone I care about."

The king whimpered, pleading for his life. Gunz and Aidan shouted, begging him to stop. Mrak Delar was deaf to everything and everyone. Placing his hands on either side of the king's head, he tilted it to the side and then twisted it with one sharp movement, killing him instantly.

Breathing hard, he let go of the lifeless body and it came tumbling down to the piles of debris, which used to be city walls. Mrak glowered down, his face a stone mask, and slightly moved forward, gradually lowering down.

"Ding-dong… the fucking king is dead…" he muttered, his lips curved in disgust. Suddenly, his eyes rolled back, and he fainted, plummeting to the ground.

CHAPTER 42

~ ZANE BURNS, A.K.A. GUNZ ~

After Mishka broke their connection, Gunz felt drained and strangely hollow, and with Mrak Delar being unconscious because of multiple injuries and overuse of his power, they had decided to spend a few hours in Alisa's house to let the Ancient Master get some rest and heal his wounds at least partially.

Gunz didn't mind a quick shuteye either and even though Alisa offered him her bed, he just folded his arms on the table, resting his forehead on top of his arms, and was asleep right away. He slept without the ring, and in his dream, he noticed a dark shadow lurking on the outskirts of his mind, but something stopped it from entering and when he woke up, he felt a lot better.

Alisa gave him one of Nik's shirts and he returned the leather coat back to Yaroslav, which he accepted with relief, shrugging it on immediately and sheathing his katana under it —a move accompanied by a soft metallic hiss.

Tessa sat on a wide bench by the wall, her head resting on Aidan's shoulder, her fingers playing with his absentmindedly. She was still too weak, and Aidan wanted her to stay with Alisa no matter what they would decide to do. She wasn't happy with it but had to admit that he was right since even the simplest task, like getting dressed or walking from the bedroom to the living room were taking too much out of her, making her dizzy and sick. Drained by the gray stones, she couldn't restore her magical energy in the given conditions.

Gunz was still in the same chair he fell asleep in, sitting with his head bowed down, his arms resting in his lap. With his Salamander senses, he detected that all his friends were here, but without opening his other sight, he couldn't see any of them. With relief he recognized the Master of Power's energy signature, and even though it wasn't as powerful as usual, he knew his friend was back on his feet and he was fine.

"King Alexander is gone, but the nexus is still polluted, and the winter rules the land," said Mrak Delar. "Any ideas on how to purify it?"

"You shouldn't have killed the king," said Aidan softly. "We could have used him to get some information."

Mrak laughed darkly. "I doubt that he knew much," he objected, his fingers drumming a nervous rhythm on the table. "He was just a pawn in someone's capable hands. A stupid and dangerous maniac—nothing more than that. I don't think that whoever was truly in charge would share any important information with this evil idiot."

"Be that as it may, Mrak," objected Aidan, "the Destiny Council is not going to be happy with you. They could have put the king under the Destiny Oath and get at least something out of him."

"The Destiny Council has been unhappy with me for years. Nothing new." Mrak Delar sighed. "They've been looking for a reason to put me on trial for ages. Well, now they have it. I have ripped the fabric of reality and killed a human in cold blood. I am shocked they are still not here."

Gunz shook his head, rubbing his cheeks, feeling the overgrown stubble under his touch. "Mrak, I'm not going to let them take you." He felt the Master of Power's fingers touch his hand in a light tap and then heard his short laughter.

"No, Gunz, you will let them do whatever they want with me," he objected, his voice hoarse. "You can't stop them and fighting the Destiny Council is not something I would recommend. Even the gods don't argue with them."

Gunz heard the sound of a chair being moved as Mrak Delar got up. "Aidan, I think we should visit the World Tree. Perhaps Sirin and Alkonost can provide some information that would help us cleanse the Land of Dreams."

Gunz also got up, supporting himself on the table. "I'm going with you," he said in a no-nonsense tone. "After all, among all of us, I'm the only one who wields the purifying fire. Mrak's and Aidan's fire power is a lot weaker than mine."

"We go together," suggested Yaroslav, his voice as calm and even as ever. "Peyton?"

"Of course, I am with you. Did you have to ask? All three of you," replied the young witch and chuckled. "Friggin' musketeers."

There was a little commotion of shifting chairs and steps and Gunz felt a soft touch to his shoulder. He flinched involuntarily and stiffened, but immediately relaxed as he recognized Alisa's energy signature.

"Gunz," she said softly, encircling his neck with her arms, "promise that you'll come back one day. Just for a visit?"

Gunz pulled her closer, planting a soft kiss on her cheek. "I will, but you have to promise something too."

"What is it?" she asked, tones of surprise in her voice.

"The beaten one is carrying the unbeaten one?" He chuckled, a lopsided smile tugging at his lips. "Don't ever do it to me again."

She giggled and kissed his cheek. "I promise."

He said his goodbyes to Tessa, Alisa and Nik and felt Mrak's hand on his shoulder.

"Are you ready, young Salamander?" asked the Master of Power and snapped his fingers without waiting for his response.

THE AIR WAS STILL COLD AND CRISP, BUT AROUND THE WORLD Tree, it seemed to be a lot warmer. The snow was melting slowly into puddles of icy water and it slurped under their feet at every step. Gunz opened his other sight and quickly assessed their position. He stood in front of the Alatyr stone and Mrak was leaning against it, his arms folded across his chest. Most likely, the Master of Power knew that he could see him, because a sad smile lit up his strong face.

Aidan, Yaroslav and Peyton stood a few feet away from them, looking around. Gunz assessed the health of the Tree, with relief noticing that even though the demonic infection wasn't cleared yet, the pure energy of life was surging through the Tree's powerful trunk and heavy branches.

"Mrak," asked Aidan, "do you want me to summon the birds?"

"You would do no such a thing, god of the Otherworld. All of you will remain where you are until I am done. Am I clear?"

A loud male voice spoke up from somewhere on Gunz's left and he snapped his head. A man in long dark robes stood in front of them. He was tall and his body shimmered with a brilliant white light, his energy signature similar to that of Gwyn ap Nudd and Aidan. Gunz watched all his friends lower down to one knee, bowing their heads before the stranger and everything inside him crashed as he realized who he was.

"The Destiny Keeper," Gunz whispered, slowly taking a knee. He didn't need to ask. He knew why he was here without asking.

Yet, he was a little surprised to see the Destiny Keeper coming to take Mrak Delar himself. Usually the Council would send a group of armed Destiny Enforcers for assignments like this.

"Master Mrak Delar," said the Destiny Keeper, his voice betraying no emotions, "the Destiny Council summons you. Your hands, please."

Gunz watched Mrak Delar silently holding out his hands as the Destiny Keeper produced a pair of handcuffs, shining with the energy of magic that was brighter than his own. Everything inside Gunz crashed. He didn't know what to do. The only thing he knew was that he couldn't let this man put the Destiny cuffs on Mrak, draining him of all the magic and power he had, leaving him a weakened, helpless human.

"Please, my lord, stop," he said, rising. "You can't take him."

The Destiny Keeper turned around, his eyes blazing with the light of his magic. "Young Salamander?" He approached Gunz and put his hand on his forehead. "You are blind. So, it is true then—you retrieved the Dark Codex."

"Yes, my lord."

"Chernobog has it?"

Gunz bowed his head, unable to tell the lie.

The Destiny Keeper smirked. "Let's assume he does. So, why can't I take Mrak Delar, Salamander?"

"I need him, my lord," said Gunz quietly, not meeting the Keeper's eyes. He cleared his throat and added, "If you want me to cleanse the Land of Dreams, I need Mrak Delar."

"First of all, you don't need Mrak Delar," objected the Keeper, taking his hand off Gunz's head. "You need a Master of Power. Summon the Master of Kendral."

Gunz shook his head, a lopsided smirk curving his lips. "I would love to do that, sir, but I can't," he objected. "Kendral is still sealed and so is the Land of Dreams. And as long as the nexus remains polluted, I can't summon him here. So Mrak Delar is the only Master of Power who can help me."

"Clever little Salamander," muttered the Destiny Keeper. "Well, then I'll have to take one of your friends to make sure that Mrak Delar is not going to try to escape."

"You have my word. Isn't that enough?" growled Mrak Delar indignantly, his power spiking around him. "I swear on my power, I will be at your disposal as soon as the Fire Salamander cleans the nexus."

"Not even close, Ancient Master," replied the Keeper calmly.

Through his other sight, Gunz watched him approach Aidan, Yaroslav and Peyton. The constant use of his magical sight was draining him, but he had to see what was going on, so he kept it open.

"I think, I'll take him," said the Destiny Keeper. "Your hands, Prince Potemkin."

"My lord…" whispered Yaroslav staggering back, fear making his voice shake.

"Take me!" yelled Peyton. Jumping to her feet, she forced her way between the Keeper and Yaroslav. "You put these cuffs on him and you'll turn him into a pile of dust. And you know it! He is a vampire, for God's sake. Magic is what sustains his life and the cuffs will suck it dry out of him, killing him. No! Please take me instead."

"But Peyton, sweetheart," purred the Destiny Keeper, his magic fluctuating around him, "you know that you are more human than all of them here. These cuffs may kill you just as fast as they may kill your undead lover."

"And I would gladly give my life for his," said Peyton, meeting the Keeper's steady gaze as she pushed Yaroslav back, shielding him with her body.

The Destiny Keeper grabbed Peyton's hand and walked her back to Gunz, an all-knowing smile on his face. "When the dark becomes light, and the light becomes darkness… When the predator gives its life for its prey," he said, staring pointedly at him. "Do you know what you need to do now, young Salamander?"

"The prophecy," mumbled Gunz, reciting the words of the prophecy in his mind as understanding flushed over him. "Yes, my lord, I know what I need to do, and I still need Mrak Delar to do that."

"But of course you do." The Keeper laughed openheartedly, but his humor was short-lived. He sobered up quickly and continued, "You need him and you also need what's inside here"—he tapped with his finger on Gunz's forehead—"and I don't mean just your brain. Do you understand me?"

"Yes, sir."

"Ancient Master," said the Keeper. "Peyton and I will be leaving now. Once the nexus is cleansed, please summon me at once and I'll bring her back." He arched his brow at Yaroslav. "Something tells me, Prince Potemkin will make sure you do."

A low hiss escaped Yaroslav's lips as he covered the space between him and Peyton in a heartbeat, pulling her into a tight embrace. He kissed her, but she pulled away and took the Destiny Keeper's hand.

"I'll see you soon," she whispered so softly that only the vampire's and Gunz's overly sharp Salamander hearing could catch it.

The Destiny Keeper snapped his fingers, and they both vanished from the Isle Buyan.

CHAPTER 43

~ ZANE BURNS, A.K.A. GUNZ ~

"You shouldn't have done it," said Mrak Delar, approaching Gunz.

"And you should have stayed out of it!" yelled Gunz. He closed his sight and exhaled as darkness surrounded him again. "I told you!"

"I couldn't let Chernobog control you, could I?" asked Mrak Delar, tones of anger in his voice. "The infamous god of Destruction controlling a Great Fire Salamander with your power? What could possibly go wrong with that scenario?"

Gunz just shook his head. "If the god of Destruction wants you on your knees, he'll find a way to get you in the right position. One way or the other..."

Mrak didn't say anything. Gunz took a few deep breaths to calm down and reached deeper into his own mind. He wasn't sure what needed to be done or what he was looking for, but the connection with the Dark Codex came easy, almost immediately. The book presented itself and, in his mind, he could browse it as if he were holding it in his hands. He formed a question, and a spell materialized in his head, glowing words of Dragon tongue lingering before his eyes.

Gunz sighed with relief and his lips twitched at the corners. "Anyway, Mrak, I didn't lie when I said I needed you," he continued. "Besides myself, I need three more magical beings of fire, the darkness and the light."

"And may I ask how you know all that?" Mrak Delar's iron fingers squeezed his shoulder, turning him a little in his direction.

"I just do," replied Gunz with a nonchalant shrug. "I'm the Fire. I'm everywhere and I know everything."

"Fire my ass. Kal you are not," grumbled Aidan, approaching him, and then addressed Mrak Delar. "He is lying."

Mrak Delar laughed. "Of course, he is. And he is the world's worst liar. Gunz," he growled, "you will tell us the truth."

"I will," agreed Gunz, stepping back, "but not today. It's time to do some spring cleaning."

He reached into his pocket and stilled, shivers running down his spine. His Swiss army knife was missing. With horror, he remembered King Alexander taking his sword. For a moment, he stood with his head bowed down, grieving as if he had just lost his best friend, but then sighed and turned to Mrak Delar.

"Mrak, may I borrow your sword?" he asked apologetically, his voice hoarse. "Mine was... I lost it."

"Yes, sword, of course," said Mrak Delar and with surprise Gunz detected those lighthearted tones in his voice which usually indicated a smile. "Give me your hand, Gunz."

Gunz held out his hand and felt a touch of plastic to his skin. He wrapped his fingers around it and raised his head in the direction he assumed the Master of Power was in. A soft chuckle was the response to his move.

"I couldn't leave your weapon in the hands of an evil bastard," said Mrak Delar. "Don't lose it again, boy."

"Thank you," replied Gunz, his throat dry, and murmured his sword's name, manifesting it.

He called to the fire within him, producing a small flame in the palm of his hand. "Kal, I summon thee," he whispered and without waiting for his mentor to appear, he drew a flaming rune in the air and slammed his hand over it, shouting, "Semargl, I summon thee."

The Fire Elemental and the Slavic god of Fire materialized at the same time. Gunz didn't need to open his sight to know that both his summoning calls had worked.

"Semargl," said Kal, greeting the Fire deity.

"Hello, brother," replied Semargl. "Your young one called us?"

They both turned to Gunz, and he heard Kal take in a sharp breath.

"Gunz, my child, what happened?" he asked, seizing Gunz's chin with his hot fingers, and gently lifted his head up. "You're blind…"

"It's okay, Father, I'll tell you everything later," replied Gunz, stifling a sigh. "I'm not done yet. I need two more beings of magic—the light and the darkness. When they arrive, I'll explain what we need to do to purify the nexus."

Gunz bit his lip, locking and unlocking his fingers. After everything Chernobog had done to him, the idea of seeing him again was making him shake with fury. Slowly, he approached the Alatyr stone and drew a rune on its surface, summoning the god of Destruction. A black portal opened up next to him, enveloping him with the suffocating energy of the Dark Nav. He ignored it and drew one more rune, infusing it with his power and whispered another name. A collective gasp rolled through the Isle as Gunz completed his spell.

Kal seized his arm, squeezing it tight, as he pulled him closer. "Are you sure you know what you're doing, my child?"

"I do what I have to, Father," replied Gunz dryly, prying Kal's fingers off his arm. "Isn't that what any Child of Fire is supposed to do?"

Gunz opened his other sight and watched Chernobog

emerge out of his portal. The second portal, filled with blinding brilliance, was still rotating, emitting a powerful vibe of light. A second man walked out from the portal and stilled, staring at Chernobog.

"Hello, brother," growled Chernobog, leaning slightly forward with his hands clenched into tight fists. "Long time, no see."

"Not long enough," replied Belobog, folding his arms.

Both men were the same size and had the same facial features, but everything that was dark about Chernobog was light in his twin-brother. Dressed in all white, Belobog had long platinum blond hair and a beard, and his glacial blue eyes shone with pure hatred as he stared at his brother.

Before anyone could do anything, both Slavic deities unsheathed their swords and charged each other like crazed bulls, quickly gaining in size. Thunder rolled through the Isle Buyan and the wind picked up, ruffling the branches of the Tree as the two blades collided, bringing the opponents closer together. The ground trembled and the world around them separated—Chernobog's side was consumed by darkness and an eye-watering light unfolded in Belobog's wake.

"Goddammit!" Gunz cursed, channeling as much power and magic as he could find and as he realized that it wasn't enough, he tapped into Kal's and Semargl's. Both the Fire Elemental and the god of Fire gasped, staring at him in shock.

Better to ask for forgiveness than for permission, he thought, cringing at the idea of facing Kal when it was all over. *I need to stop them, before these two idiots ruin our only chance of cleansing the place. Seems like the amount of their brains is inversely proportional to the amount of their powers.*

He allowed the fire to take him over, and as his body got engulfed in smoldering flames, he rose to the same height as the two deities, who were shouting at each other the kind of profanities you wouldn't hear in the world's finest construction site while hacking with their giant swords like two oversized woodsmen.

Gunz muttered a few words in Dragon tongue and two flaming circles surrounded each god. They rushed forward but ran into an invisible wall and were thrown back. Gunz folded his arms over his chest and stood, silently observing the brothers' fruitless attempts to break through his spell. After a few tries, they stopped and turned to Gunz, breathing heavily.

"Are you done?" asked Gunz coldly.

"You..." hissed Chernobog, his godly powers swirling around him like dark smoke. "How can you even know this spell! No mortal can know it, let alone have what it takes to wield this kind of magic!"

"I am the Fire!" roared Gunz, and his voice boomed through the Isle Buyan. "I am everywhere, and I know everything!"

Chernobog cast a quick glance at Kal, but the Great Salamander just shrugged, a derisive smirk stretching his thin lips under his hooked nose. "Well, he is," he said, suppressing his laughter.

"Now that we've got that out of the way," continued Gunz, realizing that the two gods were staring at him intensely and their expressions promised nothing good, "let's talk about why I summoned the both of you here."

"Please, little lizard, enlighten us," hissed Belobog, the brilliant light of his power making Gunz's eyes water. "While you can that is. Because when I break through this enchantment—"

"Silence!" barked Gunz, sending a jolt of electricity through the invisible walls of his spell. The twins cried out in pain and fell silent. "You will have to put your sibling rivalry away. I don't care to hear any of your mutual grievances. Bring it up to your father Rod, if you must. But here, you will listen to me and do as I command, because this is our only chance to cleanse the Land of Dreams and save magic. Am! I! Clear!"

He shouted the last three words, one at the time, and the fire responded to his anger, rising higher. Then he took a deep breath, getting his emotions under control, and looked around, his other sight seemingly brighter and clearer than ever before. Mrak Delar stared at him, his face pale and tensed, a thick vein pumping in his neck, and Gunz could hear his erratic heartbeat. As far as he could see, the Ancient Master was the only person who realized what was going on and Gunz gave him a barely visible shake, asking him to be silent.

If Kal understood, he didn't show it, and Semargl, Aidan and Yaroslav remained shocked and motionless, staring at him in awe.

"Release me," demanded Chernobog, sheathing his sword. "Let's clean this mess. But if you think I am not going to deal with you later—"

"You will not deal with me later, Chernobog," said Gunz calmly, interrupting. "You don't have what it takes, and frankly, I won't allow you to bully me any longer." He turned to the god of Light and Creation. "Belobog?"

"I am ready, Great Fire Salamander," replied Belobog, throwing a scorching gaze at his brother.

Gunz waved his hand and the flaming circles disappeared. Both deities exhaled, relief reflected in their eyes, and morphed back into their normal size, looking up at him, awaiting his instructions. He assumed his human form and then rose high, levitating under the first branches of the World Tree.

Closing his eyes, he reconnected with the Dark Codex. He wasn't looking for the words of the spell. He didn't need that as every word was etched into his memory. But connecting with the Codex gave him a new kind of power that wasn't affected by the demonic pollution. Even though the effect of the dark energy had subsided a little after the City of Gold fell, it still had a strong enough hold over the Land of Dreams, making all of them weaker, forcing them to channel the magic from within.

Gunz looked down, his gaze powered by his magic slipping

from one familiar face to the next. *"Aidan, I need you to take Yaroslav and teleport back to Alisa's house. I am going to wield an enormous amount of purifying Fire, and I want him to be as far away from the epicenter as possible. Yaroslav is the only one among us who is in true danger. He will need extra protection. Do whatever you must to keep him safe. You'll know when it's over."*

Aidan gave him a curt nod and placed his hand on the vampire's shoulder. With a snap of his fingers, they both vanished from the Isle.

Once Aidan was gone, Gunz focused on the spell, the words of Dragon tongue forming in his mind. He waved his hand and a large flaming circle surrounded the World Tree. He whispered a few words and pointed at the circle. As soon as he finished his spell, the ground trembled slightly like the distant aftershock of an earthquake, and a small flame separated from the fire.

He flicked his wrist, watching the flame dancing over the snow, melting it in its wake. It rushed fast crossing the circle from one end to the other, and soon a large star was burning within it. Gunz snapped his fingers, and the flame merged back into the fire. He looked down and through the prism of his other sight, he saw Mrak Delar glowing with the power of Fire. He smiled at his friend, appreciating him understanding the task at hand without any explanations.

"Mrak, I need you to stand at one of the points of the pentagram," he said. "Any of them is fine." Then he turned to the twin-gods who stood separated by Semargl and addressed them. "Chernobog, take position on Mrak's left, if you please, and I need Belobog to stand on Mrak Delar's right."

Both gods hated the idea of some lowly Fire Salamander ordering them around and while they didn't voice their displeasure, it was crystal clear without a need for words. Despite that, they assumed their places at the burning circle and stood with their arms folded, fuming physically and magically. Kal and Semargl took the last two points of the pentacle.

Kal looked up and waved at Gunz. "What do you need us do?"

"I just need all of you to channel your powers and be ready to share it with me when the time comes," replied Gunz, switching his attention to his sword. "I'll do the rest."

He channeled the elemental power through the blade and once it was on fire, he tossed it lightly in the air, making it levitate in front of him. As he started to chant, carefully repeating the words of Dragon tongue presented by the Dark Codex, the sword began to spin. Slow in the beginning, the rotation became faster and faster until the blade looked like a solid disk, glowing with the red energy of fire, cutting the air with a low whistle.

Gunz reached forward and gently touched the burning disk. The sword stilled and a smoldering jet of fire blasted down, hitting the center of the pentagram. At the same time, he spread his arms wide, connecting with the five magical beings, and channeled their power through the pentacle.

He threw his head back and screamed as if he was in unbearable pain as the combined power of three gods, the Master of Power and the Fire Elemental settled in his blazing body. For a moment, he dissolved into his own element and a giant golden Salamander took his place, but he forced himself to revert into his human form and continued chanting.

Glancing down, he saw that the fire rose higher, now surrounding the Alatyr stone and the World Tree with an impenetrable wall of smoldering flames. He could no longer see anyone, but he was aware of their presence, still connected to their powers.

He wasn't sure how, but he knew that it was time. He stopped chanting and seized his sword, wrapping both hands over its grip. Slowly he stretched his arms up to full extent, pointing it at the sky. As he did that, he said the last words of the spell, pronouncing each word loud and clear, and an undiluted ray of purifying Fire energy escaped the sword, spreading around him like a blast wave.

All sounds disappeared, and the fire ceased. As Gunz looked down through his other sight—at least he thought he was using his other sight—he saw a massive golden wave spread through the Land of Dreams, rushing in all directions. It moved with astonishing speed, replacing the winter with the new greenery of spring. The snow was melting, and fresh grass was sprouting in its place like in a time-lapse movie.

The air cleared, no longer polluted by the demonic essence, and the stench of sulphur was gone, replaced by the delicate scent of spring flowers. For the first time, since he had arrived into the demonically challenged Land of Dreams, he saw the blue sky—at least on the dayside of the World Tree. The dark midnight sky, shining with myriads of stars, unraveled over the nightside of the Tree.

The sword trembled in his grip, and he lowered it. Gunz glanced down and saw Kal, Mrak Delar and Semargl staring up at him. Chernobog and Belobog stared at each other and judging by the position of the swords in their hands, they were ready to spring into action. Gunz sighed as exhaustion settled in his every bone and slowly descended to the ground.

As soon as his feet touched the soft grass, his legs gave in and he fell to his knees, sitting back on his heels. Feeling both relief and debilitating exhaustion, he closed his other sight, but to his shock, he could still see. Mrak Delar squatted next to him. Seizing his chin and lifting his face up, he stared into his eyes, troubled.

"Your eyes," he exhaled. "Oh, God, Salamander, you are the—"

Kal was by his side in a heartbeat. He grabbed the Master of Power's long hair, yanking it back and hissed into his ear, "You will remain silent, Master. Say nothing!"

Then he turned to Gunz, lowering down to one knee and

whispered so only he could hear him. "Gunz, my boy, I need you to close your eyes and disconnect from whatever magic is stored in your head. No one should know, you understand me?"

Gunz nodded and closed his eyes, just now realizing that he was still channeling the Dark Codex. When he opened his eyes again, he found himself surrounded by darkness and slowly got up, slightly swaying. He sighed and turned toward the twin-gods.

"Chernobog," he said with a light wave of his hand. "Thank you for your assistance, but I no longer need you. You may return to the Dark Nav."

A deep throaty growl escaped Chernobog's lips, anger spiking his dark power. "We will meet again, Fire Salamander."

"I'm sure, we will," agreed Gunz sensing the god of Destruction opening his portal and then disappearing through it.

Then he turned to Belobog and bowed to him. "My lord," he said, "thank you for coming to my call and assisting me."

He sensed the god of Light and Creation approach him and then felt his large hand on his shoulder. "Something tells me, it isn't our last meeting, Young Salamander. I hope it will be under better circumstances. I'll bid my farewell now."

And just like that, the Slavic deity was gone.

As soon as Chernobog and Belobog were gone, Mrak Delar approached him. He just stood in front of him, but Gunz could detect the vibe of unease lingering over him.

"Gunz, you did it," said Mrak Delar, his voice hoarse, "but now I must bring Peyton back and face the Destiny Council."

"Mrak—," Gunz started, but the Master of Power put his hand on his arm, squeezing it lightly.

"I have no choice," he said. "I wish things were different, but I still hope to see you one day."

Mrak Delar walked away and Gunz made a step forward, almost tripping over a root of the World Tree. He stilled, listening intently to the words of the summoning spell as the

Master of Power called to the Destiny Keeper. Like in a nightmare, he sensed the spike in the magical energy field and then heard the soft clink of the Destiny cuffs. No one said anything, but a soft moan sounded somewhere in front of him and then Mrak Delar's energy signature disappeared.

"No, please," pleaded Gunz, stepping forward toward the place where he thought the Destiny Keeper was. "Please, my lord. I did what I was supposed to do. I cleansed the nexus and saved magic. Please let him be. If Mrak Delar hadn't come here, I still would be imprisoned by King Alexander. He saved us all, sir."

He felt someone's hand on his arms and jumped aside before recognizing who it was. "It's me, Gunz. Hush." Kal's voice sounded from above.

"Fire Salamander," said the Destiny Keeper, "you're still very young and don't know the ways of magic. Please understand that taking the Ancient Master to face trial wasn't my choice. I am but a messenger. By showing up here myself instead of sending the Destiny Enforcers, I showed my respect to the Master."

"Gunz, it's true." Mrak Delar's voice was weak and shaky. "I must go now, but I'll be all right. Don't worry."

"Farewell," said the Destiny Keeper and disappeared, taking the Master of Power with him.

"Peyton?" asked Gunz tentatively.

"I'm here, Gunz, can't you sense me?" He felt her touching his hand, and caught it, squeezing it in his.

"Aidan, Peyton is here." Gunz reached his friend through their psychic link. *"Is Yaroslav okay?"*

Before he knew it, Aidan with Tessa in his arms and Yaroslav stood by his side. He smirked, detecting their presence, but their reunion was short-lived.

"Now, Aidan," said Kal, approaching them, "the Land of Dreams is no longer sealed. I suggest you take the happy couple here and go visit the Gatekeeper. She'll open the door for you, so you can teleport all of you home."

"How about Zane?" asked Aidan, worry shadowing his voice. "He needs assistance until he learns to live with—" He cut himself off, choking on his words.

"I'll take him home," said Kal firmly. "My son and I need to have a word."

Gunz sighed—a word with Kal could never be anything fun, especially when the Great Salamander had an added growl in his voice. But to his surprise, as soon as his friends left, Kal directed his growling anger away from him.

"Semargl!" roared the Fire Elemental, squeezing the back of Gunz's neck with his burning hand. "Is there anything you want to tell me?"

"Surely, I do not understand what you mean, brother," huffed Semargl.

"You don't, do you?" hissed Kal and his grip on Gunz's neck got tighter. "Look into his eyes and tell me the truth, god of Fire!"

Semargl seized Gunz's chin, forcing his face up. A split-second later, he let go and Gunz heard a light squeak as the deity clenched his teeth.

"It's the Dark Codex. He merged with it," Semargl said after a moment. "But how is it possible?"

"This is why I am asking you if there is anything you want to tell us," repeated Kal, fury heating up his giant body. "Stop playing games. Is he your son? Are you his biological father?"

"What?" Gunz and Semargl yelled at the same time.

"Calm down, Kal. I knew my biological father... well, I didn't really know him. He was killed when I was too young to remember," said Gunz attempting to sound as calm and peaceful as he could muster. "He was mundane. No magic. Nothing! I am a Fire Salamander. You told me yourself—all Fire Salamanders are born human. And you are the only man I call father."

"Kal, I am not his father, but there are other gods of Fire in other pantheons. You may want to ask them," added Semargl snidely and vanished.

Gunz stood with his arms dangling by his sides, not sure what to say. He felt a small nudge on his back as Kal guided him toward the Alatyr stone and helped him sit down. The Great Salamander sat down next to him with a grunt and gave him a short tap on his lap.

"Well, my child, we have work ahead of us," he said, chuckling. "You are a Great Fire Salamander, but you are more than that."

"Why?" asked Gunz.

"You merged with the Dark Codex. The power of this artifact is so great that only anyone of equal or greater power can merge with it without dying," explained Kal.

"Aren't we immortal?" Gunz shrugged.

"Yes, the Dark Codex couldn't destroy you, but it would reject the merging process if you couldn't command it," explained Kal patiently. "It's not only that the Codex accepted you, but you were able to command it. Anyway, I think I overreacted a little…"

"You think?" Gunz chuckled. "I'm just a little Fire Gecko, Father. Trust me. It's not me. It's the dark soul of Ivan the Terrible that made it possible. He commanded the Codex, not me."

Kal stopped talking and Gunz relaxed against the stone, his mind blank. Magic was back in the nexus, flowing with its full force and after so many days of being deprived and drained, he felt intoxicated and drowsy.

"Father," he called quietly, "can you do something for me?"

"What is it?" asked Kal, absently.

"Take me to Gwyn ap Nudd."

"You want to go after Mrak Delar," said Kal softly. It wasn't a question. The Great Salamander stated the fact.

"Yes."

"It's stupid, reckless, and dangerous."

"I know," mumbled Gunz. "Mishka thinks these three words should be my middle name." He chuckled humorously.

Kal laughed but returned to a serious mood almost immediately. "Mishka is as wise as they come. But in all seriousness, there is nothing you can do for the Ancient Master now, my boy. He knew what he was doing and the consequences of his deeds."

Gunz nodded, biting his lip. "He did it to help me, Father. I have to try. It's the least I can do for him."

"I wouldn't expect anything less from you, my boy. I guess we are going back to the Otherworld then," said Kal, unfolding the flaming curtain of his portal.

EPILOGUE

* * *

~ Aidan ~
Coral Springs, South Florida
Evening

GETTING OUT OF THE LAND OF DREAMS WAS EASY, ALMOST habitual. After a short conversation with the Gatekeeper, she opened the door into the realm of humans. Carrying Tessa in his arms, Aidan walked through it followed by Yaroslav and Peyton. Once outside the nexus, he snapped his fingers teleporting into Tessa's place.

His penthouse and his school had been destroyed by the explosions, and Tessa's small apartment was the only place he could go. He would have to take care of finding a new place for his school and purchasing a new house, but right now he didn't want to think about it, all his thoughts focused on the precious cargo in his arms.

As soon as Gunz purified the Land of Dreams, Tessa started to feel a lot better, recovering in no time, but Aidan refused to let her walk on her own until they were at home. He gently sat her on the couch, going down on one knee in front of her and taking her hand into his.

She gazed down upon him, a kind smile on her face, and he couldn't take his eyes off her. Seemingly, she hadn't changed, but there was something different in her expression, in the way she tilted her head or pressed her lips together, and all that made him love her so much more.

He brought her hand up to his lips, planting a soft kiss on her knuckles. "Tessa," he whispered, his throat dry like old parchment. "Don't ever do this to me again. I was dying every moment of every day when I didn't know where you were and what happened to you."

"I'm sorry," she mumbled, her fingers softly threading through his hair. "I made a mistake…"

"You think?" Aidan chuckled. "Are you sure you and Zane are not related? You definitely have similar personality traits."

She giggled, and this familiar little laughter sent electricity down Aidan's spine. "And what might those traits be?" she asked, seizing his ear and pulling it up slightly. "Think hard before you say anything, oldie, or your ear will get it."

"Ouch, ouch…" Aidan laughed. "I was referring to the stubbornness and pathological inability to ask for help when you need it." He thought a moment and then added, "And also the need to protect and take care of everyone around you, except yourself. In that—you and Zane are like brother and sister."

Tessa smiled, but then sighed and patted the couch next to her, inviting him to join. "Listen, Aidan, there was a reason to my madness," she said softly as he lowered himself down on the couch, leaning back.

"I'm sure you are going to tell me why you left the Guardians HQ without notifying anyone," he said, staring at her intently, his fingers playing with a pendant on a long silver chain. "You know that every time you break any of the Guardians' rules, it's my head on the line."

"I know, Aidan, and I'm sorry. I'm sure, we will have to face the Guardians Council sooner or later," she whispered, bowing her head.

"I'm surprised, they didn't summon me yet," he murmured, dropping the pendant. "So, what happened?"

She pulled her legs up on the couch, folding them, and leaned against Aidan's chest, resting her head on his shoulder. He moved her up a little and wrapped his arm around her shoulder, playing with her long hair.

"I received a summoning call," she said without looking at him. "I mean it wasn't quite a summoning call, but rather a communication." She took a deep breath. "From my father."

"Perun?" asked Aidan, his eyebrows rising. "It's not possible. No one knows where he is, sweetheart."

"I know that now," whispered Tessa. Her hands found his, entwining their fingers. "But at the time, I was sure it was him. He knew the kind of things that only my parents would have known."

"Like what?"

"Like the fact that my parents left me on the steps of the Church by the Sea with only my name written on a piece of paper," she said. "He told me about how they did it and why. He made me believe, Aidan."

"I'm sure it wasn't hard," mused Aidan. "You wanted to believe."

"True that," muttered Tessa, tilting her head up to see him. "Anyway, he told me he was in the City of Gold and he needed my help right away. The only reason he was seeking my help was because he had no one else he could trust with the Lord of Chaos rising again."

"Oh, Tessa, why didn't you tell anyone? Me or Missi, the Guardians, Zane? Anyone at all?"

She bit her lip, tears gathering in her eyes. "I know now that it was a mistake, Aidan," she said with reproach, her voice fluctuating and breaking with high notes. "But at the time, this man sounded so sincere, convincing and urgent... I believed him. Besides, I think he placed some kind of spell on me to make me do it. I wanted to call you, but as soon as I picked up my phone, I had the strongest urge to drop it and just leave. The same happened when I went to the Archmage Allerton's office. It was like a turn-away spell, but so much stronger, you know? I can't believe I didn't recognize that..."

She sighed, tears running down her cheeks. She wiped them with her hand angrily, smearing dirt over her skin. He lifted her onto his lap and wrapped his arms around her, softly rocking back and forth as if she was a little girl again, abused by her mean classmates.

"It's okay, Tessa, it's over now," he whispered into her ear soothingly, feeling her slender body relax in his arms. Then a deep shudder ran through her and she shook her head.

"It's not over, Aidan," she objected. "This is just the beginning. When I arrived at the City of Gold and the king imprisoned me, he said something... I am sure it was just a slip of the tongue. Besides, he was positive I would never see the light of day. He said that only Perun can stop the Lord of Chaos, but since the god of Thunder is no longer around, the Zmey is free to rule. Well, almost." She stared at her dirty hands with blackness under her broken fingernails, an expression of surprise reflected in her eyes. "He told me that without my father, I was the only one who had that kind of power—"

Tessa cut herself off and twisted in Aidan's arms, hiding her face in his chest, sobbing quietly. He held her tighter as he got up. Shifting her weight slightly to the left arm, he snapped his fingers, teleporting them to her bathroom.

She giggled, tears still running down her cheeks. "You know

I can walk on my own, oldie," she said, wiggling to regain her freedom.

"I know," he replied, filling the bathtub with warm water. Once the tub was filled, he helped her undress, shedding the dirty rags she was wearing on the floor and lowered her into the tub. With horror, he noticed welts and cuts on her back and stomach, and anger spiked in him, making his eyes shine with white light.

She met his blazing eyes and smiled weakly. "It's okay, Aidan. I'm okay…"

He swallowed hard and reached for a luffa and soap. Gently, he ran his hand with the luffa over her shoulders and chest, washing away the dirt, wishing that he could make her painful memories disappear just as easily. She closed her eyes and relaxed, her lips parted slightly as her breath quickened under his touch. Longing whispered through him and it took all the power of will he had, to remain outside the tub and continue to take care of her.

"Aidan," she whispered, and the sound of his name on her lips was like the best music he had ever heard. "There is more…"

"Oh?" Aidan exhaled, gathering his scattered thoughts and focusing on Tessa's words rather than her lips.

"Angel is in trouble," said Tessa, turning in the tub a little to face him.

"What kind of trouble?" he asked, his daze gone. "You know what he is. He is Death. What could happen to Death?"

"I don't know," replied Tessa, and he detected her nervousness and agitation. "Remember, I am part Reaper, so in a way, Angel and I have a connection. And right now, I can sense his distress. I believe all Reapers can. Something is terribly wrong."

Aidan got up and closed his eyes, channeling his power. He took a deep breath, connecting with the Otherworld, searching all the deathly realms for the presence of Death. After a moment, he let go and frowned.

"I think you're right," he muttered. "I can't find him anywhere."

He drew a rune in the air, infusing it with his power and placed his hand over it, summoning Uri. Nothing happened. He grunted, silently cursing himself for leaving Uri alone to face the demons in his demolished school.

"Both Uri and Angel are missing," he whispered. "Death and Archangel Uriel... Dammit. And here I thought I could take a short break..."

He glanced down at Tessa, and she smiled weakly at him. "Maybe a thirty-minute break? Can we allow this to ourselves?"

She got up in the bathtub, pulling the plug open with her toes to let the dirty water out and opened the shower. Aidan observed her, his eyes taking in every inch of her willowy body and held his breath. She was beautiful with her wet skin glistening as rivulets of water ran down her small breasts and firm stomach, plastering her long dark hair to her face and shoulders. Desire percolated between them, setting his blood on fire.

"The Guardians may summon us at any time," he exhaled, breathless.

"I don't give a damn. They can wait thirty minutes," objected Tessa, pulling his shirt off over his head.

"We should talk to Zane and Yaroslav... Angel and Uri could be... in serious trouble," he panted as her hands quickly unbuttoned his pants, sliding inside.

"Dammit, Aidan!" she yelled, yanking his pants and underwear down, leaving him completely naked. "I love you! And I want to have a few minutes with the man—um—god I love. I was dreaming of this moment all those endless days and nights I spent in the king's dungeons. Scared and alone! Thinking about you was the only thing that kept me going." She fell silent, breathing hard, but then her eyebrows lifted, making her look younger than she was. She stamped her foot in the water, splashing it, and commanded, "Nothing is going to change in thirty friggin' minutes. Get into this tub at once, Aidan McGrath!"

"Yes, my lady. I'm at your command," Aidan said, smiling at her bossy tone and her slightly rough manners. "Just promise that no matter whose call you receive or what destiny throws our way in the future, we'll take care of everything together."

"Always... and together..." She stretched her arms to him. He took her hand, kissing her slender fingers, and stepped under the downpour of warm water, giving himself to her.

* * *

~ Yaroslav ~
Ft. Lauderdale, South Florida
Later on same evening

THE LAST RAYS OF THE SETTING SUN BATHED IN THE SMOOTH surface of the ocean, throwing playful pink and yellow flares of light on its infinite waters. In this area, the shore was thin, mostly devoured by the encroaching water, and despite the beautiful sunset and pleasantly cool weather, the beach was empty.

Yaroslav sat on top of his leather coat thrown over the cool soft sand, his back rested against the concrete wall running along the Ft. Lauderdale beach. Peyton relaxed next to him with her head on his chest, her fingers playing with a golden lock of his hair, twirling and untwirling it.

"How did it happen?" she whispered so softly that only his vampiric hearing could catch her words.

"What?" he asked, gazing down at her, a dreamy smile playing on his lips.

"This... you and me... you know," she mumbled, raising her bright eyes at him.

He laughed, slightly readjusting his position. Then he

lowered his face and found her lips, gently kissing her. She responded to his kiss by turning a little and encircling his neck with her arms.

Peyton pulled away a moment later, gazing up at him, her eyes slightly drunk and her lips still parted. She ran her fingers over his cheek and a tender smile touched her lips.

"You look like a boy, young and innocent," she said, brushing his hair off his face.

"Young and innocent," muttered Yaroslav, smirking. "Yup, that's me."

"How old are you, Yaroslav?" asked Peyton, sitting up to see him better. "No one really knows. Some say you are three-four hundred years old."

"No, I am not that old, but my mother likes to keep those rumors up," he replied, his mind traveling back to the day of his second birth when Akira found him, ending his miserable human life. "I was twenty when Akira turned me in the year of our Lord 1779. So that makes me two hundred and sixty years old in human years. Just a little older than you."

Peyton laughed and punched him in his shoulder, but then turned around and straddled his hips, gazing down at him, her hands on his shoulders. Her copper curls framed her tender face, her blue eyes sparkling brighter than the rising moon, and Yaroslav stilled, enjoying the moment of closeness.

Her eyelashes cast long shadows on her cheeks, giving her a mysterious and captivating look. As he gazed up at her, warmth spread through him—the kind of warmth he hadn't felt for quite some time. He pressed his hand to his chest, feeling as though his heart was beating again.

She touched his lips, running her fingers down, tracing the shape of his jaw. "Do you like it?" she asked, curiosity in her eyes. "You know, being a vampire."

He dropped his head, breaking their eye contact. "I wish Akira had left me to die. The things I did when I was a new vampire..." He shuddered. "But it is what it is. I can't change what I am now. I learned to live alongside humans without harming them. It's been many years since I killed a human."

She leaned forward, pulling him to her chest and planted a soft kiss on top of his head. "Well, I am glad you are here," she said into his hair. "But can you promise me one thing?"

"What is it?" he asked drawing back so he could see her face.

"Never attempt to turn me." She got up, offering him her hand. "I would rather die than be one of the creatures I learned to hunt and kill since I was five. My mother was one of the Sisterhood's most formidable hunters and when she was killed in the line of duty, the Sisterhood brought me in and raised me hating and killing the likes of you. It's in my blood..."

"So, am I a creature? A bloodthirsty, disgusting leech?" he asked, crumbling inside. He took her hand and got up, picking up his coat and shaking the sand off of it, his every move sharp and rough.

"No, Yaroslav, you are not," she replied, hanging her head. "You are a vampire, but you're not like the others. I've never met anyone like you—human or otherwise..." Her voice trailed and she shook her head.

Taking his hand, she pulled him off the beach onto the brightly lit street. As they headed toward the *EverSafe* building, she put her arm around his waist, and he draped his over her shoulders.

"Listen, there is something I need to tell you," she continued after a while. "There was a reason I was next to the *EverSafe* building that day."

"Oh?" He glanced down at her.

"Yeah... I was following you, watching you and your mother," she said, shame prominent in her voice. "I want you to know that the Sisterhood of the Sun is after the Scarlet Queen and her entire organization. I was sent here to gather information, and when Missi asked me to take care of her restaurant for her, I said yes, seizing the opportunity to get closer to Zane Burns and Aidan McGrath as both of them were in your mother's trust circle."

"If you hate vampires so much, why did you step in to help me?" asked Yaroslav. "Like you said, it was just another internal altercation between vamps."

She stopped, pulling at his arm to turn him around. Her eyes met his and he saw tears gleaming under her long eyelashes, sliding down her pale cheeks. "Because..." She swallowed but didn't look away. "Because I love you. I think I fell for you long before you even noticed my existence. The first time I laid my eyes on you, I knew I could never harm you."

"Peyton—," he whispered not sure what to say or do, but she shook her head, making her curls bounce.

"Don't say anything, please. I know you don't feel about me the way I feel about you and it's okay," she pleaded, her hand finding his and squeezing it. "You have no idea how hard it is for me to tell you all this." She cleared her throat. "It's been my worst nightmare—loving the man I was taught to hate. I have no idea what to do and how to deal with my feelings. I got used to being a cold, thoughtless killing machine, and all these emotions were scrambling my brain.

"So, I tried to stay away from you, which didn't work, of course. Not seeing you was making it even worse. But when I finally had a chance to be close to you, I felt so conflicted that I treated you like shit. I think I hoped to provoke you to do something that would change the way I felt about you. I was scared and angry, Yaroslav... scared of the way I felt about you... angry at myself for breaking my oath to the Sisterhood... Most of all, I was terrified that you would learn the truth about my—" She exhaled a rugged breath, silent tears sliding down her face.

"Peyton, please don't cry—"

"No, let me finish," she interrupted him, wiping her tears. "There is something you need to know, Yaroslav. That night when Akira sent you to Miami Beach… I was the one who gave the false intel to your mother through our man in your organization. We didn't expect that she would send Zane Burns to deal with the situation. We thought she would send her usual fighters—vampires and upirs—and we were waiting for them there, ready to destroy them. The goal was to weaken your mother's organization, killing her subjects one by one."

She shook her head biting her lip, and he didn't interrupt her, unease spreading through him.

"But that demonic team—that wasn't us. Obviously, it was King Alexander's pawns, following his orders," she continued. "However, it was our enchantment that blocked your connection with your mother at that time. This is why Akira couldn't feel that you were in trouble, even though you were fighting on the steps of her building."

Since he didn't say anything, she pulled on his arm, continuing on her way to the *EverSafe* building. They walked up the steps and halted a few feet away from the door.

"Now that you know it all, do you hate me?" asked Peyton, gazing up at him, scared and vulnerable like he had never seen her before.

A soft smile touched his lips as he lowered his face and kissed her, cupping her face with his hands. He stepped away and glanced down at her. Her eyes were still closed, her slightly swollen lips inviting him to kiss her again.

"Did I answer your question?" he asked, pulling her into his chest.

"I don't know if you answered her question, but you sure answered mine!"

An unfamiliar female voice rang behind his back, and Yaroslav spun around to see a young woman, dressed in a black shirt and jeans, standing a few steps below them. She held a strange-looking gun trained at his chest, her eyes burning with hate. Peyton gasped, and her fingers squeezed Yaroslav's.

"You are done here, Peyton! I have orders to bring you back to headquarters," growled the woman, her hand not wavering. "Let me do what you were supposed to have done a while ago and kill this blond leech."

Before Peyton could say anything, the woman pressed the trigger of her strange weapon. A bullet erupted from the barrel of the gun, producing no sound and no fire flair. All he saw was her hand slightly jerking up from the kickback, and then Peyton threw herself in front of him, shielding him with her body.

The bullet hit her square in her chest. For a split-second, she stood there, her hand clasping her wound as thick blood streams spilled between her fingers, her eyes wide with shock. Yaroslav caught her before she could fall and gently lowered her on the marble steps. Then he rose, anger the likes of which he hadn't felt for a long time seared through him, making him shake from head to toe.

Without taking her eyes off Yaroslav, the woman tried to reload her strange weapon with her trembling hands, but she was too slow. He reached her before she could do anything. With a feral growl, he grabbed her head, his fangs expanding, and ripped it off her shoulders with his bare hands. The head dropped to the ground with a dull thud, rolling down the steps, and bright red blood pumped from the headless corpse splashing his face and chest as it collapsed. He wiped his face with an expression of disgust as he turned around and walked back to Peyton.

Lowering down beside her, he pulled her up, cradling her in his arms. Then he bit his wrist, pressing it to her lips. She didn't object, allowing some of his blood to spill into her mouth. Yaroslav pulled down her shirt, noticing that the bleeding didn't stop, and the wound wasn't healing.

She smiled at him faintly. "Your blood..." she whispered. "It's sweet. I never knew."

"Why are you not healing?" he asked, his heart wrenched.

"It's the bullet," she whispered and coughed, more bright red blood escaping her lips, coloring them scarlet. "Wooden... enchanted to block the healing... kills vampires... You can't save... me..."

"No, please..." Yaroslav moaned, pressing her limp body closer to his chest. "Let me turn you. Please, I can't let you die."

"No, never... Yaroslav?" Her eyes rolled back, and she exhaled, her head tilting lifelessly to the side.

"Peyton?" he called, still unable to believe it. He touched her face with his shaking fingers, sharpening his hearing—there was no heartbeat. "No..."

He saw some red liquid dripping on Peyton's tender face, for a brief moment not realizing it was his own tears. Slowly, Yaroslav lowered her body on the steps and got up to his feet. He looked down at her, feeling numb. Then he threw his head back and howled, as if it was his own heart torn apart by the wooden bullet.

The door of the *EverSafe* flew open and Akira rushed outside, katana in her hands.

"Yaroslav!" she yelled, but he ignored her and spun in place, turning into a large bird. Hearing Akira's constrained gasp, he glanced at his reflection in the dark windows—his normally white feathers were dripping with blood, and his eyes shone with a furious scarlet glow.

He screamed, a loud throaty sound, and flew away, disappearing into the dark sky.

* * *

~ Zane Burns, a.k.a. Gunz ~
Somewhere outside the human realm...
Outside of time...

"Gunz, are you sure you want to do it?" asked Gwyn ap Nudd, giving a light tap on his shoulder to attract his attention.

"Yes, Gwyn, it was never a choice for me. It's something I must do," he said. "Mrak would do the same for me."

Gwyn ap Nudd sighed. "You're a good man, but as you probably know, no good deed goes unpunished," he said, kindness in his voice. "Anyway, once I open the last door, there will be no way back."

"Understood, sir," replied Gunz, feeling nervous and jittery.

"I know you can't see, so I'll let you know once we're in place. When I tell you, open your other sight but be careful. Do not tap into the magic of the Dark Codex accidently. Except us, no one should know about it."

Gunz nodded.

"I have no idea what we will find there—most likely nothing good, but you must keep your cool and stay respectful. You understand?"

"Yes, sir. I guess I'll behave the way a Child of Fire should," he replied with a nervous lopsided grin.

"That's what I'm afraid of." Gwyn chuckled, and in his mind, Gunz could see his unnerving white eyes crinkling at the corners. "Kal needs to lighten up a bit. You are a modern man, not a medieval knight," said Gwyn. "Well... Ready or not, here we come."

He put his hand on Gunz's shoulder, softly directing him through a door of blazing light.

* * *

Gunz felt a gust of cold wind ruffle his hair and then the light touch of Gwyn ap Nudd's hand to his arm.

"Open your other sight," the King of the Otherworld whispered, gently nudging him forward. "Watch your steps."

Gunz did as he'd been told and looked around, taking in his

surroundings. He stood in a large stadium seating circular hall. A light scent of lavender lingered in the air and since it seemed artificial, he figured it was some sort of air freshener. At the far end of the room, he saw a large desk with three people sitting behind it. Through his other sight, he couldn't see them clearly, and they appeared to shine brightly with the magical energy that was almost identical to Gwyn's. No doubt they were the infamous Destiny Council and being so close to them sent cold shivers down his spine.

As he walked down the stairs, following Gwyn ap Nudd, he realized that two of the people at the desk were men and one was a woman. Their eyes blazed with the light and even if he had his normal vision, the brightness of their magic wouldn't allow him to distinguish their features.

He was looking for Mrak but couldn't see him anywhere. Other than the three people in front of him, there was no one else there, and his steps echoed loudly through the empty hall.

Gwyn halted in front of the desk and slightly inclined his head, while pushing heavily on Gunz's shoulder, signaling him to kneel. Gunz took one knee, lowering his head, watching the Destiny Council from under his eyelashes.

The man in the center got up, his honey-sweet smile shining brighter than his eyes. "Gwyn ap Nudd, hello, brother," he sang, holding out his hand to him.

Gwyn ap Nudd stared at his hand a moment too long but then shook it, demonstrating his complete unwillingness to do so.

"Brother?" he huffed, the corners of his lips quirking up under his well-manicured mustache. "It's been centuries since I had the misfortune of calling you my brothers." He shrugged. "And I prefer to keep it this way."

"Aw, Gwyn, please, old friend, let's forget our old disagreements," continued the man, oblivious to Gwyn's less than warm greeting. "Tell us to what we owe the pleasure of seeing you in our modest realm."

"Modest!" muttered Gwyn under his breath. "You don't know the meaning of this word." But then he waved his hand in Gunz's direction and said out loud, "You owe it to the young Fire Salamander. He is here to speak for the Ancient Master."

The man waved his hand at Gunz. "Please rise, Fire Salamander."

Gunz got up, looking at the members of the Destiny Council calmly. The man frowned and walked around the desk. He approached him and placed his hand on Gunz's forehead.

"But you are blind... cursed, actually," he whispered, throwing a quick glance at Gwyn. "Mr. Burns—I believe this is your name in the human realm?"

"Yes, my lord," replied Gunz, making an effort to sound calm and even. "My name is Zane Burns, and yes, I'm blind. To see you, I'm using my other sight."

"Fascinating," he murmured to himself. "What can we do for you, Mr. Burns?"

"My lord," said Gunz, his chest tightened with unease, "I'm here to speak for Master Mrak Delar as I believe he is innocent."

The man walked back behind the desk and sat down, leaning slightly forward. "Innocent?" he asked and smirked. "I think not. The Ancient Master admitted his guilt. The trial is over. You are too late."

"He admitted his guilt? Not if he was in his right mind," Gwyn growled, the light around him glowing brighter than that of the Destiny Council. "Where is he, Magnus?

For a moment, Magnus looked a little lost and Gunz could swear he noticed a shadow of fear crossing his shining features, but he recovered quickly and leaned back in his massive chair.

"He admitted his guilt and accepted his punishment," he said coldly. "There is nothing you can do now, Lord of the Wild Hunt."

"You are lying, Magnus," said Gwyn ap Nudd, his jaw set. "I hate it when people are lying to me. Besides, you're forgetting I know how you operate here."

He growled a spell and waved his hand at the empty space to his left. All three members of the Destiny Council hopped to their feet, but Gwyn muttered another spell and they fell back into their chairs.

The air on his left shimmered, revealing a view that made Gunz's blood run cold. Mrak Delar was sprawled, chained between two tall poles, not unlike those he had seen at the City of Gold. He had only a pair of light linen pants on, and since he had no shirt, Gunz could see a brand of a slave burnt into his shoulder. A thick leather collar was fastened around his neck. His head was bowed down low and Gunz didn't know if the Master of Power was conscious.

He made a move, but Gwyn ap Nudd seized his arm, holding him in place. "Don't look at Mrak," he whispered so only Gunz could hear him. "Look through what you see. The Destiny magic can mislead even the magical sight. It's an illusion created to make Mrak suffer and hide the truth from those on the outside."

Gunz narrowed his eyes, sharpening his other sight, and looked at Mrak again. The illusion shimmered away, but the reality wasn't much better. The Master of Power was sprawled on the floor, his wrists locked by the Destiny Cuffs. His long hair, spread around his pale face, was no longer obsidian black, but regular dark brown with a touch of gray on his temples. Dark shadows lay beneath his closed eyes and under his high cheekbones, and he looked like he was a step away from dying.

Gunz grunted, jerking his arm out of Gwyn's grip, and approached Mrak. He extended his hand forward, sensing an invisible barrier surrounding his friend.

"*Latentius revelare,*" he whispered with a slight move of his fingers.

The barrier of magic disappeared, revealing thick iron bars. Gunz lowered to his knees and reached through the bars. Grabbing Mrak's wrist, he searched for his pulse, and when he found a soft uneven beat under his skin, he sat back, wiping cold sweat off his forehead.

Glancing over his shoulder, Gunz nodded at Gwyn ap Nudd, then got up and approached him, turning to face the Destiny Council.

"What are you charging Mrak Delar with, my lord Magnus?" asked Gunz with a respectful bow.

"He is guilty of many crimes, young Salamander," replied Magnus dryly. "Mutilation of the fabric of reality was the final nail in his coffin."

"I assure you, my lord, everything the Ancient Master did, had been done for the good of the realm. All of them," said Gunz, struggling to remain calm, facing this aggravating, arrogant man. "If Mrak Delar hadn't done what he had, the Land of Dreams would still be sealed and controlled by the followers of Chaos."

Magnus rose, brilliant white light getting brighter around him betraying his boiling fury. "Let's agree to disagree, Salamander," he hissed, slamming his hand on the desk, sending the giant gavel flying to the floor. "Mrak Delar has been walking this world as though he is a king, positioning himself above the law. It's about time we showed him how wrong he is."

"That's not true," Gunz objected frostily, his hands clenching into fists.

"How dare you!" Magnus rose, leaning over the desk, but Gwyn stepped forward shielding Gunz.

"Magnus," he growled warningly. "The young Salamander tells you the truth. We owe this victory to Mrak."

"Don't talk about things you don't understand, Gwyn ap Nudd," shouted Magnus, quivering with fury. "I'm talking to the Fire Salamander and the conversation is finally getting interesting." He straightened, breathing hard, and an icy smile stretched his lips. "Mrak Delar failed. Again. He failed to reveal Rasputin's intentions and he killed King Alexander—the only source of information we had. Now, we have no way of finding out who is leading the followers of Chaos and how they are planning to raise the Lord of Chaos yet again! Without this knowledge, we can't stop them!"

He folded his arms over his chest and glanced to the left and to the right at the other two members of the Council. They nodded, agreeing with him. Gunz dropped his head, trying to organize the scattered thoughts in his mind. The situation seemed to be hopeless. There was nothing he could do to help his friend.

"The Ancient Master failed his mission and broke multiple rules while failing," added Magnus mockingly. "Even Gwyn ap Nudd knows that I am right, otherwise he would be at my throat by now."

Gunz threw a glance at Gwyn ap Nudd and bit his lip. Then he raised his eyes, staring straight into the blazing holes of Magnus' eyes.

"Then I failed too," he said tiredly, his voice just above a whisper. "We all did. May as well put the Destiny Cuffs on me and throw me into this cage next to Mrak."

"Be careful what you wish for, Child of Fire," hissed Magnus. "And do tread lightly. By arguing with the Destiny Council, you are cutting the branch you are sitting on."

"What are you talking about?" asked Gunz with a half-shrug. "I've never heard of you, let alone got any help from you all."

"Gunz," whispered Gwyn warningly, squeezing his shoulder.

"Wait, wait, Gwyn. Let him talk." Magnus raised his arm up, stopping him. "I find his ignorance just as amusing as his hubris."

He waved his hand and a big screen TV materialized in the hall. He snapped his fingers, and the screen lit up with a soft blue light. Like in an old, silent movie, Gunz watched his younger self fight in front of his house with a group of demons, one of them over seven feet tall. He watched himself killing the demons and setting the dead bodies on fire.

Magnus snapped his fingers again, and the picture on the screen changed. He saw volkolaks running in the Quiet Waters Park, biting and killing humans, while he was fighting the air demon under the cover of Uri's protective dome.

Magnus gave him a pointed stare, waving at the screen. "Who do you think has been covering all your fireworks and magical shenanigans all this time?" he asked mockingly. "If not for the Destiny Council, all of you would be either playing lab rats somewhere in Area 51 or in prison for multiple murders—let me remind you that human police don't distinguish between you killing a man and you killing a demon wearing a dead man's body. They have this nifty word for it"—he glanced heavenwards as though he was trying to recall a word—"oh, yeah… homicide."

Gunz stilled. There was no doubt Magnus was threatening him, and he had to admit that his threat was valid. Many times, lying in bed at night, he wondered how come no one ever caught on camera him wielding the fire. Or why neighbors never called 911 while demons were attacking his house, throwing energy orbs and lightning bolts.

"My lord, please," he said peacefully, raising his eyes at Magnus. "I'm not here to argue with you. I'm here to beg you for mercy… not for myself but for my friend." He waved in Mrak Delar's direction.

"So, I've heard," said Magnus dryly, approaching Gunz. "I've heard that you would do anything to protect people you care about. Blind and vulnerable, you are here to beg for your friend. So beg. Let's see how far you are willing to go to save him. Bend your knee and kiss my hand." He laughed derisively. "I don't see you begging, Salamander."

"Screw it," growled Gunz and walked back to the iron bars, surrounding Mrak Delar. He channeled all the magic and power he could find within and his body dissolved into flames. He placed his hands on the metal bar, heating them up. Sensing that what he had wasn't enough, he tapped into the magic of the Dark Codex, allowing the magical artifact to unveil in his mind completely, surrendering to its full power.

He stifled a scream, as the book presented him with multiple spells at once, causing a searing pain in his head, and then laughed diabolically as he realized that now he had the power he had never had before—the forgotten knowledge, some of which had been forgotten for a reason. He could see it all—all the secrets preserved in the Dark Codex, including the knowledge of how to break a curse. Any curse...

This is why the followers of Chaos wanted the Codex—to break Veles' curse. The thought rushed through his mind, but he put it away, focusing on his present situation. He started to chant the words of an ancient tongue he didn't understand, and the metal bars dissolved under his touch.

Gunz walked inside the cage and put his hand on the Destiny Cuffs. They clicked, releasing Mrak Delar's wrists, and fell to the floor with a metallic cling. As soon as the cuffs were gone, Mrak's appearance began to change. His hair turned jet-black, and some color returned to his ashen face. His dark eyelashes fluttered, but he didn't wake up.

He turned around and stared at the Destiny Council, a cold, uneven smirk curving his lips. Searching through the Dark Codex, he placed his hand over his eyes and a blinding white light erupted from his palm. When he removed his hand, Ivan the Terrible's curse was broken, and his vision was restored. He disconnected from the Codex and closed his magical sight, blinking a few times to get used to the light, and pinned the Destiny Council with his igneous gaze.

"Screw you," he growled. "I don't need your goddamn help

and I'm done begging. I'm done being blackmailed and bullied by the likes of you—good, evil and in between. You need me! You hear me? If you want to keep Zmey and other supernatural beasts under control, you need the Fire Salamander fighting them! And Mrak Delar? You don't have a fighter on the side of good who is as loyal and honorable as he is. How dare you—" He cut himself off, shaking his head. Bending down, Gunz lifted Mrak Delar with a strained grunt, draping him over his shoulder. Then he turned to Gwyn ap Nudd and addressed him. "Can we go now, Gwyn?"

Gwyn stared down at him, a chain of emotions flashing through his angled features. Then he raised his head and his blazing eyes pinned the members of the Destiny Council to their seats.

"Gwyn, what's going on here, brother?" hissed Magnus, fear reflected on his face. "His magic is more than that of a Great Fire Salamander."

Gwyn laughed. "Brother? Don't you dare call me that. Never again." He raised his hand, slowly extending his middle finger as he arched his brow. "You've heard the young Salamander. Screw you!" He laughed again and there was so much icy hatred in his laughter that Gunz cringed inwardly.

King of the Otherworld moved his hand, drawing a bright rectangle in the air, then he infused it with his power, creating a door, and bowed ceremoniously to Gunz.

"After you, my lord," he said, a smirk playing on his lips.

Gunz walked through the door straight into Gwyn's living room. Carefully, he placed Mrak Delar on the couch. The Master of Power opened his eyes and looked at him, a weak smile warming up his features.

"What did you do now, Fire Gecko," he whispered hoarsely, his eyes darting to Gwyn ap Nudd for the answer.

"Nothing you need to worry about, Mrak. Get better and I'll see you soon," replied Gunz, giving him a light tap on his shoul—

der. Then he turned to Gwyn ap Nudd. "Gwyn, is there a chance you will allow me to open my portal from your house? I'm too exhausted... I want to go home."

Gwyn shrugged. "You are a Great Fire Salamander, little one." He laughed. "Nothing can stop you. Your portals burn through the fabric of reality itself."

"Then how come Kal never opens his portals here and is always waiting for you to open a door?" asked Gunz, flabbergasted.

"Because he respects my rules," replied Gwyn ap Nudd, chuckling, as he dropped into a large armchair. "The wards are down. Go home, boy. You need a few days of uninterrupted sleep. Open your portal."

Gunz bowed to Gwyn ap Nudd and waved his hand, unfolding the flaming curtain of his portal and walked through it. For the first time, he didn't open his portal into his backyard but straight into his living room. He closed his eyes and took a deep breath, enjoying the silence and solitude.

Now that he didn't have to worry about anything or run for his life—at least not yet, he started to feel how truly sore and exhausted he was. Glancing at the stairs, he wasn't sure he could make it all the way to the second floor and was considering sleeping in the living room on the couch.

A loud knock on the door interrupted his train of thought and he spun around, his nerves stretched to the limit instantly. He scanned the area around the house, realizing that the people knocking were human, and headed toward the door.

As he swung it open, he stilled, his mouth open. A few men in police uniform stood before him. The street in front of his house was filled with police vehicles and a couple of fire engines were parked at the side. The firefighters stood in front of their trucks, holding fire hoses in their hands, aiming at him.

"Mr. Zane Burns?" asked the man closest to him, his voice cold and official.

"Yes," replied Gunz, a dreadful feeling taking hold of him. "What can I do for you, officer?"

"You can turn around and put your hands behind your back," said the man seriously, producing a pair of handcuffs. "You're under arrest."

"I don't understand," mumbled Gunz. "I work for the FBI, give me a second and I'll show you my badge."

"That won't be necessary, Mr. Burns," objected the policeman dryly. "We're well aware of who you are and what you are. Agent Jim Andrews can't help you. He is busy facing his own problems. Turn around, hands behind your back."

Gunz observed the area, noticing all the neighbors, police officers and firefighters watching him and sighed. Perhaps exposing the World of Magic in front of all these humans hadn't been such a bright idea.

I can break out of any human jail at any time, he thought, forcing himself to calm down. *I need to figure out what's going on first.* Slowly, Gunz turned around and crossed his hands behind his back, feeling the handcuffs biting into his skin.

"You have the right to remain silent," went on the policeman, directing him toward the police vehicle parked in his driveway. "Anything you say can and will be used against you in a court of law—"

"Excuse me, officer," Gunz interrupted him as they halted in front of a car. "But what did I do? What am I charged with?"

For a moment, the man stared at him with interest. "Double homicide, Mr. Burns. You are charged with the murder of Hazel Wells and Sophia Porter."

Gunz stilled, staring at the officer in shock. But the man opened the car door for him, forcing him inside.

"Now, go—Fire Salamander," he said with a smirk and shut the door behind him.

BOOK FIVE: EXCERPT

*Read on for an excerpt from
N.M. Thorn's new book:*

**The Fire Salamander Chronicles.
Book 5**

* * *

***Zane Burns, a.k.a. Guns
Somewhere in the United States... Probably...
Date—unknown...***

The room was absolutely white. Except for unblemished white walls, polished white tiled floor and white ceiling, there was nothing else in this room—no furniture, not even a mattress on the floor. A small area in the back was separated for personal needs by a low white wall. Long white light panels were embedded into the ceiling all around the perimeter.

The lights never went off, not even at night, and since there were no windows or a clock, it was impossible to count time.

BOOK FIVE: EXCERPT

Gunz sat on the hard floor, resting his back against the wall as he stared at his reflection in a one-way mirror at the other end of the room. If not for his dark hair, he would be invisible against the white wall in the white medical scrubs he was wearing.

He got up, pushing off the floor, and swayed slightly. Since he'd been brought here and locked up in this room, he hadn't been able to take a deep breath as the air in this chamber of torture was infused with halon, a low-toxicity fire extinguishing agent. There was enough oxygen here to keep him from dying a human death, but his fire was suppressed, and he experienced a constant nagging pain, accompanied by lightheadedness and fatigue.

Despite feeling weak and unsteady, he assumed the initial stance of Koryo—a Taekwondo pattern Aidan had taught him a while ago—and closed his eyes, focusing on his breathing, as shallow and uneven as it was.

The loud clank of the lock made him flinch and open his eyes, staring at a small window in the entrance door as a guard knocked on it with his baton.

"Inmate 802313," he said dryly. "You've been summoned."

Gunz sighed. Usually that meant nothing but trouble for him. Approaching the entrance, he pushed his hands through the window, allowing the guard to lock the handcuffs on his wrists. The restraints were just a human variety toy, and normally something like this wouldn't keep him restrained for longer than a few minutes.

Here, however, everything was different. Magic detectors and heat detectors were installed in his cell and as soon as the magical energy field around him spiked up even a little or if his body temperature went up by a few degrees, a large dose of halon was released, incapacitating him, leaving him curled up on the floor, screaming in pain. The muscle weakness was so debilitating that he had to wonder if it was only the fire

BOOK FIVE: EXCERPT

suppressants that made him feel this way or if there was some powerful dark magic in play too. In this facility, he was disabled as a Fire Salamander, as a wizard, and as a man.

The guard opened the door and seized his shoulder, roughly yanking him out of the room. As a reaction to the sharp movement, everything around him spun and his stomach heaved. He leaned forward, bracing himself with his handcuffed hands against the wall, and rested his forehead against his elbow.

The guard pulled him away from the wall, shoving him farther ahead. "Keep moving, inmate," he said icily, adding an extra push into Gunz's back, which almost sent him flying to the floor.

Gunz glanced back at the man, shaking his head. In this hellhole, all guards wore strange helmets, covering their faces. All he could see was a pair of blue eyes, staring at him with icy contempt. He walked the already familiar path along the well-lit corridor and stopped in front of a door with the name plate on it stating, "Dr. Roger Harris".

The guard knocked and once he heard a loud buzzing, pushed the door open. He grabbed Gunz by the back of his neck, forcing him inside the room.

"He's all yours, Doc," he said, pushing Gunz toward the table.

Gunz grunted as he lost his balance and fell forward, hitting his forehead on the edge of the desk. The room flipped upside down as he dropped to the floor. With his blurry vision he saw the guard leave and close the door. Then he felt someone's hands grabbing him under his armpits, pulling him up gently. Doctor Harris helped him sit down and walked around the desk to his own chair.

Gunz leaned back in his chair—it was a large leather office armchair—and closed his eyes, taking a few deep breaths to fill his lungs with clean air. When he opened his eyes again, he saw Doctor Harris observing him with interest.

"Feeling better, Mr. Burns?" he asked.

Gunz nodded, staring at the doctor with a deadpan expression. It wasn't their first meeting and every time he was in this room, the good doctor tried to take his mind apart, block by block, as if it were nothing but a bunch of Legos. He hated these sessions and couldn't understand their purpose. Everything here was designed to torture him, which he still couldn't figure out why. It seemed like whoever held him captive was torturing him for the sake of torture.

"I'm fine, Doctor," said Gunz, his voice raspy from constant coughing.

"Great, great." The doctor rubbed his hands together, an expression of delight on his face. "So, Mr. Burns... or should I call you Gunz? Or maybe Fire Salamander?" he asked, arching his eyebrows at Gunz.

Gunz tensed—that was the first time the good doctor let it slip that he knew his nickname and his true nature. But he suppressed his emotions and smiled lazily.

"No, you should not," he replied. "Only my friends can call me that, and you're not one of them."

"Aw, Mr. Burns," purred the man, leaning back in his chair and making a steeple of his fingers. "I was just trying to be nice. There is no need to be so offensive. Not just yet, but I'll give you the opportunity to fight once we're done here."

That's something new, thought Gunz, cringing inwardly.

Since Gunz didn't say anything, the doctor continued, "So, Mr. Burns, what do you think about your stay here?"

"Your five-star accommodations could do with a good interior decorator," replied Gunz, sarcasm clear in his every word.

"And why is that?" asked the doctor.

"I'm not the biggest fan of the color white," replied Gunz, an uneven smirk curving his lips. "Besides, sleeping on a cold floor with lights on doesn't promote a healthy life environment."

"Are you suffering from sleep deprivation, Mr. Burns?"

"No, Doctor Harris, I suffer from infinite boredom," he

replied dryly. "I don't even have reading privileges. Come to think of it, I didn't even get my phone call when I was brought here, which is a violation of my rights."

"You mean it's a violation of *human* rights, Mr. Burns," replied Harris with a sugary smile. "We both know, you're not human. Legally, there is no human rights violation here."

Gunz grunted, clenching his teeth to stop himself from saying anything that would trigger some painful consequences.

"I see," purred the doctor, observing his reaction. "How does it make you feel?"

"Hmm," hummed Gunz. "How does it make me feel? Good question. Well, like strangling you with these very handcuffs, for one." He lifted his chained arms with a cold smile, his fingers clenched into tight fists.

"I see." The doctor nodded, calmly observing him like he would any lab rat. Then he cocked his head and smiled as if Gunz didn't just threaten his life. "Do you read a lot?"

"I used to," replied Gunz with an indifferent shrug. "Until you threw me in this hellhole, that is."

"Hellhole? Hardly." The doctor laughed. "So, Mr. Burns, if I give you reading privileges, which book would you like to read?"

Gunz smirked. "Infernal Justice."

"Interesting choice," mumbled Doctor Harris, writing something in his notepad. "Why did you choose this particular book?"

Gunz raised his eyes at him, his jaw set. "Because I would prefer Infernal Justice to that of the Destiny Council."

For a moment, Doctor Harris stared at him mortified but quickly pulled himself together and his lips stretched into a forced smile, the corners of his mouth twitching a little.

"I have no idea what this Destiny Council is. Never heard of it," he said frostily, putting his notepad away. "Our session is over for today, Mr. Burns. I will make sure you receive the book you requested. In the meantime"—he pushed a button on the intercom panel—"your guard will escort you to the training facility. You're cleared for training."

He grabbed a piece of paper with his name printed at the top and quickly wrote something on it. Gunz heard the door open but didn't turn around. Doctor Harris waved his hand at the guard and once he approached the desk, he offered him the paper.

"He's cleared to begin training," he said coldly, motioning at Gunz. "You can escort him there now and give my note to the Commander."

The guard grabbed Gunz's shoulder and yanked him up to his feet. A low growl rumbled in Gunz's chest as he jerked his shoulder out of the guard's grip. He stood staring at the man who'd been abusing and torturing him for the last—he had no idea how long—and his chest was rising and falling with heavy breaths as he struggled to suppress his fire.

"Mr. Burns," hissed the doctor, "you would do well to cool down. Literally. If you don't want to trigger the fire suppressant system in my office that is." He pointed at the magic and heat detectors on the wall. "In a minute, you will be in the training facility where you can safely let out some steam."

He quickly walked around the desk and put his hand on Gunz's shoulder. Gunz snapped around, death staring from his eyes. But then he took a deep breath and relaxed his tense shoulders.

The doctor glowered at the guard. "Can you *please* take him to the training facility without insulting or abusing him?" he hissed, throwing his hands up.

"Yes, sir," replied the guard, but his voice carried his displeasure.

It seems like this man has something against me personally, thought Gunz as he headed toward the door.

* * *

The training facility looked like a high school gymnasium equipped with all kinds of martial arts training equipment. Gunz looked around, taking in his surroundings. About fifteen men were already training there and even without using his other sight, he could sense that except for one man, none of them were human.

Gunz stood barefoot on the hardwood floor, not in a rush to make a move. The guard who brought him here approached the man who was the only human in the room and gave him the letter from Doctor Harris. The man stopped what he was doing and took the letter, dismissing the guard with a quick flick of his wrist.

Once the guard was gone, the man approached Gunz. Standing no more than a foot away, he stared down at him, a vibe of arrogance exuding from his every pore. He glanced at the paper in his hand again and smirked.

"So, you are the infamous Zane Burns I've heard so much about," he said, his voice raspy like the voice of a man who started smoking in his early teens. He gave him one more once-over and laughed, slapping himself on his thighs. "Nothing much to see, is there?" He glanced at the rest of his team that gathered behind him. Then he switched his attention back to Gunz. "So, boy, show me what you're good for."

Gunz met his mocking gaze calmly. Then he sighed and sat down on the floor, crossing his legs. The man looked back at his crew and snickered.

"Do we have a little rebellion on our hands?" he asked snidely and flicked his fingers at one of his fighters.

A man separated from the crowd, stepping forward. He was tall, no less than six-foot-eight, and had long white hair flowing freely down his back and shoulders. His eyes were angled and shone with an electric green light like that of a feral feline.

Despite his size and considerable bulk, he moved with the grace of a dancer and his chiseled features didn't betray his emotions as he glanced down at Gunz.

"Lucan," said the man, "help him to his feet. Our new friend needs assistance."

Lucan closed the distance between them in one step and easily lifted Gunz to his feet as though he weighed nothing. When he bent down, Gunz caught the sight of Lucan's pointed ear. *He's an elf,* he thought, shivers running down his back. *How did they break him?*

Elves possessed powerful magic only they could wield, but in the realm of humans, they were quite rare and capturing them was practically impossible, whereas breaking one into submission was unheard of. Yet, as Gunz stood slightly swaying, he had no doubt he was staring at an elf.

"Lucan," said the commander, "would you like to try out our new recruit and have a quick sparring match with him?"

Lucan's leaf green eyes darted to Gunz, and he shook his head no silently.

"And why not?" asked the commander.

"He's a Fire Salamander," replied the elf, his voice as void of emotions as his face.

"Don't be scared, Lucan." The commander snickered. "Here, he is just a little man. He can't use his magic or his element unless he wants to get a nice dose of a fire suppressant."

"My apologies, Commander Moore," said the elf, crossing his massive arms behind his back. "As a man he is too small. Even without me using my magic, it won't be a fight but cold-blooded murder. I'll kill him before the fight ever begins. There is no honor in that."

"You dare to disobey a direct order, elf?" hissed the commander, heat rising from his thick neck to his bulldog-like face. "Who gives a damn about your honor?"

The elf froze, his angled eyes widened in unmistakable fear. Gunz smirked and sat back on the floor with his legs crossed.

"I'm not fighting for you," he said flatly. In other circumstances, he would probably be burning with anger, but right now, he could barely speak. "You are starving me, torturing me with sleep deprivation, abusing me physically and poisoning me with halon. How the hell do you expect me to be able to move, let alone fight an elf who is almost a foot and a half taller than me?"

"First of all, we are not poisoning you with halon. The fire suppressant we use is not halon but halotron—works just as well and environmentally friendly," grumbled the commander sarcastically, anger permeating around him. "We're all about a green earth here, you know. Second, you're going to do as I command. You have no choice."

"We all have a choice," replied Gunz quietly, his eyes sliding over the faces of the fighters, "and I already made mine."

The commander approached him and swung his arm, punching him in his jaw. Gunz cried out as he fell to the side, his weakened body not complying with the demands of his mind. His mouth filled with blood and he spat on the floor, pushing himself back up into a sitting position.

"We'll see about that," hissed the commander, turning toward the elf. "Lucan, since he already made up his mind, now the choice is yours. Who is going to be punished today, you or him?"

"Me," said Lucan, dropping his head, his long hair falling over his face and chest. "I refuse to fight a man who is not in his best shape."

"Fine," growled the commander, distaste curving his lips. He turned to his team and waved his hand. Two more men stepped forward, their eyes glowing with a scarlet glow, betraying their vampiric nature.

Naturally, elves had pale white skin, but as soon as the

BOOK FIVE: EXCERPT

undead monsters approached Lucan, his face became ashen, bordering with blue. Nevertheless, he didn't make a move when they put their hands on his shoulders. The vampires pushed him down to his knees, and to Gunz's shock, the elf didn't fight them even when they stripped his thin shirt off. One of the vamps tilted Lucan's head to the side, exposing his jugular, and his fangs expanded.

Lucan froze in place, his eyes wide, his lips slightly parted as his chest shuddered with short breaths. Gunz shook his head, clenching his jaw. *I am so going to regret this,* he thought as he got up to his feet and raised his hand.

"Hey, Commander Moore," he said as loud as he could, "stop it. I'll spar with your elf."

The vampires let go of Lucan, waiting for the next order. The commander nodded, a cold smirk curving his lips, and both vamps walked back, joining the others. Lucan got up and approached Gunz, his heavy green gaze boring into him.

"Follow me," he said quietly, directing him to the mats in the center of the training room.

Gunz stepped on the soft mats, bowing, but then smirked and bit his lip. Showing respect to the dojang was so deeply rooted in him that he was doing it automatically. For a moment, his memory flashed back to his training sessions at Aidan's school and his soul bled as he thought of his friends.

At least they are safe, he thought, regarding Lucan calmly as the elf took a position facing him. *Now that I'm blacklisted by the Destiny Council, they're safer away from me.*

Lucan stepped closer, placing his hand on Gunz's shoulder. "Thank you for taking the punishment for me," he whispered so only Gunz could hear him. "I'm deeply sorry, Salamander, but you will probably regret your decision."

Gunz looked straight ahead, his gaze landing on the firm squares of the elf's stomach. As he slowly raised his eyes up, he felt like he was staring at a high-rise.

BOOK FIVE: EXCERPT

"I think I already do... Jesus, man, what did they feed you when you were a kid? You're as tall as Kal..." He scratched the back of his head, a lopsided grin crossing his face. "Do you worst?"

The elf squeezed Gunz's shoulder, and he sensed a wave of elven magic surging through him. It felt like an adrenalin shot—his heart sped up and everything inside him came to life. He shuddered from the unexpected sensation, struggling to keep his fire under control. As his gaze fell on the magic and heat detectors under the ceiling, he wondered why the magic detectors didn't sense the elven magic, but he couldn't even get in touch with the Dark Codex in his mind without triggering them.

"Better?" asked Lucan quietly, and Gunz gave him a barely visible nod. The elf laughed coldly and asked loudly, "Are you ready for pain?"

Gunz smirked and quickly drove his arms up, sending his body into a backflip while he whipped his right leg, kicking the elf lightly under his chin. He didn't intend for this kick to be hard, but rather wanted to show Lucan that despite the height difference he wasn't an easy prey.

"Jumpy little lizard, aren't you?" asked Lucan, rubbing his chin, as excitement lit up his cat-eyes. "I'm still going to destroy you."

"Like I said—do you worst."

Lucan stepped back into a guarding stance, and for the first time a true smile changed his cold features.

"Fire Salamander—go!" growled the elf, turning his hip as he threw his entire body into a powerful hook.

DEAR READER

Thank you so much for reading The Burns Codex. I hope you enjoyed the book and will join Zane Burns' next adventure in the fifth book of the series.

If you would like to stay up-to-date on the latest information about new releases, special offers, and more, sign up for my mailing list. www.nmthorn.com

For more information follow me on Facebook and Instagram.
  www.facebook.com/nmthornauthor
  www.instagram.com/nmthornauthor/

BEFORE YOU GO...

Your reviews mean the world to me and are greatly appreciated. If you enjoyed the Burns Fire, please take a few minutes to leave a review. It doesn't have to be long. It can be just a few words or stars rating.

Please help spread the word by taking this small extra step and leave your review on Amazon and/or Goodreads.

ALSO BY N. M. THORN

The Fire Salamander Chronicles

The Burns Path (Prequel Novella Book 0 - for my subscribers)
The Burns Fire - Book 1
The Burns War - Book 2
The Burns Defiance - Book 3

ABOUT THE AUTHOR

N.M. Thorn currently lives in South Florida with her husband and son. Owner of a digital marketing agency by day and a writer by night, she loves spending her times creating new worlds, paranormal planes of existence and anything that could be described as supernatural.

When she is not busy working with everything digital or exploring fantasy worlds, she enjoys spending time with her family, reading, painting and martial arts.

If you would like to share your thoughts, ideas or just send N.M. Thorn a message about the Fire Salamander world, feel free to contact her at: nmthornauthor@gmail.com

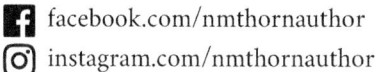 facebook.com/nmthornauthor
instagram.com/nmthornauthor

Printed in Great Britain
by Amazon